Benjamin Stevenson is an award-winning stand-up comedian and *USA Today* best-selling author. He is the author of the globally popular 'Ernest Cunningham Mysteries', including *Everyone In My Family Has Killed Someone*, which is currently being adapted into a major HBO TV series, and the sequels: *Everyone On This Train Is A Suspect* and *Everyone This Christmas Has A Secret*. His books have sold over 1.5 million copies in twenty-nine territories and have been nominated for nine 'Book of the Year' awards.

Follow Ben to keep up with news,
events and latest releases!

ALSO BY THE AUTHOR

The Ernest Cunningham series
Everyone In My Family Has Killed Someone
Everyone On This Train Is A Suspect
Everyone This Christmas Has A Secret

The Jack Quick series
Greenlight
Either Side of Midnight

Standalone
Fool Me Twice: Two Twisty Mysteries
Don't Hang Up (audio only)

EVERYONE IN THIS BANK IS A THIEF

BENJAMIN STEVENSON

PENGUIN BOOKS

UK | USA | Canada | Ireland | Australia
India | New Zealand | South Africa | China

Penguin Books is part of the Penguin Random House group of companies whose addresses can be found at global.penguinrandomhouse.com

First published by Penguin Books in 2025

Copyright © Benjamin Stevenson 2025

The moral right of the author has been asserted.

All rights reserved. No part of this publication may be reproduced, published, performed in public or communicated to the public in any form or by any means without prior written permission from Penguin Random House Australia Pty Ltd or its authorised licensees.

Penguin Random House values and supports copyright. Copyright fuels creativity, encourages diverse voices, promotes free speech and creates a vibrant culture. Thank you for buying an authorised edition of this book and for complying with copyright laws by not reproducing, scanning or distributing any parts of it in any form without permission. You are supporting writers and allowing Penguin Random House to continue to publish books for every reader. Please note that no part of this book may be used or reproduced in any manner for the purpose of training artificial intelligence technologies or systems.

Cover images: butterflies by Stock gallery 01/Shutterstock;
parrot by sssimone/Adobe Stock (generated by AI)
Cover design by Adam Laszczuk © Penguin Random House Australia Pty Ltd
Bank plan by James Mills-Hicks, Ice Cold Publishing
Other internal images by Adobe Stock Photo
Typeset in 11/17 pt Sabon LT Pro by Midland Typesetters, Australia

Printed and bound in Australia by Griffin Press, an accredited
ISO AS/NZS 14001 Environmental Management Systems printer

 A catalogue record for this book is available from the National Library of Australia

ISBN 978 0 14377 997 1

penguin.com.au

We at Penguin Random House Australia acknowledge that Aboriginal and Torres Strait Islander peoples are the Traditional Custodians and the first storytellers of the lands on which we live and work. We honour Aboriginal and Torres Strait Islander peoples' continuous connection to Country, waters, skies and communities. We celebrate Aboriginal and Torres Strait Islander stories, traditions and living cultures, and we pay our respects to Elders past and present.

For Aleesha Paz
Thief
(Heist #6)

Maybe last words should therefore be included in those lists of hackneyed devices or props that theorists have been outlawing for decades ever since Father (!) Ronald A. Knox (1924) and S. S. Van Dine (1928) or the decalogue of the Detection Club Oath (1932). These lists ban motifs such as unknown and untraceable poisons, more than one secret passage, the wrong brand cigarette butt, identical twins or doubles . . . servants as killers, forged fingerprints, the dog that did not bark, supernatural agencies. Some authorities would include love, but last words are not included in anybody's list of contraband.

    Karl S. Guthke, *Revelation or Deceit: Last Words in Detective Novels*

The robb'd that smiles steals something from the thief
                                  William Shakespeare, *Othello*, Act 1, Scene 3

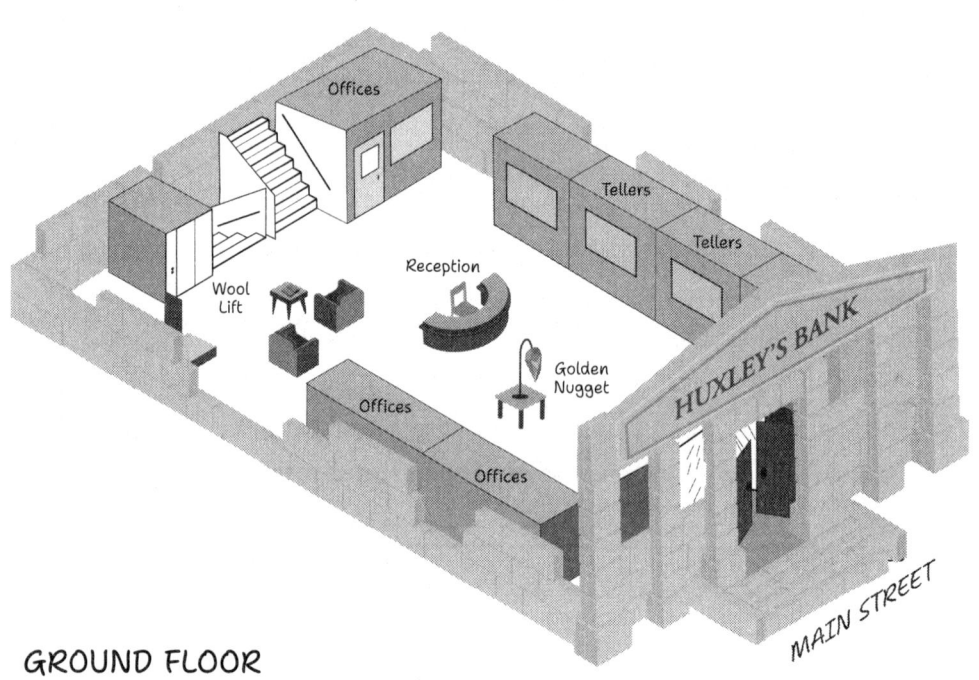

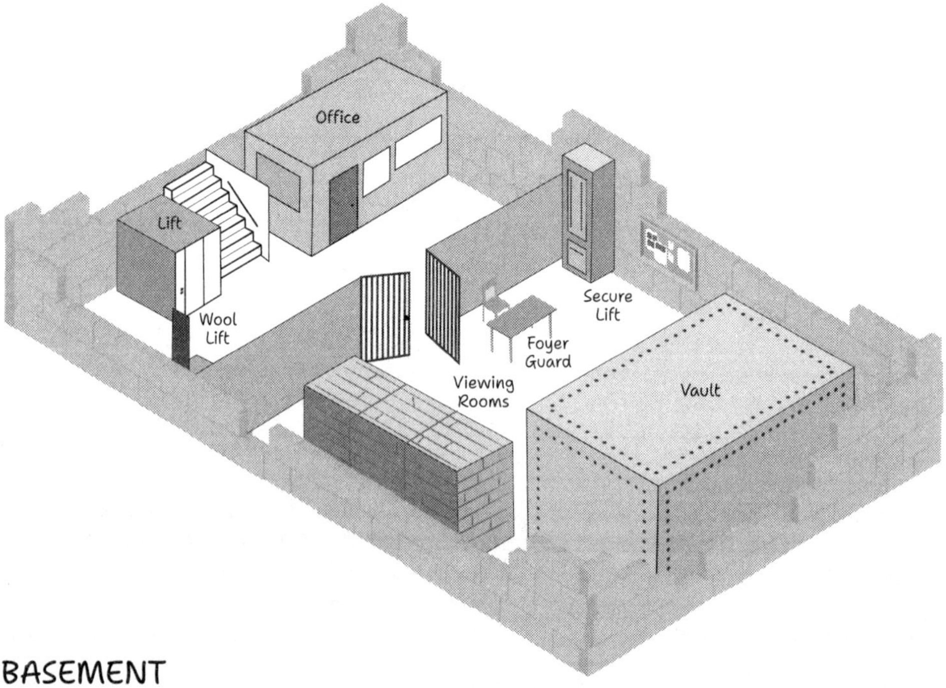

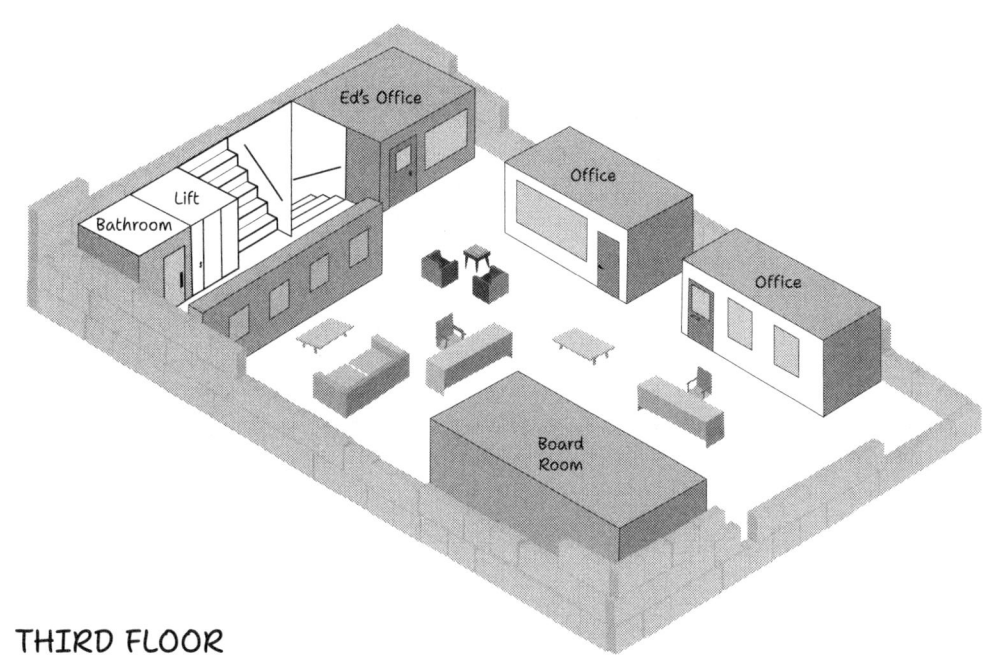

THIRD FLOOR

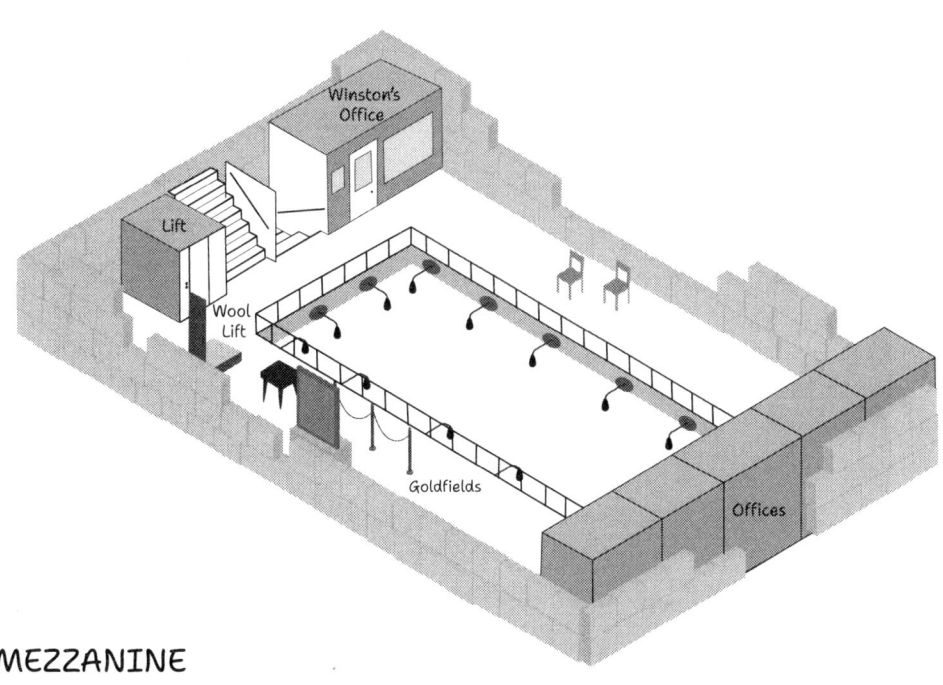

MEZZANINE

PROLOGUE

Given I'm dying, and have just the one pen, let's motor through the pleasantries.

My name's Ernest Cunningham. Up until today, I would have said that I'm a passable detective. Not professional, and a long way from expert, but so far three murderers would likely attest (if the two dead ones could talk) that I am quite the nuisance. So: passable. Factoring in the whole dying thing knocks me down a few notches, though.

If it seems like an odd time for me to jot out a memoir, I'll clarify that I'm not catastrophically injured. There are no missing limbs spurting crimson, no poisons coursing through my body, and nor am I, unlike some other unfortunate souls in the pages to come, aflame. I'm just sitting here on the ice-cold floor of a steel box, about the size of a fridge, with, I've calculated, fifteen hours of air inside it. That is, of course, not factoring in any oxygen wastage from my screaming and banging useless fists against the inside of a door only I know the code to. Some of my curse words were quite inventively lengthy and required deep breaths. Call it fourteen and a half hours, then. Worth it.

Neither my dwindling ink or air has time for backstory but,

generally speaking, if you're reading something I've written, it's because I've solved a murder or several. I was raised on a diet of Golden Age detective novels – the 'fair-play' mysteries where the clues are front and centre for the reader – which came in mighty handy when I found myself getting caught up in, and transcribing, real-life murders. I've always prided myself, when I chronicled those three cases in my first three books, on being a reliable narrator. Everything I show is the truth, exactly how I saw it. The reader and the author solve the mystery together. There are no hidden facts or deliberate omissions. That's how 'fair play' works.

I say 'generally speaking' because this time's a little different. Yes, there's been a murder. Several, actually. And in fourteen hours and, let's see . . . twenty-nine minutes, there'll be another. I will, as promised, write down and present to you every clue I see. Against form, however, I must make one omission not usually permitted in the Golden Age: the name of the killer.

That's because I haven't solved it yet.

Usually, once I'm up to the writing, I've satisfied all the requirements of the genre. I've had my stitches and book deals sewn up – not necessarily in that order. I've generally also spilled some blood and had some poured back into me – definitely in that order. I've stood in front of a room full of suspects and whittled them down, one by one, to the real killer or killers. That's usually my favourite part; the parlour scene, it's often called. The climactic unravelling that both reader and detective *earn*. It's really the only reason people read murder mysteries.

Knowing the ending usually means I can tell you where to look, point out the important clues along the way so you are as well armed an armchair detective as I am a real one come the finale. Without knowing who the killer is, I can't assuredly point you in the right direction. Sure, I can tell you some things to pay close attention to: that the pieces that look *too easy* probably are, for example. But it's not the same. A book without an ending is swallowing your greens and not making it through to dessert.

I have theories, of course. I managed to weed out a few red herrings, expose a few lies and stockpile several motives before being sealed in here, but I am still a killer short of a murder mystery. It's small consolation that I must have been getting close enough for someone to want to get rid of me. Perhaps that is my final clue. What did I discover, just before this all went down, that turned me from a nuisance into a liability?

I keep trying to trace the size of the pair of hands against my memory of their pressure on my back – did I feel a ring? – or to dissect the patter of the retreating footsteps – what was the length of their stride, the type of shoe? – under the iron clank of the door sealing. But it doesn't help.

Irony is quite neat in fiction, but in real life it's smug and annoying. I spent the better part of twenty-four hours trying to get into this safe. Now I'm going to die in it.

My supplies are as meagre as my oxygen. I have this notebook, pen and a few other bits and pieces: a thumb-sized flashlight to write by, a thick black marker, a broken radio, a magnet, a high-school chemistry textbook and a near-empty gun. The gun is a revolver with a visible chamber: I'm no weapons expert, but I can tell there are two bullets left. I won't die of thirst: I have a glass jar of water – yes, a jar – that I'm putting off drinking because it's not mine. And I'd feel really guilty if I drank it. I need air more than water, anyway. I guess, if suffocating really is as bad as I think it might be, at least I have those two bullets. One spare.

Eventually the police will crack open the safe. They'll want to check what's been taken. But that will come second to corralling the surviving hostages and dealing with the mess in the vault in the basement. Even if I am still alive, what's to stop me getting pancaked against the wall by a two-inch-thick steel door when they blast it off its hinges? They won't have cause to be careful. No one knows I'm in here, because no one knows I was robbing the damn bank in the first place.

Oh yeah. I robbed a bank. I should've led with that.

I'm not the only one. Everyone in this bank is a thief.

Ten suspects. Ten heists. That much I've deduced. If that sounds insane, trust me, it is. While I've become accustomed to being a murder magnet, I'm still new to the whole burglary thing. Here's something I've learned: there's more you can steal from a bank than just money.

From what I can tell, the stolen items are: a gold pen, a single dollar, other varied amounts ranging from a few thousand to twenty-five million dollars, a coffee cup, a life, and, to be cute about it, a heart.

That list doesn't quite cover the promised ten heists; there are more thefts and thieves for me to puzzle out. That'll be my framework for solving this, to assign each suspect a robbery. If they consider something worth stealing, maybe it's also worth killing for. Inside these thefts lies motive for murder. The question is: which one?

So, back to the page. Why spend these final hours writing? Because I write these things the same way I solve them. By pretending there's a reader out there, I can assemble the clues in a fashion befitting the fair relay of information of the Golden Age detective novel. I figure if I go back over all the clues, maybe a solution will emerge. And if I can't get there in the next fourteen hours or so, maybe I can put enough of what happened on the page so whoever winds up reading this might be able to piece it all together.

I'm not saying, like, *avenge* me or anything. But it does have a nice ring to it.

So there you have it. Maybe by writing it all out I can help you solve the murders so far and, in doing so, solve the one that's coming next.

Mine.

THE FIRST HEIST: A GOLD PEN

CHAPTER 1

Ernest Cunningham is dead.

While I've stared down my own death on several occasions, I was surprised to read about it, if only because comprehension is one of the faculties greatly reduced by dying.

It took a quick self–pat down and a refocus on the photograph accompanying the breaking news article to accept that I was still in one piece. Pre-trapped-in-a-box me, even in the dimly lit café, passed as pallid but definitively alive. The gloom was not from lack of effort by the morning sun outside, currently putting on a furiously ignored show like a five-year-old's trampoline routine at a backyard barbecue. A thick and mobile shadow blocked it, blanketing the town of Huxley. In any other mystery, this shadow would be clouds foreboding a brewing thunderstorm, ready to cut me and a group of suspects off from the world. Not here. The atmosphere was going for something much more biblical. While people outside still hurried as if through a storm, foreheads tucked into elbow crooks, there wasn't a drop of wind or rain. The black shadow moved across the sky like it was alive.

The news headline wasn't a misprint: the victim *was* indeed me. Or, rather, the actor Laurence Birch, hired to play me in the upcoming television adaptation of the first of three murder cases I've solved. I'd met him enough – twice on Zoom and twice in person – to feel guilty about how quickly my eyes skipped over his obituary to seek out the inevitable words: *production delayed*.

'Reports of your death have been greatly exaggerated,' my fiancée, Juliette, said, plucking her phone back from me and shoving a gooey, buttered slice of banana bread into her mouth at the same time. Juliette has a list of careers as long as the rib-cage tattoo of a poetry-loving surfer: ski-resort owner, writer, murder suspect. All former. Also former was her long hair. She'd recently cut it for a charity initiative, and her style was now abrupt, slick and deserving of an invite to a prohibition-era soiree. She was, as usual, lightly sunburnt, from inhabiting the outdoors as much as I did hospital beds. We'd spent the Australian winter in the mountains, her in a transient ski-instructor role and me recovering from a bullet wound.

'He doesn't even look like me,' I said. I took out my phone to look up the article myself and read it properly, but Juliette whipped it away.

'He looks a little like you. Stop stalling.'

'I'm not stalling. Although I have been meaning to mention that the photographer is too expensive. We'll have to cut the canapés.'

'We're not cutting the canapés.'

I was fretting about our upcoming wedding, though not for the usual reasons. We met during one murder and got engaged during another, so it only stands to reason that someone will die at our nuptials. That's how it happens in books. Turns out life events are very dangerous for a recurring series detective.

'Four grand for photos. What's he taking them with – the Hubble?' I continued, quickly tallying the numbers in my head. 'It puts us up to thirty-eight thousand. Unacceptable.'

'Where is this coming from?' Juliette's mouth dropped open a little. 'Who's counting?'

'I am.' It had been spinning around in my head for a while, but I finally blurted it out. 'The average divorce rate in Australia is forty-three per cent. And the more you spend on a wedding, the more likely you are to get divorced, statistically speaking. Now, the average wedding in Australia costs thirty-six thousand dollars. So if we spend more than thirty-six kay, we're increasing the odds of divorce.'

'If I drink four mimosas while getting ready, and then I'm denied canapés, I reckon that would drastically impact the divorce statistic. And this wedding talk is definitely stalling,' Juliette said. She leaned back and folded her arms to appear formidable. 'Take me through it one more time.'

'Okay, um. Well, you see—'

'We've come a long way for an *um, well, you see.*'

If you want to put Huxley on a map, you can estimate the distance from any country town to Sydney by the thickness of their banana bread. We were working with at least two inches, which computes to about seven hours' drive north, up to the Queensland border at the foot of the mountainous barrier that separates the eastern Australian coastline from inland: the Great Dividing Range. We were fuelling up before a by-invitation loan meeting with Huxley's Bank, one of the oldest family-owned banks in the country. It should be no small hint to their influence that the town itself is named after them. So I was a little nervous.

'Do it for real. And stop slouching.' Juliette cleared her throat and put on a deep voice. 'I'm a very busy man.'

'By all reports, Winston Huxley is actually a very reasonable—'

'Ernest—' Juliette broke character with a whine. 'Work with me.'

I pulled myself up in the chair and straightened my tie, which I'd lost the argument over wearing. Apparently a tie helps secure a bank loan – must be something to do with displaying a willingness to hang oneself. 'Okay. But if you're taking feedback, people don't say *I'm a very busy man* in real life. It's just a shortcut in stories for *I'm a wanker*.'

'Are you calling me a wanker?'

'Are we still in character?'

'Is that a risk you're willing to take?'

'Mr Huxley, you have a beautiful office.'

I feigned looking around the café. There were a thousand little *tap-tap-tap*s against the bay window (not hail, if you're guessing ahead), peeling gold paint spelling *Liz's Café* across it. Country town shops are often eponymous, I've found. To further my point, we'd parked in front of a *Darren's Thai Food* that morning. No shade to Darren's culinary skills, but I'd sooner eat Liz's banana bread than Dazza's pad thai. This opinion was seemingly shared, judging by the For Lease sign in the restaurant's dusty window, clinging on by one remaining corner of Blu Tack. Inside the café, across from us, I glimpsed two parents consoling their daughter over a photo of Laurence Birch on her phone. She was pale and sunken-eyed with shock. Fandom is a funny thing. A parasocial relationship with a Hollywood star gives a young woman as much grief as I've seen actual families express around murder victims.

I tried to block the café out and get into character, picturing myself in Winston Huxley's office.

'So tell me about this proposition,' Juliette said, still speaking from the chest.

'I have, in recent years, become quite renowned for solving crimes. All of my cases have made the national news, and I've published three memoirs chronicling how I solved them. I'm proposing to translate this skill set into a more, um'—I caught Juliette's eye and steadied my voice—'professional arena. *Sir*. The loan will allow us to become operational: rent premises, pay for IT support. Possibly hire staff.'

Juliette stroked an invisible beard. 'Well, it'll surely be the first detective agency we've set up with a business loan. What are your qualifications?'

'I used to write books about how to write mystery novels. I'm a huge fan of Golden Age mysteries – Agatha Christie, Ronald Knox and all that. The foundation of our business will be that by applying the rules of the classic fictional detectives, we can solve real-life cases.'

'Zero experience,' Juliette muttered under her breath. 'So how much do you charge to solve a murder, then?'

I bristled. 'He's not going to ask that.'

'He might and I am.' She broke character, then passed a flat hand over her face as an actor does to reset. Her voice dropped a register. 'It's a business, and a business has to make enough money to be trusted to reliably repay its loan. I might like to think about how that money's going to come in. Do you give a discount for serial killers? A loyalty card?'

I slipped back into my role. 'Actually, I'm hoping to get away from murders. There're lots of people in need of a professional detective's services without being tied up in anything quite so grisly.'

'How much did you get paid for your first three cases?'

I eyeballed Juliette. She was having too much fun with this. 'Huh?'

'How much?'

'Well, nothing. You know that.'

'Who does? We've never met. My name's Winston. You expect to make money off this when you're out here solving murders for free?'

'I stumbled into those murders, more than anything.'

'Stumbled?' Juliette thumbed through an official-looking document on the table between us, for which I'd even paid an extra dollar for premium spiral binding. She frowned. 'I don't see that in your marketing plan.'

'It's a word-of-mouth business.'

'But your clients are dead.'

I fiddled with my tie. Juliette evidently found it delicious to hold back a lifeline for another few seconds, but eventually she let me off the hook. 'What are you working on now?'

'Nothing.' I tried a laugh. 'Unless Laurence Birch was murdered.'

He was. Of course he was. But we'll get to that.

'What about your previous case?' Juliette continued.

'They'll have to recast.' I was still focused on Laurence. I didn't realise I'd said it aloud until Juliette responded.

'Touching. I think that's quite far down the list of priorities.'

'They'll have to have a funeral, *then* they'll have to recast.'

'Can we keep focus please? Your last case?'

'Eight months ago. Christmas. I was shot. I had to take some time to recover— Can we . . . can we just be ourselves for a bit?'

'I'm perfectly myself.' She threaded her fingers through her belt loops, as if her imagined banker had a jeans-strainer of a torso, leaned back and sniffed theatrically. 'Tell you what I'm seeing? I'm seeing a disorganised, low-return business proposal. Drowning in insurance and, let's be honest, occupational health and safety risks. I'm sorry, but three murders isn't a business. I don't think anyone's going to want to hire you—'

If a baker's generosity improves by the metric of distance from an airport, so too does the ricketiness of a loan application. That much I'm sure was obvious from the jump: no one drives seven hours when their business idea is a good one.

Juliette wasn't doing an impression of Winston Huxley, she was doing an impression of everyone who'd turned us down from every glass-doored corner office to every felt-cubicle basement-desk across Sydney. We'd gone up and down the ladder – and I mean *down*. Having a diamond-toothed loan shark, assumedly taking a break from knee-capping to squeeze in our meeting (I did not wear a tie), describe your business venture as *high risk* is a real confidence killer.

Of the more legitimate avenues, some had never heard of me and thought the idea of a detective agency was too old-fashioned. I'd been prepared for that. What had shocked me was the response from those who *had* heard of me. Rather than prove I was a good detective, my books, it was repeatedly explained to me, captured a series of risky near-death experiences. One banker told me my books were only shelved in bookshops as 'murder mysteries' because there isn't a section for 'insurance nightmares'. I'm not oblivious to my frequent perils: I'd signed up to be an organ donor after my most recent scrape with death, just in case. But now I understood why the eyes of the lady who handed me my donor card lit up like a cartoon character with dollar signs for pupils, accompanied by a near audible *ka-ching* sound effect, as if my inevitable demise filled all her quotas at once. No bank could invest in someone whose every case might be their last. Of the many annoyances of dying as I write this, this might be the worst one: proving those *very busy men* right.

And not only is this case killing me: I worked it for free, too. *Again*.

The offer to come into Huxley's Bank for a meeting had been a rushed, and out of the blue, lifeline. Winston had asked how fast we could get here, so we'd driven overnight for our 10 a.m. It was well and truly our final shot.

It all bubbled over. I pushed myself out of the chair and went full method, pressing my finger on the table with each point. 'Three murder*ers*. Over a dozen murders, thank you very much. Huxley's Bank could help save lives. I've been on talk shows, radio, national news. My phone number leaked a few months ago and I was so inundated with calls I had to get a new one. But that's not the most important thing here.'

Juliette was trying to control the twitch of a smirk. 'What is, then?'

'I solve impossible crimes. People don't want to hire me. People *need* to hire me.' I collapsed back into the chair, spent.

'I knew that was in there somewhere.' Juliette reached over and squeezed my shoulder. 'How could he say no?'

'Like everyone else, I guess – gleefully.' I reached for the banana bread, but Juliette slapped my hand away. I was reluctantly dieting for the wedding; given the number of times I've been stabbed, it helps to have a little extra protection around the middle. But a new suit would, even without the photographer, tip the wedding budget perilously close to the magic thirty-six. Besides, eight months' recovery had gone twelve rounds with my savings. Sure, I had royalty cheques from the memoirs, but they were dwindling. And TV money isn't all it's cracked up to be. I was told by my agent that the producer who optioned the rights was coming off an enormous stinker and 'needed a low-budget project to right the ship; you're just what he's looking for'. I think she meant it as a compliment. Laurence Birch was the only thing of any value attached to the project. And now he'd carked it.

'How'd he die?' I changed the topic, wanting to get my mind off money and onto the far more comfortable topic of death, as we stood up and joined the queue to pay.

The family I'd noticed had split up; the mother and daughter had headed off and the father was in front of us itching for the cashier to hand over his change. He kept rolling his neck and checking his watch. I caught a glimpse of the digital display: 5.30. Whatever he was in a hurry for, he needn't have worried; his watch was four hours behind. It was currently 9.30. Receiving his change, Mr Twitchy knocked my shoulder on his way past, several of his coins spinning on to the floor. He didn't bend to pick them up, just surged towards the exit as if on a wave of stress. A quick note: just like people don't drop dead in first chapters of mystery novels without consequence (hello, Laurence Birch), neither do people bump into each other in coffee shops. I didn't know it yet, but this was the start of Bryce Fredericks' very bad day.

'Birch? Uh.' Juliette shook her head in light memory. 'Hit by a delivery van or something, yesterday. Article said they switched off his life support half an hour ago.'

'You talking about that actor?' The cashier, ponytail tight and high like a cat's tail, piped up. 'That happened near here. Over in Byron Bay.'

Near is a relative term in the countryside. Byron Bay was over the mountain range and on the coast, two hours' drive. Brisbane, at least ninety minutes away, would be described by plucky real estate agents as *practically next door*. Byron Bay is a gentrified beach oasis populated by equal parts spiritualists and backpackers, amid multi-million-dollar mansions. It's where positive thinking meets negative gearing and people walk barefoot to connect with Mother Nature, provided that *Mother Nature* is the name of their wi-fi network. In recent years Byron's popularity had exploded, and it boasted a bit of a celebrity portfolio. Evidently Laurence had chosen it as his Australian base.

'Settle a bet,' I said to the cashier, cutting in ahead of Juliette to tap my card. Even broke, I wanted to pay for things. 'Do I look like Birch?'

'Nah.' She sized me up. 'You're too tall. Bigger shoulders too. Dude's tiny.'

Fair enough. That, too, had been the first thing I'd noticed when I'd met Laurence. I'm no beanpole – Juliette's a head taller than I am – but Laurence was surprisingly small in the way that actors sometimes are, when we're so used to seeing them projected on a giant screen and filmed from the knees up so they can stand on phone books. Laurence also had a set of obscenely white teeth that he flashed with the frequency of someone caring to show off their expensive dental work. He smiled like parking a Lamborghini on the street. Unnecessarily and so you'd see it.

The other oddity from our first meeting was that he'd asked to flick through my wallet. Figuring that a celebrity wasn't about to nick off with my loyalty card that was three coffees away from a freebie at *Bean There Done That*, my local, I'd been curious enough to let him.

'That's not a fair comparison. She's only seen his films,' Juliette complained as we walked to the door. 'She hasn't met Laurence two-point-oh.'

This was our running joke. The second time I'd met Laurence in person, at a breakfast meeting with the television adaptation's producer, a mousey Frenchman named Remy Allard, he'd changed completely. You still wouldn't mistake us for brothers, but you might think he'd robbed my house, because he was wearing my clothes. The same brand of jeans, a buttoned shirt with the sleeves rolled up and a baseball cap with my football team's insignia. I'd never even told him who I barracked for; though, on second thought, the membership card was probably in my wallet. He'd grown his previously buzzcut hair (he'd just filmed a war movie) and curated a dusting of stubble, but thankfully hadn't gone so far as to dye it my shade of brown. He had a takeaway coffee cup from *Bean There Done That* with him (he had, indeed, stolen my loyalty card) and was experimenting with an atrocious Australian accent. This was how I learned, first-hand, about his reputation as a method actor.

It was a little creepy but, just in case you're thinking it, it wasn't anywhere near a good enough impersonation to sustain a mistaken identity mystery, that old chestnut of Golden Age plots. I'll consider the possibility in the hours to follow, given what was written on Birch's takeaway coffee cup, but I'm still having trouble reconciling it. Besides, who would want *me* dead, especially before the murders I'm about to investigate even kicked off? It's not like many people knew I'd be in Huxley's Bank today, let alone that I would need to be prevented from being here in case there were murders to solve.

I digress. The point is, and this probably says more about me than him, but, in dressing down to my level, all Laurence Birch really looked like was a celebrity trying to pass incognito at an airport. It was nothing more than low-budget cosplay. An assassin would have to have their eyes shut to mix us up.

Juliette had paused by the café door, summoning the courage to face the windless, rainless maelstrom outside.

A thought occurred to me. 'If you think we look alike, does that mean you found him attractive?'

'Careful, Ern.' She pushed open the door. 'You've already died once today.'

CHAPTER 2

Outside was a plague. Told you it was biblical.

Butterflies. Millions of butterflies. A once-in-a-decade confluence of weather patterns and thermal air currents had deposited an entire species migration onto Huxley. While it wasn't a white-out, there were enough in the air that you had to keep your eyes down and your mouth shut unless you wanted a visitor in either of them. Don't get the wrong impression. These weren't regal, colourful butterflies. These were tiny white-winged pests – a moth with a good agent. They moved like moths in light too, skittish and darting. As dozens of them careered into us like careless Christmas shoppers, Juliette and I put our heads down and hurried across the inventively named Main Street as if through a hailstorm.

Chemically, gold is not magnetic (I know this courtesy of the chemistry textbook I've got beside me in my soon-to-be coffin, which we'll get to), but try telling that to this patch of land in the late 1800s. The whole town sprung up practically overnight after great-granddaddy Huxley struck a rich vein of the stuff in his backyard, and the prospectors flocked. Where once there was a lone farm, suddenly there was a makeshift canvas town. Services were needed. A doctor and then, swiftly, due to the quality of medicine, an undertaker. Little fact: Huxley has one of the country's earliest crematoriums, annexed to the church. Next: a butcher, scurvy, then a grocer. In that order. Of course, fortunes found are fortunes often squandered: beer, bread and brothels followed. Canvas became wood. All before it had a name. It takes a short piece of string to join the lion's share of the gold to the town's christening and, the last piece of the urban puzzle, its own bank. A lone farm to a loan farm – that's the alchemy of building a town.

Main Street could have been a postcard of this history. It was as wide as a freeway, despite being single lane, designed for horses and wagons and unchanged since. The town had as many pedestrian crossings as it did traffic lights: none. Crossing the road was pot luck. One modernist touch was parking zones – two hours maximum on weekdays, though I reckon you'd have to be the unluckiest sod in the world to get a parking ticket here and the fine would only run to spare change.

Each side of Main Street was lined with terrace buildings, adorned with the type of ornate, colonial furnishing where each looked like it was wearing a brigadier's hat. The facades had all been freshly painted in different bright pastels, so the street's horizon moved from pink to blue to yellow. Moulded plaster words adorned roofs and awnings, because a heritage building is like a toddler; they're always keen to tell you their name and how old they are. *Brewery, Since 1912*. The mountains rose up behind the town, appearing rippled from a distance, like a body in a noir film lying under a silk sheet. It's no surprise that Huxley is often used as a film set for period dramas. Park a few vintage cars outside the courthouse and scatter some petticoats on the street and it would be as if you'd travelled back in time.

Even in the dappled light, Huxley's Bank cast an imposing shadow across the cluster of history. Four storeys high, built with hulking sandstone blocks, the top floor shrunk inwards like a wedding cake. Four storeys mightn't sound like much, but it dominated the roofscape of double-storey terraces. The bell tower of the church behind it was the only higher point in town. This being a gold rush town, everyone knew where the worship really happened. As if to show off its status, the bank was the only building without a fresh coat of paint, indifferent to modernity. The windows were braced with iron cages, looking like Hannibal Lecter's mask.

Wide steps led through a dozen stone columns up to large brass doors, complete with a peppering of polished rivets and a twisted metal wreath of a knocker. Juliette and I hurried up the stairs, desperate to get out of the butterfly tornado. Above us a huge contingent flocked together in a shadow, moving across the sky like silk. Flickers of light escaped through the beating of wings.

The brass door opened smoothly – helped by some hidden piston, given its weight – into an antechamber of sorts, a small room with an ATM to one side, an umbrella rack to the other, and a set of glass doors, this time electric, straight ahead. Looking back, I wish I'd lingered on the threshold. Just to taste the air, see those flashes of sunlight. As a detective I'm supposed to stop and notice clues. No one really tells you to notice everything else.

I'm hanging on to this moment because it's been twenty-six-odd hours since I first set foot inside this bank. I haven't left it since. I'm beginning to accept that I probably never will.

Banks are supposed to feel safe, an interior designer once told me, without intending the pun. The key is to build confidence in one of two ways. Either the bank is humble, just like you, and they'll treat your money with respect and surety, or it's the opposite: the bank is *nothing* like you, and their luxury is your aspiration. The end result is the same: hand over your hard-earned.

Huxley's Bank seemed to invest their design budget across both philosophies. Grandiose, dark-stained wood met green leather and soft lighting throughout the atrium. The ground floor was a wide-open space with a circular desk console like a ship's bridge in the centre manned by a lone receptionist. The atrium was cavernous: the ceiling was three whole storeys high. The building had no first floor, and what would have been the second was simply a balustrade-ringed mezzanine. Orange-hued lamps jutted from walls like torches in pyramid crypts. The whole vibe was expensive but, surprisingly, not garish. On a little podium by the door, a gold nugget the size of my forearm was suspended by a chrome stalk. Tapering to a sharp downward point, it looked like an ancient ceremonial dagger. The plaque on the podium beneath read: *Harold Huxley's First Find, 1892.*

'Some people frame their first dollar, I suppose.' Juliette shrugged, appraising the nugget. 'I know nothing about gold. How much do you think it's worth?'

'Enough to start a detective agency, I'd bet.'

A security guard stood by the display. His name tag read *Felix* and he was Chinese-Australian, in a crisp white shirt with black epaulettes, hands grasped either side of his belt buckle. A revolver was clipped near his hip. A plastic chair and a bottle of fluorescent orange sports drink, tucked behind one leg, completed his station. He shifted his weight between his feet and cleared his throat to signal that he was watching us. As if a judgemental cough had ever deterred someone from robbing a bank.

I held my hands up. 'I wasn't gonna.'

Juliette dragged me away, our shoes clicking on the black-and-white diamond tiling as we headed to reception. 'Why do you insist on needling people who have guns?' She prodded my chest, right where my gunshot scar was. 'You've either got a short memory or you love hospital food.'

'Or I have such a short memory I've forgotten how bad hospital food is,' I countered. 'The guard's an ornament anyway. He wouldn't pull his gun even if I was robbing the place. All the money here is insured, and an inexperienced security guard isn't going to risk escalating the situation with a firearm. It's all part of the design. The same as the bars on the windows. They don't *do* anything, but they make you feel like the building, and therefore your money, is protected. Besides, everything is digital these days. Who even robs banks anymore?'

Juliette sighed. 'Are we practising your detective skills again?'

'Go on.' I cricked my neck like a boxer preparing for a fight. 'Shake the cobwebs off.'

She knew her script, though the delivery was a little stilted in my opinion. 'Why do you think he's inexperienced?'

I looked back over at the guard. 'Well, for one thing, he's got a chair next to him but he's standing. Given that they've provided a chair, the policy must be that he can sit down if he wants. So I think he's trying to make a good impression. He's also clutching his belt, which is too heavy because of the aforementioned gun clipped to it, which means his pants don't fit properly. Which could mean he's lost weight, but then you'd shop accordingly, so it probably means he's not accustomed to having such a loaded belt. In any case, I'm extra safe from him quick-drawing on me because if he did, his pants would fall down. Shall I go on?'

'We get it, you're a detective.'

'He's actually standing because it puts him in eyeline of the receptionist, who he keeps chucking glances over at.'

Juliette's head swivelled to take in the red-headed receptionist – mid-thirties, the guard's age – scribbling in a notebook with one hand, her other forearm strapped in a blue wrist guard.

'And she's been reciprocating. But the glances are coquettish, not intense. They're exploratory. They don't really know each other yet.'

'What's an *exploratory* glance?' Juliette asked.

'The opposite of the one you're giving me.'

'Okay, genius.' I was winning her over; her tone had spun back to playful. 'The bank's only been open forty minutes. Even the laziest employee might do their job properly for an hour. Besides, we're here to meet the head honcho. He could be trying to make a good impression because his boss is about to walk past.'

'Fair points, but you forgot about the glances.'

'I'm exploring them.' Juliette tapped her lip. 'What if the receptionist is the new hire?'

'Her laptop is currently asleep and it's playing a screensaver of her most recent holiday.' It wasn't the hardest game of travel bingo, though I'd been advantaged by playing a lot of GeoGuessr in the hospital. 'I spied the Marina Bay Sands of Singapore, Macau's skyline and Vegas neon.'

'So she travels.'

'All in the same trip though. She's wearing a cast in the photos, courtesy of a broken wrist. A trip like that crisscrosses the world; it would take a while to do, and ages to save up for on her salary. So it must be long-service leave or she's accumulated a stack. And her wrist is healed enough to ditch the cast but still be strapped in a guard. So she just got back. Ergo, Felix the security guard is the new guy. How'd I do?'

'Confident, if not entirely convincing. And'—she jabbed me with a finger—'not fair play. You didn't tell me about the travel photos before you started deducing. That's hiding a clue. Naughty.'

Fair play means that the clues must be presented clearly to the reader, and Juliette is right. While I could reasonably have expected her to notice, because she was there, for the purposes of this notebook I really should have disclosed the photographs in my original descriptions. That is, of course, assuming that they are clues to the woman's years of employment at the bank.

We'd approached the desk and Juliette turned her attention to the receptionist, who looked up as we approached. A magnetic name tag read *Michelle*. 'Hi there. We're here to see Winston Huxley.'

It was no surprise she'd broken her wrist on holiday, given her clumsiness in knocking half the pens off her desk as she rummaged for, I assumed, an appointment book. I thought it strange she didn't just log in to the computer, given she had both a laptop and a desktop. She shuffled the papers around and looked up at us with a blush. 'Sorry, first week.'

Juliette kicked me righteously under Michelle's sightline. As a happy consequence, given they are a clue to something else, consider the holiday snaps now fairly introduced.

'It's for the Cunningham loan application,' Juliette said, then added with a smirk, 'This man's magnificent deductions deserve to be funded.'

'Oh, Cunningham, yeah.' Michelle nodded along without actually checking anything. 'Mezzanine level. Take the stairs. You'll see his name on the door.'

I started, 'Where—'

'If you find yourself in the basement surrounded by cash, you're in the wrong room.' She checked her watch. It occurred to me that a lot of people I was running into today were concerned about the time. She had the tone occasionally found in people whose job it is to answer questions, in that they are affronted by the audacity of someone asking them one.

'—are the stairs?'

'By the wool lift.' If she could have added *obviously* with any level of professionalism above subterranean, she would have. After a few seconds, I realised we had been dismissed, by virtue of her attention no longer abiding us. God forbid we asked where the wool lift might be, let alone why a bank had one.

We peeled away from the desk and found the stairs at the back of the room. A row of teller windows ran along the side of the building to our right. Only one was operating, the staff member attending to a teenage boy with a literal pink ceramic piggybank with a black squiggle for a tail. 'My lucky number's eighty-five,' the boy was saying. 'I'm superstitious like that.' A tinted glass screen blocked the teller from my view.

The wool lift was an antique flat wooden platform, obvious among the tiles, next to an ancient deathtrap of an elevator and the stairs. It was formerly operated by a rope-and-pulley system between floors and was now preserved as part of the floor, the ropes stationary, though still hanging for ornamental effect. A plaque nearby explained how in the early days of the bank the lift, normally used by shearers for wool, was used to raise gold from the vault in the basement to the mezzanine and third floor. I looked up. The rope line sailed into the roof, a reciprocal square hole in the mezzanine floor. I imagined them lifting gold a hundred years ago, grunting as they pulled the rope. Another fact I've recently learned about gold: it's heavy. Both on the arms and the heart, it turns out.

I clocked the glint of similar plaques all around the room. From the gold nugget to the building's historic components to oddities like a rusty teapot in the corner, the whole place was a gallery to the Huxley family's history.

Tempting as it was to see if the wool lift would take our weight, and not trusting the tiny elevator beside it to even fit the two of us, Juliette and I took the stairs. From the mezzanine level, the bird's-eye view of the space made the whole lobby feel even more resplendent, more like a ballroom than a bank. The entrance was across from us, tellers now to our left, alongside a fern-peppered waiting area, a collection of couches and some scattered tables and chairs for casual meetings. On one of the couches below was a priest, scrolling an iPad. To the right were offices, I assumed, based on the walnut-stained doors with rippled glass windows and silver-lettered names. A young woman holding a portable IV drip and an elderly woman, who I took to be her grandmother, waited by a self-service tea and coffee station. In the ceiling, four equidistant skylights shone rectangular prisms of butterfly-dappled light down from each corner, giving the whole room an eerie, aquarium-like atmosphere.

I rested my forearms on the balustrade and leaned out over the space.

Juliette braced next to me. 'We're walking out of here with Huxley's money, one way or another.' She squeezed my arm. 'I've got a vibe on this one.'

'I got it wrong,' I said.

'You got the glances right.'

'The wrong way around. Backwards isn't correct.'

'Backwards might be correct. Ever heard of a palindrome?'

I refused to lighten up. She pulled my shoulder upright, turning me away from the railing to face her.

'Wait. You're upset about that silly game? We were just messing about.'

'Exactly,' I said. 'What if that's all I'm doing? Just playing dress-up?' I flicked the tie, uncomfortable on me, to make my point. 'I'm not a detective. And every office we get laughed out of just proves it further.'

'You've solved three murder cases. You're being ridiculous.'

'That is precisely what I'm realising.'

'First of all, Winston *invited* us. And urgently. This won't be like the others. Second, you think because you didn't figure out some inane fact about someone you've never met it means you're not a detective? This is real life. You don't need to walk into a room and dissect every little thing about a person, from the way they take their coffee to their relationship with their mother, based on the length of their nose hairs. That's for fiction. Everything's a puzzle if you want it to be. You've saved lives. You don't need to solve every little thing. Just solve the things that matter.'

Her voice is in my ear now as I write this, though that may be the oxygen deprivation. Almost as if, somewhere in my subconscious, the answer to who did this to me, to the others, is trying to break out – something in this conversation bubbling up as important. What are the things that matter? Ten robberies. Ten things I suspect have been stolen. Present company excluded, all but two of the thieves – both future and current, both planned and opportunistic – were below me as I stood on that mezzanine. One hadn't entered the bank yet; the other waited for me at our 10 a.m. appointment.

I'll pause to clarify. They might all be thieves, but not everyone is conducting a full-on *heist*. That would be ridiculous.

There are only three of those.

One's already happened by this point. One's in progress. And one's about to kick off.

What else about Juliette's words is ricocheting in my brain? Palindromes. *Backwards might be correct.* How can a bank robbery happen backwards? Now that's a brainteaser. Can you rob a bank by putting something *in* it?

The answer feels . . . close. But it's water in my palm; I can't hold on to it. Best I keep on with the telling. Juliette might be a memory, but she is still waiting by the mezzanine railing for a response.

'Tense. And nasally,' I said.

'Huh?'

'That's what someone's nose hair might reveal about their relationship with their mother. And how they take their coffee. Which explains the first.'

Juliette cracked a smile and I forced one to accompany it as she pulled me towards Winston Huxley's monogrammed office door.

I took one last look at the bank's ground floor layout – schematics are important in heist narratives – and caught the guard lobbing another flirty gaze across at Michelle.

I'll just clarify one more thing. I did say *everyone* is a thief. So yes, I'm including Felix the security guard. I think I've figured him out.

Now's a good time to remind you I'm not above using a technicality, either. Not all thefts are criminal. Like I said, someone steals a heart.

CHAPTER 3

'I want you to solve a mystery.'

I was as surprised by Winston Huxley's words as his head seemed to be to have hair on it: a manic and random selection of silver tufts among liver spots and balding. He grasped my hand – cold, bony fingers like lockpicks – as he ushered Juliette and me into his office and towards two Chesterfield armchairs by a glass table. I sank into my seat, the springs softened by use. Winston gestured towards a little pod-coffee machine and kettle, and offered us tea, which we both declined. He must have been in his seventies but moved like he was younger.

I managed to shove the prospectus at him before he retreated behind a green-leather-topped writing desk with a matching emerald banker's lamp. He had on a peach-coloured shirt that was far too big, pooling around the elbows and shoulders, paired with a navy-blue vest and trousers that fit him perfectly. He leaned back in his chair and surprised me by putting his feet on the desk, revealing a pair of Air Jordan sneakers. No socks. It was as if Jekyll had dressed half of him, and Hyde the other.

Behind Winston was a black-and-white photograph of two men

holding up the dagger-esque nugget from the foyer. One I took to be Harold Huxley, with a bristly black moustache, a thick canvas shirt open across his chest and suspenders. The other was a shirtless Chinese man with work-hardened sinew. It's not a twist to reveal now that this man is related to Felix – I don't have the ink or oxygen to mess about.

The walls around us were ringed with bookshelves, mostly heavy economics hardbacks. There were also several display cases, one of which had a collection of clicking pendulums as well as an antique abacus with coloured wooden balls on four lightly rusted steel stems, accompanied by yet another small gold plaque, assumedly mentioning how it had once been used by Harold Huxley to count the number of abacuses he owned. If you're wondering, the abacus currently displayed a count of 1011. Another display case was filled with toy trucks, proper diecast metallic ones from the 1950s when lead poisoning and swallowable parts were standard in children's toys. The boxes had various brands; I recognised *Hess* and *Corgi*. I'm no collector, but these appeared to be perfectly preserved: they gleamed inside unbroken packaging. Adjacent to the desk was an upright safe, one of the old-fashioned ones with the dial on one side and a pirate-ship-looking wheel in the centre to open it. It was chin high. I can also tell you it's just big enough for me to sit cross-legged in one just like it.

Not to play a game of *Where's Ernest?* but this is not the safe I'm dying in. Neither is the code to open it 1011.

Back to the conversation at hand. 'A mystery?' I repeated, confused.

'We've already got a parrot upstairs.' Winston tossed the business plan across his desk without even looking at it. It skidded perilously close to the edge, where it would have dropped into an empty bin. 'You do disappearances, right?'

'It's not my specia—'

'You've lost it, he'll find it.' Juliette cut me off. It was not a catchphrase we'd agreed on.

'Excellent. I have found myself in a bit of a'—I would learn Winston had a habit of pausing his speech – for reflux, not thought – as if his sentences were hitch-hiking up from his throat and halting when they missed a ride—'predicament. Sign this and we can get started.'

He frisbeed a loose-leafed folder to us, which by some miracle managed to stay together long enough for Juliette to catch it.

She flicked it open. 'A non-disclosure agreement?' She raised an eyebrow.

'I think there's been a mistake,' I said. 'You invited us here to talk about a loan application.'

'For the detective agency?' Winston extended his leg and tapped the heel of one Air Jordan on our business plan, which I found quite disrespectful to the premium spiral binding.

'Yes. But we're not exactly—'

'What good is a detective agency if you won't take a case?'

'What good is a bank that doesn't lend money?' I snapped back.

A pregnant pause is a cliché in writing. This one was having triplets. Juliette stared daggers at me across the silent office. Eventually, Winston snorted. As I'd hoped, here was a man so rarely corrected that it amused him.

He spun his legs off the desk and rolled his chair around to us, hands on his thighs as his feet paddled the floor. 'For some reason, I thought you'd be less prickly in real life. The books are spot on.'

'I'm a reliable narrator. I write the complete and accurate truth.'

'I know. I know. I just assumed you'd'—he twirled two fingers around each other in the air—'finesse it a little.'

'Fair-play mysteries have no room for finesse.' I tapped the NDA. 'I can't sign this.'

'Don't be obstinate. Didn't you think it was'—his words waited for a ride, thumb out—'strange that you were invited to discuss a loan with a bank you'd never applied to?'

'Word gets around,' I offered feebly.

'That it does. Particularly when the *word* is to watch out for one Ernest Cunningham and his money-sieve of a detective agency idea.' He scoffed at my reaction. 'Don't look so surprised, of course we all talk. It's business. And you're the flavour of the week. Everyone finds you hilarious. From Sydney to Perth, it doesn't matter which bank you go to, you're tarred.'

'Is that a threat?'

'It's an offer. You're in need of a bank. And it just so happens I'm in need of a detective.'

'I hear there are big buildings filled with those. They generally have a blue and white sign out the front. Can't miss 'em.'

'I don't know if you're waiting for me to literally hand you an olive branch—' He drew a gleaming pen from his breast pocket and offered it. 'But maybe gold will do? Sign the NDA and we can discuss fees.'

'Look, I appreciate the offer,' I said, aware of both Juliette fidgeting beside me and the fact that I was tanking our last chance at financing the agency. 'But this has more red flags than a golf course. You duped us into coming up here. You won't involve the police. And the NDA. Disclosure is kind of my thing.'

'Not this time, it isn't.' Juliette plucked the golden pen from Winston's hand, signing with a flourish before I could protest. She gave me a look that, early on in our relationship, I would have misinterpreted as apologetic. Now I knew it meant *fight me*. 'What's the case?'

'Missing person,' Winston said.

'Persons,' I added, trying to reinject some professionalism. 'Even when it's just the one, it's still plural.'

'Semantics.'

'Semantics solve cases.' I made a mental note that this would be a better catchphrase for the agency.

Winston rolled his eyes and turned to Juliette. 'Is he always this argumentative?'

'Yes.'

'I disagree,' I said. Then decided to finesse myself. I won't lie in the books, but it doesn't mean I can't lie in real life. I do it quite often, actually. I held out my hand and Juliette offered me the pen. 'Who's missing, then?'

'My brother, Edward. He and I are co-directors here. He's been missing since yesterday.' Winston put a finger to his lips in thought. 'Or the night before, I suppose – that's a possibility. I assume timing is important.'

It is.

'The point is, I haven't seen him at all since I left work the day before yesterday. So far, so normal. It's not like we sleep in bunk beds. But then yesterday he didn't come into work.'

'Odd to mention your bedding. I'd assume you didn't bunk together. You share a house?'

He shook his head. 'Separate houses, but both built on the old farm. We're neighbours, not roommates.'

'How close are the houses?' Juliette asked.

'Close enough to see his car coming and going, if I take your meaning correctly. Especially with headlights on at night.'

I jumped back in. 'Is Edward the younger or older sibling?'

'Younger, by ten years.'

'Married?'

'Had a wife, Martina.'

'Had? How much did they spend on the wedding?'

'Hundred grand? I don't know. How much does a wedding cost?'

I raised a knowing eyebrow at Juliette. Don't mess with statistics.

'What does that have to do with it?' Winston continued. 'She died five years ago.'

I scribbled on the back of the manila folder. 'Foul play?'

'Definitively.' He looked at the ceiling. 'But by the big guy upstairs. Not that I believe in any of that stuff. Cancer. That can only be described as foul.'

'Kids?'

'One. Died last year. An accident.' Winston pulled at the oversized shirt absent-mindedly. 'He was only seventeen.'

'What type of accident?'

His voice tightened. 'I don't see how that's relevant.'

'Everything's relevant.' I levered some compassion into my voice. 'Your brother's lost his whole family in half a decade. That might have impacted his mental health. The biggest killer of men in this country is—'

'Edward's not the type.' He folded his arms and straightened his back. 'He's solid. Doesn't need all that wishy-washy, talking-about-your-feelings crap. And I'm not talking any more about his son. Ask him yourself when you find him.'

I nodded. 'All right. How about you? Family?'

'Married to the job.'

'And when was the last time you saw Edward?'

'In his office, Wednesday afternoon. Dusk, I suppose. I left before him, around five. He told me he had to stay back and take care of a few things.'

'A few things?'

Winston crossed his heart sarcastically. 'His exact words. I know you want it precise. I'm sure many a crime has been solved with *things*.'

'That and *stuff*. And he didn't come home?'

'That's not what I said. I said I didn't see him.'

'But you saw his headlights, I'm guessing?'

'Came through the drive around . . .' He wrinkled his nose in thought. 'Maybe seven? And then headed back out a couple of hours later – ten or eleven. Before you ask if the lights came back a second time, I was asleep. His car's still here, in the employee lot, though.'

'You can't be sure they were his headlights,' I proposed.

Winston flung his hands up, the oversized shirt avalanching down his wrists. 'My curtains were closed, there was a light outside for a bit, then there wasn't. What else is it going to be? Aliens?'

'That would not be permissible under the rules of fair-play mysteries. So you're not sure whether it was Edward, or Edward's car, or whether it was even a car. Got it.'

Winston squeezed his fist, then took a deep, nasal breath (in such a rehearsed fashion that I concluded it was a therapist-taught method, despite his adamance that therapy was *wishy-washy*) and offered me a trite smile of acknowledgement. That was what I wanted: him to be disgruntled enough to expose a little more truth than he wanted in his answers.

I pushed on. 'Do you usually see Edward every day?'

'Mostly. It's not like we're in each other's pockets, but normally he'd tell me if he's off for a weekend—' He thumped his chest; I saw his neck tighten. I wondered if it was purely biological, or some kind of truth-telling tic. 'He goes up to Brisbane mainly, or sometimes he likes to go camping. Besides, at least he'd pick up his phone.'

'Has he been to Byron much?' Juliette asked. Good job, I thought, seeking to tie the two disparate plot threads together this early in a mystery. Of course they will come together, but not quite yet.

'Hates the place. Too touristy.'

'You've called him?' I continued.

'And texted. I thought I'd try that before hiring a detective.' A twitch of his lips failed to hide his sarcasm.

'Asking the obvious questions can help find the unexpected answers,' Juliette said, which was a far more moderate response than mine would have been. Then, as if I needed another reason to marry her, she tossed in, 'For what it's worth, you're mixing up hiring us with blackmail.'

'It rang at first,' Winston capitulated. 'But now I think it's out of battery – it goes straight to voicemail.'

'Your relationship is good then?' I took the volley. 'Brotherly?'

'Depends on the definition. Didn't you kill your brother?'

I waved a hand. 'Semantics.'

'We got on well. I mean, we worked together, lived next door. Pub dinner twice a week or so, texts and email— I'm sorry, do you mind?'

It took me a second to realise he was pointing, agitated, at my face. In thought, the pen I was holding had drifted up to my lips.

'I had that fashioned from a chip off Harold's first nugget. You might have seen it in the entryway. I'd appreciate you not chewing the back of it. Gold is soft. You'll mark it.'

I made an apologetic grimace and lowered the pen back to the folder. 'And you're telling the truth? That five o'clock, two nights ago, was the last time you saw him?'

'I didn't kill Edward and then hire you to find the body, if that's what you're asking.'

'Maybe not. But then why are you wearing his shirt?'

Winston did a little surprised burp. Eventually he got out, 'How do you mean?'

'Your vest and pants are perfectly tailored, but your shirt is far too large. I'm also sinking into this chair, which means someone heavyset made the springs surrender. I assume Edward sits here when the two of you have meetings, given you guided me to it for ours, which means it's your default guest chair. And a brother's closet is fair for pilfering.'

'I spilled coffee on myself this morning, and Edward keeps a change in his office.'

'No, you didn't. You have a coffee machine, but you only offered us tea when we sat down, not the usual "tea or coffee". Which means the machine is broken or you're out of pods. The bin's empty, so you didn't have the last one, and I don't see a takeaway cup. So, no, it wasn't coffee. But you're not ready to tell me that just yet.'

Winston shuffled in his seat. Thumped his chest and let out a little hiccup. 'It's not important.' His eyelids fluttered, as if he was worried he'd given the wrong answer. The next words scurried out of his lips. 'It wasn't blood.'

Juliette leaned in. 'You'll tell us what it's not, but not what it is?'

'This isn't about my clothes. I'm looking for a missing persons.'

'Person.' I pointed with the pen. 'That usage would be singular. And it *is* about you. Thirty-six hours isn't really search-party appropriate for a grown man. Especially not someone with good physical health, a high-profile job that requires full mental faculties, and no family obligations. You called us yesterday afternoon, and at that point he hadn't even been gone a full day by your measure. Edward could have been sick, hungover. Hell, he could have just slept in. It means nothing that his car's at his workplace. He could have stumbled home from the pub, cabbed it home. Yet you called a private detective, not the police, as a matter of urgency. That's what we call, in my line of business, a bit suss.'

Winston's nose twitched as I snookered him.

'*Something*'s going on here. The only way we can find Edward is if you tell us what it is.'

'All right, all right. Jeez.' Winston leaned forward and lowered his voice, despite the privacy of his office. 'I was hoping you'd just pick around his place, phone records or whatnot, and track him down. I know he's missing, because, well . . . because he wouldn't have done this.'

'Done what?' Juliette asked.

'He's changed the code to the bloody vault.' He followed my gaze as it darted behind him to the Ernest-sized safe. 'Not my personal safe. The vault. Cash, safety deposit boxes. The beating heart of the place. If we can't find him, then I can't float the tellers, fill the machines. We've got reserves, but we can only put on a face of business-as-usual for so long.'

'You don't have a failsafe?'

'Of course we have a failsafe,' he snarled, insulted to be asked. 'Edward's in charge of security though. He's obviously interfered with it.'

'So close the bank. Drill the vault open.'

'And admit we have a problem? It'd be real subtle, bringing in a demolition team to blast open the door. You can't just drill it, you've seen too many movies. People are scared enough in this economy. I've seen it in real time: larger withdrawals to keep in mattresses, bury in backyards. We're proudly old-fashioned. Our customers are the rural and the elderly. They don't want an app. We have all that stuff – we're not in the stone age – but we work primarily in *cash*. If this got out . . .' His jaw set firm. 'This can*not* get out. I've already sent everyone home except for a skeleton crew, just to make it look normal. But we can't do withdrawals of any significance.'

'Got a photo of Edward?' I asked.

Winston slid a small picture out of his wallet and handed it to me. The two brothers, each with an arm around the other's shoulder, holding a beer in their free hand. The photo was taken indoors, a cluttered office of some kind. Bookshelves were in the background, and magnetic lettering on a metallic door spelled half a sentence between the frame and Winston's body: *THERS' DAY, LOVE B*. It was obvious who was who. I'd been right about Edward: he was twice his brother in weight, hair and cheerfulness. His cheeks were an ebullient rose.

'Anything else we need to know?' I prodded.

Winston stood up and walked over to his desk, opened a bottom drawer and pulled out a cloth sack, which he tossed on the coffee table. There were a few bundles of cash inside it, of various denominations, looped together with paper bands. The money and the cloth bag were dyed a faint red. 'I found this in his desk yesterday morning. When I first realised he wasn't here, I snooped around his office.'

I withdrew a bundle and flipped through the notes. It wasn't a huge stack. I held the red-stained money up to the light.

As if reading my thoughts, Winston added, 'It's ten grand. The red isn't blood. There was an ink pack – a radio sensor that detonates a blast of dye so stolen money can be tracked. It's not like in the movies when it blows once you open the bag, it's supposed to go off ten or so metres from the signal, which means detonating just outside the front door, but that's assuming a burglar leaves by foot. I'd never thought it would apply to vertical metres. Ed's office is on the third floor. It must have been exactly at the maximum range. I picked up the bag from his desk, and the extra height set it off. That's why I had to change my shirt.'

'You think he stole from the vault and changed the codes so you wouldn't notice?' Juliette asked. 'For a measly ten thousand dollars?'

'Of course not.' Winston scoffed. 'I think he left it behind.'

'A bank that can't open its own vault. And you're not even sure if you've been robbed or not,' I surmised. 'I see why you want an NDA.'

'Find Edward.' Winston held out his hand. 'Open my vault, and I'll open your agency. That's what we call, in my line of business, a deal.'

CHAPTER 4

Back out on the mezzanine, Juliette punched me lightly in the arm. 'That's the most exciting loan meeting I've ever been in.' She was jubilant. 'Couldn't have gone better!'

Winston had shooed us from his office and told us to wait for a teller to show us around the rest of the bank, Edward's office and the basement housing the locked vault. Two things were obvious: that he regretted having to turn to us, and that he had no other choice.

'I'm not sure,' I said, trying to match her enthusiasm but getting stuck halfway. 'He hired me because he thought I'd be a *bad* detective. His group chat with his banker buddies was mockery, not praise. So why approach me on that basis? You saw how annoyed he was having to tell us about the money and the problems with the vault. He wanted this fixed quickly by someone he could push around, someone who he had leverage with. Someone who desperately needed him enough to mask the fact that he desperately needed them.'

'Makes sense.' Juliette shrugged. 'He doesn't want to advertise that he's running a bank with, possibly, no money in it.'

'He lied to get us here.'

The *so what* was unspoken but somehow louder than what Juliette said next. 'He works in *banking*, Ernest. That he'll tell a few porkies should be assumed knowledge. Focus on his offer. Solve this one, and we get what no one else will give us.'

'It feels . . . too simple,' I said slowly.

'That's the thing about you, Ern. There always has to be a complication. Just because something's easy doesn't mean it's not good.' She squeezed my shoulders. 'A couple more murders and you'd be much more interested, I'd bet.'

It is one of the key facets of detective stories that only a murder will suffice as the central crime. It's just not interesting enough otherwise. Even if it doesn't look like a murder, it must be revealed to be so eventually. We're in the middle of several here, though I don't know it yet, even if my gut and the back of my neck is starting to tell me we might be. I've already given you advance warning that Laurence Birch was knocked off the block, and, to tell the truth, he is just the first. If complicated was what I wanted, complicated was what I was about to get.

'Why else would you change a shirt?' I understood – hell, I agreed with – Juliette, but I couldn't see past the gift horse's mouth. 'What if the red dye is the perfect cover for an actual blood stain? Red on red.'

She knew when to play along. 'It's not blood.'

'Why not?'

'Not Edward's blood, at least. Winston believes his brother's still alive, because otherwise he wouldn't pin his hopes on opening the vault merely by finding him again.'

She was right. I sat on that thought for a minute. 'I believe he wants us to find Edward,' I said eventually. 'I'm just not so sure it's for the vault code.'

'Try, please, to just take this as it is. It's good news. You have your shot, and all we have to do is find some guy who can't have gone far. You said you wanted to get away from murders anyway, right?'

As she said this, shouting floated up from the ground floor. It was a diction filled with slippery s's and mispronunciations. I caught the words *withholding* and *disgusted*. The voice was unmistakable, but impossible. It was very . . . French.

'Is that—?' Juliette and I said at the same time, leaning over the railing.

Sure enough, below us, Remy Allard, television producer in charge of adapting my first case, who was supposed to be half a world away in Hollywood, was yelling at the bank's lone teller.

We arrived on the ground floor just as Felix, the security guard, was approaching the kerfuffle. Remy was standing on his tiptoes in brown sailor's loafers to block the window's shutter against the pull of the bamboozled bank teller. He mistook the guard for coming to his aid, as people with money tend to mistake approaches as service.

'Thank you,' Remy said with a sigh, his spare arm wobbling in the air. His hair was perfectly cut to make it look like he needed a haircut. He had on a plain white t-shirt with a diagonal black stripe across it, tucked neatly into calf-baring pleated pants that were short enough to look ridiculous, and ridiculous enough to give the impression that they were fashionable and *you just don't get it*. A brown leather satchel hung over a shoulder. His top lip was pinched in the middle, which gave him a lubricated way of speaking. 'Could you tell this *moron* to serve me? You can't close a bank at ten thirty in the morning.'

'Everything all right, Milton?' The guard spoke over Remy's shoulder at the teller. His serious voice was fake, garnished with gruff. His posture was loose – shoulders relaxed, feet apart. As far as security gigs went, I assumed Huxley's was a cushy one: those electrolytes in his drink bottle were wasted here. This was not a bank often robbed. Until today, that is.

'Felix. Finally,' Milton began. He was clean shaven, dark haired but with a spot of white on his left temple, though I was unsure if it was genetic or had bleached only since the stress of meeting Remy. Milton was wearing a polo shirt, black with orange sleeves, embroidered with *Huxley's* above the pocket. 'As I've explained to the customer, we're not closing. We're short-staffed today and I have to attend to an urgent matter. I told him I'd serve him afterwards.' He directed his words to the guard, but said them loud enough so Remy would overhear, like a child in trouble.

'What do you suggest I do until then? *Go bankrupt?*' Remy was prone to exaggeration.

'If that is a pressing issue,' Milton countered, 'I might not be much help regardless.'

Remy doesn't take well to plain facts or sarcasm, possibly because his conversations are so hyperbolic he often can't tell the difference. He would only know the price of milk if he owned the cow. As such, he started to boil. Felix, sensing this might tip over, tapped a sign by the booth. *Please don't abuse our staff – we're all on the same team!*

I love passive-aggressive office signs, because it means not only has an indiscretion happened, it's happened enough times to warrant a trip to the printer. Remy, who believes signs are written for other people, inhaled to retort but then spotted Juliette and me and, at last, deflated. He shrugged off the staff with a grunt and slid over to us. That's another thing about Remy; he rarely walks anywhere – he sidles, slides and hovers. He is so propped up by his own self-belief it enables him to tread lightly. It means he has a habit of arriving by your shoulder unannounced.

After a quick, too-wet kiss on Juliette's cheek, he thumbed back at the teller window. 'Unbelievable.' Then, as if it were a restaurant, 'The service around here.'

'I think we might be responsible,' I said, waiting for Remy to acknowledge the bizarreness of us bumping into each other in country Australia, but he didn't look surprised at all. Beside me, Juliette subtly wiped her glistening cheek. 'We're the urgent matter.'

Remy sized me up. In the hierarchy of filmmaking, the writer was often at the bottom. I could see his imagination trying to stitch together a scenario where I was more deserving of urgency than he was and completely failing. Then he landed on one possible scenario: 'Has there been a murder?'

'I expect one was just prevented,' Juliette chimed in. 'Aren't you based in LA? Why are you all the way out here?'

'Our set's not far,' he answered.

'You've built a set? How did I not know that?' I asked, feeling like there was a party I hadn't been invited to. 'If you're making progress, does that mean there's another instalment of the rights fee?'

'Not at this bank!' Remy said, loud enough for Milton to hear.

'Hang on.' I thought it through. 'It's far too hot.' My first case, the one being filmed, was set in the mountains, at a hotel caked in snow.

'Potatoes,' Remy said. Then, irritated at my confusion, spoke insultingly slowly to explain. 'We don't use *actual* snow in television. How would you keep it together for a dozen takes? And confetti looks fake in hi-def. So we use potatoes. Shredded, mashed. Dyed white. Whatever. Every time someone eats an ice-cream in a film: potatoes.'

'It seems your whole production is *on potatoes* then. With Laurence Birch and all.'

Remy's brow furrowed. 'Laurence is dead, haven't you heard?'

'That's what I meant. On ice.'

'Don't get me started,' Remy said, as if he were having a harder day than the guy who'd headbutted a delivery van. 'I mean, I've worked with actors who insist on doing their own stunts before. People who might get themselves killed, just so they can brag about jumping off trains or whatever. It could screw the whole production – we've got to make the insurance watertight. But Laurence was supposed to be low risk. He doesn't even do his own pick-ups—'

I didn't get the chance to admit my cluelessness at the term before Remy rolled his eyes and explained.

'—reshoots. In movies we film a double from over the shoulder to pick up dialogue. Let alone his own stunts.'

'I've jumped off a train,' I offered, not that it was a competition. 'Laurence wasn't insured?'

'Oh, he was. Heavily. Though not as heavily as some.' He sucked in his cheeks. 'Tell you what, absolutely, devastatingly'—he sniffed, shook his head and for a second I mistook him for sincere—'*selfish*. A lead actor getting himself killed like that. No respect.'

'I'm sorry for your loss,' I said with zero sincerity, placing a hand on his shoulder.

Remy took it at face value, grabbed my hand and clasped it. 'Thank you, that means a lot.'

'Do you bank with Huxley's?' Juliette asked. It was strange for Remy to have any Australian bank accounts, let alone one in a rural town, even if he was filming nearby. Any Hollywood production budget was probably more than this bank would have in the vault on a good day. If Remy did have local banking servicing the TV show, no wonder Milton couldn't meet its demands with what he had on hand. Winston had just told me they couldn't do significant withdrawals without vault access. Is that what Remy wanted? *Withholding*, he'd said.

I'll flag that I'm aware of the genre requirement here. This is a murder mystery. No coincidences allowed. Now, of course, any group of people, in any place, gathered together, is some kind of coincidence. But Remy Allard simply can't be in this bank, halfway around the world, for no reason. It wouldn't be fair. Which is why he's about to lie to me.

'I have a little bit everywhere.' Remy waved off the question. 'Huxley's handles my clothing company.' I didn't know he had a clothing company, but it didn't surprise me that he had as many pies as fingers. A film and television producer is like an investor. Remy followed the green. I'd watched his latest film, *Touchdown*, after our first meeting. It had over a dozen twirly logos before the credits, which I'd been surprised to find were all, by some administrative trickery or another, Remy's businesses. He was the babushka doll of filmmaking and every company owned a smaller company: from the cameras, to the batteries in the cameras, to the bags to put the batteries for the cameras in. The film, by the way, was awful: expensive visual effects and A-list actors couldn't save a story about space monsters learning about American football and falling in love along the way. Who'd have thought? Even the title was bad. I would have gone with *Pitch Invasion*.

Remy pointed at his shirt. 'Do you like it?'

I weighed up his plain white t-shirt with the diagonal black stripe. 'It's minimalist.'

'It's not about fashion, you imbecile. We live in a surveillance world. Cameras on every corner. You ever gotten a ticket for not wearing a seatbelt?' Remy had a habit of hurling an insult and then immediately chatterbox-ing over it, as if not acknowledging it made it less offensive. He gestured at his torso. 'You won't get a ticket wearing this. The cameras think you're wearing one.' He showcased the black stripe like it was a sash at Miss Universe. 'Company's called BeltBuster. We're still in the investment round, if you're interested.'

'No.' I said it too quickly and chucked in, 'Thank you.'

'Your loss.'

'What happens with the show now?' I couldn't resist asking. My cheque was due on the first day of principal photography – the day the cameras start rolling – but without a star, there was no shoot.

'It's a shame. Laurence was going to be really great. I foresaw awards. Big things.' And here, at last, was the misty-eyed eulogy. Not for the man, but for the production. Remy's money dripping down the drain like Birch's blood through the gutter. 'And he loved this role. Said you had *meat on your bones*.'

'He was playing me, not eating me.'

'Means you have depth.' He sized me up. Crinkled his nose. 'Personally, I don't see it. But that's what a great actor does. He was finding angles to you I bet you haven't even discovered. Embodying you.'

'That's not embodying. That's fictionalising.'

'That's *acting*. I wish you could have sat down with him. You might have learned something about yourself.'

'He doesn't even look like me,' I sulked.

'Of course he doesn't. This is the movies. The point is to upgrade things.'

I must have blanched, because Remy seemed surprised to have offended me. His phone started to ring, and he answered in the way where he spoke the last of our conversation directly into it, as if to impress on both the caller and me that he was too busy to direct his speech to either and we should just tune in to what was relevant to each of us.

'Don't take it personally. He might be more handsome, famous and rich than you. But you're better at crossing roads.'

CHAPTER 5

Juliette and I had taken a seat among the waiting area's grid of couches while Milton finished chatting to Felix. They were occasionally pointing over at Remy, I assumed discussing whether it was worth the aggravation of kicking him out. The priest I'd seen from the balcony was fanned out on the couch opposite the one we took, legs open in a position that would be described as *greedy* were he on a bus, and gave us a mild nod as we sat down. It's pointless describing a priest but here goes: all black, trousers and shirt, white collar like a midnight cat's nose.

'You buy Remy's clothing story?' I asked Juliette.

'I buy that he's made a bad investment. I don't buy that's why he's here.'

A clicking interrupted us. I looked up and saw the priest snapping his fingers and gesturing animatedly to get our attention. I gave him a curious wave. He had short curly blond hair with dark roots, thin wire-framed glasses and a nose so small it was as if he were built from clay and it had been forgotten, thumbed on last minute with a ball of scavenged scraps. He turned to his iPad and tapped quickly, then spun it around. I saw white blocky text on a black screen, like a chauffeur might hold up at an airport.

ERNEST CUNNINGHAM?

'Yeah,' I said.

The priest pointed at his throat. Then made an X with his forearms. *Can't talk.*

I nodded my understanding.

He pointed to his ears, gave me the thumbs up. *Can listen.*

I nodded again, then felt like I should say something aloud and went with the first foolish thing that popped into my head, which was, 'You're a priest.'

He flipped, tapped, then re-flipped the iPad.

NAH. JUST EARLY FOR HALLOWEEN.

I must have looked concerned – it was 22 August – as he followed it with:

WE'RE ALLOWED TO MAKE JOKES.

'This is Juliette.' I gestured towards her.

The priest nodded deeply in greeting. GABRIEL. DON'T WORRY ABOUT THIS. He pointed at his throat. TEST OF FAITH.

'I thought only monks did vows of silence.'

SOMETIMES IT'S NICE TO STOP AND LISTEN.

'How do you know my name, Father?' I asked.

FATHER. He crinkled his nose in disgust and retyped. GABRIEL'S FINE. I READ YOUR BOOKS.

'How'd you like them?'

I'VE READ A BETTER ONE. He smiled.

'Not fair. That one has co-writers.'

The conversation risked drying up. Banks are like doctor's offices: if it's rashes or cashes, you can't ask the person across from you what they're in for. So we didn't have much more to talk about. The priest was keen to continue though. He held up a finger for me to wait and turned back to his iPad. It took him a while to type.

I HEARD YOU TALKING ABOUT LAURENCE BIRCH. I GAVE HIS LAST RITES THIS MORNING AT DAWN. THAT FRENCH GUY HIS AGENT? Gabriel's glasses bounced on his nose as he wriggled his brow expectantly at me.

'No.'

HE WAS HANGING ABOUT. KEEN TO UNPLUG.

'Why are you telling me this?'

YOU'RE HERE. He tapped at the screen. MURDER?

'Not yet.'

BUT SOMETHING'S OFF. He leaned forward. I'M A FAN OF LAURENCE. KNOW HOW HE GOT HIS START IN MOVIES?

'He can sing,' Juliette said slowly. Then, in revelation, 'Maybe that works. Damn it, I didn't even think—' She realised the company. 'Oh. Shi— Damn. Shoot. Sorry.'

Gabriel was clearly unfussed by casual blasphemy. He offered a magnanimous smile.

Juliette turned to me and said plainly, 'Laurence started in musicals.'

I frowned. I didn't get it. Gabriel tapped away. Juliette pointed in vigorous agreement at what he'd written.

AND DANCE. TRIPLE THREAT. IF YOU GET MY MEANING.

'He's got good balance,' I replied. 'A dancer isn't going to trip in front of traffic. Is that your point?'

His eyebrows shot skywards, expecting my excitement, and fell when they didn't get enough to hold them up. He tapped determinedly on his iPad. I HEARD YOU TALKING WITH THE FRENCHMAN ABOUT INSURANCE. I THOUGHT . . . He paused. He'd managed to get tongue-tied without speaking. He deleted and started again. GIVEN HE WAS SO KEEN TO UNPLUG.

I cocked my head in surprise.

Gabriel gave a non-apologetic shrug. EAVESDROPPING ISN'T A SIN.

He tapped some more, but this time he wasn't writing. After a moment, he passed over his iPad showing an eBay auction page. There were several listings from the same profile, *CelebrityEstateSale69*: a signed photograph of Laurence Birch, a lock of hair, a pilot script with a red cover on it, and a pale-blue takeaway coffee cup. Gabriel made a drinking motion, so I tapped on the link for the coffee cup. The heading read *Laurence Birch, coffee cup, holding during fatal accident. GENUINE DNA!!!*

There was a gallery of photos. The cup was slightly crumpled, no lid. The bottom was stained dark brown by either coffee or blood. There was nothing significant about it, except for the price.

'Fifteen hundred bucks?' I snorted. 'That's insane.'

I thought about the inconsolable young superfan in the café and wondered if she'd lay out fifteen hundred big ones for a piece of trash with DNA on it. I really didn't see the point, unless a mad scientist wanted to clone the dead actor.

'Celebrity death market,' Juliette said. She held up her phone, where she'd done a quick search. 'Locks of hair. Water bottles with lipstick smears. Look, two weeks ago a piece of Laurence's used chewing gum sold for fifty dollars. I guess dying must increase the price.' She scrolled. '*Eurgh*, some people buy *bathwater*. There must be demand for coffee cups.'

Gabriel swiped his finger in the air. The meaning was clear: *scroll*.

I scrolled through the images, which showed the cup from all sides. I stopped on the final one. On the side of the cup, scrawled in black texta, was a name.

ERNEST.

'Embodying,' I muttered under my breath.

It's becoming clear that I can't escape the beckoning of the classic mistaken identity plot. I still wasn't convinced we looked similar, but if Laurence was trying on method acting, going by my name in public places, that gave it another level of plausibility. Was it enough? One of the key points of some old-fashioned mistaken identity mysteries is that the character may have never met the doppelganger. *But the victim can't possibly have died yesterday*, a character may exclaim, *I had a meeting with him this morning!* They don't even have to look the same if the killer merely adopts the persona, and not the face, of the victim. It doesn't really hold up in the modern day, with Google Images and social media profiles. I suppose you've twigged that this morning was the first time I've met Winston Huxley in the flesh, and he might be Edward, but that kind of bamboozlement had run its course once we hit the 2000s.

As for me and Laurence 2.0: if someone had genuinely never seen me, could they mistake Laurence Birch for Ernest Cunningham, overhearing him give my name to a barista?

I handed the iPad back to Gabriel, who typed, CURIOUS?

'I'll admit it's interesting.'

Gabriel performed a smug charade of brushing dust off each shoulder. Having got his reward of acknowledgement, he checked the time, then stood up and headed over to Michelle at reception. She gave him a head shake in clear commiseration.

'If, and I say that heavy on the *if*,' Juliette said, dissecting plausibility the same way I had, 'someone had never met you, they might get you mixed—'

'Why would someone who'd never met me want me dead?'

A grin twitched. 'Yes, much more likely from people who *have* spent time with you.'

'It's still more likely that someone hasn't jumbled us up. Remy, for example, couldn't possibly confuse the two of us. If he was involved, it has to be for different reasons.'

'Involved? You mean his desire to switch the machines off?'

In the background, Gabriel was holding up his iPad for Michelle: HE CAN'T IGNORE ME FOREVER. EVER HEARD THE PHRASE 'PATIENCE

OF A SAINT'? If it's not a sin to eavesdrop, then neither can it be to eaves-read, I figured.

'Sounds to me like if you insured a film correctly,' I continued, 'you might make more money *not* making it.'

'There's a leap between insurance fraud and murder, Ern. I love the way your mind works, but you have a tendency to catastrophise.'

'I know.' I mulled it over. 'And I know what you're going to say – that I'm turning this into a murder. That I should focus on Winston's request to find his brother. But I *am* thinking about Edward. Isn't it strange that Laurence is dead, Remy is here, and Edward is missing? Feels like there's something connecting them.'

I took out a pen and wrote each of their names in the points of an imagined triangle. What could go in the middle? 'I need to see the vault. What is taking Milton so long?' I swivelled around and looked for the teller. Surprisingly, he was once again behind the window, serving a person with a baggy hoodie, head cocooned in it.

Remy spotted this at the same time I did and strode over to declare his disgust. He rested a hand on the hooded person's shoulder. '*Some* of us have been waiting!'

'Ern.' Juliette plucked the pen out of my hand. I looked down; it was Winston's gold pen. I'd forgotten to give it back. 'He'll be livid.'

I was only half-listening. Juliette said something else, but it came to me muffled, as if spoken through a car window. She hadn't seen it yet. Milton had, based on the beads of sweat rolling down his forehead. Gabriel probably hadn't, though I wondered if he'd break his vow to call out. Michelle had her back to it. The teenage boy, the sick girl and her grandmother were too far away, and Felix too inattentive. Unfortunately for Remy, though he was closest, he hadn't seen it either.

'Hey! I was first.' Remy pulled on Hoodie's shoulder and spun him around. 'I'm talking to yo—'

His hands shot up like an action figure that's had its lever pulled and he staggered backwards. Now he'd seen it.

'Are you listening?' Juliette rapped my knuckles playfully with the pen. 'I said congratulations – you just robbed a bank.'

'Turns out,' I said, as we heard the gunshot, 'I'm not the only one.'

THE SECOND HEIST: A SINGLE DOLLAR

CHAPTER 6

It wouldn't be much of a murder mystery if the thief had shot Remy square in the gut, in full view of the detective. Instead, they'd raised the gun and fired it into the ceiling. Plaster and dust sprinkled down, speckling the thief's hood with its own form of dandruff.

Juliette and I slid off the lounge to the floor. I'd caught a quick glimpse under the hood but hadn't seen a face, just the glint of a silver mask. Across the room, I saw Michelle hunched inside her circular reception desk and Gabriel taking refuge on the other side of it. I couldn't spot the patient and her grandmother, but I could see the IV stand, upright, by the tables, so I assumed they were huddled under one of them. The teenager with the piggy-bank was closest to the exit. He made a break for it, through the sliding doors to the vestibule. My eyeline to the main brass door was blocked, but I could see the boy's lower half. The way his back hunched, legs bracing, told me he was pushing against a locked door. Trapped.

I risked a peek up. Remy, for his part, had fallen to the floor. He scrambled backwards, shoes finding no purchase and squeaking against the tiles. Felix had his hands behind his head, wet patches in his armpits already. I'd been right about him being a quick surrender: his gun was already on the ground, a snub-nosed revolver with a brown grip. He kicked it over to the thief with a clatter, wincing like it might go off.

Nobody moved, the whole atrium frozen like a chess set in an indecisive match. Gunsmoke curled in the air; the smell of burning tickled. The tap of butterfly wings on the windows outside was the only noise.

Then, in an instant, chaos. The sprinklers came on first, hissing out a deluge strong enough to drench us immediately. The water was freezing. An alarm kicked up next, piercingly loud. The thief whirled back to the teller windows. Milton's hands, which had crept under the desk towards a panic button, I assumed, shot back to vertical. But the damage was done, the alarm's wail swelling. It was hard to tell if I imagined the twitch of the thief's trigger finger among the sheets of water, but the automatic security shutters rattling down might have saved Milton's life. The steel curtains slammed into place, cutting off the teller booths.

The thief scanned the room. Not wanting a third eye in the centre of my forehead, I ducked back down. After a few minutes, the sprinklers bled out to a drip. The plonk of the last fat drops in puddles echoed. The alarm still raged. But, underneath it all, there was a new sound. The click of a heel, and the slap of a toe. Footsteps on wet tile. The thief was moving.

What now? Juliette mouthed to me. Droplets hung from her eyelashes like dew on blades of grass. Forgive me a moment of fond reflection on this detail. I am dying, after all.

Click-slap. Click-slap.

It was getting louder. I didn't want to become a target by poking my head up, so I glanced over at reception instead. Gabriel was tapping at his iPad.

Click-slap. Click-slap.

Juliette tugged at my sleeve. She was shivering, but I couldn't tell if it was fear or the impromptu ice bath. I tried to focus on the footsteps in the cacophony. They might have been fading a little. Had the thief changed path, or were they simply treading more softly?

I looked back to the reception desk. Gabriel was holding up his iPad with the answer.

Run.

CHAPTER 7

Hostage is a new identity for me. Both being one and taking one: but it's a day of firsts.

It might be a valid test of faith, but Father Gabriel's iPad was useless as a timely warning signal. A gun barrel introduced itself to the bridge of my nose as I stood.

Aside from a slight shuffle to put myself between the thief and Juliette, I didn't dare make any larger movement. The thief tilted their head slightly, sizing me up. I took the same opportunity. Up close, I could see the hood was pulled over the convex silver mesh of a fencer's sabre mask. I peered into it, but it was like looking at a mannequin. I couldn't make out anything else.

Under the jumper, I could see fabric matching their pants poking out at the wrists: a navy-blue boilersuit, like a mechanic might wear. With the layers of clothing, it was hard to guess their body shape: man or woman, heavyset or lithe, Edward or Not-Edward (as I'm sure you're thinking). Yellow canvas gardening gloves that looked well soiled, and stiff army-surplus boots completed the outfit. This heist was clearly planned, but not far enough in advance to get the costuming down. It reeked of a hasty solution to a forgotten dress-up day at school.

I could hear the thief's breathing pulsing against the inside of the mask, ragged with adrenaline. The gun in their hand stayed eerily still, as if daring me to underestimate their composure. They were standing on the other side of the couch. I doubted I had the reflexes to vault over it before they pulled the trigger, so stayed put.

The Fencer flicked the gun to the side. *Move.*

I found my voice. 'No.'

I heard a hiss of annoyance from the mesh. Then a deep, nasal inhale. The Fencer was trying to keep themselves calm. After what I assumed was an internal and therapeutic count to ten, they jabbed the gun again, repeating the flick to the side, this time more emphatically. I realised it was pointing to the reception console, where Gabriel and Michelle had bunkered down. They wanted us together.

To be honest, I was happy with safety in numbers. I'd only refused the first instruction to test the thread of the thief's patience, to see if they were trigger-happy or not. I'd also wanted to imprint on them that *I* was the potential troublemaker of the group. Should things go south, this made it more likely I would be targeted first, therefore protecting the others. Satisfied I'd achieved both of those goals, I pulled Juliette up from the floor and we were obligingly herded towards the desk, the border-collie-with-a-gun a few steps behind us.

The alarm gave a dying low-power squawk and called it quits. The whole space felt like a cyclone had just come through, a crippled place coming back to life. The sheen of water on the tiles bounced the light around the atrium, and the air held a tang of chlorine amid the damp. I thought I heard a siren, a long way off, but I couldn't tell if it was just my ears still ringing.

We reached Michelle and Gabriel and, again, the thief silently gestured with the gun. The Fencer and Gabriel would have a hell of a time catching up.

'A gun? Seriously?' Michelle snorted, shaking her head at the Fencer as she joined the pack. We started moving towards the entrance. The thief heralded Remy and Felix with another wave of the gun and they hurried over. We picked up hostages like a magnet collects filings. Now we were moving as six.

'Type faster next time,' I hissed at Gabriel, as he fell in step.

We arrived at the interior vestibule doors, which slid open to reveal the teenager sitting inside. He had his knees up, back against the brass door, which I could now see was firmly chained in a figure-eight between the two handles and padlocked. Unlike us, the teenager was dry, there being no sprinklers in the annex. He must have been fifteen, peak acne. His face looked like cheap fried rice: pasty white, flushed with occasional pink spots. His piggybank sat on the floor beside him. When he saw us all approach, the gun holding us in line, he dragged the pig protectively into his lap. As if that was worth robbing a bank over.

Piggybank secured, the boy needed little encouragement. Juliette gave him a reassuring squeeze on the shoulder as he joined the huddle, but his gaze kept drifting to the gun.

She grabbed his chin and forced him to look at her. 'Hey. I'm Juliette. Stick with me.'

'Eric,' came back a quivering voice.

Our un-chained chain gang moved back to the atrium, where we approached the collection of tables and chairs, the abandoned IV drip in the middle of them.

There was no one there.

The Fencer moved to the front of the pack, holding out a hand for us to stay put. They bent and looked under the tables. When they stood up, I could tell they were shaking. Then, with a sudden burst of violence, they flipped one of the tables. Then another, kicking and heaving until every chair and table and possible hiding spot was upended and the furniture lay strewn around them. The IV stand crashed, the bag rupturing and clear fluid glugging out onto the tiles. Then they went over to the reception console, swiping everything off the desk, looking underneath it, ripping the computer from its station and hurling it across the room in a tornado of plastic shards and circuit boards. The thief's shoulders heaved as they stood in the middle of the carnage and regained their breath. I started to regret outing myself as the troublemaker.

'They don't have enough hostages,' I whispered to Juliette.

If there was a plan, it was clear this wasn't it. They can't have been worried about alerting the police: the silent alarm had already been pushed. So the wrinkle must be that all of us were needed as hostages. I couldn't make sense of why seven hostages instead of nine was such a problem.

Mathematically, I figure you really only need one hostage to make your point. Or two, I suppose, if you're the showman type and plan to kill one. Point is: I saw no objective difference between seven and nine hostages, or ten if I include Winston, assumedly hiding upstairs, in my count. Even if we ruled out Milton, safe behind the lockdown shutters, there seemed to be enough of us.

To the Fencer, by the way they were stalking the room, kicking at chairs as they passed, it seemed more crucial to get their house in order. They scanned the room. The only places to run were the offices that ringed the ground floor, the basement or upstairs. The thief's head swivelled between the three. The growl of breath hummed against the wire mesh.

Indecision.

There were bars on most windows, I'd seen that coming in, but I hadn't viewed them from every angle. Maybe there would be a way out in one of the offices, or the bolts in the sandstone were rusted enough to be kicked out of the wall. Likewise, perhaps there was a fire escape upstairs, or roof access. The basement would be a dead-end, so it could be ruled out as an escape route. The dilemma was obvious: two possible floors, one searcher. If the thief really did need all of us, they didn't want to risk the extra two hostages getting away while they searched the wrong floor.

They tapped the gun casually against their hip. Then they turned and strode over to the group with the confidence of a decision made. I'd love to say I threw myself in front of what was about to happen, but they had Eric by his collar before I even registered the threat. The Fencer dragged the boy from the group, spun him around, then took a step away and held the pistol out, arm's length, right to the back of Eric's head.

'No!' All of us, excepting Gabriel obviously, shouted in unison. The gun spun on us, and our voices fled, our advance slowed.

The Fencer cleared their throat loudly, returned to their stance, arm outstretched, the gun back in place at the base of Eric's skull. Eric was shaking, jeans darkened. Gabriel woke up his iPad.

A sound came from inside the mask. A long, clear whistle. Two notes: high then low. *Yoo-hoo.*

I thought I saw a flutter in the curtains on one of the ground floor office windows.

The Fencer put a second hand on the gun, steadied their aim. Whistled again.

I could hear Gabriel tapping at his screen behind me. I was just about to turn and say something pithy about the uselessness of typing out a protest, when the iPad sailed past my ear, spinning across the room in a near-perfect frisbee, and smacked the thief right in the side of the head.

I stand corrected.

As the iPad clattered to the tiles with the distinctive *tink* of a glass screen breaking that triggers humanity's Pavlovian wince of *expensive*, the thief seemed to short-circuit. Their mask had been knocked askew, revealing white skin, stubble, a blade of a chin. A man, then. He wrenched it back into place. He stared down at the device in silence, while we all took a collective breath and held it. I saw him take the same deliberate quivering inhales he'd taken when I'd been uppity before. As if he was asking some higher power for the strength not to shoot anyone.

Hate to break it to you, buddy, but the Word of God just smacked you upside the head.

Then he was marching over. Credit where credit's due, Gabriel had succeeded in making the thief forget about the youngest hostage; Eric was now safe and forgotten. Instead, the gun now pressed against each of our foreheads in silent accusation. Most of us, me included, wilted away from the barrel, still warm from the first firing. Juliette pressed herself against it in rebellion, which seemed to be enough for the thief to decide that she was the culprit. He didn't shoot. Instead, he raised his arm, ready to swing the pistol down across her brow.

Every one of us has a fuse burning inside. I've solved enough murders to know that's all a murder is, a spark fizzing to the end of it. *Boom*. You might think you don't have a murder in you, but you do. It's just at the end of a very long fuse. A murder happens when that cord is clipped, shortened, inch by inch, by motives and transgressions, until it has nowhere to go but right into the dynamite in the pit of your stomach. For everyday people, that fuse is long enough to bear the snips. Murderers are a mix: for the psychos it's too short, sure, but some people have weathered too many snips.

Watching this guy preparing to pistol-whip my fiancée snipped all my remaining fuse at once. The spark hit the bomb inside, and I leapt up with a roar. I'll be honest, I was ready to kill this guy. Rip his mask off and make him eat it. He saw me move and turned—

'Ever fired one of those before?' A new voice hit us from across the room.

We all froze. An office door was now open. The elderly woman was standing in the doorway. This, I will learn, is Laverna. She wore an aqua silk blouse rolled up to the elbows and tucked into pleated white pants. Blue and black ink curled up both her arms, colour dipping in and out of crinkled skin like a mottled ocean. Her voice suffered the weight of thousands of cigarettes, and her straight-backed indignance that of thousands of fools. A set of wide brown eyes and a pasty forehead occasionally poked over her shoulder as she moved towards us.

'Pulling a trigger takes a lot more than a twitch of the muscle,' Laverna said. 'It takes desire. It takes heart. Maybe desperation. Something deep inside, to bubble up. It takes something volcanic.' She stopped walking a few metres from the group, as the Fencer turned his attention, and aim, to her. She wrinkled her nose, unfazed. 'I see steam but no lava. And if I'm wrong, well, that'd be the same mistake my second husband made.'

The gun tilted up to the roof, finally away from anyone. Juliette closed the gap between us and pulled me into her arms.

'Thank you,' Laverna said. 'This is what you wanted, us to join your little crew, correct?'

The thief gave a nod.

The eyes reappeared over Laverna's shoulder as she waved an open palm in a semi-circle. 'The floor is yours. On with it.'

The Fencer hesitated. He'd got what he wanted, but perhaps he didn't want it to seem like he needed Laverna's permission to proceed. Deciding to keep the bird in the hand, he pointed the gun at the stairs and flicked it in an upwards motion.

As we headed for the stairs, Gabriel scurried over to his iPad and picked it up. It was as good as a confession that he'd thrown it. I got a quick glimpse. A spiderweb of cracks on the right of the screen obscured half of the word he'd written, but I could still piece it together: COWARD.

Juliette was in front of me; I'd made sure to place myself between her and the gun again. She was muttering platitudes to a snuffling Eric. Well, to be honest, I couldn't actually see the snuffling, just hear it. I assume it was Eric, but it may well have been a grown-man movie producer. I felt a tug at my arm. Laverna had her hand out. She introduced herself in a whisper, then gestured to the pallid girl with her. 'Being we're all in this together, we might as well get to know each other. This is my granddaughter, Cordelia.'

Cordelia gave a timid nod, her eyes glued to the floor. She didn't take up much space, both physically – she was short, thin-boned – and with her general energy. She had cascading blonde hair that went to her hips and was walking in tiny, shuffling steps. I pegged her as early twenties, even though her attitude felt younger.

I pointed over at her IV on the floor, the bag of fluid now leaked out and empty. 'Is she okay without that?' I asked, checking over my shoulder. The thief didn't seem to notice us talking.

'She'll be fine. Won't you, love?' Laverna squeezed Cordelia's shoulder. 'One battle at a time.'

'Once the police get here,' I said quietly, 'this guy'll give his demands. It'll be give-a-little, get-a-little. We just need to go along with it until we know what he wants. We'll make Cordelia the first trade.'

Remy butted in, making no effort to lower his voice. 'The dying girl's got the least reason to go first.'

Cordelia glanced up.

'No offence.'

Gabriel gave him a sharp elbow to the ribs.

'What?' Remy was wide-eyed. 'Am I wrong?'

Gabriel flashed the iPad at him, no need to retype the word already on there.

'Offence taken,' I said. 'You'll go last.'

The thief cleared his throat from behind us, hushing the conversation. As we reached the stairs, Cordelia pushed out in front and I fell behind Laverna, the stairwell reducing us to single file.

'Thank you,' Laverna whispered back to me as we trudged upwards. 'First to the lifeboats, that one.'

'In a wig,' I agreed. 'I'm sorry, but I just have to ask—'

'Faster than some, slower than others.'

'Huh?'

She kept her voice low. 'You were going to ask me if Cordelia is dying.'

'I was actually going to ask if you really shot your second husband.'

'Gosh. No. Glad the intimidation worked though.' She chuckled. 'I've never even seen a gun before.'

'That makes your composure even more remarkable, given it was pointed at your head.'

She shrugged. 'I was a dangerous cargo specialist in the eighties. Those are fancy words for *truck driver*. And the words *truck driver* are simple words for *a volatile environment for women*. I knew what was in the back of my truck might kill me, but I hadn't been prepared for the real danger being outside of it. Not much scares me these days. I figured I'd just let him know where the balance of power was.' She turned to look at me, and I saw a spark in her eye. Her voice lilted with amusement. 'It *was* a bit of a thrill. I mean, who even sticks up a bank anymore? How deliciously old-fashioned.'

CHAPTER 8

With full respect to my fellow hostages, the nine of us didn't seem the most high-value group of detainees. A silent priest, Gabriel; a patient and her carer, Cordelia and Laverna; a teenager, Eric; a trainee-receptionist and a surrendering security guard, Michelle and Felix; a film producer with a dead star, Remy; and a pair of amateur detectives.

We were sodden and sullen, seated around a large oblong mahogany table, locked in a boardroom on the third floor. The Fencer had gone down a floor to find Winston, a hostage with some actual value. I assumed, given I hadn't seen him peering curiously over the mezzanine's balustrade, that he had barricaded himself in his office on hearing a gunshot.

The top floor had been spared the sprinklers, so the carpet didn't squelch. People squeezed out their soaked cuffs or tried to lean into the slivers of sunlight coming through the barred windows to dry. Through the barrage of white flutters, I could see down to Main Street. Two police cars sat in a V, bonnets together, blocking the street. The whole hostage round-up had taken maybe fifteen minutes, which seemed enough for the local police response but not enough for any specialty units.

'Why are we just waiting for him to come back?' Remy asked, wringing out his socks and draping them over the back of a chair, despite the fact Eric was sitting in it. Remy is clearly the type of airline passenger whose feet wriggle onto your arm rest from the row behind. Eric, the type to take it, just leaned away. 'He didn't explicitly tell us to stay here.'

HE DIDN'T SAY ANYTHING. Gabriel showed off his grasp of irony.

'He's locked the door,' Felix said matter-of-factly from the other side of the table. He might have been the only person benefitting from the robbery so far, given he was towelling off Michelle's hair with a micro-fibre towel he'd had in his pocket. 'Speaks for itself.'

'And? You don't kick doors down in security training?'

'He has a gun.'

'He has two,' Remy sneered. 'You gave him yours.'

Felix made to stand, but Juliette put a hand on his shoulder. 'We don't know what this guy wants, but we're going to be here until he gets it,' she said. 'Let's try and tone down the posturing.'

Our phones hadn't been confiscated, so of course we'd called the police (except for Eric, who had decided to stream a live feed from his phone, the viewership already in the tens of thousands). The cops had told us basically the same thing: sit tight and don't antagonise. They'd get there as fast as they could.

'Agreed,' I backed her up. 'The best way to manage this is as a united front. Felix, Remy's just as scared as you are. And, Remy, Felix did the right thing handing over the gun. The money is insured. Huxley's will get back what he takes. Let him have it. He can't take anything from us but time.'

This got Eric's attention. He turned his phone camera to face me. His previously floppy hair was pasted to his forehead. 'Is that true?'

'I don't really want to be on camera.' I put a hand up, but I felt it made me look like a criminal on the news, so I put it down.

'Have you heard of Twitch? I've got two million subscribers.' Eric spun a finger on the screen, and I saw a blur of emojis. 'Comments are saying you're some kind of detective. Are you famous?'

'In certain circles.'

Remy snorted. 'Which ones?'

It was an odd comment from the guy who'd paid for the television rights. 'Murderers, mainly.'

Eric started again. 'So if the money's insured—'

'Your piggybank's safe, love,' Laverna said from the head of the table. She leaned across, peeled Remy's socks from Eric's chairback and flung the wet slugs at him. He looked more offended than when he'd had a gun pointed at his face. 'I'm with these two, we need to approach this as a group.'

'What about the safety deposit boxes?' Eric asked.

'You have some Lego squirrelled away or something?' Remy sniped. 'Leave it to the adults, little boy.'

'I'm fifteen.' Eric put his head on the table and spoke to the wood in a sulk. 'And I was just curious. If Fencing Guy rounds up Manager Dude, there's no issue handing over the cash. We can all go home. But we might be here longer if he's after the boxes.'

'He's got a good point,' Michelle said. 'Things might be insured to cash value, but some stuff is irreplaceable.'

On the word *irreplaceable*, Laverna squeezed Cordelia's shoulder. Cordelia didn't respond; it looked as though she was barely listening to the conversation, picking at a scratch in the table's varnish.

'The next step is negotiation.' I attempted to refocus the group. 'This guy clearly wants us here, which means he plans on using us as leverage, which means he wants something he can't get in a smash and grab. It also means he needs our cooperation; hence we can ask for things too. So what do we want?'

'Towels,' Felix said, holding up the cloth he'd scrubbed Michelle's head with. 'This is for polishing, not drying.'

'Food,' Michelle added. 'I'm starving.'

'Pizza?' Eric said hopefully.

My stomach rumbled at the mention. Though not much time had passed, the fading adrenaline was kicking back up my previously muted functions. I was hungry and starting to shiver with cold.

'Water,' Juliette added. 'In case it gets shut off.'

Eric's voice was meek, barely audible. 'I need, um—'

'Spare clothes.' I talked over him, remembering his darkened jeans and sparing him the embarrassment. 'For all of us. I'm soaked through and freezing.'

From the iPad in the far corner: WHAT ABOUT MEDICINE?

'Good idea.' Juliette turned to Cordelia. 'How quickly do you need a new IV?'

Laverna answered for her. 'It's not as urgent as getting dry.'

'We may as well put it on the list. What medicine is it?'

'Milrinone. It's not a big—'

'Jesus.' Felix blew the word out through his teeth. 'Poor thing. My dad was on that – he had a gammy ticker.'

Cordelia glared at her grandmother. It appeared she had been trying to hide the severity of her condition and was annoyed to have her frailty revealed this way. Through the window, I saw the two police cars back up, letting a large black van pull through, before closing the gap again. A man in a bulletproof vest stepped out, revealing a glimpse of flashing lights and computer screens inside. A command centre.

Juliette nudged me. 'I knew I recognised her,' she whispered.

I looked down at her outstretched phone. On screen was a FundAble website with a picture of Cordelia, smiling wide, taken in that just-before-sunset moment that's a favourite of social media influencers everywhere.

I knew FundAble. It was one of those websites where people could run their own fundraisers, ranging from entrepreneurial (business start-ups, invention ideas), to silly (one man put up a fundraiser with a target of $10 to make a potato salad and, once the internet caught wind of it, raised $50,000), to the serious (rebuilding destroyed homes or lives). I knew it because I'd made one myself for my detective agency. The problem was, FundAble's unique system meant it only released the money when the total goal was met. I'd put what I thought was a reasonable $25,000 target, given the media profile of my cases, but had only raised a paltry eleven hundred dollars. One hundred was from Juliette, and the rest was from my uncle Andy who, later, asked for half of it back because he'd mistakenly thought it was tax deductible.

Cordelia's first post was on 2 May, last year. *New Hope!* was the title in bold. *On Monday, my life as I know it ended. But after a week crying, I've decided to look towards the future . . .* The box was cut off by a 'read more' link. Her fundraising target was $150,000, to cover a litany of things including *in-home care* and *employment difficulties* and was displayed using a cartoon thermometer filled right to the top with a red line. She was on $150,050. The donations themselves were listed as rolling comments in a live feed. The most recent, $150, from a 'Bryce', whose name meant nothing to me yet but should to you, had tipped her over her goal.

I guess dying was more financially attractive than a detective agency.

'Okay.' I returned my attention to the room. 'We need towels, food, milrinone—' I counted them off on my fingers.

'Hang on,' Remy said. 'If this is a team effort, we should have a vote.'

'On what?'

'On whether we should rush the guy.' He said it like it was the obvious choice.

'He has a *gun*.'

Two GUNS.

Felix looked guiltily at the floor.

Remy held up a finger to announce his plan. 'When we hear him coming down the corridor, we hide beside the door, and when he unlocks it we burst out, bowl him over, pick up a gun and—' He made a motion of pulling the trigger.

'We're not going to kill him,' Juliette said.

'We could just'—Michelle didn't bother hiding a hint of disappointment—'tie him up. At least we'd find out who he is.'

'I've made horror movies,' Remy said. 'The teenagers always beat up the masked killer, and then they all stand around and take the mask off to see who it is. *BAM.*' He clapped his hands together. 'The killer *always* wakes up. Don't waste time. Shoot them dead first, incapacitate the threat, *then* take off the mask and find out who it is.'

'Incapacitate the threat first, be curious second: I agree with you,' Juliette said. 'But this isn't a psycho horror movie killer. It's just some guy. I know it's scary, but he hasn't actually hurt any of us. Shoot him in the leg or something.'

'He's just a petty thief,' I agreed. 'Our best plan is to wait it out.'

'Burglar,' Michelle corrected. 'He's a burglar, not a thief.'

'What's the difference?'

'Burglars take things by force. Thieves are more elegant.'

She is, of course, correct. And semantics solve cases. If you're wondering, given I now know the distinction, I believe I have described him correctly as *thief* in the previous chapters. I might be oxygen deprived, but I'm not going to let a clanger like that slip through.

'How is this not force?' Remy petitioned.

'Burglar, thief, whatever. He's scared us – certainly.' I glanced out the window, where there were now at least a dozen people milling about in various costuming: uniforms and suits. 'But the police are here now. There's no need to be rash. He hasn't even taken anything.'

'Not yet.' Remy put his hand in the air, a vote. 'All in favour of rushing the door?'

'What do you think?' Eric asked, and it took me a while to figure out he wasn't talking to us, but to his live stream. He was outsourcing his decision to an internet poll. 'Sorry,' he said to Remy. 'Chat says sit tight.'

After a second, Michelle's blue wrist guard lifted into the air. Felix followed suit, partly to agree with Michelle, it seemed, and partly because Remy's needling had got under his skin and he wanted to prove he had stones. I wasn't worried. It was still three on six.

And then Gabriel's hand went up.

'What the hell?' I turned on the priest. Blasphemy felt appropriate.

'No influencing the election,' Remy shot at me.

'Are you going to be the one at the front of this charge, then?'

'Let the man vote.'

Gabriel held up the iPad sheepishly. He couldn't meet my eye. SOME THINGS ARE PRICELESS.

I forced myself to calm down. 'It's still four against five, that's a majority for—'

Cordelia's hand went up.

Everyone's gaze spun to the silent young woman. Even Remy's mouth dropped open, he was so surprised to have won an argument. Laverna made to speak, but Cordelia set her jaw, straightened her back.

'It's just death,' she said plainly. 'What are you all so afraid of?'

CHAPTER 9

Credit to Winston Huxley, the man can take a tackle.

In retrospect, it was an obvious flaw in the plan: that the thief might not be the one to open the door. Well, the one in the sabre mask anyway. Those charging the door – Michelle, Felix and Gabriel (Laverna had put a forearm across Cordelia's attempt to join, and Remy had, predictably, taken on a supervisory role) – tumbled into the corridor in a stack on top of Winston, while the Fencer stood in bemusement, not even bothering to lift the gun as the failed rebellion unpicked their limbs from their game of Twister.

Winston, at the bottom of the pile, bucked and screeched, at Felix in particular, tossing barbs about deducting his salary to pay for a pair of glasses. Felix helped his boss up, despite being swatted off, a river of apologies flowing. Remy, sour at his plan's failure, dropped into a seat like he'd been impaled from on high.

Back where we started, scattered around the table, the only thing the vote seemed to have accomplished was dividing us into pacifists and aggressors. We had subliminally taken different sides of the table; I was with those who'd voted for restraint. I know I'm playing against type by not aligning with the danger-seekers – after all, I have a habit of being endangered. But that's only after I get a murder case to solve, and I didn't know I had one yet.

The Fencer tossed a black duffle bag on the table without instruction. Eric, mistaking him for a highwayman, placed a sad little Velcro wallet in the bag. There's just something financially insecure about a Velcro wallet; it's like riding the Tour de France with training wheels. The Fencer, as if offended by this donation, picked out the wallet and flung it back to the boy. Then he raised a fist-sized black plastic box in front of the mask and spoke for the first time. 'Phones. Smart watches.'

His voice came out distorted: slowed down and deepened, like a mythical giant talking underwater. The box was some kind of voice-changing device. That was important. A mask is basically part of the bank robber's uniform, and of course he'd want to fool any security cameras pored over after the robbery, but going to the effort of disguising his voice meant something extra.

One of the hostages knew who he was.

'This is not the way to do things.' Michelle spoke up for the group. 'You've proved your point.'

'Phones. Smart watches.'

'Unbelievable,' she muttered, stepping forward and chucking her phone in the bag. She locked her gaze on the Fencer, not the least bit scared of the gun, and spun a pointer finger in the air. 'Could you just hurry it up a bit?'

Winston, rubbing his shoulder, unclipped a smart watch and tossed it in. I followed with my phone. Remy handed his phone to Eric, as if he were an assistant, and Eric obliged, waving goodbye to his live stream as his phone joined the pile too. Laverna threw an object in that could have been either a phone or a house brick, given the clunk it landed with. Cordelia and Juliette followed. Gabriel started typing out a protest, deleted it and slid the iPad, and a phone, in too.

If it seems like we're giving up easy: we are. We'd already called the police, texted loved ones, the only thing left to do was wait it out.

I noticed Felix tilting away from the group, trying to hide his phone under the table and tapping away at the screen. He was so focused on typing, he didn't notice the entire room become silent and the gun point towards him. The Fencer cleared his throat.

Felix turned, holding up his screen meekly. 'I haven't done the Wordle yet,' he squeaked. 'I'm on a hundred-day streak.' He presented the screen, proving he was in the middle of the popular *New York Times* word puzzle. His first guess, of all things, was THIEF. (No correct letters.) I swear I thought I heard a mask-muffled chuckle as the Fencer lowered the gun and flicked it in a *get-on-with-it* gesture.

Cordelia leaned forward slowly enough to be stopped and, when there was no effort to impede her, retrieved her phone. She held it up in a loose grip, the way you'd surrender a gun, and said, 'If this is going to take all day, I haven't done my Duolingo.' It's hard to give stink-eye behind a fencing mask, but our thief was giving it a red-hot go. And yet, no objections. She hurried off with her phone to a far corner where she started yammering hushed Spanish phrases into the language-learning app.

'All day?' Eric piped up, seemingly surprised.

The Fencer stared at him as blankly as the mask would allow.

'I mean, uh, how long is this going to take? I have a stream. A tournament.'

'We're hostages,' I said.

'Soooo . . . like early afternoon? Or—' He mistook the silence for negotiation. 'I could probably do four o'clock?'

The Fencer tapped the gun on the table.

'*Five?*'

'Maybe cancel,' I offered.

'But it's the Australian Championship League Univer—' The hope didn't just retreat from his voice, it was deported, as realisation dawned. He couldn't even finish his sentence, aghast the robbery might take so long.

Now I was sure it wasn't my imagination; the mask was ever so slightly shaking back and forth in disbelief. I'd always thought bank robberies went out of fashion due to the digitisation of the profession, but now I'm thinking it was probably due to the attention spans of Gen Z hostages. Everyone's so used to their opinions being validated on the internet that even gunpoint can't conquer main character syndrome.

Dopamine preserved, puzzles solved and languages learned, phones were returned to the bag. If you're keeping track: I glimpsed that Cordelia completed Day 480 of her Spanish lessons (*bueno*) and Felix barely conquered the Wordle.

You might think Winston, who was the one actually being robbed, would try to take his device back, but he just spun on his seat like a bored child. He must have already made emergency calls from his office, and his vault was sealed so tight even he couldn't open it: a robbery didn't bother him. 'Well.' He used his heels to scupper the spin, held both arms in the air. 'Buffet's open. What will you be having then?'

'First of all, I'd like to apologise.' The glitchy, digitised voice floated through the room. 'This is a last resort. I am not a violent man.' The Fencer paused as the weight of the gun in his hand seemed to surprise him. He placed it behind his back as if, like Clark Kent wearing glasses, we'd forget he was the thief. To be fair, given a sabre mask and a voice-changer, I've learned it can be tough to tell who's who. 'We've done the hard bit. If you do as I say, you will all be in your own beds tonight. But that's up to you. Do what I ask of you, and you'll go home. Do something stupid, and you'll have made the decision for me. Don't see me as a threat. See this as an opportunity to walk away with the best dinner party story of your life.'

'We're cooperating.' I self-appointed myself as spokesman. 'We need food, water—'

The Fencer held up a finger. 'There'll be time for that.'

'This young girl is sick—'

'I'm twenty,' Cordelia said, ignoring the fact that, given this is a murder mystery, it is customary in book titles to relegate any female, no matter their age, to *girl*.

'She needs milrin—'

'I'll live,' *The Girl In The Bank* said firmly.

The Fencer's attention lingered on her. A calculation, perhaps factoring in if there was room in his plan to make allowances for medicine. The bag full of phones started vibrating, a heavy burr that could have only come from Laverna's decades-old anvil. He checked his watch. Shook his head. 'Not now. You'll be—' His voice caught, a blink of empathy. 'Fine.'

'Well?' Winston honked. 'Do you have demands or whatnot?'

'Yes. Well. Uh.' Robbing a bank must be like asking someone out, all that mental rehearsal deserting you in the moment. 'I want, uh, money.'

'We figured,' Felix said.

Winston waved it away. 'Let me save you, and all of us, the time.' He thumbed his chest. 'Winston Huxley. Yes, that one. Name's on the building. The tellers might have a couple of thousand in them, so that's low enough to keep you below the maximum sentencing threshold. But if you touch the money in the vault, we're suddenly at a higher offence level. We're talking decades of jail time versus community service. It's not worth it.' The explanation was smooth. It was impossible to notice the lie at its core: *we can't open the vault*. 'We'll forget about the gun. Gentlemen's agreement. That lowers the severity too. You have my permission to plunder the tills.'

'There's a gold nugget in the foyer,' Juliette said. 'That'd be worth more than the tills.'

Winston's glare probably dried her clothes.

'That's not enough,' the Fencer said.

'What do you bloody want then?' Winston folded his arms. 'We can sit here all day; I'm not opening the vault.'

A landline phone in the middle of the table rang. The Fencer waited for it to ring out before he spoke again. 'A dollar.'

'I told you, there's a few thousand in the—'

'One dollar. Just one.'

This was greeted with silence and confusion. Who robs a bank for a single dollar?

'I've got a buck,' Eric said, over the excruciatingly loud tear of his Velcro wallet. 'Or, at least, I thought I . . . Somewhere in here?' He flipped it inside out and produced two silver coins. 'Will seventy cents do?'

'I'll spot the other thirty,' Michelle offered, actually smiling at the ridiculousness of it all. 'If that's what you need. It's too easy, if it's not. Just get it over with.'

'Too easy,' Remy repeated, working his tongue around it. I appreciated his confusion, Michelle hadn't exactly used the phrase correctly. I've written her dialogue exactly as she said it, by the way, grammatical ineptitude and everything. 'You Australians have the strangest phrases. How can something be *too* easy?'

'Depends if you're here to fuck spiders,' Laverna said, rummaging in her handbag.

Remy looked horrified and concerned.

'I can give you a dollar,' Laverna continued. 'Let me see—'

Everyone followed suit, holding up wallets and tossing coins onto the table. Gabriel feebly held up a credit card, shrugging as if to ask if the burglar would accept a tap payment. Remy, from whom neither cardboard sign nor pistol has ever compelled a donation, was the only one who stayed silent, pretending to inspect the roof.

In the end, our meagre collection totalled, by my count, $4.80, two pieces of chewing gum and a button. Some haul.

'And this too.' Remy plucked the piggybank from Eric's elbow, shook it and, satisfied with the jangle of coins inside, placed it in the middle of the pile.

Eric scowled and snatched it back.

'Four dollars and forty cents?' Juliette appealed, throwing my counting skills into doubt. (Surely a pre-requisite of any good detective, on reflection.) I recounted. She was correct. We all peered up, as if waiting for a deity to accept our sacrifice.

The Fencer shook his head. 'One dollar,' he repeated. 'From the vault.'

'Here's the thing—' I started.

'Another word and I'll sue,' Winston hissed. 'You signed.'

The phone rang again. The Fencer picked it up and promptly slammed it back in the cradle so hard the casing cracked a little.

I turned to him. 'Point the gun at me.'

The digital voice faltered. 'I don't have any further need—'

'Do what you came here for. Point the gun at me.'

The Fencer gingerly raised the pistol. I turned to Winston, putting on a pantomime frown. 'I'm under duress. Given my life is facing imminent – no, keep it pointed at me, thank you – threat, I can't be obliged to uphold a non-disclosure agreement at the risk of my personal safety.'

'The disrespect!' Winston threw his hands up, knowing I was legally correct, then told the Fencer in a grumble, 'Feel free to shoot him.'

'He can't open it.' I pointed to Winston. 'No one here can. The head of security, Edward Huxley, changed the code, and has now gone missing. Okay, you can actually lower the gun now, if you don't mind. I'm a private detective. Winston hired me to find his brother and open the vault again.'

'*Missing?*' Michelle echoed.

'Does this mean the bank has no money?' Cordelia asked.

'You're not getting paid for this.' Michelle was laughing at the thief now. 'I'd take the four dollars.' She plucked one of the pieces of gum from the bounty and popped it in her mouth, leaning back to watch the show unfold. The only thing missing from her attitude was a box of popcorn.

'It doesn't mean anything,' Winston said, sulking, then to the Fencer, 'except that you're the unluckiest bank robber in the world, because you've chosen to stick up the one bank that can't open its own vault.'

There was a little twitch of the head under the sabre mask, the hint of a *just-my-luck* smirk. The phone on the table rang again and the Fencer picked it up. This time, he raised it to his mouth, holding the voice-changer between the receiver and his mask. 'I have no demands.'

He hung up again, then yanked the cord out and dropped into the seat closest to the door. He propped his feet up on the table, the gun resting in his lap. 'I'm not leaving until I get my dollar. So I guess you'd better find where this Edward fellow is.' The Fencer seemed decidedly relaxed for someone who'd just been told that their whole plan was a bust. 'Otherwise, Winston Huxley, start figuring out how to rob your own bank.'

CHAPTER 10

'*You are dead. Dead!*'

Last words are key clues in many a murder mystery, and I've encountered plenty across those I've solved: from discreetly hidden photographs to messages scrawled in a victim's own blood. Arthur Conan Doyle's last words, though he wasn't murdered, were to his wife: *you are wonderful.* My current situation is no exception – last words abound. Heads up, there's the abacus in Winston's office (1011) and, I am resigned to admit, probably this notebook. But this was the first time they'd been squawked at me by a bird.

I'd been granted a thirty-minute hall pass to prowl the bank for clues to the vault code. Once I'd revealed my identity as a detective to the Fencer, Winston assured him I was his best chance of getting it open. This was purely self-serving: if I succeeded, Winston got entry to his vault, and if I didn't, he got the smarmy pleasure of watching me fail. I tried to rope Juliette into the mission, but the thief, sensing our relationship, preferred to split us up.

'She stays here to make sure you come back,' he'd said. 'You can take the guard instead. Thirty minutes. Or I shoot someone.'

Felix seemed a fair choice, as at least he knew his way around, and I doubted I would have found Edward's office without him. It was on the opposite end of the third floor to the boardroom. Most of this level was a wide, open-plan office space filled with hot desks and break-out spaces and various other hyphenated corporate buzzwords designed to remind employees they are replaceable. The single elevator I'd seen on the ground floor, wrapped in an old-fashioned lattice cage like foam mesh on an apple, was down the far end, before a corridor headed off to bathrooms and the like. On the floor by the lift was a bolted square panel – a trapdoor that sealed off where the wool lift used to service this floor, I realised. In the centre were the stairs to the mezzanine. Beside them, an inauspicious slate-grey door without a nameplate, just shy of a set of bins, led to the co-director's office.

'Dead!'

I'd almost had a heart attack as I opened the door.

Of course, the animal-as-witness is par for the course in mysteries: the mimic bird who retains a vital statement, squawked back to the detective at an opportune moment. Winston had even helpfully foreshadowed this earlier, though I hadn't caught his meaning, which is why the Amazon parrot nearly scared me to death. It was a fluffy thing with a bright green body, a beak like a red clown's nose, and a white patch around each eye. While Amazon parrots may not have the timbre of, say, a starling or a myna, to perfectly replicate a human voice, try having one shout '*You are dead!*' in your unsuspecting ear and see if it freaks you out.

Felix, for his part, stumbled into the nearest bookshelf. 'I hate that bloody thing,' he said, clutching at his chest.

'*You can't kill me.*'

'Don't test me, bird.'

To say Edward's office was less extravagant than his brother's would be to say that an anthill is less extravagant than Everest.

It was musky, dark and cluttered. Filing cabinets stuck their tongues out. Shelves bowed into smiles, lopsided books like crooked teeth. There was a chance Edward wasn't missing at all, he was just buried under all of his files.

'Does it have a name?' I asked, pointing at the bird. It was in a large cage that sat on a head-height podium, perched on a tree branch skewered between the bars. The newspaper lining the bottom of the cage was scattered with pistachio shells and bird poop. Beside the cage was a shelf with a few photographs and a gold bar, the size of a sausage roll, on the red velvet tongue of an open wooden box. There was a little plaque on the front of the box, though unlike the memorabilia downstairs this was modern, dated 18 March last year. It read: *The sea fears you.* The gold bar had a little dent in one end, and I was reminded of Winston telling me not to chew his pen.

'His name's Ditto,' Felix said. 'Figures.'

'How well do you know Edward?' I asked while fumbling in the gloom for a light switch. 'He's head of security, right?'

'Yeah. He's my direct report. He's an okay dude, for a Huxley that is. Sets my roster, updates the security protocols.'

'Such as?'

'You know, the usual. This might come as a surprise to you, but we don't get robbed all that often.'

I found the light switch and flipped it. At first I'd taken the gloom to mean there were no windows, but there was a door-sized one hidden behind a drawn shade. Rolling up the blind would have been pointless, as any light was blocked by the exact same man-sized safe as in Winston's office, like it had been bought in a two-for-one sale. It fit in front of the window almost perfectly. The only difference was Edward's had alphabetical magnets on the front of it, spelling out: *HAPPY FATHER'S DAY, LOVE BEN!* I realised the photo I'd seen in Winston's office, the fridge-like object showing half this message, had been taken in here. Though Edward had fixed the errant apostrophe between when they'd taken the photograph and now: I remembered it reading *THERS' DAY, LOVE B* in the picture. Semantics.

'You must have procedures though.' I started sifting through envelopes and papers on Edward's desk. I knew I was out of my depth: my deductive skills had been completely reduced to hoping I'd find the vault code written on a post-it note.

'For sure,' Felix said. 'Silent alarm, like you saw. Surrender first, it's all insured. We're not supposed to stop a robbery. Same as any bank in the country.'

'The security shutters on the teller windows – once they're down they can't be lifted, right?'

'Not without a full system reset.' Felix cut off my next question with a tone that implied what he was saying was obvious. 'Which you can't just do from here, in case you're wondering. Once the alarm's been triggered, everything moves off-site with a third-party company. It's pretty annoying if there's a false alarm, but in the event of an actual robbery, it means that no matter who has a gun to their head, they can't bring up the shields.'

I spied a printer-copier in the corner, a clanking thing that belonged in the last century, which had a stack of paper in the out-tray. I picked it up and leafed through it: every page was blank. Curious, I picked up one of the files from Edward's desk and placed it in the copier. It came out as a perfect replica, despite a smudge of ink down the left, so the copier was fine. Why would you print out more than a hundred pages of blank paper? I folded one and put it in my pocket, dropping the rest of the stack back in the out-tray. 'Is there an emergency exit behind the teller desks?'

Felix shook his head. 'Another exit would be another entry point.'

'So the teller, Milton, is still behind there?'

Felix shrugged. 'Where else would he be? It'd be stupid for him to join us.'

I didn't know. 'And this third-party security – once the building is locked down, it doesn't automatically deactivate access to the vault?'

'Look, I don't really know, okay? My general responsibility is technically client control, in case someone, like your mate, arcs up at a teller. But to be honest, I'm not even really here to do that. The Huxleys think my main job is to guard their museum.' He blew his cheeks out, bored. 'What exactly are we looking for?'

'Any receipts, bookings, hotel phone numbers where Edward might have gone. Failing that, a big neon sign with the vault code on it.'

'Right. The code'll be six digits. Edward was pretty sensible. I doubt he would have written it down.' He turned. 'Unless you know it, bird?'

'*Dead!*'

'When you say museum,' I continued, 'you mean the nugget?'

'Yeah. I spend more time polishing that stupid thing than guarding the bank. Winston always wants it spotless. There's a valuable painting, a Sidney Nolan – *Goldfields*, if you've heard of it – on the mezzanine, and then there's a few knick-knacks that are decidedly *not* valuable, but Winston seems to think someone might run off with them.'

'Like what?'

'Well, there's a rusty teapot that'—he put on a toffy, lecturing voice—'*Harold Huxley used to sustain himself in the cold nights sifting the river.* Honestly.' He scoffed. 'You'd think it brewed holy water.'

I'd seen the decrepit teapot earlier – it definitely didn't warrant stealing – so I nodded along, still looking around. A computer on Edward's desk wouldn't let me in without a password. In the top corner of the office was a mounted television screen, the image bisected into quarters but all screens black. 'The cameras are off,' I observed. 'Edward doesn't even bother to put a gold bar in a safe.' I pointed to the shelf. 'And Winston's worried someone will steal a teapot?'

'I just do the legwork, I don't supervise the systems,' Felix said. 'Edward does that all himself. Hell, we don't even have overnight guards. As for the teapot, think of it like art. Put a painting up in a frame: so what? Sticky-tape a banana to a wall and put a security guard next to it, voila – it's valuable, purely because you make it look like it might be. I'm just lipstick on this place, to make it look like it's worth protecting.'

'I assume you didn't say any of this in your job interview.' I fossicked in the drawers, then through the scattered files on the desk, tossing aside sheaves of paper that would take more than my thirty-minute hostage-recess to read. Next to a mug filled with pens sat a single toy petrol tanker. It was in complete contrast to Winston's collection, scuffed and paint-chipped, with a wheel missing, and I could barely read the word *Hess* on the tank. It was similar to those in Winston's cabinet, fossilised in their plastic boxes, but the difference between the brothers was obvious: one liked to use things, the other liked to own them.

I kept looking. A folder with eBay receipts for collectibles. The Hess truck was worth a whopping two-hundred-and-twenty grand. An invoice from a company called Security Solutions stood out because of the date – 20 August – which was the last time anyone saw Edward and the date he changed the vault code, but the actual contents of the invoice was business as usual: eleven grand for a 'systems review', a streak of sputtering ink down the left side of the page from his tired printer.

Felix had just told me about the third-party control centre. Had they found something in this review that had compelled Edward to change the vault code? Had the review uncovered a risk, or revealed an opportunity? I put the invoice down and started looking under the desk.

The invoice is obviously more important than I'm giving it credit for. Why else would I be describing it, given my precious air reserves? It's actually on me right now. (Well, sort of. It's in my pocket but, given that I'm currently naked – don't worry about that though – it's not exactly *on* me.) So it's clearly important enough that I came back for it later. Let me slide it in after this chapter in the spirit of full disclosure. Fair play and all that.

I picked up a small rubbish bin and tipped its contents onto the desk: the shells of a few dozen disembowelled pistachios – it seemed Edward had the same diet as the bird – some chocolate bar wrappers, a few receipts and a thankyou card. Opening it, I was surprised to see a picture of Cordelia standing in a flowering garden of pink roses, wearing a white dress embroidered with purple flowers and a smile that didn't reach her eyes: *Thank you for your donation. Life shines so much brighter knowing that you're in my corner.* Smaller font running along the bottom read: *Photography courtesy of Meg Pickham, Dress courtesy of Queenie Fabric Designs, Printing courtesy of Darren's Printers.* I pocketed it, wondering if Darren was some kind of local baron, what with the printing press and the Thai place.

'That's the thing about banks though, isn't it?' Felix pored over a far bookshelf, where Edward had a small collection of Arthur Conan Doyle. He was far from a completist, having only the second volume of Sherlock Holmes stories, *The Adventures of Sherlock Holmes,* and two of the four novels, the first, *A Study in Scarlet,* and the third, *The Hound of the Baskervilles.* Felix glanced over them. 'They're this ivory tower of wealth, but all the money inside it is someone else's. They say they keep my money safe, but they lend it to you. Then when I want mine back, they get it from some other schmuck. The only thing you need to run a bank is the *perception* of value. Is this a clue?'

He was holding up an unfolded umbrella.

'No,' I said incorrectly. 'And it's bad luck to open it indoors. I'm beginning to think you might be in the wrong business.'

Felix collapsed the brolly and rested it against the wall. I noticed a small tear in the fabric on the outer edge of the webbing. He turned to me with his hands on his hips. 'So how does all this work, then?'

'How does all what work?'

'You're a detective, but you don't seem like a cop.'

'I'm not. I've just solved a couple of murders.'

'Are you like those TV ones? Just a walking encyclopedia of knowledge?'

I shook my head. 'I'm an expert in crime novels. Specifically detective ones. I follow the tropes. You'd be surprised how much of the genre actually applies to real life. The whole world works on rules. There are rules to writing crime fiction, too. You can't do anything that breaks the reader's suspension of disbelief, for one thing.'

'Like aliens?'

'Yes, exactly like aliens.' I'd said the same to Winston about the lights outside his window. 'Something wild can't just show up at the end of the mystery and resolve everything. I can ask if something's plausible. Is it *fair*? So I eliminate everything that's *unfair* – or unrealistic – and then apply everything that's *fair* to rational logic. That's my skill, I guess. I know what to look out for.'

'Are these fair?' Felix plucked *The Hound of the Baskervilles* from the shelf and held it up. 'This is the only one I've read, but I liked it.'

'For the most part,' I said. 'Though the dog would have died.'

Felix flipped to the end of the book, the great pain of mystery writers, and tried to understand my point. Spoiler alert for *The Hound of the Baskervilles* in this paragraph, by the way. I went on. 'The suspected ghostly hound is revealed merely to be painted in glow-in-the-dark phosphorus, to give the illusion of a haunting. Phosphorus does give off light, but it is also poisonous if absorbed through the skin. The dog may well have glowed in the dark, but it would have done it lying very still. Deadly still. Quite a pathetic ghost.'

Felix snapped the book shut. 'You're no fun to watch movies with, I imagine.'

'I tend to guess the endings.'

'Where does a talking bird sit on your fairness spectrum?' Felix raised an eyebrow over at Ditto.

I looked at the parrot, who was currently pecking a meal from under one of his wings. Not the most reliable, but a witness all the same. 'It's a fairly common trope to get an animal to witness something,' I said. 'There are a few classics: Dog That Doesn't Bark, for one. That means the victim knows the suspect, as they've met the dog before. The Cat Sneeze: a killer who has an allergy is often revealed by a passing cat. This is The Blithering Bird: a parrot might squawk out a suspect's name, or record a victim's or a killer's final words. Last words are a bit of a classic too, now that I mention it. It's all par for the course.'

'You think Ditto is parroting Edward's last words?'

'We don't even know if Edward's been murdered.'

'Okay.' Felix thought for a second. 'But Ditto clearly overheard something. And it sounds like a threat. *And* Edward is missing. Is that fair?'

'Yes, that would be fair. We can't assume Edward and the bird are linked, though – that's the red herring. But clearly this bird heard *something*.' I turned to Ditto. 'Are you a clue, mate?'

'*I am not a clue*,' the bird squawked.

Felix laughed, shrugging. 'Straight from the horse's. Clever bird.'

'Birds don't know what words mean.' I held up a finger for quiet, hoping Ditto would speak again, and whispered, 'It's not a conversation, it's a recording. They regurgitate, act on cues. He's not chatting to you. This is *also* something he's overheard.'

'*I am not a clue.*'

'Soooo'—Felix was trying to work it out—'him saying he's not a clue . . . is a clue?'

'Honestly, I have no idea.'

I turned it over in my mind. If Edward's disappearance was sinister, most of the bird's recollection made sense when pieced together as two halves of the same conversation. In the bird's singular tone, it could have been multiple speakers. If Edward had changed the code to the vault, someone might have been driven to murderous anger. But Edward could feel his safety was insured as the only one who knew the combination. Hence *You are dead* and the swift rebuttal, *You can't kill me.*

The most likely conversationalist would be Winston, which would mean he'd lied to me about the last time he'd seen Edward. Not an impossible scenario.

But *I am not a clue* perplexed me. It didn't fit that imagined conversation. I was certain I hadn't misheard it, given Ditto had said it twice. The bird, surely, couldn't be self-aware. I'm the only one allowed to do that in these books.

I'd seen everything I could without a computer password or a safe combination, and I checked the clock on the wall. 'Take me to the basement. We're due back in about ten minutes.'

'*You are dead. Dead! You can't kill me.*' The bird's chattering followed us out the door. '*I am not a clue.*'

Security Solutions

GST Registered

INVOICE

INVOICE #	DATE
700 345Y	20/08/2025

BILL TO

Huxley's Bank
12 Main Street
Huxley, NSW, 2496

DESCRIPTION	AMOUNT
Security Review	10,000.00
Goods and Services Tax (GST) – 10%	1,000.00
TOTAL	**$ 11,000.00**

CHAPTER 11

'Any other non-avian clues in Ed's office then?' Felix said, as we walked down a flight of stairs to the basement. This was a longer stairwell, with several angular turns leading us underground.

'Not many,' I said, even though I now know there are plenty.

For a start, the magnets on the safe. I'll remind you it was 22 August at this point. Father's Day was two weeks and spare change away, the first Sunday in September. And, of course, Edward's son was dead. Then, of course, the thankyou card from Cordelia. Don't forget the umbrella and the hundred sheets of blank paper on the copier. The bruised gold bar. *The sea fears you.* And the pistachios, too. No one is allergic, just in case you're trying to get ahead of me. It made sense they were in Edward's trash; he's a heavyset man and they're good for lowering cholesterol, given they are filled with healthy oils, but every clue counts.

And, of course, the safe holds more importance than just what's written on it.

It is to be my coffin.

'The magnets might be a clue. Father's Day's not for weeks,' I summarised for Felix.

He looked over his shoulder at me, squinting in confusion. 'Well, yeah. Weren't you just talking about the importance of last words?'

'Ben's?'

'He died just under a year ago. Terrible accident.' He put up his hands, in a *don't ask me* gesture. 'I don't really know the details. Police came out to their estate, not sure what for, but whatever it was they didn't find it or didn't get it, because I've never heard a follow-up. The poor kid must have scared one of the officers during the raid.' He made a little gun motion with his fingertips. I got the picture. 'Like I said, an accident.'

I blew a whistle out through my teeth. Be it a delivery van or a botched police operation, the word *accident* was doing a lot of heavy lifting today.

'You know,' Felix continued, 'I wouldn't be surprised if it was just all a bit much for Ed with the anniversary coming up. After something like that, I could understand wanting to just throw the towel in and get away for a while. Bet you he's sitting in a hotel room somewhere, staring at the ceiling, and all these shenanigans are just a fluke of a badly timed Menty B.'

Even psychiatric conditions had slang these days, I thought but didn't say.

'You're suggesting Edward kept the *last* message from his son on the safe's door?' I clarified. That made sense, like a voicemail message someone can't bring themselves to delete. He was preserving his son's final missive. 'It's from last year?'

'I thought you were good at this stuff?'

'I said I knew the rules. Besides, I focus on murder mysteries, not bank robberies.'

'What are the rules for bank robberies, then?'

It was a good question. Unfortunately for me, my Golden Age detective heroes didn't really tackle many bank heists. Of course there are the requisite jewel thefts and recoveries, and Poirot grapples with a million dollars in bank bonds at one point on an ocean liner, which technically counts (and I am all about technicalities, see: burglar/thief), but the only story I can bring to mind that features a bank robbery *in situ* is Sherlock Holmes' 'The Red-Headed League'. In it, Sherlock deduces that a contingent of burglars has rented out an office beside a bank with the purpose of tunnelling between the two and he waits for them inside the vault. Interestingly enough, thieves admitted to using the story as the inspiration behind the real-life tunnelling robbery of Lloyds Bank in London in 1971. That bank's location, of all places: Baker Street.

Quick side note: 'The Red-Headed League' is one of the stories included in the collection *The Adventures of Sherlock Holmes*. Yes, the one on Edward's shelf. Make of that what you will.

The real-life robbery of Lloyds is renowned for several reasons beyond the Holmesian circumstances: first, that despite all of the conspirators being caught, and between one and three million pounds being stolen from safety deposit boxes, only two hundred thousand was ever recovered. The second is that reporting on the robbery was rumoured to be kiboshed by a government suppression notice, leading many to believe that the thieves had inadvertently stolen something sensitive from a deposit box (the most popular chatter involves compromising photographs of a member of the Royal Family). Of course, that is all rubbish, but it's a fun-enough urban legend. But thinking of this did fire up one possibility in my mind to answer Felix's question.

'The main heist is not the main heist,' I said aloud. 'That's a rule for a heist narrative. Whatever you *think* the heist is, the real heist is going on underneath it.'

'Oh yeah, like swapping the bags and that. I've seen *Oceans*.'

'There's another contender for a rule,' I decided. How many heist films have you seen where the bags of cash are opened at the end and are filled with paper, while a flashback reveals a diamond being palmed off midway through the heist? Or the cops pulling the mask off the finally captured thief to find they are one of the hostages with duct tape over their mouth? 'There's always a switch.'

The stairs levelled out into an enormous subterranean bunker. In front of us was a set of iron bars, secured by a traditional key lock. Beyond that was a polished concrete antechamber, an unattended desk with no chair and a single computer monitor to the left, and a row of wooden booths with red velvet curtains to the right. Further back was a gleaming silver circular door that took up almost the entire wall. The vault.

Above it was a square wooden-planked section in the otherwise concrete ceiling, the base of the wool lift. While the vault was gleaming and modern now, a hundred years ago I imagined that the gold might have been piled right here, and the wool lift used often. There was a scattering of fine dust and flakes on the floor underneath it.

'There's always an inside man,' Felix said, fighting with a key ring so overburdened it was like a possum with its entire family on its back. He eventually found the right key and opened the grille. He let me in first and then followed, locking up behind me. 'Another rule, maybe?'

While we might have just been chewing the fat, from the perspective of hindsight, these three pillars of heist narratives will hold obligingly true. First, you'll have clued in that there's no way our thief is seriously after a single dollar. Which means he just wants to open the vault, and what he really wants is something else inside it. Photos of the Royal Family, perhaps. And police don't just raid a house, guns drawn, for nothing. My logical progression was that whatever was wanted from Edward's house in that raid a year ago must have been moved to the vault, possibly a safety deposit box. It would fit the first rule: the main heist is not the real heist.

I'll tell you now that the other two rules will be satisfied: there will be a switch, and there is an inside man.

Felix was giving me a verbal tour of the room: the desk on the left was a guard station, and the velvet confessionals were viewing rooms for the safety deposit boxes. The bank had two hundred and eighty boxes housed inside the vault, in fourteen rows of twenty. He explained that security amounted to a foyer guard upstairs (his job), and a vault guard in the basement. Given the vault couldn't be opened and Winston had already told me he'd sent as many staff home as possible to try to keep it quiet, it made sense the second guard wasn't here.

'There's no chair,' I observed, pointing to the guard station. 'You had one in the lobby.'

'Everyone got sent home the last few days,' Felix said, as if it closed the matter. 'No guard, no chair.'

'Yes. But who takes their *chair* home on a day off?'

By the desk were the polished silver doors of an elevator, far more modern than the antique death-trap in the main building. By my mental schematics of what I'd seen so far, this elevator could only go up one floor, so it must go up behind the teller desks, where perhaps a secure room was annexed to them. It made sense to move the money behind the security shutters. Did this mean Milton could have moved between floors, into the vault?

'Does Milton have keys to this gate?' I asked.

'Yeah,' Felix said. 'There's a set in the teller's secure room. He could use the elevator, but he'd only get through the grille. He wouldn't have the vault code. But why go through a gate when a guy with a gun is on the other side?'

We walked over to the vault. Beside the giant circular door was a small digital keypad, glowing a dim blue.

'How functional is it that only Edward knows the code?' I asked. 'Him going missing is an inconvenience at best and a disaster at worst, but it's not the only thing that could have gone wrong. What's your hit-by-a-bus plan?'

'We might be low-key but we're not stupid,' Felix said. 'The code resets every month and can be accessed, or reset, by a three-factor authentication process. That's above my station, but Winston has it on his computer, for sure. Keep in mind I had no idea anything was even wrong until an hour ago. If Winston really can't open the vault, it means Ed's turned the failsafe off. And in that case, yes, whoever set the code is the only one who knows it.'

There was nothing more to be gained from staring at the keypad. I poked my head into the booths but noticed that Felix was shifting anxiously behind me.

'Thirty minutes,' he said.

'We've still got a few, but okay.' I started walking back towards the entrance. 'How do you open the safety deposit boxes?'

'Two-key system,' Felix said. 'Bank has one, customer has the other. The box is brought from inside the vault and opened in the private viewing room, where items can be retrieved or deposited.'

'The customer never sets foot in the vault?'

'No. We bring the box out.'

'So the customer stays out here, unguarded, while the guard fetches the box?'

'Well – yeah?' Felix hesitated, looked around the room. 'There's nothing to steal out here though.'

'Do you always lock people in, then?' We'd arrived at the grille, which Felix had locked behind us.

'Force of habit.' He seemed a little flustered by this, like he hadn't expected me to notice, and started on his ring of keys that belonged in a horror movie, judging by the number of incorrect choices and jiggles of the lock he made. The gate finally opened and he gestured through it. 'Hurry up, thirty minutes is in the rearview.'

He left the grille unlocked and we started up the stairs again. He took them two at a time. I wondered if he knew something I didn't. 'You don't seriously think he'll shoot anyone if we're a few minutes over, do you?'

'It's not a risk I want to take.'

'We might not get let back out. What about protecting the mon—'

Felix whirled around at that. Above me on the stairs he was an intimidating foot or so taller. 'Don't you get it? People, not pennies. What have the Huxleys promised you to get into the vault?'

'I'm hoping to get a loan for my agency,' I admitted.

'Well, that's how they work,' Felix said. 'It's always one promise into the next into the next, but each one isn't worth the air used to give it. But you can keep handing out promises if people *believe* they can keep spending them. It's . . . it's . . .' He seemed to have a revelation. 'It's like a bank with no money in it.' He'd worn himself out with the outburst and was breathing heavily. He rubbed his brow. 'I'm sorry. I'm just stressed.'

I weighed my next words carefully. 'What do the Huxleys owe you?'

'Everything. My family's worked for them for generations.'

'That's a relative of yours in the photograph on Winston Huxley's wall? Someone who was here at the start. They were a team.'

Felix nodded, turned and kept going up the stairs.

I spoke to his back. 'And that means they owe you?'

I could see the frustration in his shoulders. 'Solving this for *them* . . . it doesn't make you the hero. It's the Haves and the Have Nots, and you're helping the Haves. And they'll give you a bread-crumb or two but never the loaf, and then you're on the leash and they own you. A little lap dog. Actually, now that I think of it, your very job title is classist. *Private* detective. You're charging people to solve murders? None of that public-funded regular crap for our murder cases, *my good chap*. Not to get all political on you, but in my opinion it's quite simple really: close the banks. Money is *a lie*. Society should be free education, free healthcare and free bloody murder-solving.'

'I'm not being paid for this,' I grumbled, wishing people would stop bringing it up.

'My point stands.'

'An abolitionist who guards a bank. Now I've heard everything.'

'I'm not a radical.'

'I believe it.' I didn't hide the sarcasm.

'Do your own research. It's very sensible stuff. And that's just general economic theory: if there's anyone who deserves to be robbed, it's the Huxleys.'

'Why'd you vote to attack the thief if you didn't care whether he got into the vault or not? What's your ideal outcome here?'

Felix cleared his throat guiltily as we entered the atrium. 'I gave him my gun. If someone got hurt with it, that'd be on me.'

'But if he didn't have a gun?' I pressed.

'Ideally? I'd give him what he wanted.' He paused, then added, 'And he'd take his mask off. Show his face.'

'You think he's a coward?'

'No. I want to see his face so that when all this is over, I can buy him a drink.'

I was panting keeping up with Felix as we crossed the lobby. I'd been itching to get over to the teller booths and see if Milton was still hunkered down behind them, if we could help him. But Felix had no time for a diversion, keen to get back to the other hostages within a defendable window of tardiness.

'Can we just take a quick look . . . Maybe we could go a bit slo—' I grabbed Felix by the wrist and pulled him backwards.

'Listen. I felt this guy's energy up close. He might have started out aggressive, but that was the adrenaline. Once he had us all corralled, he chilled out. Even when Winston told him the safe wouldn't open, which seems like a real snag in a bank robber's plan, it seemed to relax him *more*. He doesn't want to kill anyone. He's not going to mind if we're a few minutes late. We might not get out again.'

'You might like to bet your life on things, Ernest, but don't bet other people's.' Felix hurried across the room.

I knew he was right. I could gamble my life, but I couldn't gamble someone else's. I couldn't gamble Juliette's. Still, my feet seemed stuck to the floor. I called after him, just to have the last word, 'I really don't think he's going to shoot anybody.'

At that exact moment, a gunshot rang out across the room.

CHAPTER 12

Turns out a brass knocker sounds very similar to the *whip-crack* of a bullet firing. It was coming from the front door.

Felix, despite his haste, recognised the importance. 'I'll try to buy you time,' he said, bolting up the stairs. I moved through the wreckage of the foyer towards the knocking.

Only a few hours ago it had been a regular morning at a country bank, all murmured conversations, impatient queues and too-cold air conditioning. Now, courtesy of the Fencer's furniture flipping and the sprinkler system, the atrium resembled the ballroom on a capsized cruise ship. The air was humid, swamp-like. I waded through it. Past the icicle of Harold Huxley's gold nugget, a bulbous golden droplet distending from its point, the electric doors to the antechamber slid open. I stepped in. The thick chain that bound the door was rattling. While the chain was taut, wrapped around itself and the handle several times, a column of light could be produced by a hard shove from the outside. Not enough to squeeze even a rake-thin twenty-year-old through, I considered, but enough to slide an arm in. Or talk through.

There was a navy-blue uniform flitting across the gap.

'Hello?' I called, keeping my distance, in case I was mistaken for a thief and not a hostage.

The door stopped jiggling.

'Are you armed?' The returning voice was nasal, high in the throat.

'Hostage,' I called back.

'Alone?' The inflection swung up. Surprise.

I checked behind me. 'Alone.'

The chain strained and a blue-grey eye appeared in the sliver of air. 'You escape?' The man had lowered his voice to a hiss. 'I can't get you through the front, but we've got the bars off one of the windows in a downstairs toilet.'

I stepped forward and put my toe in the door to hold it open. Closer now, I could see through the gap. A short man who filled up so little of his navy-blue bulletproof vest it fit him like a turtle's shell was standing on the threshold. Underneath he wore a collared shirt with the sleeves rolled up, and a pink tie. I could only see a slice of him at a time, but it was enough to see that his hair was flat and jet black, receding variably, his forehead traced by a big M. But the sides were robust: a widower's peak with mistresses. His features didn't quite fill out the available space; his eyes, nose and mouth clustered together in the middle of his face, like a farmstead in the centre of acreage. His pinched mouth, which a straw would need to turn to spelunking to get into, didn't help cover any more ground. He wore a tactical Kevlar helmet that was also too big for him, the strap loose around his neck.

'Don't worry,' I said. 'I'm not in any danger. I don't need a way out.'

A wiry forearm squeezed through the door. It had a light fuzz of white hair, like mould on fruit. 'Tobias Cuthbert. I'm the negotiator.'

'Ernest.' I shook it. 'Cunningham.'

'How many bad guys?'

'One. Two guns.'

'How many hostages?'

I counted quickly in my head. 'Ten.'

'Anyone hurt?' He spoke fast and direct, like he was answering questions in a buzzer-beater round on a quiz show. All fact, no fat.

'No, but we need milrinone. I don't know the dosage. It was in an IV drip. Maybe eleven, actually – hostages, that is.'

'*Maybe* eleven?'

'There was a teller. He triggered the silent alarm. He's not a hostage per se, but he'll be trapped behind the shutters.'

'Milton? We've got him. There's a secure elevator to the vault. So ten hostages, one gunman, two guns. Automatics?'

I nodded at the numbers, neglecting to factor in the rules Felix and I had just established. There's always an inside man. In writing this I have the benefit of hindsight. So let's exclude Milton, given he's escaped, and yet still call it eleven for the number of people trapped in here.

'Pistols,' I said. 'Uh, I think. Small ones. One's definitely a revolver. The other more . . . I guess the technical term is chunky?'

'And he's – a male, correct? We've interviewed Milton, who thought he walked like one.'

I nodded.

'This fella's just happy for you to wander around?' Tobias shifted his weight between his feet and I saw a bright yellow taser on his hip.

'Not exactly. I was given a job to do. Me and the security guard.'

Tobias plucked a notebook from a shirt pocket and checked it. 'That would be Felix Gao?'

I nodded, though I didn't know his surname.

'Milton didn't know everyone's names,' Tobias explained. 'I also have Winston Huxley, Father Gabriel – hard to miss – and from the description of the out-of-towner, Remy Allard, I think. If IMDb is to be trusted.'

'That's right.'

'Could you help me out with the others? A grandmother and a girl?'

'Young woman.'

'Huh?'

'Don't worry about it. Yes, the older one is Laverna. Cordelia is her granddaughter. She's the one who needs the medicine.'

'Ah, the Brights. Whole town did a fundraiser for Cord.' There was a pause while he wrote something in a notebook. 'Brave girl.'

'There's a boy named Eric,' I offered. 'I'm sorry, I don't know his surname.'

'Very good.' Tobias didn't write it down, and I assumed as Milton had served the boy before the robbery he would have relayed that information already, but Tobias proved me wrong. 'Full disclosure, that'd be Cuthbert. Eric's my son. Is he okay?'

'He's a little shaken, but no worse off than anyone else.'

'Could you look out for him? For me?'

'Of course. He's clutching some piggybank tightly though, but I don't think the thief's after it.'

'He might be if he knew what was in it. Silver dollars,' Tobias said. 'Eric won them in a video game competition. It was pirate themed. Second place was silver.'

I struggled to hide my surprise that the pig was actually worth something. 'I didn't realise you could make money playing video games.' I remembered Eric saying he had two million followers on Twitch, the platform he'd live streamed to. I didn't know what that equated to in dollars, but I did know that if I'd sold two million books, I wouldn't have had to come begging to Huxley for a loan.

'They call it Esports, actually.' Tobias filled me in with the air of someone used to being corrected himself. 'Electronic sports. Though they barely need the E – it's like a legit sport these days. The local university even has a team, *with* scholarships. Kid'll retire before

I do,' he said, then looked back at his notebook. 'And you're here with someone?'

'My fiancée, Juliette Henderson.'

'Gotcha. And there's a woman from reception, I hear?'

'Ah, yes. Michelle. Also at a loss for her surname. We haven't really had the chance to sit around and do any icebreakers.'

'Right.' His tone was flat. It made sense: he was putting the technical aspects of the job first so he didn't get worked up worrying over his son. Treating it like any other day. 'Should we get you out?'

'He said he'd shoot someone if I'm not back in time. I'm already late.'

'Do you believe him?'

'I'm talking to you, aren't I?' I thought about Felix's warning. 'But let's keep it quick.'

'Where's he holding everyone?'

'There's a boardroom on the third floor.'

Tobias disappeared. There was a rustle as he unfolded and traced his finger over what I assumed were a set of blueprints he was holding flush against the door. 'Okay. Smart.' He returned to the slit. 'It's taller than the rest of the town, so no good lines of sight on the windows. How's the environment?'

'Honestly,' I said, shrugging, 'he's the most relaxed thief you could hope for. You going to shoot him?'

Tobias swatted his arm back and forth, scattering half-a-dozen white butterflies that had been making themselves at home in his hair. 'Not through the plague of locusts we aren't. Snipers wouldn't get a clear shot even if we could get them high enough. The church's bell tower is the best bet, but there aren't as many windows on that side.'

'He hasn't hurt anybody.'

'Just over two hours.' Tobias checked his watch. 'Probably a record for Stockholm syndrome.'

'I'm just saying.'

'How do I know it's not you?'

'You don't.' I respected the question; it's what I would have asked. 'But I'd be asking for more than a dollar.'

Tobias's forehead crinkled. 'Is that what he wants?'

'Yep. Just one.'

'And so? Just give it to him. Hell'—he started patting his pockets—'I'm sure I've got a dollar here somewhere.'

'We've tried that. He wants it from the vault. Which, unfortunately, no one in this bank knows how to open.'

'Don't you have a Huxley?'

'We've got the wrong one. Edward Huxley changed the code two days ago, and he's gone missing. Besides, I don't think our bank robber *really* wants a dollar. That's just what he's telling us. There are two hundred and eighty safety deposit boxes in here.'

Tobias sucked his teeth as he turned this over. 'Can you give me a minute?'

I heard him hurry off, the tap of his shoes down the stairs, and the door settled closed. I wondered how far past my designated thirty minutes I was. It's surprising how absolutely useless humanity has become at guessing the time without our phones. I was still rattled by what Felix had said. Specifically, one word: *gamble*. I'd always thought I was helping people, the same as I'd told Juliette in the coffee shop, the same as I'd said in every meeting, and as was printed in our premium-binding-for-a-dollar business plan. I really believed it. Of course, I *liked* solving crimes. I *liked* the pay-off of being proved right, the feeling of everything clicking together at the end. I *loved* a parlour scene. But I'd always thought I could like something and help people at the same time. Maybe that wasn't true.

Was I just an addict, chasing a high?

The textbook definition of addiction is when it starts to interfere with your personal relationships and your work. In my previous cases I've had half my family murdered and accused my fiancée of being a killer (during a marriage proposal, no less). Some would classify that as interference. The diagnosis writes itself.

Maybe that was why I'd got into so many scrapes. Because it was like rolling the dice another time. I'd built up a tolerance to solving a case; now I had to risk dying to get the thrill.

When I write it out like that, it doesn't sound very healthy. And that's not even taking into account what I'm about to do next, which is another nail in the coffin.

Also, with the beauty of hindsight, dying is not thrilling *at all*. At least not the way I'm doing it. There's more sitting around than you'd think.

The door pulled ajar again, and Tobias's arm snaked through, a plastic bag dangling from his fist. He had to turn away from the door to get his shoulder in, and the taser on his hip jiggled in the gap. I considered stealing it. Another risk of the Fencer letting us wander the bank unattended was that we might come back with a weapon. There was something worrying in that: he was either the worst bank robber ever, or he simply didn't care.

I took the bag, and Tobias's face came back into view. 'We can't get him on the phone,' he said, as I peered down into the bag. Inside was one half of a two-way radio. It rattled against something small: a one-dollar coin. I snorted a laugh. 'Worth a shot,' he said. 'We've tried all the internal numbers.'

'I don't see the point. He doesn't have any demands. He just wants to get into the vault.'

'There's always something. No offence, but the ten of you are currency. I can convince him to spend you. And talking's the first step.' His eyes softened. 'Will you help me get some people out? Cordelia, for example.'

'Not Eric?'

'Everyone's equal here. I wouldn't be on this assignment if the team had any other choice.' He tugged at the shoulder strap of his ill-fitting Kevlar vest.

The mismatch of body armour and the suburban accountant shirt and tie made sense. I didn't think the police would have a full-time professional hostage negotiator based this far out of the closest city.

'I'm a divorce lawyer. I have a practice in Huxley. This isn't my regular workday.'

'A *divorce* lawyer?' I said, my disbelief barely hidden.

'Aren't you an *amateur* detective?' he retorted. 'I'm capable, don't you worry about that. Obviously I want my boy out and safe, but I need you to trust that I will make the right decisions, not the ones that benefit me personally. That's my promise. The sick girl comes out first. Okay?'

I closed the bag and nodded. It did seem strange that the Fencer hadn't asked to trade us for anything yet. He'd flipped his lid at the risk of not having enough hostages, and yet now he didn't seem to care? Sure, I was apparently his best shot at getting the vault open, but he was risking letting Felix and me escape by having us go off on our own. The place was locked up, but it wasn't exactly a fortress. The police had got Milton out, for example.

'So what happens now?' I asked. 'How long until people start rappelling from helicopters and kicking in windows?'

Tobias shook his head. 'We're not coming in. No one's injured, and from the sounds of it no one's under any immediate threat. Plus, hostages like yourself are wandering the bank alone, which is, to be honest, surprising. If we go in, all we'll do is antagonise. Sure, we could send an SRT – Special Response Team if you're wondering – cut the power, lance through this chain and fling some flashbangs in, the whole lot, but one stray bullet is all it takes. I've never lost a hostage, and I'm not starting now. Besides, as cinematic as blasting through the skylights might seem, we couldn't get a chopper in the air even if we wanted.' He swatted the butterflies again. 'Because of these bloody things. We tried, and they all got sucked into the engine, jammed it all up, like lint in a washing machine filter. You tell him that, if he's watched too many movies and thinks he can ask for one as a getaway. No go on the chopper.'

'Never lost a hostage,' I whistled, impressed. 'How many bank robberies is that?'

'None.'

'Believe it or not, you and I are equally qualified.'

'Settle. It's not my first day. Police use me to consult every now and then. Though it's usually one-on-one, domestic violence incidents or suicide prevention. Talking them down is the same as any bank robbery – a guy behind a locked door with a gun in his mouth. It's still a hostage situation. It's just themselves they've taken hostage.' He leaned into the door. 'A bank or a bathroom, it's the same, I promise. Get me on the radio with this guy, and we'll get through this.'

'There's no registered psychologists in Huxley to consult?' I asked.

'What's it going to take for you to trust me? The first time, yes, I got the call because they had no one else to turn to for someone threatening to jump off the bell tower. I was in over my head, but I bumbled through it. Surely you can relate.'

I could, but I stayed silent.

'I've done the training in my own time since. Hell, I can do bomb disposal. I only died three out of five simulations. And if that doesn't convince you'—he threw his hands up—'I'm a *divorce lawyer*. My job is literally to stop people killing each other. A bank robbery? Piece of piss.'

This got a laugh out of me. 'Okay. I'm buying it. I'll deliver this.' I clutched the bag with great solemnity. An idea hit me. 'Ben Huxley's death – did you work on that? Was it the result of a domestic violence issue? Was that why the house was raided?'

'I'm not a police officer,' Tobias reiterated. 'I couldn't tell you what went down because I wasn't there, because it's not my job. I only get called when there's talking involved, and there was no one left to talk to by the time they might have called me. Sorry.'

There was a pause, like the end of an awkward date. I chucked a thumb over my shoulder at the bank's interior. 'I need to get going. Let's do this again sometime.'

'You've got my number.' Tobias nodded at the bag with the radio in it. 'And tell your hostage taker, if you can, not to get comfortable. Just because we're not coming in doesn't mean we won't. I say *we*, but I mean *them*.' He glanced towards the street. 'The guys with the big guns. They hear a gunshot or anything that increases the threat level, and they don't have a choice.'

'Towels,' I remembered, just as I stepped away. 'We need towels. Clothes of various sizes. And some food and water. Pile them up here and I'll try to get back to pick them up. And I need you to have the police run their missing persons' magic on Edward Huxley. Phone, credit cards, hotels. Have a dog sniff a pair of underwear. Whatever it is you do. Find the guy.'

'Got it. That and the milrinone.'

'You could give me a gun?'

'No antagonising.' It was the answer I was expecting. 'Gotta protect my clean sheet.'

'Does that perfect record include the hostage *takers*?'

Tobias was quiet. He spread his arms. 'Last chance if you want out. No shame in it.'

'I'm staying.'

'Thought you might. You have that air about you.'

Looking back on it, I still choose to believe he meant brave.

CHAPTER 13

My tardiness was barely noticed, given that the Fencer wasn't even there when I got back and, in fact, everyone was spread out in the main office space rather than cramped in the boardroom. Felix tapped his wrist as I walked in, warning me of the dangerous game I was playing. Eric was with Cordelia, making a sport of tossing tiny wads of chewed-up paper into a cup, his piggybank tucked close to his hip.

I went over to them. Both were pale, though for different reasons. Cordelia was sick, stubborn and defiant. Eric was just scared.

'I talked to the negotiator. Things are going to be okay. Whatever this guy wants, it'll be you first, Cordelia, then you, Eric.'

Eric looked a little disappointed by that. He'd clearly guessed his dad would have been brought in and hoped nepotism would get him out first. He was shaking.

I sat down next to him and squeezed his shoulder. 'Your dad wants you to be brave. You have to stay in here so she can go. She's sick. It wouldn't be fair if he put you first. Can you do that?'

He gave an accepting sniffle.

'Must be hard having a professional negotiator as a dad,' I joked. 'Try bargaining your bedtime with that.'

This got a grunt instead of a laugh. I floundered to connect, half aware that Juliette was watching my grapple with teenage communication, a glint of affection in her eyes, from across the room.

'Your dad said you liked video games?'

'Esports,' Eric mumbled.

'Of course. You've got a tournament tonight?'

He nodded.

'Let's get you home for it. What's the game called?'

'*Buccaneers*. It's a shooter.' The attitude was fading, Eric warming up as he talked about his passion. 'You play as pirates. I stream as well as play competitively.'

'And you're pretty good? I hear you placed in some competitions? Won some prizes?'

A little nod, then his eyes nervously darted to the pig with his tournament winnings nestled inside, six silver coins. The message was clear: *how much has he told you?*

'It's okay. I can keep a secret.'

'There's six coins,' he admitted. 'A couple of grand each.'

'I was wondering, does the phrase *the sea fears you* mean anything to you?'

'Yeah. It's the announcement when you win a game. Like'—he put on a deep voice—'*Flawless Victory* or *Game Over*.'

'Ben Huxley was pretty good then?' I asked it casually, but I already knew the answer. Tobias had said the silver coins were a *second-place* prize. It made sense that gold would be for first, and Eric had just confirmed it. The bar in Edward's office was a trophy.

'We played on the same team,' Eric said quietly. 'We were friends. He won some, I won others. We made each other better. Sparring partners.'

'He was two years older than you?'

'Yeah, I play up. I'm trying to qualify for ackle. That's Australian Championship League.'

'You mentioned tonight's tournament before. I thought you were already in it?'

'University division. Tonight's the finals. I could get promoted to the full league.'

'Did Ben play in your division?'

'Yeah, but I did it younger.' Tears welled for his friend, and he lowered his voice. 'He died.' A little hiccup. 'I miss him.'

I rubbed the pig's head. 'I'll protect you,' I promised. 'You have my word. Hey, you reckon I could swap careers? I was pretty good at *Super Mario* back in the day.'

Finally, a genuine smile. 'How *old* are you?'

Michelle, spinning idly on a chair by Felix, who sat on a desk opposite her, overheard this and whispered something to Gabriel, cross-legged at her feet. He passed her a new notepad and black marker he'd scrounged up to replace his confiscated iPad. She scribbled on the pad. Held it up.

N008

Eric laughed out loud at that. Michelle seemed pleased with herself.

'What was that about?' I asked, wandering over.

She thumbed her chest. 'I play *Buccaneers*. I was just calling you an amateur. *Noob*, short for newbie. You have to type quickly while mid-game, so everything's truncated.'

'With numbers?'

'It's one way. That's called leetspeak. Elite, opposite of newbie, shortened to leet, shortened to one-three-three-seven.' She could see my confusion and wrote it on the pad.

1337

'It looks like the word *leet*, see?'

'Does it?' I wrinkled my nose. 'So 1337 is shorthand for leet, which is short for elite, which is short for *good at a game*. And that *saves* you time?'

She patted me on the back condescendingly.

'What about one-zero-one-one.' I wrote it out for her. The number on Winston's abacus.

Michelle examined it. 'Could be binary. Ones and zeros. But it would just be the plain number eleven in binary. Which is nothing.'

'In gamer talk?'

'Nothing. L O L with an extra L?'

'Laugh out loud? Even I know that one. Laugh out loud . . . lots?'

'Stick to *Mario*.'

I headed over to Juliette. Laverna had found herself a mug of tea – we weren't completely abandoned for supplies; this was still a functional office space – and had been watching my conversation with amusement. It was nice that there was a little trauma-bonding going on between a few pairs: Michelle and Eric; Eric and Cordelia. Little pockets of friendship blooming like spring flowers after frost. The group had a strange sense of unity after a few hours. Well, most of us. Remy was using his satchel as a pillow underneath one of the desks, and Winston was nowhere to be seen.

Juliette wrapped her arms around my neck, kissing my cheeks. 'Goss from up here is that Gabriel is *pissed*. Someone vandalised the church graveyard last weekend.'

'Maybe that's what he wanted to talk to Winston about this morning.'

'Even juicier – he thinks Edward did it.'

'Why would Edward kick over tombstones?'

'Couldn't say. Also.' She held a finger up. 'I've thought about the wedding. Once you get into the vault, if we fill our pockets and blame the robber, that doesn't count towards the thirty-six-thousand wedding budget does it? Then we can get the photographer.'

It was hard to tell if she was joking. 'I've had a better idea,' I said. 'The photographer is four grand and we're on thirty-four already, right? Well, remember we looked up private detectives' fees to compare for our business plan?'

She nodded slowly, trying to figure out where I was taking this.

'They charge fifteen hundred a day to follow an unfaithful spouse with a high-quality telephotographic lens. Here's the idea: I *hire* a private detective to take photos. Then we come in at thirty-five and a half.'

'I don't know if I want my wedding photos all zoomed in, taken from behind the wheel of a black sedan across the street.'

'That's the beauty of it,' I explained.

Juliette's smile faltered a little when she realised I wasn't kidding.

'I tell the PI that I suspect you're up to something *during* the wedding. Make sure they keep an eye on you. Photos getting ready, at the altar. I request shots of everything, just to check if you're throwing side-eye to my groomsmen—'

'Eurgh. Andy. Yuck.' She paused. I could see the idea growing on her. 'Fifteen hundred, you said?'

'*And* you get canapés.'

She stuck out a hand. I shook it. Rules aren't just important for murder mysteries or bank robberies: our wedding was now, in my mind, officially divorce-proof. Thirty-five thousand, five hundred dollars, with five hundred left over for incidentals.

'Okay, one problem solved,' she said. 'Now, to present matters. What happened downstairs?'

I showed her the bag. 'Police want to start up negotiations. Towels, medicine and food should be en route soon. Where is our Fencer?'

'Don't know,' she said, baffled. 'He ferried us all to the bathroom – one at a time, mind you, which seemed like a slow process. Then he took us out into the main office space and had us all do yoga to help blood flow. Then he took off.' She lowered her voice to a whisper. 'I don't think he's ever robbed a bank before.'

Looking around the room, it did feel more like an airport lounge for a delayed flight than a bank robbery. It was decidedly threatless.

I checked the clock on the wall: 1 p.m. 'Are you starting to get the feeling he doesn't really care enough about this?' I ventured.

'Maybe he's got post-hostage depression. Oh sure, taking hostages is fun, but then you're like'—she rolled her eyes—'*I didn't realise how much work it is.*'

'We said we'd get "the snip" at two hostages,' I added, and it felt good to laugh. 'Suddenly I'm looking after ten.'

'What if he's already left?' Juliette said, serious again. 'You know, set us up with a perceived threat, while he's already off with the stash. Cops waste their time outside planning how to get us out. The longer we keep ourselves here, the bigger the head start he has.'

'Except he hasn't been in the vault.'

'No.' Juliette prodded me on the chest. '*You* haven't been in the vault. That's not the same thing.' She paused, weighing me up. Walked her fingers up from my chest, my neck, and onto my temples. 'Something's going on up there, isn't it?'

'I know as well as anyone that I have a tendency to overcomplicate things. But—' I hesitated. It was impossible to put into words, as *vibes* aren't allowed as clues in Golden Age mysteries. 'We're in a nucleus here, and I just get the feeling something is colliding. We've got a dead body in Byron, two hours' drive from here, a police raid a year ago that resulted in another dead body, a missing banker, a vault that can't be opened, a bank robber who doesn't seem to care about money, and a guard who doesn't care about protecting it, plus a priest who can't talk and a bird that won't shut up.'

I took a deep breath. Juliette looked momentarily buried under the avalanche of words. I realised she didn't know the context for half the things I'd just rattled off. She stuck a metaphorical hand out of the snow. 'Did you say a talking *bird*?'

'Is that what you got from all that?'

She wrinkled her nose. 'It *is* the coolest bit.'

'What does the word *clue* mean?'

I could see her assessing if this was a trick question or if I was having a stroke. I'm supposed to be a detective after all.

'It means a hint,' she said cautiously. 'A piece of an answer.'

'The bird, it said *I am not a clue*.'

'That's meta, even for you.' She chuckled. 'Did you mishear it? *I haven't got a clue? Glue?*'

'It said it three times.'

'Welcome to school, then.' She cracked her knuckles performatively. 'I'm surprised you don't know this, mystery expert and all. A clew, c-l-e-w, is a ball of thread. It's from the Greek myth: Ariadne gave one to Theseus to lay a trail out of the labyrinth and find the exit. You know, the minotaur story and all that. The word can still mean a ball of yarn, though it's a little old-fashioned, but that's where the modern word *clue* comes from.' She puffed with pride at her knowledge. 'Because, quite literally, Theseus followed a *clew* to the answer.'

'So the bird is talking about a ball of wool?' I told her the full message. *You are dead. Dead! You can't kill me. I am not a clue.* 'What in the world does that have to do with knitting?'

'You ever met a Country Women's Association? Cut-throat.'

'I'm being serious.'

'So am I.'

Around me, I became aware that the space had tensed up. Everyone except Eric seemed to feel it; he tossed one more wad of paper at the cup, bouncing it off the rim and scurrying over to pick it up, only to find himself looking at the black army boots and boilersuit cuffs of our resident captor. Eric bounced back to Cordelia like he was on a bungee cord.

The Fencer took in the group from behind his glinting metallic face, then raised an arm and counted us off manually. He came up one short. The gun hung lazily by his side, as he tapped it against his thigh.

Suddenly there was a clatter and the sound of breaking glass from the stairwell. Winston stood guiltily on the top step. Coddled to his chest in folded arms was a crystal decanter and a collection of glasses scavenged from his office, one of which had just tumbled out of his grasp. He hurried over and scattered the glassware on to a table.

'Thought we could use a drink,' he said meekly.

Everyone held their breath. And then the thief put his hand out.

Winston, hurried and fussy like a servant who's just spilled wine on a king, poured out a dram and handed it over. The thief manoeuvred the glass under his mask, giving another glimpse of his chin, then knocked it back. It must have been strong: he coughed and thumped his chest. Then, without the voice-changer, wheezed, 'Jesus.'

'Not a bourbon man?' Winston smiled, relaxing, and poured himself one. He raised it to the thief. 'Polish your shoes and light your fireplace with that.' He turned to me, as if he and the Fencer were some kind of team. 'Any luck?'

I shook my head.

The Fencer checked his watch, pulled the mask back down, then held out his glass so Winston could top it up. Then he retreated to Edward's office. I saw him brush the contents of my rubbish-bin dumping off the desk and sit behind it, door open. The only way out was by the stairs or elevator, and he'd see us easily. For the first time, the gun left his grip: he placed it on the desk.

Though I killed a few minutes pretending to think about what to do next, I knew I had to follow. I clutched the plastic bag tightly and hoped Tobias was as good a negotiator as he'd promised.

I moved slowly, like a zookeeper approaches a tiger, both hands in the air and from a clear angle of sight. The last thing I wanted to do was surprise him. But he was in some kind of melancholy stupor, staring deeply into his glass, rather than drinking it, and

I had no choice but to rap lightly on the open door. As difficult as it was to make out any expression in his blank face, I would suggest he looked up in mild surprise. He didn't pick up the gun, but slid it gently across the desk to be closer to him. Not worried, but prepared.

I held out the bag. 'There's a radio in here. They have a negotiator outside. They're waiting for your instructions. They say you can have whatever you want.'

Okay, so I ad-libbed a little. Sue me.

The Fencer didn't move. He raised the voice-changer and said, in his deep and digital boom, 'I have no demands for them.'

'You do want to get in the vault, right?'

The Fencer nodded.

'They're looking for Edward. He's the one with the vault code. If they find him, how are they going to give it to us if they can't get in contact? Skywriting?'

The Fencer considered this, then nodded at the desk. I tossed the bag onto it, careful not to get too close. He found a pen and used it to lift the bag open and peer inside, confirming it was a radio as promised. I thought I clocked a small twitch of his chest, a chuckle even, as he saw the dollar coin. It didn't seem to be enough of a bribe. He closed the bag.

'*You are dead!*' Ditto said from beside me.

My job done, I should have left. To be honest, I'm not sure where the brashness came from. Perhaps the bourbon fumes had marshalled my confidence a little.

'Or,' I started, my voice jigging like a tattoo needle, 'can we just drop the pretence that what you're after is in the vault at all?'

The Fencer cocked his head at this. Curious. His fingers drummed the table.

'I have a knack for this kind of stuff. Tell me what you really want, and I'll help you get it. In the meantime, why don't you let everyone else go? Just make it you and me.' This didn't win him over, so I risked a guess. 'What is Edward Huxley hiding? Something the police want, but didn't find.' No response. I tried another line. 'Did someone here hurt Laurence Birch?' The finger drumming stopped. Something there. 'Come on, people out here are scared, sick. You don't want to kill anyone. I don't think you're that heartless.'

He pushed the chair out from behind him so aggressively it bounced off the wall and tipped over. Suddenly he was advancing on me, the gun in his hand. Any idea I had that he was not the type to pull the trigger evaporated, and I backpedalled out of the room.

It was like watching a glitch in real life. He held the voice-changer up, then the gun, then the voice-changer again. As if he wasn't sure whether to insult me or shoot me. I thought it wise not to remind him he could do both. His shoulders were quivering. Was it anger? Or was he . . . crying?

There's an infamous case from Pennsylvania where a burglar was locked into an explosive collar and forced, by threat of detonation, to rob a local bank. A puppet controlled from afar. The story popped into my head.

'Is someone making you do this?' I asked.

He chose to neither shoot nor speak, retreating into the gloom of Edward's office and slamming the door behind him.

CHAPTER 14

On my walk back to the hostage crèche, Winston spied me and raised his glass lazily. 'Opened my vault yet?'

It was a taunt instead of a question, given he knew the answer. He sounded a little tipsy, his tongue a dog off-leash, sniffing around his cheeks like park bushes. I changed path and headed to him, showed him my palms. Empty.

'Oh, is that . . .' He pretended to be watching something flutter past him in the air, just out of grasp. 'Is that your agency?'

I didn't take the bait. 'Did Edward knit, by any chance?'

'Knit?'

'Or crochet.'

'I wouldn't have the foggiest.' Winston blew bubbles in his drink, then with a surprising amount of disgust, said, 'Though I suppose that's something you'd keep to yourself if you were into it. How does that open the vault?'

'It doesn't,' I admitted. 'Just curious. I think we're being made to look one way so we don't see the real truth. What else is valuable in this bank? I know you have *Goldfields* by Sidney Nolan on the mezzanine, the gold nugget in the entry, some bullion in Edward's office. How about your collection of model trucks?'

'Childhood knick-knacks,' Winston said airily. Given his toys were preserved in the original packaging, I'm sure he was a lot of fun as a child. Edward at least bashed his about. 'Worth a little more than you'd expect, especially in good condition, but a lot less than the rest of the stuff you just mentioned. A few grand for the best.'

That wasn't what the eBay printout on Edward's desk had said. The Hess tanker was supposed to be worth two-hundred and twenty grand. I wondered if Winston was keeping the real value a secret in case it attracted attention. I pushed. 'Anything else?'

'Me.'

'Now's not a time to be pithy.'

'My time is the most valuable thing in here,' Winston said, opening his arms, completely sincere. Then he looked around and settled his gaze on Cordelia and Eric. 'Oh, you want me to say something lame like *the youth of tomorrow*?'

'I'm not talking in riddles, Winston. Is there anything else valuable in this bank?'

'Monetarily?' Winston sobered, furrowed his brow to give it proper thought. 'No. The Nolan's got pedigree, sure, but it's only worth a hundred grand. The nugget's a kilo and a half, so one-fifty, one-eighty on a good day. But you'd have to rinse both of them through the black market, so you'd lose half. Chump change. It's not worth robbing a bank over.'

'Neither's a dollar.'

'Why bother then? You may as well'—the words curled around his tongue with disgust—'*get a job*.'

I decided not to mention that a hundred grand was life-changing money for plenty of people. Although, he did have a point: it seemed a meagre payday for such an extravagant robbery. 'There's more you can steal from a person than just their wallet,' I said.

Winston snorted, personally affronted at the very notion of doing anything not for financial reward.

'Is that going around?' Felix's approach interrupted us; he was nodding at the bourbon.

Winston's lip twitched downward, as if it would be vulgar to share the drink with an employee, but he realised I was watching him and relented. I did notice he only poured half the amount he'd served himself. Out of obligation he offered the spout of the decanter in my direction, but I waved it away.

Felix examined his glass, then nodded towards Edward's closed office door. 'Should we, like, just sneak past and leave?' he whispered.

As he said it, the door clicked open. The Fencer was a shadow in the dim light, holding one hand up to his mouth. The shape of the object in his other was no longer the gun though, but the radio. I'd succeeded: he'd talked to Tobias. 'Medicine is downstairs. And clothes,' the voice-changer crackled. It was hard to dissect tone amid the digital warping, but it sounded almost . . . apologetic? An olive branch.

'Thank you,' I called back.

I thought, in the shadow, I saw a nod, and then the Fencer took his seat again. This time he left the door open. The permission was implicit: we could go and fetch supplies, but he was watching.

'What about Edward?' I asked Winston, keen to finish our conversation because, if we were allowed to make the trip downstairs, I was starting to think I could kill two birds with one stone. Not the talking ones, of course. 'Anything personally valuable? Or illegal?' This was my current line of thinking. If Edward was hiding something worth raiding his house for, maybe he'd realised it wasn't secure enough there and moved it to the vault. That would be one reason for him to review the bank's security.

Winston snorted. 'Now that's an accusation.'

'Until we open the vault, we don't know he hasn't robbed you barren,' I reminded him.

'I'd be surprised if he was mixed up in anything. Crochet or criminal.'

'Then why'd his house get raided?'

Behind us, I heard a splutter and a cough. Michelle had taken a sip from Felix's glass. She reached for Felix's orange sports drink, but he selfishly pulled it away from her. She folded her arms and huffed off to the office kitchen, the honeymoon period so swiftly ended.

'It got raided because he had that stupid new surround sound system.' Winston poured himself another glass. 'Do your research before you start throwing such tripe around.'

'Surround sound?'

'Video games. His son used to play them. I got Ed a surround sound system for Christmas. Real hi-tech stuff, top of the line, a very generous gift.' He seemed to read my face as unimpressed with the brag. 'I know you think I'm a heartless brother. That I care about the vault more than I do him, but you don't understand. We got the business *together*. But I'm the one who has to be a hard-arse and make the decisions no one likes. For both of our benefits.'

'One of you gets to play with the trucks, the other has to keep them in their boxes,' I offered.

'Exactly. Otherwise who'd have a new truck ready when Ed's has found its way down the stormwater drain *again*?'

My mental image of Winston shifted. No longer was he stiff-edged, boxing up his collection and keeping them for his sole enjoyment. Now, in my mind, they were kids, sitting in a driveway playing trucks. And Winston was bending over to his sobbing brother, handing over a private, protected, treasure. In my imagination, the torn packaging was clutched behind his back. Hidden.

'How much is the Hess petrol tanker worth, exactly?' I asked, an idea forming.

'Two, three thousand. Mint.'

He was sticking to the valuation. Which meant Edward had overpaid.

While it's a bit of a stretch to believe that Winston's entirely deplorable persona was merely a facade to let his brother believe he came to success easily, it's also true that in every comic duo there's a straight guy and a funny guy. In every steamboat there's someone shovelling coal and someone tooting the horn.

'What does this have to do with a surround sound system?' I asked, though a little more warmly.

'It makes bangs go bang and booms go boom. A passing patrol car hears gunfire from the house, kicks in the door and shoots—' He droned off. 'They weren't searching for anything.' For the first time he looked at me square, instead of over my shoulder. His voice wobbled. 'It's my fault. Ben's dead and I'm to blame. That's why Ed's doing this to me.'

I was surprised to find myself taking on the role of comforting him. I understood it: he was used to taking responsibility for his brother. If he wore this on his shoulders, too, it protected Edward. Gave him someone to blame except the universe. 'It's not your—'

'If I hadn't bought—'

I stopped his glass going back to his mouth. 'Mystery writers won't admit it, but death is just a big sequence of coincidences. That you're there on that day, at that time. That the wind is blowing just right. That you missed your bus because you bent to tie your shoelaces, and the next one is the one that crashes.'

That a delivery van hits you on the street while you're holding a coffee cup with the name *Ernest* written on it, I thought but didn't say.

'The chain reaction of bad luck is both very simple and an astronomical series of fractional incidences,' I continued. 'Like all of us here today.'

'You think?'

'Is that why you didn't want to talk about Ben this morning?'

'I want you to open my vault.'

I thought back to our initial conversation in his office. *Edward's not the type. And I'm not talking any more about his son.* Him brushing off the conversation about Edward's loss, moving me away from even the slightest hint that Edward's grief might have led him to harm himself. I realised it wasn't because Winston didn't believe it. It was because he did. He desperately wanted it not to be true. He couldn't *let* it be true. Opening the vault was important, but he only talked it up to save face. The vault code was Edward and Edward was the vault code. I had to find one to find the other. And that was the real reason he'd hired me. To make sure Edward hadn't broken down, almost a year on from his son's death. He needed me to find Edward. Alive.

'Yeah, I know. The vault, sure.' I reached out and touched his arm. 'Edward didn't kill himself.'

His eyes begged me to be right on this. 'How can you know that?'

'He eats a *lot* of pistachios, right?'

'Yeah,' Winston sniffed. 'All the time. Health kick. Carries them around in his pockets. It's disgusting.' He said it with affection, not true distaste.

'Nobody planning to kill themselves cares about lowering their cholesterol,' I said. 'There you go. Getting what you paid for. A bit of detective work.'

Winston wiped his nose on his sleeve, sniffed deeply and checked around the room, as if the most embarrassing thing he could be caught doing was showing emotion. Post-outburst, I could see him consciously trying to set his expression back to normal, and I had the feeling that if I wasn't standing in front of him he'd have stuck his fingers in his mouth and pulled his cheeks up manually.

'Okay, genius.' He settled back into cantankerous like the mood was a pair of slippers. 'Then why'd he change the bloody code?'

'I've been thinking about that,' I said. 'I can't say why, but I've been trying to get into his mindset. He's a sensible guy, Felix told me. Yet he's bypassed the failsafe, which means the only place the new code exists is in his head. It needs to be a number he won't forget. It's too risky otherwise.'

'I'm not an idiot, I tried all the birthdays.'

'What about deathdays?'

INTERLUDE: KEYPAD ENTRY

020924
Access denied.

CHAPTER 15

If you ever want tactile proof of Einstein's theory of relativity, try paying with a debit card you're not *quite* sure has enough money on it, or typing the wrong code into a bank vault: the millisecond between the final *boop* and success or failure is infinite. It's even worse when you have an audience.

Gabriel held up a frowny face on his notepad.

Winston, Juliette, Eric and Gabriel had come for the show: one for hope, two for boredom and one for humiliation, but I'll let you figure out which was expecting which. Gabriel spent the walk there scribbling on his pad and shoving it in Winston's face; I took it as taking the opportunity to have his say about the vandalism to his graveyard.

'I don't know what you want.' Winston swatted the pages away and sped up. 'I think there are more important things at play right now.'

Gabriel scratched a frustrated black star on the pad.

It was interesting that we'd gotten five of us out into the bank so easily. Our unspoken permission to fetch supplies hadn't specified how many of us were allowed downstairs, so we'd paraded past the office door with enough obvious slowness for the Fencer to object. Again, he didn't really seem fussed about half his hostages being free range.

We were a miserable lot as we trudged up through the foyer, but at least we weren't empty-handed. We'd collected towels (most of us were dry by now, but gift horse and all that), clothes (jumpers, jeans, and t-shirts of various sizes), sandwiches, a disassembled pallet of bottled water that had been rolled through the door one by one into the antechamber, and a clear plastic IV bag of milrinone, along with plastic tubing and syringes.

I was walking next to Gabriel. 'You think Edward vandalised church property?'

Gabriel shifted the towels he was carrying into one arm and wrote in wobbly cursive as he walked. THINK? KNOW.

'You saw him?' I asked.

HIS CAR.

'Cops probably won't take that as hard evidence.'

Gabriel affirmed this with a solemn nod.

'What kind of damage are we talking?'

SMASHED MAUSOLEUM. CRACKED STONE DOOR DOWN THE MIDDLE.

'Why are you taking this up with Winston instead of Edward?'

Gabriel's pen hesitated above the page, like he was voting on the scrap of paper on *Survivor* and hadn't decided. He wrote the start of a letter, an S, changed his mind and scribbled it out.

WANTED SECURITY FOOTAGE. HE'S ACTING SHADY.

'Add him to the list,' I said. 'Next to you. What have you got in the vault?'

Gabriel raised a curious, slightly guilty eyebrow, so I explained.

'For one thing, you wanted to come along in case I opened it. For another, you voted to attack. You're protecting something. I assume it's in a safety deposit box.'

Gabriel spent a moment deciding what to write. DON'T LAUGH. WATER.

I looked at one of the bottles in my hand. 'Water?'

HOLY WATER. IT WAS BLESSED BY POPE JOHN PAUL II IN 2004.

I knew John Paul II had died the following year.

Gabriel turned the page in his book and kept writing. IT DOESN'T LOOK VALUABLE. JUST A MASON JAR. BUT IT'S VERY PRECIOUS TO ME.

'You were willing to charge a man with a gun to protect a glass of water?' I struggled to hide the amusement in my voice.

Gabriel almost tore the paper writing his response. IMAGINE IF YOU HAD SOMETHING LIKE THAT.

He sped up, away from me, and I felt it in my chest, not least because there's something unique about being dissed by a priest. It's obvious that I have no problem putting my life on the line. I've done it often – I've even technically died once. What would I die to protect? I think back on that moment, of Juliette walking in front of me. Did I really do all this to protect her? Or did I do this just to solve some puzzle?

If it's the latter, am I dying for nothing? I'm trying not to cry. Waste of oxygen.

Halfway up the stairs, I realised that the IV stand itself, still lying in the foyer, would probably be useful for administering the new batch of milrinone, so I ladled off my armful of water bottles to Juliette and headed back to get it, checking the foyer's clock as I walked past.

It was 1.25 p.m. That's important.

As I was picking up the toppled stand, lying amid a chalky-white stain on the tiles where the spilled medicine had dried, a large shadow passed over the skylight. I looked up, thinking that maybe Tobias had managed to get a chopper in the air after all. But there was nothing in the sky except the butterfly cacophony, the clutter of winged debris. I could just see the corner of the roof: castle-like parapets, the sun behind.

I squinted into it. Then something definitely moved. And not in the air. On the roof.

Someone was up there.

What's coming is not to be my last breath of fresh air. But the next time I was outside I was dangling perilously off something, so it was my final chance to really breathe it.

I'd poked a head in on the third floor. Everyone seemed more interested in doling out food and clothing than wondering why I was taking so long, so I figured no one would notice if I kept going up the stairs to the roof exit. It was a large fire door with a hip-high lever to open it. A few scenarios played through my mind as I gripped the bar. One, that I'd bump into a fully kitted-out SRT team about to abseil down the skylights. Two, that one of the hostages was making a break for it. Or three, that Edward was on the roof.

I pushed open the door.

It wasn't dark inside the bank, but the difference between fluorescents and daylight seared my eyes. At first I only saw it in blurry silhouette. A mutant creature with four arms.

A lesser narrator would have included a chapter break here. Obviously, it was just a man. No aliens: those are the rules. My eyes adjusted. The man did, however, have an extra set of arms.

It was the thief, unmasked and half undressed, the top of his boilersuit hanging from his waist. He had on a black long-sleeved shirt. The backs of his hands were covered in blisters.

He heard me open the door, and turned, floppy sleeves swinging from his hips. It was the first time I'd seen his face. Well, second. I recognised him instantly as the harried man from Liz's Café.

Yes: the man who dropped his change and was in too much of a hurry to pick it up was now robbing a bank for a dollar.

Revealed, he seemed kinder than I expected. No leathered skin, teardrop tattoos or scars. He was youngish, early forties, though gaunt in the cheeks, hollow eyed. There were little patches of red on his neck where the mask must have irritated his skin. A bloodless white line for lips. He didn't look evil: he looked tired.

His eyes flickered down. I tracked them. The bag he'd put our phones in was by his feet. Another step away was the plastic bag I'd given him. On top of it sat the sabre mask, his gloves, the voice-changing box and both guns: Felix's revolver and the chunky one. He looked down at his arsenal like it was on the other side of the planet. If we'd both gone for them, he would have beaten me to a weapon, but instead he simply dropped his shoulders and sighed. 'It's done,' he said, checking the digital watch on his wrist. I caught a glimpse of it now that he was un-sleeved. 1.30. He'd corrected the time since I'd seen him in the café, when his watch had been four hours behind.

'What's done?' I stepped out of the doorway and onto the roof. The church spire rose up behind him, a giant iron bell hanging in the apex. Around us the butterflies beat up a storm. It was like being in the eye of a cyclone.

'I walk out of here like any other hostage.' He stepped out of the legs of the boilersuit, revealing brown chinos, and tossed it aside. 'By the time they realise—' It was desperate, rambling and pleading. His voice became quiet and small. 'It was the only way.'

'We didn't get the vault open.'

'It doesn't matter. I did it.' He laughed now; his eyes shone.

'It?'

'I'm not hurting anybody now. Not really.'

'Not really?' I was doing a good impersonation of Ditto.

I realised he'd been half trying to convince me, half trying to convince himself. He pulled at his hair. 'You're right. Oh, God. You're right.' He smacked his forehead, hard, several times, like trying to shake dust out of it. Then looked back at me. 'I've killed her. I've killed her.'

The word *her* hit me like a shot. The two – I hesitate to call them victims too early, but you know what genre you're in – corpses, Laurence Birch and Ben Huxley, were both male. I considered Edward missing, not dead. Edward's wife, Martina, qualifies as a death, but she'd died of cancer.

This is a murder mystery, not a missing person's case, though. And it's time to oblige.

'Killed who?' I tried to remember if I'd properly seen everyone on the third floor as I'd passed it. He'd said *her*. Had I seen Juliette? I thought so. But . . . had I definitely? Had my time-wasting in the foyer been fatal for someone? 'Who have you killed?' My voice rose in panic.

'I am killing her. I have killed her. Isn't it all the same?' He was no longer looking at the gun, but the edge of the building. As if the way out was over it. He turned back to me, more desperate. 'If she leaves the bank, she dies. You could just turn around? We walk back in together. No mask.'

'You just told me you killed someone.'

'It was the only way.'

'I told them there were ten hostages. You won't make it to your car.'

'Oh.' Defeat plumed from him like body odour.

'What did you do? Who is going to die? Did you'—I nodded at the guns on the ground—'shoot someone?'

'No. No.' His knuckles rubbed his forehead. 'I wanted to. But I . . . I couldn't . . . I didn't think I had it in me. And then everything . . . happened. So quickly out of my control. But opportunity knocks and you've got to grab a hold and just try to ride it. Right?'

I could do nothing but nod, though I wasn't sure what I was agreeing to.

'And . . . and . . .!' He held a finger up. 'It's all energy, right? Like, energy cannot be created *or* destroyed. All of the energy in the world is exactly the same now as it was a hundred years ago. Right? That's what they taught us in high school. A candle. Fire, heat, light. Life, death. Why is that any different? It's a shifting of *energy*. Death is life and life is death. It's hot up here. Is it hot?'

He was rabid now. It was like he'd forgotten I was there. He scratched at his neck and his eyes were glazed. I focused on the guns, wondering if, in his distraction, I could get to them first.

He moved towards the edge. I realised the truth in what Tobias had told me: this man was a hostage to himself. Guilt had a gun to his head.

'Is someone making you—'

'No one's forced me to do anything. I chose this. And you know what? I'm glad I did.' He stepped up on the parapet. 'Because who gets to choose who lives or who dies? Some stupid *list*?'

'Wait.' My protest was sincere. I realised I hadn't dared to move, barely to breathe, because butterflies had roosted across my shoulders. 'You didn't hurt any of us.'

'I didn't have to. She's dead.'

She. There it was again. My heart refused to slow. I tried to cling on to what he was saying. A list? What list? Was Ernest Cunningham on it? Scratched through as eliminated because of a coffee order?

The thief lifted one foot out over the edge. Hovered it there.

'Don't,' I said. If he had killed someone, I owed it to the family to find out what happened. 'What do you mean, a list?'

Then the thief tilted his head back and let out an anguished yell to the sky. He put his foot back down on the ledge. 'I can't even do that,' he sniffed. He started smacking his forehead again, as if there were voices in it. 'Coward. Coward. *Coward.*'

'Whoa, whoa. Stop that.' I stepped towards him. Towards the guns. 'Come back in. I'll tell them you were good to us. You didn't take anything.'

'I took the one thing that can't be given back.'

'Come on. It's over.'

'It was never about walking away.' He scratched at his neck and looked dejectedly at the deflated boilersuit on the ground. 'Not really. I think I was just trying to convince myself that there was some kind of exit, to give me the courage to go in when, really, I knew there was no going out. I'm sorry you got roped into thi—' He paused. 'I'm not going to use them.'

I froze. I must have been looking too obviously at the guns.

The thief waved a hand. 'You can pick one up if it makes you feel better.'

'I wasn't gonna,' I lied.

'I'd deserve it.' He stepped off the ledge and onto the safety of the roof, then headed towards me, pulling at his collar. 'It's hot up here, right?'

And then he burst into flames.

THE THIRD HEIST: A LIFE

CHAPTER 16

The white-hot beast consumed the thief.

The heat hit me like a wall and disintegrated the hairs on the back of my hands. I lost sight of the Fencer's body within the pyre of golden flames, the blinding white core, but I could tell he was spinning around. Perhaps even screaming, but my ears were filled with a violent whooshing bellow, the fire draining air itself from the sky, like a vampire emptying a corpse, sucking towards the blaze. Despite being outside, it was suddenly hard to breathe. Air went in but didn't nourish: oxygen sapped. It was hot enough that my wet breath evaporated inside my mouth and my throat scorched. The flame licked several butterflies and turned them into ember-missiles, swirling in the air.

The fire lost height, which I took to mean the thief had dropped to the ground. It was too hot to even consider approaching it, not that I had anything to douse him with. Or the time to make a decision. All of this had taken seconds.

The beating wings of a thousand butterflies couldn't put him out.

Among the concrete and steel of the roof, there was nothing for the fire to hold on to. The flames retreated, folding into themselves until there was nothing but a red glow, throbbing like a blacksmith's cauldron, amid a charred, smoking thing that used to be a man.

Oxygen returned. I sucked in a breath. A peculiar aroma, that of cooked meat, settled high in my throat in that awful way where smell becomes taste. My brain was unable to separate the horror of what I'd seen with the smell of barbecue and, horrifyingly, my stomach gurgled. The very notion of this made me vomit: I made it to the parapet and spattered the ground below.

I lingered over the edge, Tobias Cuthbert's words echoing in my head. *I hear a gunshot or anything that increases the threat level, and I won't have a choice.*

I'm no expert: but *human inferno* seemed, to me, an increase to the threat level.

As such, I expected to see some commotion down below, but I saw nothing. We were at the back of the building. The rear wall was sheer, the wedding-cake design only on the sides and front of the top floor. Below was the church graveyard – grey and white stone crosses peppered in green moss like bad teeth, the mausoleum with its cracked-open stone door, black space like the dead had crawled out of it – and the church itself. The church had a terracotta tented roof bookended by the high bell tower at one end and a squat little building signposted with *Funerals* at the other. Behind the church was a glassy lake with a small pier, a rowboat bobbing beside it. The whole back of the bank was deserted. The closest thing to a police presence I could see was the reflection of red and blue lights off the church's sign at the tip of its driveway: a roadblock on the drive to Main Street.

Had they even seen the commotion from their command centre out the front? Tobias had said there was no point deploying snipers given the butterflies were blocking the sightlines. That meant they had no one up high. The bank's roof was the highest point in the street except for the bell tower, and I couldn't see anyone in there. There hadn't been much smoke; the fire was white hot and fast. Maybe they had no idea of what had just happened.

I marched across the roof, ready to wave the white flag down. The equation should have been simple: dead bank robber equals freed hostages. As I walked, my foot got tangled in the arm of the abandoned boilersuit. I shook it off. But – and maybe this was ego, or maybe my memory is skewed by oxygen deprivation – the arm stayed outstretched towards me.

As the shock wore off, my rational brain started to kick back in. And with it, questions. I looked at the charred hunch of the body, cradled in the foetal position. Everything felt wrong.

Spontaneous human combustion is a scientific myth.

It was popularised in the 1800s as the reason for several unexplained fire deaths: the key factors being that a body was often incinerated beyond recognition, that nothing else in the room was burned, and that, gorily, the hands and feet were often the only parts of the body remaining. The most convincing explanation was, naturally, that the body had lit *itself* on fire. Victorian-era forensics often attributed the cause to alcoholism, believing that ketosis of the body led to internal ignition. Charles Dickens even knocked off one of his characters in *Bleak House* by the method, defending it as scientifically valid when questioned.

But modern examinations have almost universally attributed these cases to a nearby ignition source that was overlooked in an investigation. Many victims were believed to have died of natural causes and then caught fire *after*. Imagine a slackened, sleeping mouth and a lit cigarette edging closer and closer to a flammable robe; a log rolling out of a fireplace; a dressing gown draped on a gas heater. The presence of alcohol or sleeping pills, rather than creating the ignition, is more likely a reason why the victim, passed out in a stupor, didn't wake up when ablaze.

Despite this, the myth persists. As recently as 2010, an Irish coroner put down the cause of death of a 76-year-old, found burned in their home, as spontaneous combustion.

My brain knew it was impossible, but my eyes, still blinking away their medium-rare sear, were telling me differently. I'd just seen the thief burst into flames. I was standing right in front of him; there were no external ignition sources. He didn't light a cigarette. And I'm supposed to be a detective. I would have noticed a gas heater or a fireplace.

I reminded myself of the rules of murder mysteries. It *cannot* be impossible. And if spontaneous combustion doesn't exist, then . . . it means someone lit the fire. And if someone lit the fire . . . it meant I had a murder to solve.

It was easy to jump to why someone might want the Fencer dead. The vote to attack him said as much. But *this* seemed to push the boundaries of self-defence. He was robbing the bank for, on the surface, a single dollar. But it was more about opening the vault, wasn't it? He'd also just confessed to a murder. Would whatever was in the vault redeem him? Condemn someone else? Either way, if whatever was in there was worth marching into a bank and taking ten hostages over, it was probably worth killing for too.

All of these thoughts happened in seconds. The sound of a phone ringing interrupted. It was coming from my feet, inside the pocket of the boilersuit. I pulled it out. It was cheap and dated, fist-sized with a keypad and a green digital screen. Older than Laverna's brick. I pressed *answer* and held it to my ear without saying anything.

'Bryce? We're in. We're in! Get out of there.' An exuberant female voice crackled through without waiting for acknowledgement. 'You are *so* brave. Thank you.'

The Fencer had a name: Bryce. Through the phone line it was impossible to be sure, but I didn't recognise the voice as any of the hostages. Unless Father Gabriel, who I hadn't heard speak yet, secretly had a high-pitched voice.

'Bryce? Bryce?' There was a pause. Then, darkly: 'Who is this?'

They hung up.

I rang back but the caller had turned their phone off. The rest of Bryce's phone was empty: no messages, no contacts, and too old a device to have any apps, let alone a Duolingo streak. There were only four received calls, all from the number that I'd just tried, in the call log. None outgoing. A burner phone.

We're in. The words echoed. And what Felix had said about the rules for heists came back to me too: *There's always an inside man.*

I feel the need to defend the decision I made next. Not all of you will agree with it.

The thing about detective stories is that they are best solved by focusing on the certainties. I was certain of two things.

One: if spontaneous combustion is impossible, then the bank robber had been murdered.

Two: there were only ten people with close-enough access to commit the crime. The hostages themselves. Exclude myself and Juliette, and it's down to eight.

Those were my certainties. The rest was only possible. It was *possible* that someone didn't want the vault open. It was *possible* that this was motive for murder. It was *possible* that someone else – this woman on the phone – was on the inside.

I moved towards the front edge of the building, where I could signal down to Main Street and let the professionals take over. I could see the pulsing of lights reflected in shopfront windows, but not yet the road unless I leaned over.

Currently eight suspects were trapped in the one place. If the bank robbery ended, they'd be scattered to the wind. By the time the police, so relieved to have the hostages safe, even realised there was a murder to solve, the culprit could have fled. Not to mention the crisscrossed alibis, evidence destroyed under police boots, and the general unreliability that extreme stress creates in a witness. The murder would be impossible to unravel.

If she leaves the bank, she dies. I didn't know whose life hung in the balance, but those words were enough that, as I stepped back from the edge, one more certainty emerged: what I was going to have to do next.

If I was going to solve this, I couldn't let anyone out of the bank.

Which meant the robbery had to continue.

I put the sabre mask on.

CHAPTER 17

The boilersuit pulled over my clothes, the yellow gardening gloves on my hands, and the guns settled in the deep mechanic's pockets, I passed well enough for *a* bank robber, but not *my* bank robber. My black leather shoes, worn against my will to impress Winston Huxley, would give it away immediately: the thief had been wearing army boots.

I pinched my nose and approached the body. The inside of the mesh helmet was surprisingly easy to see through. Luckily the torso had been the centre of the fire, and aside from one partially melted heel, the shoes were intact. I wriggled the shoes free, choosing to shut my eyes so I didn't have to witness any skin peeling off like socks, and put them on. They were two sizes too big and squeamishly warm, like a recently vacated seat on a bus. I tried not to think about it. At least now I looked the part.

I rolled the body onto its back. From the waist up was rubbery and red, and I had to force myself to look. His brown pants were in tatters, singed with holes, bright pink pieces of shiny flesh poking through. I patted the pockets. The left one had melted, courtesy of something plastic inside it, but the right one had escaped the flames.

It held a small pen light, which I pocketed (and am now using to write by), and a folded piece of paper, torn from a grid-lined design scrapbook, with three two-digit numbers written in pen.

29-39-34

A six-digit number. Like a vault code. I couldn't be sure until I tried it, but the strangeness kept piling up. I remember thinking: why the hell would you go through with this charade when you potentially had the vault code in your pocket?

There was nothing else on the body. No wallet, no ID. I was stuck with the name the mysterious woman had called him on the phone: Bryce. I opened the bag of confiscated phones to be greeted with a tinkle of broken glass and metal, all of them smashed to pieces.

My next problem was how to move the body. Right now, should Tobias change his mind and put a sniper in the bell tower or manage to get a chopper in the air, they'd spy the corpse immediately. A dead body would have them storming the place in seconds. I grabbed Bryce by his now-bare ankles and dragged him around to an air-conditioning vent, muttering pointless apologies along the way. It didn't count as desecration if I was avenging him, I figured. The boilersuit heated up quickly, and the foam inlay of the sabre mask already felt plastered to my forehead with sweat as I rolled Bryce under a duct. I thought he was fairly well covered unless someone actually came up on the roof. The spot where he'd died just looked like an oil stain. The smell was lessening, drifting off into the wind.

The crackling of the radio almost gave me a heart attack.

'You there, mate?' It was Tobias. 'We, uh, we think we've spied something on the roof. Everything okay?'

Damn. I whirled around, wondering where the viewpoint was and how much they'd seen. I managed to calm down by figuring that if they'd really seen me stripping a dead body for a costume, Tobias might have said something more dramatic than *we've spied something on the roof.*

I noticed my shadow stretching long, dropping off the edge. The same as I'd seen through the skylight. I breathed out in relief: they couldn't see me, just the shadow hinting at movement. Even so, I hunched down as I hurried over to the meagre pile of Bryce's possessions and picked up the voice-changer, tried to figure out how it worked. It was a little black box with a button on one side like a walkie-talkie, and a dial just below. I imagined the dial selected the different sound warps, and I wondered momentarily if one of them could change male to female.

'Answer right now or we are coming in.' Tobias's switch from ally to hard-nosed was immediate. I liked it. 'Five . . . four . . .'

I had no choice. I placed the voice-changer in between the mask and the radio. 'Uh, yeah. I'm here.' I was surprised by how little I recognised my own voice in the bassy drawl. 'Everything's fine. All accounted for.'

'Glad to hear it. Confirming no one is hurt? Yourself included.'

'Hostages are fine. I'm doing okay.'

'We've spotted some movement on the roof. It's cause for concern, you understand?' Tobias had moved back to soft, buddying up with a silky expertise.

'That's me,' I said in my fake voice. Then I had an idea. 'With Ernest, the detective or whatever.' That sounded convincingly dismissive, though it stung to say it. 'He needed a . . . smoke break.'

I don't smoke, but Tobias didn't know that. I lowered the voice-changer and said in my own voice, 'Yeah, Ernest here. Everything's okay.'

'Glad to hear it. Big cigarette. Could swear I saw smoke.'

I cleared my throat, lifting the box again. With the butterflies around, I hoped he hadn't got that good a look. Could I bluff this out? 'No. I don't think so. Just a regular cigarette. Right, Ernest?'

Box down. 'Yep. Nothing unusual.'

Box up. 'You see, we're all fine.'

Tobias paused for a long second. 'You okay, Ernest?'

Of course he was onto me. A crack of nerves in my voice, perhaps. I steadied it and lowered the voice-changer. 'I'm completely fine. He's treating us all civilly. Thanks for the supplies.'

'You understand I have no choice but to send someone up the bell tower to confirm everyone's wellbeing,' Tobias said. He kept saying *you understand*, as if to imply I had a say. 'Sit tight up there.'

I spoke through the voice-changer. 'Fine by me.'

It was very not fine by me.

I risked a glimpse over the edge. A man in black tactical gear and a helmet, holding a vicious-looking sub-machine gun, was hurrying across the church graveyard to the bell tower. I gathered up the last of Bryce's possessions into the plastic bag and checked the roof for debris and obvious evidence. My discarded leather shoes had to go, so I flung them into the stairwell. All clear. Then I realised Bryce's foot was sticking out from behind the air-conditioning vent. I stepped in front of it just as I saw the black helmet emerge by the bell.

I didn't know what else to do, so I gave a wave.

'Where's Ernest?' Tobias came through the radio.

'He went inside.'

'I said sit tight. Show me.'

'Show you?' The black helmet was staring at me, unmoved, assumedly narrating down to Tobias at the command centre. I subtly tried to kick Bryce's foot out of sight.

'Ernest Cunningham. I want my guy to see he's okay,' Tobias said. 'Fetch him back.'

'Yes.' I kicked Bryce's foot harder. 'Of course, I'll just . . . go inside and get him. Give me one minute.'

'Thirty seconds.'

'He might be downstairs already.'

'Twenty-nine.'

I kicked out as hard as I could, and Bryce's knee finally crumpled, his foot sliding behind the vent. I gave a gloved thumbs up to the bell tower and hurried back to the roof's entrance, opened the door, then slammed it closed behind me and rested my head against the cold metal. I was at a crossroads. How the hell could I show Ernest Cunningham *and* the bank robber at the same time?

I'm aware I was doing all this for the memory of a criminal who'd held us at gunpoint *and* confessed to a murder himself. But murder is murder. And the family of whoever Bryce had killed deserved closure, just as whoever had killed him deserved justice.

I took a deep breath. Then I did the only thing I could do. I wrenched the fencing mask off and wriggled out of the boilersuit. I kicked the army boots away – easy, given their size – and looked forlornly at my shoes, toppled down the stairs from where I'd thrown them. By this point I only had about ten seconds left. I'd have to hope the man in the bell tower didn't notice I was only wearing socks.

I pushed open the door and stepped onto the roof, this time as Ernest Cunningham. I put on a big cheesy grin and waved to the bell tower. Then I headed back inside and closed the door.

'Thank you for cooperating. It helps put us at ease,' Tobias was saying as I picked up the radio and rummaged for the voice-changer.

'I understand,' I said through the box, mimicking his technique to make us feel like a team. 'We're heading back to the main group now on the third floor.'

'You helped me out. Normally now we'd do a bit of quid pro quo,' Tobias said. 'Still no demands?'

I had a moment of dizzying power. He was asking *me* what *I* wanted. I know I wasn't really robbing this bank, but it flitted across my mind what I could steal if I was. No more begging for loans. If solving crimes is addictive, maybe so too is robbing banks. I shook it away, embodying the dead man again.

'I want a dollar, from the vault. Have you found Edward?'

'We're working on it. How about Cordelia?'

'What about her?'

'Come on. She's sick. How about we trade? There must be something you want.'

'A dollar,' I repeated. Because that's what Bryce would have done. I couldn't let her out, no matter how sick she was, until I knew the meaning of Bryce's cryptic threat: *if she leaves the bank, she dies.*

I hurried down the stairs, considering skipping the third floor to go straight to the vault. I decided I had to check on Juliette – to make sure she wasn't Bryce's *her* – but I heard her voice just as I was about to open the door, which made the decision for me. The potential vault code was burning a hole in my pocket. I slunk away from the third floor. I figured if Bryce had finally gotten the code, and someone had killed him to prevent the vault from being opened, hiding that I was going to try it myself was a good idea. Not to mention, time was of the essence if I wanted to catch the '*We're in*' lady. Depending on her definition of *in*, of course.

'Can Ernest still hear me?' Tobias asked through the radio, as I hurried through the foyer and down the vault stairs.

'He's with me,' thief-me said.

'I'm here,' me-me said, holding the radio at the tip of my reach so it'd sound like I was a few feet away.

'My guy noticed something strange on the rooftop.'

I held my breath, resigned to being caught.

'Put some bloody shoes on, Ernest. I don't want to rescue you and then have you cark it from tetanus. This is a hostage situation, not a vacation.'

INTERLUDE: KEYPAD ENTRY

293934
Access denied.

CHAPTER 18

I've decided to take a momentary diversion from the retelling to try to get out of this box.

Let me remind you of the items I have to hand. I have this gold pen, which is real gold, and the notebook. I have quite a powerful magnet, a high-school textbook (*Chemical Insights: Junior Edition*), and a mason jar of water. Holy water. I'd be lying if I said it wasn't tempting me now; it is quite hot inside this safe and my throat is tickling. I suspect Father Gabriel would be a bit sour if I uncorked it, though, so I'm holding off. I also have one of the guns (the other was taken from me), with two bullets left in it (four were fired), and the now-smashed two-way radio with two D batteries clinging to the shattered casing.

It's a pretty lean set of ingredients for MacGyver-ing.

I've thought about firing the gun, perhaps pressed up at the corner of the door, but the ricochet in here could be lethal. Even if I stripped, wadded up all my clothes around my hand and held the gun at full stretch, I'd probably blow several fingers off. And that's best case. Yes, I did try to do this already after writing Chapter 9, which is why I mentioned writing Chapter 10 in the nude, but

I wussed out before pulling the trigger. I'm fully clothed again now, never fear.

Strap in, it's about to get science-y. Even I know that water is made of hydrogen and oxygen. H_2O. I don't need the textbook to tell me that. I figure if I can separate the two, I can create another little bit of air out of any released oxygen. It might be the difference between dying and the extra five minutes until someone thinks to check the safe in Edward's office. The chemistry textbook tells me that this process is called electrolysis and that a cup of water should give about half an hour's oxygen, if I pull some information from another chapter on gases. Granted, the relevant page is a practical experiment designed for *Ages 12–15*, but my understanding is if I electrify one of the batteries from the broken radio in the water I can create oxygen at the positive terminal of the battery, and hydrogen at the negative. Sounds simple enough, but the first problem is how do I *catch* the one I want to breathe, the oxygen, but not the other, the hydrogen?

The next problem is that pure oxygen isn't breathable, it's explosive. So is pure hydrogen. And while explosives sound just the ticket to get me out of this box, I would rather get out in one piece. I figure the oxygen will mix with my expelled breath and be safe, but water is two parts hydrogen to oxygen, which means for every bit of breath I create, I make twice as much explosive. It's a moot point regardless, because I'm missing a key ingredient for electrolysis: salt. Apparently it makes the whole thing more conductive. So that's pretty much dead in the, well, water.

My last idea centres on the magnet. It's super strong. I'll tell you how I got it in a bit, but remember that the outside of this safe has the message HAPPY FATHER'S DAY, LOVE BEN! in alphabet magnets on it. I'm going to try something. Hang on.

Okay. I think I've done as good a job as possible. What I did was trace out where I think the letters are on the inside of the door with the black marker. Next, I spent some time very carefully holding the magnet up to the door and manoeuvring select letters up and out of their original position. Now, I don't know if the door is even thin enough for the magnet to work, but my hope is that I've managed to extract the H from *HAPPY*, the E from *FATHER'S* and the L from *LOVE*. The trick was then to move one of the Ps from *HAPPY* up even higher, over the whole lot, and slide it back down on the end. Voila.

HELP

Honestly, I know the odds of me getting this right are astronomical. I have a slight advantage in having studied the original arrangement of the letters very carefully – because the apostrophe helped me solve something already – so I figure that even if I've whiffed the exact lettering, it will still look like *some* kind of message. Or of course it's possible that the magnet hasn't worked at all, and I'm in the same position. I'm a little peeved at Ben Huxley for not having enough foresight to write a longer message with enough letters for me to assemble into HEY, I'M STUCK INSIDE THE SAFE. But beggars can't be choosers.

It's funny, I'm weighing everything up in the currency of oxygen. This little experiment cost me an hour's air. I hope it was worth it.

I am starting to feel groggy. I suspect, when it's time, I'll just slowly go to sleep and not wake up. I really don't want to go in for the throat-clutching theatrics. It's not even that I'll run out of oxygen, it's that I'll fill the space with too much of my own expelled carbon dioxide and that will poison me. Once I get nearer the end, who knows – I might be willing to risk a renegade bullet or even blowing myself up. For now, I just have an imagined SOS. Even if it doesn't work, I can fantasise that it has, and it makes me feel a little better knowing I've tried. It is nice to believe in something.

And look, courtesy of Pope John Paul II, if it gets desperate, I'm lucky I won't have to go all survivalist and drink my own urine.

Wait a second!

I have everything I need, according to page 224 of *Chemical Insights: Junior Edition,* to conduct electrolysis *except* salt. I need a water-based solution with salt in it.

I don't have to *drink* my own urine.

Maybe I can breathe it.

The bad news: I don't have to pee. The good news: there is an obvious solution to that.

Forgive me, Father, for I have sipped.

CHAPTER 19

As I wait for the divine urine to pass through to my bladder, I'll try to get the rest of this down. If you're wondering, twenty-year-old holy water tastes much the same as tap. Divinity lacks tang.

My mind was a maelstrom of numbers as I again trotted up the stairs with failure hanging on to my coat-tails. For those keeping track, I'd now tried two codes – *020924*, the date Ben Huxley died, and *293934*, the number I found in Bryce's pocket – to no avail. Neither of them seemed to say anything in *leetspeak*, the gaming language, but I reminded myself to ask Eric for a youthful opinion in case there was something I was missing. Of course, I had the safes in both Huxleys' offices to consider, which seemed to be the type opened with three two-digit numbers, and the hyphens on Bryce's scrap of paper imply that is more likely those numbers' purpose, so the offices were my next stop.

It was just past 2 p.m. The sun had moved across the sky enough to no longer be cast through the skylights and was instead coming laterally through stained-glass half-moon windows around the mezzanine. I was wearing the full outfit, including sabre mask, just to be on the safe side. If I bumped into anyone I thought it would be easier to explain that Ernest Cunningham was missing than to explain why the real me had a boilersuit tucked under my arm. I was still figuring out how I was going to pass myself off as the thief *and* interrogate the suspects at the same time. There was no point me keeping up this facade unless I could investigate the murder.

Equally important was getting into that vault. If I could find out what Bryce really wanted, I could find out why someone had wanted him dead.

I was thinking all this as I paused on the mezzanine to take in Sidney Nolan's *Goldfields*. Nolan was a famous Australian painter, best known for his works depicting bushranger Ned Kelly in his armour, a slit for eyes in a metal helmet (I can relate), often in contrast to harsh, bright landscapes. *Goldfields* predates Nolan's major fame and centres on the hanging suicide of a gold miner in a field ravaged with mineshafts. Its meaning is not hard to decipher: chasing fortune is a dangerous game. There's a reason Huxley has one of the country's first crematoriums from the 1890s, before cremation became common practice in the 1930s: efficiency. Gold-mining towns were brutal places, over-inflated to the point of breaking, where disease and violence ravaged. Not much has changed, as far as money is concerned. If Nolan were here right now, I thought, he could have painted a man burning to death on a bank's rooftop instead.

A snatch of voices flitted past me. I pulled the mask down tight, just to be sure, and turned around. No one was on the balcony. I leaned over the railing and the foyer beneath, too, was empty. I waited a second in the quiet, until I heard the voices again. This time they were slightly louder. An argument. And it was coming from Winston's office.

Words crystallised. 'Ow. Stop. That hurts!'

I sped up. Yellow and green light sluiced the mezzanine in shards around me. I reached Winston's door and leaned against it. It was closed, but I could make out two blurry figures, one pacing back and forth, through the fluted glass.

'I'm not a pincushion! No more needles,' the first voice sulked. Cordelia. 'You promised.'

'I promised we'd do everything we could. This is what this is: everything.' It was easy to peg the mileage of the second voice to a name. Laverna. 'You just want to give up now? After everything?'

'We were so close.' A sniff. 'I just want it all to be over.'

'You don't mean that. Give me your arm.'

'I *do* mean that.' While the words were argumentative, this time her voice was without fight, relenting. There was a sharp hiss, I assumed in response to the needle going in. Then her breathing slowed, followed by more tears. 'Let it be over. Just let it be over.'

'Not just yet, my love.' The wet smack of a kiss on the forehead. 'Don't quit now.'

I was straining so hard to listen, pressing against the door, that when it opened I spilled, pinwheeling, into the room. Laverna took a step back in surprise. Cordelia was in the same chair I'd sat in this morning, the IV bag hooked into the stand I'd abandoned downstairs and they must have retrieved, clear plastic tubing snaking down and into her arm. I steadied, brushed my front and tried to look casual. Handy thing about masks, no one can see you blush.

'Everyone okay?' I asked digitally. Then I realised that was too sympathetic for a hostage-taker, so I added, 'I warned you not to wander off.'

While I might have fooled a man I'd never met in a bell tower half a block away, this was the first time I'd come face to face with anyone under my new disguise. Laverna folded her arms, examining me. I wondered if she could hear my heart galloping, and tried to read her for recognition, for surprise. *Is this someone that you think is supposed to be dead?*

'We wanted some privacy,' Laverna said, completely unperturbed by my presence. 'We'd rather not do this in front of everyone. You have a problem with that? Then let us go to the hospital.'

'No one leaves.' I nodded to Cordelia. 'Milrinone. That's for hearts, right? Do you need anything else?'

'Yeah,' Cordelia said from the chair. 'A new one.'

'Honey—'

'Am I wrong?'

Laverna appealed to me. 'She's had a tough week.'

'I understand I am causing you some stress. I don't want to hurt anyone.' I took in the two of them. The elderly and the sick: possibly the least threatening combination here. Tobias wanted me to trade Cordelia. Maybe I should have. I'm aware the decision to keep her is likely to draw contempt, and there's no point softening the truth given these are my last words. In order to solve the crime, I needed the full pool of suspects. It only worked if I had everyone. Letting her go was letting everyone go.

But was a dying woman really a valid suspect?

That was the problem. Of course she was.

And behind it all, if I let the wrong person leave the bank, someone would die. *If she leaves the bank, she dies.*

'I can't let you go.' It hurt to say it. There's a reason all the famous fictional detectives are cold. The puzzle comes first. But I am not without empathy. 'Are you in any immediate danger?'

'You mean aside from the gun?' Cordelia drawled.

'Medically.'

'No,' Laverna answered. 'She's not high risk. It's myocarditis. But it is better if she is relaxed. In her own space.'

'I'll see what I can do about that. First, I need you upstairs with the other sus— ah, hostages.'

Cordelia stood up, wheeled her IV stand past us and out the door. I heard the rattle as she stomped up the stairs. I felt like a parent, not a bank robber.

'Ten-four,' Laverna said with a mock salute, embodying her past life as a trucker, and started to follow her.

I held an arm out. 'Why were you in the bank this morning?'

'Really?' She examined my mask. It was an odd question, but I figured if I could rule them out, I might be able to consider releasing them. But only if I was sure. 'Our FundAble campaign hit its target, if you must know. The money was authorised. It's life-changing.'

I remembered the full-to-bursting thermometer on the FundAble page and the condition being that the money was only released once the target was reached. It made Cordelia's misery all the more tragic. The whole town wanted this girl to live, and she wanted to give up. 'You sure she's okay?' I asked.

'Didn't I already tell you this?' She squinted at me. Interesting, I thought, that Bryce had asked after Cordelia's welfare. Probably while I was fossicking about with Felix. I recalled that the username 'Bryce' had been the one to nudge the fundraising campaign over the goal with a final $150 donation. Another mystery: who donates to charity and *then* robs a bank? At least Robin Hood did it the other way around. Interesting that Bryce had cared enough about the hostages to check in on them, but not enough to let them go, though. I'm aware of the irony.

'If you care,' Laverna continued, 'what would you do if I just told you she'll die? Let us go?' My awkward throat-clearing answered the question for me. 'Exactly, so just let us be.'

'She doesn't want the medicine,' I observed. 'I overheard.'

Laverna seemed annoyed as she thought about what to tell me. 'And you wonder why we want privacy. What do you expect? She's twenty. She's had all manner of things sticking out of her and pumped through her the last year and a half. And, you know, it's fantastic that this town has lifted her up, embraced her journey with such positivity. But they chuck their dollar in and then they want it all to be good news. Because everyone's pinned their hopes on fixing everything that's wrong with *their* lives on the fact that this inspirational girl can get better. *No, you can't be sad*, they say, *we bought hope*.

And they want what they paid for. Some days, she can't be a role model – she's just a sick girl. Do you blame her for reaching her limit?'

Looking back, I understand this conversation much more clearly. Do I keep fighting in this tomb of mine? Do I bother writing out the end of this story that both has no ending and a very definite one? Or do I lie down, shut my eyes, and let it happen? Tiredness washes through me now, and I know that if I sleep, I won't wake up. And maybe that's easier than fighting. Always fighting.

'She'll be the first I let go, as soon as I can,' I assured Laverna, and I meant it. 'In the meantime, is there anything else I can do?'

'Yeah,' Laverna huffed, pushing past me. 'You can hurry up and rob this damn bank.'

I turned my attention to Winston's safe and tried the combination on the scrap of paper: 29-39-34. Twice. Spinning the wheel left, right, left and then right, left, right. A bust. I wasn't too disappointed; I figured I could get Winston to open it anyway, now I had a gun. I would hold out hope for trying this code on Edward's safe instead.

Before I left, I spent an extra minute examining Winston's office with a closeness that I hadn't managed during our meeting. The abacus displaying 1011 still meant nothing to me. There was no bird in here to squawk the absence of clues either, only Harold Huxley and Felix's forefather looking down from the photograph, holding the nugget that would, like a seed, grow the town of Huxley. They were holding it together, one hand each, I noticed. Felix had said the Huxleys owed him *everything*.

At the time I'd thought his opinions on economics were more general: that the people who run the banks are crooks. But now I was thinking that he was simply telling me that the people who run *this* bank are crooks. Winston's words bubbled up: *Ed's doing this to me*. Had another partnership dissolved?

On Winston's desk was a printout of a bank statement. The name at the top was *R. Allard*. Remy. There was no money coming in, only transfers out. Small amounts, a few thousand here, a few thousand there, to various accounts that were all but meaningless to me. Two thousand dollars out, to a *B & Q FREDERICKS*, caught my eye with the description 'kill'.

It seemed a low amount to pay a hitman. Do assassins take instalments?

There was a lock on the inside of Winston's door, sturdy and intact. A key hung on a nail buried close by in the wall, and I took it, testing it on the door. It worked. Fiddling with the lock, I noticed the tiniest piece of fabric lodged in the doorframe latch. It was black, too shiny and plastic to be from a regular piece of cotton clothing – Winston's missing shirt, for example – and I hadn't seen anyone wearing parachute pants so far. I took off my gloves and pulled it out with my fingernails, then put it in my pocket.

Here's where a mystery novel may obfuscate the real meaning of this fabric sliver until some grand reveal. I don't have time for that, so I'll just tell you. I suspected immediately it matched the tear in the umbrella in Edward's office. Yes, the one I told Felix wasn't a clue but, indeed, is.

I locked the door and put the key in my pocket, heading upstairs. Winston's office had given me an idea: the fact that it had a sturdy lock, and its positioning by the stairs between floors. I started to think I might get through the next few hours. I was feeling a little confident, given I'd fooled Laverna up close, as I made my way to the third floor.

But Laverna was one thing. We'd only known each other half a day and, at her age, maybe her eyesight tipped in my favour.

The real test, of course, was waiting for me on the third floor. The woman I was about to marry.

CHAPTER 20

In all my previous cases I have only ever held one gun, and I'd never pointed it at anyone. Let me tell you, it gets things done a whole lot faster.

When I'd left the hostages, back when I was one of them, they'd settled into the rhythm of being captive but not endangered. Now I noticed some small changes to the dynamic. Michelle and Felix weren't talking anymore. In fact, Michelle wasn't social at all: she was sitting on the floor, back against the wall with her eyes shut. Father Gabriel and Felix were playing noughts and crosses on the priest's notepad, and Juliette looked to be at the end of her tether mid-conversation with Winston. In the corner, several cushions and various squishy objects had been piled to form a comfortable refuge for Cordelia. Remy was currently pleading with Laverna, pointing at his mouth.

'It's actually a really painful ulcer,' he was saying, slightly muffled as his tongue explored his cheeks to prove the point. 'Surely she doesn't need *all* the painkillers.'

There was no immediate response to my throat-clearing at the far end of the room. I don't remember deliberately raising the gun, but it came up as if my arm were on a string, as if I understood its inherent power. Here's an interesting thing: guns are heavy. I felt it immediately in my shoulder. I wouldn't recommend getting into a stand-off unless you are very good at Pilates.

As soon as everyone saw the weapon, it was like the hush of an overture ending in a theatre. They seemed to remember they were hostages. A few whispered *shhh*s rippled over, and then everyone was staring at me.

Look, I think I'm a pretty good detective. I've solved plenty of murders. But I am under no illusions that my involvement with most has been accidental at best, and even more so, that it normally takes people a bit of convincing to listen to my theories. It was strange, being on the other side of the mask and having everyone's attention. My father had been a petty thief when I was a kid – it's what got him killed – and maybe it was something hereditary in me that got the blood flowing now. My immediate thought was *Oh, I get it.*

Juliette, having faced nearly as many murderers as me and not easily threatened, was the only one not persuaded. She simply blew out a blast of unimpressed air and cocked one hip.

I puffed my chest up, tried to stand a little taller, to hide my true stature better. 'There have been a few variations to our situation,' I said, through the voice-changer. Though the power was invigorating, I was careful not to aim the gun at any specific person, pointing wide of the group and to the back wall, and my finger stayed well off the trigger. 'I am asking for your patience and cooperation through these next steps.'

'What steps?' Remy asked, shuffling around the group from the back, then realising he'd placed himself in the line of the gun barrel and ducking out of it.

'Where's Ernest?' Juliette asked.

'Ernest will be, uh, helping me for the next little while,' I said.

She pinched the bridge of her nose in frustration. 'I knew it'd be something like this.' A new emotion emerged in her voice: disappointment. And not, unfortunately, about being a hostage. 'I assume you've given him a crime to solve?'

'I require enquiries—'

'Yeah. The usual. Okay.' She pursed her lips. 'How well do you know Ernest Cunningham?'

This stalled me. 'I think I've got to know him pretty well over the last few hours,' I blundered out.

'Few *hours*.' She raised her eyebrows and frowned, mock impressed.

'He seems switched on. Clever.' I stopped short of adding that I heard he saves puppies from drowning. What a guy.

'He is, but you give him a case to solve, and your bank robbery's over. You've traded the stage. If what you want is in the vault, you're not going to get it unless Ernest thinks it will help solve the case to give it to you. So think carefully about whatever it is you really want, because once you set him off the leash, this won't be your bank anymore. I've seen him make some bone-headed decisions in order to solve a crime, so just be ready for it.'

It almost hurt my feelings, but the stuffy insides of the sabre mask kind of proved her point. It felt like we were having a marital argument, but the only problem was that Juliette didn't know she was having it. 'Are you saying he's selfish?' I asked.

'I don't think he needs you to be offended on his behalf.' She spread her hands. 'If you want Ernest to help you, let us all go. You haven't hurt anyone or stolen anything yet. We'll all back you up on as small a punishment as possible.'

'Speak for yourself,' Winston piped up.

'Then we'll get to work solving your crime.' Juliette ploughed over Winston's objection. Kept focus on me. 'Look around. This is stupid. This is what bloody *Ernest* would do. Listen: I promise Ernest will take your case, once we're out of here.'

'Well, if he's so ridiculous,' I huffed, taking it personally, 'I don't know if I even want his help anymore.'

'You *don't* want his help. He's often pigheaded, occasionally ignorant.' She counted them off on her fingers. 'Dangerous. Insensitive. Good with clues but terrible with people. Interr—'

'I get the picture.'

'—upts people. Easily distracted. Not nearly as smart as he thinks he is. Plus there's a fifty per cent chance he'll get himself killed, a thirty per cent chance he'll get *you* killed and a one hundred per cent chance he'll suffer some disgusting injury.'

'Well, none of that was in the marketing plan,' Winston muttered.

I was about to snipe back, but I realised if this was going to work, I'd need Juliette on my side. 'Can I speak to you in private, please?'

'We can talk in front of everyone.'

'I would really like to speak to you in private.'

Felix stepped forward, putting half his body between myself and Juliette. 'Don't bloody touch her, mate.'

'If you've got a job to do, fine.' Michelle moved forward too. 'But this is going too far.'

Gabriel lifted his notepad up. IT'S OVER.

'It's not about that—'

'A real man does not point a gun at a woman,' Remy shouted.

I realised I'd lost track of the gun's sight; not only had it drooped a little (damn you, Pilates) but I'd subconsciously let it drift in the direction of my conversation. I quickly swung it to the side, aghast that I would even have it near any person, let alone Juliette.

'Go on. Point the gun at me,' Juliette said, brushing past Felix. 'Big man with a weapon. But not willing to point it at a woman?'

'I'm not going to point the gun at you. I just need to talk—'

'Where's Ernest?'

'I'm trying to tell—'

'Point the gun at me! Come on. Man up!'

I became aware that everyone was creeping forward. I was losing power here, regardless of the gun. If they chose to rush me, I'd be swarmed. Probably the only thing holding them back was that, if I was a real-deal robber, I might get off a shot or two. They didn't know I wouldn't fire, but they might take that risk regardless. I wondered briefly if they'd had another vote and this rebellion was the decision. The group pushed an inch forward, compounding the pressure.

I took a step back, widened my stance, and held the gun out. 'Nobody move!' I yelled. 'That is *enough*. I told you what I wanted. Now here's what's happening.'

Everybody froze. The gun wobbled dangerously in my hand. I aimed it over everyone's heads in a way that I hoped was realistically threatening, still making sure I kept it wide of Juliette. No way I was pointing the gun at her. Believe me from future experience: a fiancée aiming a gun at their partner is a tough first marital hill to climb.

'Ernest is mine.' I was getting into the role now. 'I am keeping him in Winston's office with the teller, Milton. I will be periodically allowing Ernest out to conduct interviews and investigations into the matter at hand. If Ernest does not return to me, on the hour every hour, I will kill Milton. If you do not help Ernest by answering his questions, I will kill Ernest. If anyone leaves the building, I will kill them both.'

My breathing was ragged, unsteady. I forced myself to calm down.

I could see everyone chewing on it. This was my plan. No one but me knew Milton had been rescued by the police, so I thought he was a pretty good fake hostage behind Winston's locked office door. And Ernest was the perfect alibi: only one of us would be in any given room at the same time. The threat seemed to work on the group. They'd stopped moving forward, at least.

IF YOU NEED ERNEST, Gabriel's notepad peeked over the pack, WHO DIED?

'Does anyone know a Bryce?' I asked, resigned to the fact that I wouldn't get Juliette alone. I might as well start my enquiries.

'A Bryce? A little more information?' Juliette said.

'I don't know. Small town though, right?'

'Bryce Atkins?' Remy said.

'Does he live around here?'

'Well, no. He's a composer, done a few films for me. Lives in LA.'

Juliette rolled her eyes. 'Now why would he be asking about Bryce Atkins?'

Remy was petulant. 'You asked if I knew *a* Bryce.'

'Anyone named Bryce *in Huxley*,' I clarified.

There was a little murmur. Cordelia put her hand up. 'Bryce Fredericks? His daughter Emma and I have the same doctor.'

A sick daughter. That's one reason to rob a bank: to pay for treatment or care. Australia's public health sector is one of the best in the world, but it's not cheap being sick, especially if a family member has to take time off work to care for someone, and not everyone would find success fundraising like Cordelia. A promising start. 'Anyone got a photo?'

'You took our phones. Weak,' Eric reminded me.

I turned to Winston. 'Does Bryce Fredericks have an account at this bank?'

'Not an important enough one for me to have heard of.' He shrugged. 'I don't know every client back to front. Ask Milton.'

Obviously, I couldn't do that. I moved the conversation along. 'Can anyone get into one of these computers?' I nodded at the desks that held rows of monitors.

Winston and Michelle both shook their heads, muttering some combination of *not my job* and *I work downstairs*. 'I'm not doing your job for you,' I heard Michelle add.

Felix put his hand up. 'Computers lock down once the alarm is pressed. To stop transfers or data hacks. Nothing on the building's network is still online.'

'Okay.' I thought about my next step, glancing over to Edward's office. I thought I had the code to the safe in there; it was the only place I hadn't tried the combination on Bryce's scrap of paper. The other safe's code still eluded me. One way to find out, I figured. And no more guesswork: the power of having a gun let me skip to the chase. 'Winston, I need the code to your personal safe.'

'Under no circumstance—'

'Give him the goddamn code.' It was hard to pin who said this, given it was a rousing chorus. I didn't even need to threaten with the gun.

Winston had to squeeze the words out of his gritted teeth like he was an empty toothpaste tube. 'Seventy-nine, clockwise,' he hissed. 'Forty-seven, anticlockwise.'

'Twenty-nine,' finished Felix from the back.

Both Winston and I turned to him in surprise.

Winston raised an accusing finger. 'How in the *hell* did you—'

'Atomic numbers.' Felix shrugged. 'You know, the periodic table?' Then, exasperated he had to explain it all to us, 'Am I the only one who paid attention in school? Seventy-nine is gold, forty-seven is silver.'

'And twenty-nine is bronze?' I asked.

'No. Copper. Bronze isn't an element, it's an alloy of copper and tin. So I figured it's twenty-nine or fifty. Copper's a better guess just due to colour. What?' He eyeballed Winston right back. 'Surprised the help is educated?'

'Okay. Sit tight. And, uh'—I hunted for an appropriate piece of gratitude that didn't make me sound any less imposing a hostage-taker—'thank you for your assistance.'

Winston's office being down a flight of stairs, I retreated into Edward's office first, to test the combination from Bryce's pocket. Ditto almost scared me into firing the gun accidentally. I really was on edge. This was, as Juliette had so eloquently put it, indeed *boneheaded*. My hands were shaking as I tried the lock on Edward's safe. 29-39-34, clockwise and anticlockwise. Nothing.

At least I could head downstairs and open Winston's safe now, but if this code didn't open either safe or the vault, what the hell was it for? And why did a bank robber have it in their pocket? I tried the date of Ben's death, 02-09-24, just in case. I even tried swapping the first two numbers in case Edward had used the American date style. Another failure. I smacked my fist against the locked door, an action I am now intimately familiar with, albeit from the other side.

I was surprised to look up and see Juliette leaning against the doorframe.

I let out a huge breath of relief and opened my mouth to tell her everything, sans voice-changer, until I noticed Felix lingering behind her.

'Did you rob the bank because Ernest was in it?' she said flatly.

I fumbled the box up to the mask. 'No. It's just an opportunity.'

Her eyes narrowed. 'Something's changed while we've been in here, then. You don't want what you wanted two hours ago. Otherwise you'd have put a gun to Ernest's head immediately, when you were taking hostages. Besides, if you knew who he was and wanted his help, it's not like he doesn't have a phone number. Why rob a bank when you could have just asked him?'

'Nothing's changed,' I lied.

'Whatever's in that vault is supposed to prove something,' Juliette went on, unravelling my lies so easily. 'So either you can't get it, or you already have it and it's not what you wanted. Hence, you realised you needed Ernest once he outed himself as a detective.

What's more, you suspect everyone here. That's why you needed all ten of us. You had your little meltdown and tossed the toys out of the box, flipped the tables in the foyer, when you couldn't get Laverna and Cordelia. We're not hostages, we're suspects. Am I close?'

Very. 'Maybe I should hire you instead.'

'Is it a murder? The Bryce guy?'

'Yeah.'

'How?'

'Spontaneous combustion.'

She snorted. 'That's impossible. But, to be fair, right up Ernest's alley.'

'Feel free to share any bright sparks,' I said. I leaned forward, then realised I'd moved out of the shadow and she might be able to see my eyes through the mesh. I pushed back into the gloom.

'Well, it's a myth. Scientifically impossible. A fire doesn't just start. Therefore somebody lit it. Therefore you need an accelerant. So find that first.' She dusted her hands. 'Too easy.'

Her phrasing crashed into my synapses. I'd heard that somewhere already today. Where? Chapter 9, just to save you time. I don't mind if you flip back through, that's all part of fair play. Maybe you'll figure things out faster than I did.

'You really think all those things about Ernest?' I said, unable to resist asking. It was strange to hear her unfiltered opinion of me. The stuff she'd never dare say to my face. The fact that I was in the middle of something much worse, telling her the biggest lie of my life, didn't really temper my bruised feelings.

'Oh, definitely. I'll guarantee two things: he *will* make stupid decisions and concoct harebrained schemes.'

I bit my tongue, boiled a little.

Juliette held up one finger, then the next. 'And two: he won't let you down.'

The warmth of it hit me in the chest. There was a beat of silence between us, and the air felt alive. Surely, she'd recognise it, I thought.

'You're not fooling anyone, by the way,' Juliette said suddenly.

My breath left me. 'Oh?'

She traced a finger in the air, up and down my body, letting the insult linger. Then, at last, said, 'With this tough guy act.'

'Oh.'

'You know what else? I don't believe you'll use that gun.' She balanced her hands like the scales of justice, sliding them up and down to show her indecision. 'I'm not willing to risk it yet. But hurt Ernest, and then you'll have to shoot me. Because if you don't, there's no bone I won't break in your body.'

I know she didn't mean it like this, but I think that might be the nicest thing anyone's ever said to me.

CHAPTER 21

Locked in Winston's office, I had no time to catch my breath, unpeeling the boilersuit and tossing it alongside the sabre mask and Bryce's boots into Winston's large bottom desk drawer. I also knew I couldn't keep the guns, so I dropped them in too. It was a risky move, leaving the only weapons I had when there was a potential murderer about, but I had no choice: if *Ernest* was caught carrying the guns, the hostages would think we had the power, and there'd be no stopping a mutiny against the now-imaginary bank robber. I felt a little reluctant, sliding the drawer shut, to be back in my own skin. Powerless.

Now that I was Ernest again, I needed to get Juliette alone. I'm no relationship expert, but there are a few simple rules to pulling off a successful wedding: keep it under thirty-six thousand dollars, don't go too crazy on the buck's night, don't let the mother-in-law organise the wedding, and don't take your fiancée hostage. It's not an often-quoted rule, but it seems like an important one. Besides, two brains were better than one. I could desperately use her help.

In retrospect, I should never have lied in the first place. I should have gone back to the group as Ernest immediately, but the conversation had spiralled out of control before I had a chance to realise my mistake. Now I had to fix it before it got out of hand. Of course, whether you're joining me for my fourth case or my first, you have probably come to expect that *out of hand* is kind of my specialty.

First, I had a combination to try on Winston's safe. 79-47-29: gold, silver, bronze (copper). I cranked the steel handle.

Nothing.

Annoyed at myself, I tried it again, perfectly lining up the dial each time. Again, nothing. I tried fifty as the third number, which Felix had mentioned as tin. Nothing.

I was having no luck today: cracking safes is so much harder than solving murders. Had Winston bluffed me? I glanced back at the desk drawer. I couldn't get changed and pull the gun on Winston again to make him tell me the real password. Ernest had been gone so long he needed to show his face. He? I? I'm confusing myself. Thinking it through, Winston had been steamed up at the thought that Felix might know the code. So it was probably real, somehow. Winston was a good liar, but if he was *that* good, it was a little scary.

In any case, the vault was more important than the safes were. I was just clutching at straws, looking for leads. There was no need to hold Winston at gunpoint over this. That would be a problem for later. I'd wasted too much time already.

A knock on the door interrupted my thoughts. It was a nervous little rap.

'Whoever you are,' Winston's voice came muffled through the door, hard to hear. 'Just . . . listen. You can have'—I missed a few words— 'you want.'

I held my breath. Not willing to move.

'Anything. I'll . . . the vault,' Winston continued. The door handle rattled. 'Just get rid of . . . Ern.'

Then footsteps, softening as they headed away. I was rooted to the spot. Had Winston just served me up as a sacrificial lamb? I had to find out.

I tousled my hair so it wouldn't look helmet-flattened, squeezed my face into my best impersonation of having my life threatened and stepped out into the bank. A hostage again.

Winston hadn't got far. He turned excitedly when he heard the door open, but deflated when he saw it was me. He walked back over, wringing his hands, bouncing on his toes. Worried he'd been overheard, I thought. I slid around the door and shut it before he could get a glimpse into the empty room, hiding that I locked it behind me.

'Strict instructions.' I gave him an apologetic grimace as I turned the key, deciding to play it clueless. 'If we try to leave, then Milton—' I slid a hand across my throat.

Winston had almost gnawed through his lip. 'Did he open it? The safe?' Before I could answer he rattled on, a train without brakes. 'Tell him we can, uh, come to an arrangement, I'm sure.'

He did appear to have given me the correct code, given his concern. Winston struck me as a man who did not beg for much, so the fact that there was something inside his personal safe that was worth begging for ignited my curiosity. Could it be motive for murder? Not out of the realms of possibility, but not a strong one. The *real* thief had showed no interest in the personal safes, at least not in front of me. That meant there was no reason to get rid of him.

'I'm not so sure.' I left it open-ended.

'Come on,' he whined. 'You're gonna hold this over me?'

'I'm not holding anything over anyone. I am the unwilling messenger at the end of a gun.' I was settling into this dual role. 'What's it worth to you? I can relay your offer.'

'Well, what does he bloody want?' Winston started knocking on the office door. 'Hey! Name your price. Don't ignore me!'

The door-knocking was too close for comfort. Winston was distracted enough that the returning silence probably seemed like hard bargaining, but I didn't want to risk it. I guided him away, walking around the mezzanine until we were in front of the *Goldfields* painting. Annoyingly, he didn't seem too bothered that I'd likely overheard him ask a man with a gun to get rid of me. Or about his possibly trussed-up employee, Milton. The only thing he cared about was the safe. I decided to keep it up my sleeve. 'He wants into the vault, you know that,' I said.

'If I knew the code, I would have let him in by now. I'm on your side,' Winston said. His face showed utmost sincerity, completely ignoring the irony of what the hanging gold miner painted on the wall beside us represented. 'Look, Felix is ungrateful. We have always been good to his family. Harold, my grandfather, employed his great-great-grandfather and everyone down the tree after – my father employed his father, and we employ him. You can't win with some people.'

The class divide was obvious in the hyphenated *great*s: the Huxleys' generational life-expectancy inflated by wealth. I almost asked him what any of this had to do with Felix – he'd brought him up out of the blue – but I decided to coax it out of him instead. 'Felix's great-great-grandfather was the other man in the photo in your office. He dug with Harold Huxley?'

'That's exactly it. And Felix can't let it go. If Yang had dug one metre to the left, we'd be standing in Gao's Bank and I wouldn't be complaining.'

I doubted this but let him continue.

'How is that my fault?' he said, hands raised.

'It's structural,' I offered.

'We built this place ourselves,' Winston said, mistaking my comment as being about architecture. 'With our bare hands.'

There is a photo in the lobby of Harold Huxley smoking a thumb-thick cigar in front of the bank's early scaffolding, mud-clad labourers behind him. I felt I was getting a pretty good understanding of Winston Huxley by now: a man who would find fifty dollars on the street and think he'd earned it. And Felix, the guy who dropped the money, thought it had been taken from him. *Everything*, he'd said, when I'd asked him what he was owed. He thought this whole building was his birthright. Missed out on by one metre of digging.

Outlining to Winston the prejudicial advantages the Huxleys had over Chinese immigrant miners in the goldfields would be no more use than begging an imaginary bank robber. I highly doubted a Huxley either hammered or broke any nails during the construction of this bank.

'What happened to Yang?' I asked.

'Doesn't the painting tell you? The goldfields were a harsh life. People didn't just find their fortune, they tested it. Do you have enough good luck to get out of here alive? Drinking, fighting, dysentery, depression. They all find you before the gold does.'

'He died on the fields?'

'Dysentery did him in. Harold looked after the child Yang left behind, gave him work. And then everyone after that, all the way down to us and Felix. That little brat.' He could have spat. I noticed his reflux had settled down since this morning. 'Can you just tell your . . . your . . . *boss* that I'm keen to talk directly? Man to man. Leader to leader.'

'Leadership seems a broad definition,' I said, a little offended at my designation to servant as Ernest. This felt like the TV show *Undercover Boss*. I decided to try to trick the safe's contents out of Winston instead. 'He's pretty pleased with what was in there. Why negotiate with you when he can just sell it?'

Winston squinted, then laughed. '*Unbelievable*. You don't even know what I'm talking about, do you?'

Interesting. Whatever Winston was keeping in the safe didn't hold a monetary value. I held up my hands in surrender. 'Why do you want me killed?'

'What?'

'*Get rid of* is your preferred way of putting it, is it? A bit more digestible.'

He seemed to find this even funnier. 'You heard that? You have no idea what's in the safe, do you?'

'You gave him the wrong code.'

'I gave him the *right* code.' He really believed it. 'Did he try it twice?'

An eye roll seemed sufficient in reply.

'It's the correct combination. Let me try it myself.' Winston made to move past me.

I blocked him. 'I can't let you in there. Boss says. Trust me, the safe is locked tight. Are we just not talking about the fact you want me killed?'

'This is between me and the masked man, thank you. It's not about you.'

This adamant denial, bordering on gaslighting, completely stalled me. How could he deny the very words I'd heard through the door? Had it not been his voice? I tried to find level footing on more simple questions. 'Could Edward have swapped that code as well?'

'No way, you'd have to open it to change it. And we don't know each other's combinations – it's my personal safe. There's no bank property in there, so there's no back-up auto-reset computer thingy either. The code is in one spot and one spot only.' He tapped his head.

'Gold, silver, bronze.' I parroted the code's essence. 'It's not exactly *uncrackable*.'

'Felix knew the periodic table,' Winston accused.

'It was a guess. And only after you'd clued him in on the start of the sequence,' I reminded him. He stewed on that for a bit. 'If you tell me what you have in there, I can try to get it back. When the thief does open it.'

It was more a snarl than a smile that came back. 'If you can't open it'—he raised his voice, to make sure it could be heard in the office—'I have no more deals to offer.' He seemed relieved by the whole thing.

This wasn't getting me anywhere. I refocused the conversation. 'Different topic. You don't know Bryce Fredericks?'

'I told you, the only people who get into my office are the high rollers. I don't see people like you every day.'

I let it slide – if I chose to be offended by everything Winston said, the conversation would go on forever.

'We're talking millions of dollars,' he continued. 'Not the type of people who need to rob a bank.'

'And not priests either, I take it.' I remembered Gabriel, before the robbery, ready to camp out at the front desk until Winston would see him. Usually a mystery author would try to bury that detail in the hope that the reader forgets about it, but here I am, playing fair. 'Collection plates a little thin for you?'

'He couldn't buy his way into a dollar-store. I have no business with that man,' Winston grunted. 'Witch hunt.'

'He seemed pretty keen to see you.' I played it a little dim-witted. 'Something about his mausoleum last weekend?'

'First of all, he's got nothing. A shadow in the dark? A glimpse of Ed's car? Second, that's just a flimsy pretext anyway. I wouldn't be surprised if he smashed up his *own* graveyard just to get in my office.'

'And why would he do that?'

'I cut him off. No more extensions.'

'He's in debt?'

'At this point, you'd think if God wanted him to win, he'd hand him a filly.' He pointed at the roof. 'Aren't they supposed to see signs? I'm agnostic, so I don't believe in any of that, but if you pick *that* badly, maybe someone wants you to lose.'

'Gambling?'

'The amount of money going in and out, it has to be.' He gave his little frog-like burp. 'Quite unbecoming for a priest.'

'He thinks you can help him out?'

'Everyone does. My time is val—'

'I get it.' I held up a hand. 'He did come here in person, though. That's pretty urgent.'

'It's not like he can pick up the bloody phone, is it?'

That was a fair point. I changed tack. 'Remy Allard has money. Does that earn him a seat at the high-rollers' table?'

Winston blew out his cheeks. 'That is a man who needs an unsubscribe button. He'd sell ice to a polar bear.'

Finally, Winston and I agreed on something.

'He told me he banked with you for his clothing company,' I said. 'The BeltBuster t-shirts.'

'I have no idea if he has a basic account with us – he might – but once he had my ear on the insurance deal, you'd better believe he pitched everything not nailed down. Keeps trying to shill those shirts on me – you want a free one? I've got samples. Rubbish quality.'

'Did you say *insurance deal*?' Words like *insurance* are usually important in mysteries. Like the words *will* or *invoice* or, come to think of it, *kill*. 'I assume most of the wealth here lies in agriculture, farms and acreage,' I continued. 'Speaking from experience, travelling here for business is reserved for people at the end of their tether. What are you insuring Remy for?'

'His production. The whole thing. He said he wanted somewhere local – apparently they're filming around here. It seemed like pretty easy money, though I might have thought twice if I'd actually *read* your books. I charged Mr Allard a ridiculous premium and he took it. No questions. First red flag. I should have charged him double.' Winston cracked his knuckles. 'He's smooth, I'll give him that. I didn't even think that maybe he was here because he'd burned all his other bridges. It was all very convincing. They had that movie star, Laurence Birch, attached.' He paused, examining me, clearly thinking I looked nothing like Birch. His lip curled. 'I mean, I guess he could dye his hair, cut down on sleep, come to work hungover—'

'Please. I'm uncomfortable with flattery. So you had stars in your eyes?'

'Not as much as Ed. He invested in the film personally. He told me.'

'It's a television show.'

'I guess it's neither now.' Winston held one hand up, then pushed his other palm into it with a slap, mimicry of a traffic accident. 'You heard about Birch, I assume?'

'Of course. How deep did Ed go?'

'Couple million.' He said it like we were pricing a lemonade stand. 'Give or take.'

'I often mix up my millions. Is it a couple, is it a few?' I didn't hide the mockery.

Winston didn't laugh.

'Remy's not in here to sell you t-shirts,' I said. 'He wanted to withdraw cash, and Milton couldn't give it to him because it was more than he had in the tills.' A thought I'd had earlier came back to me: that you could make more money on a film by *not* making it if you insured it correctly. 'The insurance would pay out if Laurence died, right? Seems a big enough obstacle to shut down a production. Remy wanted his payout.'

Winston nodded. 'It's called a Key Person Clause. You find it in any company: if someone who is invaluable to the business carks it, there's compensation. It's pretty obvious in a film – you can't make it if the lead actor bites it. Works the same in private though: a lead analyst, respected board member, those kinds of people.'

'The only person in a bank who knows the code to the vault.'

'For example, yes.' He considered it for a second, then shook the idea off like he'd just stepped inside from rain. 'Edward is not contractually defined as a key person, if that's what you're thinking, aside from the fact that he, literally, holds the key. But come on, we're not paying out a claim mere hours after the incident. We'll check it, make sure it's all balanced, before we pay out.'

'You mean find any loopholes you can slink through. I found Remy's bank statements on your desk. You were looking to see if there was any ammo in them to help get you out of paying.'

'You think *my* insurance is already wiring me for this?' He gestured over the shipwreck of a foyer. From the balcony, it looked like we'd played a losing game of Jumanji. 'They'll try to screw me out of it. I'll try to screw Remy. That's the game.'

'So let me get this clear. Remy accepts your exorbitant insurance offer, no questions asked. And suddenly the worst happens: Laurence and a delivery van have a meet-cute. Gabriel told me – well, wrote to me – that Remy was keen to pull the plug on Birch. Sounds like someone who might have been planning on taking you for a ride.'

Winston's eyes widened. 'You think *Remy* killed his own movie star for insurance?' He thought it through. 'No. He probably had dollar signs in his eyes over the plug pulling, sure, but not enough to plan it all out. To commit a murder. That's got to be one of the most ridiculous things I've ever heard. It's the worst plan ever.'

'You'd be well out of pocket if you had to pay up. Would that upset you?'

'It's pennies.' Winston threw his hands up. 'Sure, I'd rather not pay it. But I'm a businessman, I made a deal. Sometimes they're bad. I'll stick to it if I have to. It's not gonna ruin me.'

To be fair, I didn't know what he defined as *pennies*. A couple million? A few? 'If it's so low, why kill for it?'

'That what I'm telling you – it's a terrible plan. Not least because it *wouldn't work*. An insurance company will check a claim way more carefully than the cops would. Mr BeltBuster does not have the level of mastermind required to outwit cops *and* banks.'

'It might surprise you to hear how rarely murderers are masterminds,' I said. 'It's mostly just opportunity and pressure.'

'Open your ears. That's only half of it. Even if he'd managed to orchestrate something like that *and* get away with it, he's killed the wrong person.'

'You just said Laurence had a key person clause.'

'*A* clause. Not *the* clause. The most insured person on that agreement'—he jabbed a finger on my chest—'was you.'

It took me a second to comprehend this.

'I'll bite,' I said eventually. 'How much am I worth?'

THE FOURTH HEIST: TWENTY-FIVE MILLION DOLLARS

CHAPTER 22

Turns out I am worth a lot more dead than alive. This is both upsetting and gratifying.

Questions and scenarios rampaged through my mind as I stormed up the stairs. Twenty-five million was worth killing for, no question. But it was implausible for Remy to mix up me and Laurence. For Laurence to take my fate, Remy must have hired someone else to do his dirty work. Someone who'd never met me. Someone for whom an actor *embodying* a role in a café, for whom a coffee cup with the name *Ernest* on it, had been enough to transform Laurence Birch into a target.

'I know what you've done,' I said, spotting Remy as I emerged from the stairwell.

Remy might not have been able to plan a very good murder, but he at least had the good sense to know when his number was up. He circled me like he was a matador, hands out, crab-walking in a circle. Then he ran. Unfortunately for him, everything on the third floor was dead-ends and barred windows: the only access to the mezzanine was the stairs, which I was blocking, the elevator, which I was next to, and the antique wool-lift, if he kicked out the floor and dropped through the hole. He chose the bathroom down the corridor. I heard the chime of shattered glass on tile and the crash of metal before I opened the door. Once inside, I caught up to him easily.

Well, half of him. He was dangling from the hips, stuck in a head-high window.

I jammed a nearby rubbish bin under the bathroom door handle (the commotion had not gone unnoticed, and several people had followed us) and flicked the lock on the handle for privacy, crunching over the broken glass to his dangling legs. The crash had been a set of lockers, tall thin metal columns with two doors each, that he'd pulled down in his scramble up the wall. I leaned against the blue and white wall tiles, his toes scrabbling on the wall next to me. There were no bars on this window, but given both the expected injuries from the third-floor fall *and* the small size of the window itself, it wasn't the best escape route.

'Hey, Remy,' I said casually. We were at the back of the building, so he wouldn't be seen scrabbling by the police barricade out the front. I could take my time.

Remy's body sagged over the sill like wilted lettuce. He said something I couldn't quite make out.

'Didn't hear that.' I gave him a little tap on the ankle.

'I said,' he yelled, 'help me *down* or push me *out*!'

'Such a hard choice.'

'In my defence,' he groaned, the sill pressing on his diaphragm and making him take short breaths every three words, as butterflies hovered in and landed on his belt, 'if you'd have just died like you were supposed to, you wouldn't be so offended.'

I went to correct him, but his logic was, admittedly, sound. 'I am alive,' I said. 'And offended.'

'Don't be so precious. It's business.'

'You hired somebody to kill me! For a lousy two grand. I saw your bank statements. *Kill.*'

He physically thrashed at this and slipped further out of the window. I grabbed his pant leg and held him steady. As far as suspect interrogations, this was unique, even for me.

'Don't be ridiculous,' Remy whined. 'I don't have to hire anyone to kill you.'

'He volunteered?'

'What?'

'Bryce.'

'Atkins?'

I let his cuff slide an inch through my hand and grabbed it again. I'd never done the whole *torture a suspect* thing. Solving murders is just a series of people lying to you in succession: the detective part is figuring out which lies are worth killing for. It's an endless pinball of deceit. Holding Remy in the window gave me the same sense of control as if I had the mask on.

'Oi! Oi! Wait, wait. I don't know what the hell you're talking about,' Remy yammered, swallowed a butterfly, spat it out, and kept on rambling. 'I swear. Come on. Pull me up, please.'

The door handle jiggled against the bin. 'You insured me for twenty-five million, correct?'

'Yes. Yes! Correct.'

'Then you hired someone to kill me, but they messed it up and killed Laurence instead. Because of his method acting. Correct?'

'No. You've got it all wrong.'

A knock on the door. Juliette's voice. 'Everything okay in there?'

'Interviewing a suspect,' I called back. In turning to talk to her, I absent-mindedly let another inch of Remy's pant leg slide through my grasp.

'There is no TV show!' Remy yelled, as I caught him again with a jolt.

'I know. Birch is dead, it's off. You wanted twenty-five million, but your hired goon killed the wrong guy, so you'll settle for a few million before anyone figures it out.'

'No, I mean there never was one!'

Remy was kicking around now, erratically enough that he risked sliding all the way out the window. I might have enjoyed the intimidation, but I wasn't about to let potential answers splatter on the pavement. I grabbed him by his belt loops and hauled him inside where his knees crumpled and he fell against, then slid down, the wall. He ended up slumped on the floor, panting, his BeltBuster t-shirt covered in tiny speckles of blood from scraping against the remnants of glass in the frame.

'Explain,' I said, aware that the bathroom door had started bulging against its hinges.

'If I tell you, will you get help?' He was short of breath.

'That's why I'm here.' I struggled to hide the boredom in my voice. I didn't have the patience for more of Remy's theatrics.

'There never was a television show,' Remy confessed, clunking the back of his head against the wall in defeat. 'So you solved a murder. You know how many of those scripts I see? It's nothing special. But *you*. You are special. I read your books. Close scrapes, every single one of them. You should have died at least six times, by my count.'

'I did die once,' I corrected. Semantics.

'Exactly. I got the budget drawn up and then over-insured you as a creative consultant. Jacked up your importance to the whole thing. Imagine that. A *writer*.' He snorted, then swallowed nervously when he noticed I wasn't laughing along.

'That's why the filming location is apparently all the way out here? Even though the murders took place in the snow? Because there is no set, so it doesn't matter?'

Remy nodded slowly. His eyes were on the bathroom door, still wriggling in its hinges. I righted a tipped-over locker, dragging it over to bolster the door on a diagonal. Papers fluttered out of it, and I noticed that a cheap padlock on one of the doors had snapped in the fall. The name on the open locker was *Felix*. I tapped the cabinet, the bathroom door now firmly secured. Remy's face fell.

'Talking's the only way out of here,' I said.

'That was half the reason, and Laurence wanted to stay in Byron Bay, alongside his celeb pals. A Hemsworth lives there, you know? And the land was cheap here. The main thing was to spend enough to make it *look* like we were doing a show. I bought a few cheap discarded acres, parked a few trucks on it, sprung up a bit of scaffolding. It had to be a real-enough production without being a real production. And then, of course, there are a few companies inside companies: catering, costume, carpentry. Just enough to make it look like someone with a roll of notes is walking through town. The transfers I made are for *contract* kills. A *kill fee*. I had to cancel all their contracts, as they were bleeding me dry.'

'If you're spending all that cash, why not just make the show?'

'Did you see my last movie?'

I nodded. *Touchdown*.

'Well, you're part of a special few.' He sighed. 'I lost eighty million on it. That's where I got the idea. You know, if we never released it, we could have written down a hundred, a hundred and twenty in tax?'

I'd heard of this, studios cancelling completely finished movies as it was more cost beneficial to claim a tax deduction on making the movies than to release them in theatres.

Remy continued. 'No studio was going to fund my next picture after that. And my personal company was down to the dregs – a few million. I still had status in Australia, so I thought I'd find something down here. I didn't have enough money to make a show, but I did have enough money to *not* make one.'

'I didn't realise fraud was so expensive.'

'You gotta spend money to make money.' Remy shrugged, seemingly oblivious that this aphorism was not intended to cover insurance fraud. Neither did I point out that the phrase was aptly coined by a Roman playwright named Plautus, a failed businessman. If you could bottle and sell unintentional irony, Remy wouldn't have to make fake shows.

'You say you don't know Bryce Fredericks, but you hired him for something. Otherwise why pay him a kill fee?' I'd seen the statement: *B & Q FREDERICKS*.

'I don't really know these people, I just transfer the money.'

I had my head in Felix's locker now. A clean set of folded clothes, a pair of running shoes. An old lunchbox with a banana that could only be described as a new civilisation. Behind all that was a yellow envelope with an insignia reading *Precious Metals Laboratory*. I pocketed it. Don't worry, this isn't one of those times when I put away a vital piece of evidence until the penultimate chapter. I'll read it once I'm out of the bathroom. I emerged back into the fresh air. 'So Laurence Birch was in on it?'

'God, no. He was an essential part of the shell game. A big actor attached meant we could boost the insured budget. But he thought it was real, just like you when you signed the contract, and I had to keep him in the dark. It was all working so well, but then, well, you failed to die.'

'I don't see how any of this is supposed to make me think you *didn't* try to kill me.'

'Have you read your books? Dying is like, your thing. I don't have to hire anyone to kill you. All I planned to do was wait for you to get a new case, and you'd do us all a favour and shuffle off. *Bang*. Done.' He slapped his hands together as if dusting them. 'No one gets hurt.'

'Except . . .' I let it linger.

Remy furrowed his brow, confused.

'I would be dead in this scenario,' I reminded him.

'Oh.' The revelation seemed genuine. 'Yeah. But, but, but.' He hunted for a justification, and then something sparked in his eyes. 'It's not like *I'm* killing you. I'm just playing the market. You can bet on anything these days. Your odds of death are higher than most. It would be financially irresponsible of me not to invest.'

'How could you not?' I said flatly. I could hardly object: everyone had been telling me I was a dead man walking all day. Remy had just been prescient enough to bet on it. 'So how does that get us here? There's two people who were going to be the most hurt by your scam. Edward, who invested two million dollars, is missing. And Laurence is dead.' I didn't say aloud my other theory: that I suspected Remy had hired Bryce Fredericks, then stiffed him, and that evidence of the whole scam might be in the vault. 'A detective who has more faith in your planning skills might suspect you're cleaning house.'

'Edward didn't invest in the show,' Remy corrected me. 'If he lost two million, he didn't lose it with me.'

That contradicted what Winston had told me; I'd have to ask him about it later. 'This all doesn't sound like a very good plan,' I said.

'Well, not if you put it like that. But it's not all about you. It's about the funding. I overfund the series, I do some creative accounting, and everybody's rich. I insured you as a little'—he waved a hand—'cherry. Just in case. But then I borrowed too much money from too many of the wrong people, and suddenly that little side bet became, well, my only way out.' He realised this was a terrible attempt at defending himself. 'I still didn't try to kill you. Unless praying counts. And you were this close.' He held his thumb and pointer up, a smidge between. 'The train, that cable car, from your last cases. You just had to come into form.' He really was treating it like a horse race. 'But then you got cold feet or something. Didn't take a case for six months, and suddenly I'm spending money like I'm making a real miniseries, the investors are breathing down my neck and you're gallivanting around trying to set up a detective agency that finds missing pets and cheating husbands, talking about how you don't do murders anymore.'

'I got shot. I'm getting married. It makes you consider things.'

'Well, it's not very consider*ate*.' He groaned, pained by the conversation. 'Could you go back to getting yourself killed?'

'I'm working on it,' I said. Truthfully, it turns out.

'I had to bring Laurence out to Australia to keep up the charade, otherwise people would have started asking for their money back. Money I couldn't give them while you were still breathing,' Remy continued. 'I kept Laurence interested for a bit, telling him we were shooting exteriors, getting him into costume and all that, having him meet you, but I could only string him along for so long. I couldn't pay Birch's massive kill fee out of my pocket either. I needed your insurance payout to cover it. There was only one thing for it.' He read my eyes. 'Not *that*. I fessed up. I honestly thought Birch'd take it well. We pretend to make the show, then can it. An all-expenses-paid vacation. I even offered to bring him in for ten per cent.'

'Generous. If you're carving it up, I'll take twenty-five per cent to top myself.'

'Really?'

'No, Remy.'

'That's what Laurence said,' Remy grumbled, as if we were the ones being unreasonable. 'He was furious. Yelling that I'd wasted his time, running him around to fittings and rehearsals. Researching his character. His *method*. He stormed out of the café onto the road, and he was in such a tizz he mustn't have seen the van. I didn't push him, I swear.'

At this, there was a thump against the bathroom door and the staff locker tipped forward, vomiting junk across the floor as the door burst inwards. Half-a-dozen heads peered into the room.

Juliette was at the front of the pack. 'Why the hell did you lock the—' She took in the room. Saw Remy. Saw blood. 'Is he okay?'

'He's fine,' I said, looking over, only just noticing he was now pale, eyes fluttering. The tiny spots of red on his abdomen, which I'd thought were small nicks from glass shards, had turned into a swamp. It wasn't like, fatal, or anything, but it was a bit more than the light scrape I'd diagnosed him with. *If I tell you, will you get help?* made a different kind of sense now. As did his groans of pain. 'Oh. Damn.'

Juliette brushed past me and lugged Remy up to standing, draped him across her shoulders, and started carting him out of the room. She ignored me completely. 'Laverna, this office should have a first-aid kit,' she called. 'Check the cupboards in the kitchenette.'

'He tried to get out the window.' I made my excuses to her back. 'The thief said if anyone leaves—'

She stopped but didn't turn. 'Then why'd you lock the door?'

'I had to ask him some questions.' I might not have noticed Remy's injuries, but I am adept at detecting disappointment. 'Please, Juliette. I didn't see that he was bleeding so badly.'

She paused a moment. Then, still facing away, said, 'But you did know he was bleeding?'

A few drops of blood dripped onto the tiles. *Drip. Drip.*

'A little.'

People were peering around the doorframe, otherwise I would have told her everything. I moved to help, but she brushed me off, readjusted Remy's weight and continued out of the bathroom alone. 'A detective who doesn't notice blood. This isn't you, Ernest.'

Remy's blood had left stars on the tiles. I went to call after her and then I realised I'd inadvertently lifted one hand to my mouth. The hand I'd been holding the voice-changer with when I was playing the thief, and not the hostage.

Which one was I again?

CHAPTER 23

If one good thing comes from all this, it's that I am coming to understand murderers a little better. Know thy enemy and all that. What I'd told Winston was true: the stereotypical murderer, the mastermind who plans everything out perfectly, is actually the anomaly. Real-life murder is, at its most simple, the final decision in a long domino line of increasingly bad decisions. There are lots of names for it: a sunk cost fallacy, digging up. The reality is the same: bailing out a sinking ship with buckets made of wood from the hull.

I can solve crimes by tracing back those bad decisions, all the way to the beginning. The revelatory thing is that the first one, the 'big bang' of decisions that smashes into every atom, is often so incredibly small, even the murderer must think *How did we get here?*

Standing in Winston's office, locked door behind me, I asked myself the same thing. The sun was setting, a glowing coal horizon dripping onto the Great Dividing Range, the sky above lurid pink. The butterflies, previously confetti shadows on the bank's walls, were now long dark shapes across Winston's bookshelves; you'd have thought a flock of giant birds was coasting across the sunset. It was stuffy, so I opened a barred window slightly for a breeze.

I took out the yellow envelope I'd retrieved from Felix's locker. It was already sliced open, one single sheet of A4 paper folded inside. The top read: *EDXRF SPECTROMETER REPORT: SAMPLE.* Below was a table split into four columns. Disordered numbers ran down the left, but the next two columns explained them: atomic symbols from the periodic table in the second, and the full name of the element in the third. The fourth column had a percentage.

26	Fe	Iron	94.00023%
6	C	Carbon	3.982104%
79	Au	Gold	1.310003%
14	Si	Silicon	1.295420%

Given gold had seventy-nine in front of it, I realised the first column must be the atomic numbers. With this in his locker, no wonder Felix had known enough chemistry to guess Winston's safe code. The rest of the table was filled with various other metals, but all had a disclaimer of *environmental margin of error* against a one millionth percentage or lower.

My first thought was the same as yours will be, that the gold nugget in the foyer was fake. That Felix must have had a hunch and been testing it. The 1.3 per cent gold could have been plated over an iron core, the 94 per cent component. But I remembered Winston telling me off for chewing on the pen, made from the nugget, and his concern was genuine. An iron bar would also be incredibly easy to test: gold is not magnetic, while iron is. Harold Huxley simply wouldn't have gotten away with faking it.

Chemical Insights: Junior Edition has a chapter on gold. In the interest of fair play, I'll divulge the contents (which I won't read until later) now. Apparently fool's gold, named such because of its gold-like appearance and ability to trick prospectors, is iron disulfide. That is iron and sulphur (famously yellow) combined into a material named pyrite, which has the shiny appearance of gold. Crucially, there is no sulphur on the spectrometer report. So whatever Felix was testing wasn't pyrite either.

The strangest thing about the report was the date on top: eight months ago. Given his grudge against the Huxleys, if Felix had evidence their palace was built on fakery, why hadn't he come forward?

I pocketed the report with all of this swirling through my mind. I knew I needed to tell Juliette the truth, but she had refused to listen to me while Laverna padded up Remy with bandages. I had hovered on the fringes of the group, trying to pull Juliette away, but she wasn't having it, so I'd retreated downstairs to put the mask back on.

Remy's okay, by the way, just a few scratches. It looked worse than it was. But that's no excuse. I'm still keeping a fifteen-year-old boy and a young woman with medical issues hostage too – don't think I don't know that.

Why didn't I just fess up? Tell everyone, end the heist and let the police sort it all out? There was Bryce's final threat, sure, but I'm hiding behind that, I realise. The answer may not be satisfying, but it is simple.

Because I had come this far.

Because if I'd done all this and didn't solve the crime, then what was it for? And that's the same awful rationale that makes murders spawn from seeds. Because I'd made that first mistake, then I'd made a second, larger one to justify the first. And so on. The same as Remy and his investors, his burgeoning insurance scam. Even though I knew it was a fallacy, I still felt the need to keep going. My addiction.

The truth is, Remy was right. I've been dying for years. This box I'm in now is just speeding it up.

Every case I've solved, every risk I've taken, every life I've endangered purely because I've *come this far* was a trade. A part of me dying off each time. When I picked up the gun to take this bank hostage. When I ignored Remy's injuries. Where I was now, alone and holding a gun, was the domino at the end of that path. And if I packed it in, I'd have chipped away at myself for nothing. I had to go further. Dig up. Wood from the hull.

I have the advantage of hindsight here, to dissect myself. And nothing but honesty, in my last hours, will do. Doing the wrong things for the right reasons doesn't make them right. Maybe I'm writing this to solve a mystery. But maybe I'm writing it so you can understand – especially you, Juliette, if you get to read this after I'm dead – why I made that next bad decision. And the one after that.

I picked up the voice-changer and clicked the radio. 'Tobias. I have demands.'

He answered immediately. 'I'm glad to hear it. Let me get a pen.' It was quiet for a second. 'Go.'

'First, sleeping bags. Pillows.'

'Staying overnight?'

'Depends.'

'You know, we could just wait until you fall asleep and come in there. Our stand-off is not exactly mutually powered. I'm telling you this because honesty is important. I want you to know I'm not playing any cards under the table. You keep this up through the night, you lose ground. My guys are on shifts, they get to sleep. They'll be sharp, shoot straight. I'm not threatening you, by the way, I'm giving you an opportunity. We haven't cut the power yet, but we could do that too. Why not wrap this up early? We can all be home for dinner.'

He was good, I thought. Threatening, yet on my side at the same time.

I decided to play it tough. 'Did you write it down? Sleeping bags.'

'Yes, got that.'

'I need a science textbook. Chemistry.'

'Okay, sure. What year?'

'Preferably this one.'

'What *school* year? You want high school? University?'

'Comprehensive,' I decided. 'First-year university or just under. Though easy to understand for someone who, for example, hasn't studied chemistry at university.'

'Little bit late to be researching your robbery,' Tobias drawled. 'I'll try to get one with a section on homemade explosives, shall I? Blast your way into the safe.'

'I wouldn't say no.'

'Anything else?'

I thought about it. 'Pizza.'

Hold up. My bladder is calling.

False alarm. Where was I? Oh, adding another domino to the chain.

'That it?' Tobias said through the radio.

'I also need bank statements. For everyone in here. And a man named Bryce Fredericks.'

'We can't do that.'

'Why not? You're the police.'

'And when the police acquire such information, they subpoena it from the bank itself. Milton's briefed me on security features, and the computer network is offline. Who's Bryce Fredericks?'

'Good question. Find that out for me, please. Apparently he has a daughter named Emma. Possibly sick. Cordelia knows her – they share a doctor.'

'He's in there with you?'

'No. Found Edward yet?'

'Still looking. No trace of him. Mobile phone company records have come through, no calls since two days ago, and those were connected via the local tower. So he was here then, don't know where he is now. We'll let you know as soon as we do.'

I almost said thank you, but settled on stoic silence.

Tobias broke it first, which was a point to me. 'How is everyone? You know I have to ask.'

'Fine,' I lied. 'Eric's safe. Hitting it off with Cordelia. I'm sorry he's missing his *Buccaneers* tournament tonight.'

'You're doing me a favour.' Tobias laughed, tactically casual, I was sure, but that didn't mean it didn't work. 'Not exactly what a parent has in mind when they say to get outside and find some life experience. But I guess it technically counts. Plus if he meets a girl . . .'

'Happy to provide the service.'

'Back to business. If I get you this stuff, what do I get in return?'

'A hostage. Remy Allard, the film producer.' I could let him go, I figured. Bryce had said a *she* couldn't leave the bank.

'You know I want Cordelia first.'

'He's hurt.'

This got a crackle of indecision. 'You said everyone was fine. If someone's hurt, you're not giving me a lot of options about coming in there.'

'It's not that bad. And I didn't do it. He scraped himself on some glass.'

'If he's not badly injured, I'll take the girl. If he is, I'll take both. Final offer.'

Of course, I was partly trading Remy because I felt guilty that I'd endangered him in the first place. But the truth was, I believed him. He may have wrapped himself up in some idiotic tax fraud insurance scam, but he hadn't been pushed to murder to protect it. Which meant I didn't need him anymore. Everyone else was still in the game.

I put the radio down and walked to the other side of the room, just to avoid the temptation to take Tobias's offer. One of two things was about to happen. Either the radio would crackle to life or the windows would explode as special-ops soldiers blasted their way in. After the third minute, convinced I'd made a mistake, I strode back over to the radio, but just as I was about to pick it up, it fuzzed.

'Okay,' Tobias breathed, sounding like he'd just had an argument. I imagined there was someone more gung-ho with a gun already loaded beside him. 'We'll take Remy. Give us an hour to get your stuff.'

'Thank you.' It slipped out of my mouth. I reminded myself to be hard-nosed.

'You sure that's all you want?' Tobias asked.

'Do people normally ask for more?'

'For a hostage? Yeah.'

'That's all I need.'

'It's just . . . sunscreen, a chemistry textbook?' This caught me off guard. I hadn't asked for sunscreen. Bryce must have. He had been covered head to toe in a boilersuit, gloves and mask. What use did he have for sunscreen? Tobias was still talking. 'Those aren't in the usual requests.'

'I'm not your usual bank robber.'

CHAPTER 24

'He's trading Remy,' I said, announcing myself to the group back on the third floor, and acting as if the masquerading bank robber was benevolent instead of grovelling. I had the radio and voice-changer secreted in my inside coat pocket, just in case.

Remy was sitting up, shirtless and, thankfully, no longer bleeding. He had enough colour back in his cheeks to be enjoying the attention and couldn't hide the flush of smugness at the realisation he'd be first out. There was a TV on above our heads, sound off. The rolling news footage showed the front of the bank, almost glowing around the edges in the sunset, while reporters talked into fluffy microphones. In the bottom left of the screen, photos of all of us appeared in succession. The scrolling caption read: *Hostages include the World Junior #1 Buccaneers Esports competitor, Hollywood producer Remy Allard and part-time detective Ernest Cunningham.* I was a little miffed that Esports and a bankrupt producer got a higher mention than I did. Besides, I'm not part-time. I'm robbing a bank *and* solving a murder here. That's two jobs.

'Downstairs, they've taken the bars off one of the windows in a toilet,' I said, parroting what Tobias had told me about how they'd got Milton out. 'They can get him out of there. Our guy says we can take him down there ourselves.'

'If there are no bars, why don't we all just slip out?' Felix said.

I shook my head. 'Head count. We'd be risking Milton if we come in under.'

'If the cops come in as we go out, they can rescue him before the guy even realises,' Michelle said.

'It takes a millisecond to pull a trigger. Are we willing to risk that?'

There was a murmur among the group, agreeing it was too risky.

I realised the flaw in my plan. Remy would get outside, and he'd either be asked about or bump straight into the very person who was supposed to be held hostage – the only reason me and the thief couldn't be seen together. Milton. I could hardly back out of the deal with Tobias now, though. I guessed I just had to find a way to get Remy to keep his mouth closed.

TAKE CORDELIA. Gabriel held up his pad. SHE'S GETTING WORSE. RAPID HEARTBEAT.

I glanced over to where Cordelia was propped up on the cushions. She'd whitened, and her breathing was noticeably faster than before.

'How is he?' Juliette interrupted my thoughts. I was glad she was at least talking to me, if only for practical purposes. I could hardly pull her aside now to confess, in the midst of Remy's injury and Cordelia heading downhill, and she didn't seem interested in a private conversation either. Yes, this is one of those times where if *we just talked to each other* we'd have all been a lot better off. But things kept getting in our way.

'The thief? Ah . . .' I thought of a way to truthfully sum it up. 'Losing it a little.'

'I meant Milton. Is he hurt?'

'Define hurt,' I said.

Her jaw firmed.

I could see her marching downstairs and kicking in the door to an empty room, so I added, 'He's fine. I meant stressed out, he's a bit spacey. Milton's just, well, not really all there.' I offered what I hoped was a confidence-giving smile to the group. 'It's okay, everyone. This guy doesn't want to hurt us. He just wants answers.'

'Get him up,' Juliette said, clearly having become the hostages' de facto leader in my absence. She turned back to me. 'He told me about the murder.'

It took me a second to realise she was explaining to me because I supposedly wasn't part of that original conversation. I arranged my face in what I hoped was an expression of discovery.

'Some guy named Bryce. Spontaneous combustion, apparently.'

'I know,' I said. 'Impossible, right?'

'He didn't come in here for you, so there must be evidence in the vault,' she went on.

I rejigged my expression into mild surprise. Behind us, Remy, though perfectly able to walk, was luxuriating in being carried across Felix and Michelle's shoulders, waving goodbye to the room like he was in a parade.

'You don't have to be his dog.'

'I don't have a choice,' I said. Because, at the time, I felt like I didn't.

'I know you've got a gun to your head.' She sucked the corner of her lip. 'That just means you've got a difficult choice to make, not that you don't have one.'

I made to move past her and follow Remy, Michelle and Felix down the stairs, but she put her hand on my chest.

'Hold up. I'll handle this. You stay here and look after the kid. And *don't* interrogate him.'

I needed to talk to Remy before he got outside, but he was already disappearing into the stairwell. As it happened, he turned back to give me a gloating farewell salute at the exact moment Juliette pivoted away from me. I gave him a steely glare. Held my hands out in invisible cuffs, pointed at him and zipped my lips. Reminding him that, no matter how strange it might be to bump into Milton, he had twenty-five million reasons to keep quiet.

Remy squinted back, confused.

I pointed at my chest. Then my lips. *I keep your secrets, you keep mine*, I mouthed. I pointed at Gabriel, just to be clear. Not just silence, *absolute* silence.

The message seemed to click across Remy's features, albeit with the confusion of not knowing what my secret was, as the group disappeared into the stairwell. That left Laverna, Cordelia, Winston, Gabriel, Eric and me upstairs. I stepped inside one of the offices that had a large window overlooking the street and most of the columned entrance and front steps. Only the actual door and the far side of the building was obscured.

I heard the door click behind me; Gabriel had followed me in.

'How quickly do we need to get Cordelia out of here?' I asked, watching outside.

Streetlights had flickered on with the coming dark. Though the sun was setting behind the building, over the glittering dam, the bank itself had swallowed the last of the day on Main Street, and it was cast in shadow. Clumps of black-clad tactical police were grouped under cones of electric light. A few people in yellow hi-vis were erecting floodlights. Otherwise, there wasn't much activity. A crowd of stickybeaks stood behind the barricades. Tiny coals of cigarettes flared among the blinking red lights of TV cameras. We'd be on every station in the country.

Gabriel sidled up next to me and placed a finger on the glass. It squeaked as he drew something, then he puffed his breath on it. A frowny face emerged from the fog.

'I'll get her out,' I said. I might be bone-headed, but I'm not completely insane. I wasn't going to risk Cordelia's life. I just had to figure out how to get her out safely. And quickly. 'I'll make sure he lets her out. I think he underestimated her deterioration. Laverna told him there was no urgency.'

It was a weak excuse, but that didn't make it untrue. I heard Gabriel's pen start to scratch across the page as I kept staring out the window. Given he didn't know it was my fault, he hardly needed me to defend myself. But I suppose I said it for my benefit. To convince myself that what I'd done wasn't reckless and selfish. I think I'd already realised it was over.

I heard the pen stop, so I looked at his pad.

YOU CAN'T MAKE SENSE OF DEATH.

'I can try,' I said.

Gabriel shook his head. I KNOW YOU THINK YOU CAN. WHY ELSE DO THIS?

'I wouldn't be much of a detective if I didn't solve murders.'

YOU'RE LOOKING FOR AN EXPLANATION.

Outside, there was sudden movement. The cluster broke apart, like someone running through a pack of seagulls. Tobias was marching across the blockaded street, up the steps. It was easy to tell him apart; he was now the only one not wearing a helmet. He disappeared from view among the columns. When I looked back, Gabriel had written more.

IF PEOPLE DIE AND IT DOESN'T MEAN ANYTHING, IT'S JUST A TRAGEDY. IF YOU MAKE DEATH A PUZZLE, IF THERE'S AN ANSWER. He turned a new page. IT MAKES SENSE. IF SOMEONE DID THIS, IT'S SOMEONE'S FAULT. IF THERE IS NO REASON, IT IS SIMPLY TOO MUCH.

'You barely know me,' I said. 'How can you know all that?'

WHY DO YOU THINK PEOPLE COME TO CHURCH?

Beneath us, shirtless, bandaged Remy was being carried out on a stretcher. The hiss of a cheer, like a wave breaking on the shore, reached us on the third floor. The television cameras flocked like moths. Remy pumped a fist in the air that would almost certainly be printed on the front page of a dozen newspapers tomorrow. Then it was into the back of an ambulance. A few police officers levered open the barricades, and the ambulance trundled slowly through the crowd.

'I'm not really into that stuff,' I said.

YOU'RE MISTAKING THIS FOR A CONVERSATION ABOUT RELIGION.

'Cordelia's dying,' I said. 'She's twenty. How can that be meaningless?'

JUST BECAUSE IT DOESN'T HAVE A REASON DOESN'T MAKE IT MEANINGLESS.

'Don't give me that "mysterious plan" stuff. She wants to die.'

I KNOW. Gabriel wrote slowly. IT'S HARD TO WATCH. SHE HAD SO MUCH HOPE.

'What happened?'

THEY HAD A HEART. TOP OF THE LIST. BUT LAVERNA LOST CONTROL ON THE DRIVE TO THE HOSPITAL IN BRISBANE, HIT A TREE. NO ONE WAS INJURED, BUT THE CAR WAS KAPUT. DIDN'T MAKE IT.

'If she wasn't hurt, why give up the fight?'

DONOR HEART'S GOT A TIMER ON IT. SIX HOURS. THEY DON'T WAIT.

So much of Cordelia and Laverna's relationship made sense now. Cordelia's spark of hope snuffed out by getting so close and having it ripped from her. And Laverna, desperately trying to push her granddaughter to keep going, forcing the milrinone into her. Because if Cordelia did die, it was all Laverna's fault. She'd been the one to blow her chance at a new heart.

And the community, handing over cash. Giving for the same reason I solve murders. Because if their five dollars helps this young woman, maybe there's a reason for all this pain and misfortune in the world. Hell, it's the same reason we read Agatha Christie: because someone good, someone impeccably moral, will set things right. Golden Age fiction was popular between the World Wars because it was justice served in a topsy-turvy world. I wanted an answer because I wanted to make sense of it all too. Because one day I might come up against the wrong end of a gun – or the inside of a safe. I guess I've learned something about myself: I would rather die with a reason than live without one.

'Why are you here?' I asked, because if this was my last minute in the bank, I had to know. I was already thinking how I'd let everyone go. About the consequences of Bryce's words: *if she leaves the bank, she dies.* But I no longer had a choice. 'I saw you ready to chain yourself to reception this morning to get Winston's ear. Well, eyes.'

He was slow to write it. BUSINESS.

'It's hard to lie on a notepad,' I said. 'Winston told me he'd frozen your credit line. Gambling.'

The words became janky, rushed with annoyance. BULLYING. HE'S TRYING TO MAKE ME LOOK UNRELIABLE.

'Did you owe someone money? Is that what happened to your graveyard? They smashed up a bunch of old bones in your mausoleum as some kind of threat?'

NOT A TOMB. NO BONES. FEW HUNDRED URNS. He was writing angrily now, the lines jagged. CAME IN TO TALK MAN TO MAN.

I took a chance on something I'd noticed. 'This is about money, though. You almost told me before, when I asked you why you needed to see Winston – you drew an S to start a sentence on your notepad, but changed your mind and scribbled it out. But it wasn't an S. It was going to be a dollar sign.' I noticed he didn't deny it, so I asked again. 'Gambling?'

NO ONE'S PERFECT.

'No,' I agreed. 'Do you take confession?'

THIS MIGHT SURPRISE YOU, BUT I'M A GOOD LISTENER.

'Will you sit behind one of those screens and we pretend we don't know each other?'

You have again mistaken this for a conversation about religion. Buy me a pint.

I pointed at his pad. 'Now we're speaking the same language.'

He shook his hand out, cramping from all the writing, and started to abbreviate words to save time.

So u go talk 2 the guy. Get him 2 do another trade. I'll get Cordelia ready. Good?

I nodded. Gabriel slapped me on the back, which let me lean in close enough to swindle something from his pocket without him noticing. As we parted, he held up the pad.

2 Easy!

That phrase was like a song on the radio you couldn't turn off. I kept hearing it today. Why was it twitching some latent synapse? I stared at his pad. Suddenly it came together. I didn't realise, but I must have frozen entirely, because Gabriel had enough time to write again before I could get my mouth to start working again.

What?

'Don't make a big deal of this,' I said. 'Mysteries don't suffer divine intervention, just because you *happen* to be a priest and *you* happened to give me the answer. If you go giving *Him* credit—'

He added an exclamation point.

What?!

'I know the code to the vault.'

CHAPTER 25

I crashed into the returning envoys in the foyer. Michelle, Felix and Juliette had been joined by Winston, who I'd last seen leaning over the balustrade, surveying his bank's destruction. They were having a council of some kind and immediately hushed as I approached. The foyer had mostly dried out, so I no longer splashed through a film of water, but dried shoeprints and water stains remained. There was still a chalky coating on the tiles by the flipped tables. I knelt, putting a finger down. Detectives must use all their senses, including taste, even if it means licking a floor once in a while. Salty. There was a stack of pizza boxes on the reception counter, and Juliette was holding a thick bright-blue hardcover book with molecules on the front. *Chemical Insights: Junior Edition*. Tobias had, mostly, delivered.

'Our bank robber is a weird dude.' She held up the textbook for me to see.

'You don't know the half of it.'

'Are you okay? You seem more rattled than usual.'

'Winston tried to have me killed.' This was true and seemed like a good reason for my erratic behaviour, so I thought I'd fess up. 'Asked the thief to *get rid of* me.'

'Let me at him.' She took a step.

I held her back. 'He denies it. But what if . . . the coffee cup.' I let the implication sit in the air. 'He invited us all the way up here.'

'Why would he bring you up here to kill you? He doesn't even know you.'

'Which is why he might accidentally mix me and Birch up. If he only had a bad author photo and a misnamed coffee order to go on.'

'Still no motive. I've got something too, though no one's threatened to kill me. About Edward,' she said. 'You know he has Arthur Conan Doyle on his shelf.'

I nodded.

'*The Adventures of Sherlock Holmes* caught my eye. That has "The Red-Headed League" story in it – you know, the one that inspired the real-life robbery of Lloyds Bank on Baker Street? It's one of the quirky facts you'd usually put in your books.'

'Yeah.' I was distracted, looking over at the other hostages. One in particular.

Juliette noticed. 'Am I boring you?'

'No. Go on. Lloyds Bank.'

'Those burglars in 1971, they scoped out the bank, measured out the furniture with umbrellas and paces, and then tunnelled in from next door. What if that book is on Edward's shelf because it gave him an idea? The mausoleum is broken open. What if it's the entrance *to a tunnel*.'

I grabbed her by the shoulders. 'That is brilliant. Edward robs his own bank by tunnelling in. That could be what Gabriel saw.'

I meant it. It was clever, and something I hadn't thought of. There were a few gaps, like timings lining up – Gabriel had spotted the mausoleum break-in last weekend, but the bank had only been robbed on Wednesday night – but it had potential.

Juliette was pleased. 'It could be our way into the vault,' she said.

'I think I know a faster one,' I said, turning to Michelle. I had a piece of paper from Edward's office in my pocket that I'd grabbed on the way down. 'This whole robbery has really upset you, hasn't it?'

'Hasn't it upset everyone?' she said, bone dry.

'That's not it,' I said. 'There's something about the robbery that needled you much more than everyone else. You seemed *unimpressed* with the whole thing. If you were in your seventies and had seen it all in the heyday of bank-robbing, sure, I'd buy that you were tired of the shenanigans. But this is your first week – and you seem personally offended.' This had started right at the beginning: *A gun*, she'd said, completely unthreatened, *seriously?* 'You corrected me on the difference between a burglar and a thief.' *Burglars take things by force. Thieves are more elegant*, she'd said, almost disgusted by the designation. 'And you kept complaining about the way he was conducting the robbery. You told him *this is not the way to do things* and that *this is going too far*. You were giving a running commentary like a chef eating at a bad restaurant. It was as if the whole bank robbery wasn't up to standard.'

'I'm not in on this.' Michelle's eyes blazed. 'If that's what you're implying.'

'The entire thing has been decidedly amateur,' Juliette tempered, struggling to hide her disappointment that I wasn't following her tunnelling idea. 'We can all agree on that.'

'Exactly. But it upset you the most, Michelle. Because you're not an amateur.' I shoved the Security Solutions invoice at her. 'You're a professional. And you robbed this bank two nights ago.'

THE FIFTH HEIST: TEN THOUSAND DOLLARS

CHAPTER 26

'Milton didn't know your name,' I explained, as she guided us downstairs into the vault room. I haven't forgotten about Cordelia, but I figured a five-minute diversion might be okay, especially if opening the vault solved everything. 'The negotiator relayed his description of you as "a woman from reception". Why wouldn't he refer to a colleague, even a new one, by name? That was only one of the giveaways that you didn't really work here. You didn't check any calendar or appointment book when we showed up, you just waved us over to Winston's office. The photos on your screensaver too – Singapore's Marina Bay Sands Hotel, Macau, Vegas – they weren't from a recent holiday. Those are all gambling hotspots: big casinos, bigger vaults. All in need of security reviews. You were working. Coupled with the disrespect that you were giving our actual bank robber, that's how I figured out this was your career. You rob banks for a living.'

'I prefer the term *practical security consultant*,' Michelle huffed. 'I put people's systems to the test.'

'So Edward hired you to rob his own bank?'

'*My* bank.' Winston's correction floated over my shoulder.

'Of course he did,' Michelle said. 'This isn't a hobby.'

'Why?'

'He wanted to test the security. I don't ask questions – clients prefer it that way. It was a routine task: hack the system, break into the vault.'

'And you have a little personal flair,' I explained. 'Your fee for this job is ten thousand dollars, as per the invoice for your fee plus tax. Exactly the amount on Edward's desk. Because rather than steal it, you leave it on the hirer's desk to prove you've been in the vault. Then you change the vault code so they can't get in until you're paid.'

'I have a reputation for my method, yes.'

'Risky leaving money out like that.'

She held up her hands, as if to say *you got me*. 'It's about making an impact. If I send someone a report listing all their critical failures, it's just a piece of paper. That's like buying an umbrella on a sunny day: no one does it. But if they walk into their office and the vault's been ransacked and the money's there taunting them, you better believe they're taking notice. I have to make it rain. I made sure it was the dye-pack money anyway; it couldn't have been stolen without setting the ink off.'

'Does this theatricality extend to impersonating the receptionist?' Juliette chipped in. 'That seems excessive.'

'That was to demonstrate another flaw in your'—she targeted this at Winston as the stairs levelled out and we stepped into the vault room—'systems, yes. I stress-test everything, including the staff. I printed the name tag at an Officeworks myself and simply turned up and said I was a new hire. The real receptionist lost a fair bit of money on bad investments last year, so she was only too happy to accept a bribe to stay home for the day, then I had to top her up to take a second day. Milton believed I was new. Winston didn't seem to notice, just barked at me not to let the priest in. And Felix was too goo-goo-eyed to properly consider me. Another fail mark.'

'Goo-goo is a strong word,' Felix replied, frowning.

'You never had a shot, mate,' Winston said.

'But Edward doesn't show, or pay.' I talked over them. 'So you're backstage in costume with no one to perform to?'

'I couldn't believe it. I sat there the whole day. The bank seemed to be running as normal, like they hadn't even noticed they'd been robbed, and I'm twiddling my thumbs behind a desk. I only showed up this morning to let Edward have it for wasting my time. Charge him extra. And'—she turned to Felix—'you did have a shot.'

Spontaneous combustion does not exist, but Felix sizzled. He turned away, opening the grille.

'What's your real name?' I asked.

'Given you write books and my whole career is based on anonymity, let's stick with Michelle.'

'Why didn't you just open the vault the very second this started?' Winston pushed me out of the way. 'It's my money Edward's spending, and I'm apparently paying for these security services, so I'll handle the questions, thank you very much. It could have all been over by now.'

'It wouldn't be the first time a firm has hired more than one contractor and set us off against each other. I wasn't going to do the burglar's job for him,' Michelle explained. Hearing her now reminded me she'd said as much before: *I'm not doing your job for you.* 'It might sound stupid, but think about it: one dollar? From the safe? Who wants to get into a vault but doesn't want any money from it? Someone who is testing the system, that's who. I don't work for free.'

Okay, I've just flipped back through this notebook, and it is obvious – as soon as Bryce mentions that all he wants is the dollar, Michelle relaxes. She smiles as she offers him her thirty cents: *just to get this over with.* She thinks it's a job. An unimpressive one, sure, but not a dangerous one.

'Of course, even before that, I had my suspicions. Because who robs a bank manually these days? I also knew he wasn't a pro. For one thing, I don't use guns. You shouldn't. I assumed it was blanks or some kind of little firecracker he threw at the ceiling. But still, it's dangerous. You could never run a business approaching it like that. Thief, not burglar, remember? You're putting yourself at risk too. If a hostage rebels and bashes your head in, it's not their fault if it turns out you have a toy gun.'

The gun had sure felt real, but now I wondered if it was. I hadn't held enough real guns to know the difference. I remembered her staring down the barrel, unimpressed.

'You voted to attack,' I said, recalling that she'd been on Remy's side of the poll. 'Why do that if you thought it was a test?'

'Same reason I left the money on Edward's desk. Impact. Reputation. If I take down a competitor publicly, in this word-of-mouth business, I accelerate my own demand.'

'But that plan must have changed pretty quickly?' I surmised.

'Yes. It did. Again, once we knew he wasn't after money, it just became a game between him and the police. The most valuable thing in a bank robbery is time. And my job is to test the security to protect what's in the vault. So I considered it my ethical responsibility not to crack. But—' She looked guilty. 'Then you told me Edward had gone missing. I couldn't contact him the previous day, he hadn't paid me, and he'd disappeared entirely. Worse, I checked his phone number against the employee registry, and he'd contacted me on a *different* number. I felt so stupid.'

'What better way to cover the tracks of an actual robbery than to hire someone to rob the bank, apparently legally, just before you do. If you erase all traces of the hiring, then you've got a scapegoat,' Juliette summed it up. 'Once you knew it was off the books, you were afraid he'd used you as a stooge.'

'If you open that vault and it's empty, I only took ten thousand dollars.' She crossed her heart. 'And I put it on Edward's desk. The bag never left the building.'

'Exactly how many people did you plan to let rob this bank under your watch today?' Winston lobbed the insult at Felix, full of acid. Felix tried to herd us through the open grille, if only to stop us discussing his ineptitude. Winston turned to Michelle as we moved. 'You changed the code to my personal safe? What is it?'

'I didn't touch anything but the vault.'

'Can we skip the bull—'

'I swear. And I should have been more clear once this all went to hell, but I was worried, okay, about being framed for something Edward was doing.'

This made sense, and Michelle didn't even know Edward had lost millions investing in something. Winston had thought it was buried in Remy's production, but Remy denied it. Maybe Edward had stolen his own money to cover his losses on something else.

'I don't think he was trying to set you up,' I said. 'These were just extra security precautions. Perhaps he didn't want anyone to know he'd commissioned a security audit. He was worried enough to make Felix carry a brand-new gun, for example.'

'How'd you know that?' Felix blanched.

'Your pants were falling down because your belt's too heavy. And you handed the gun over so quickly, almost scared of it going off as you kicked it over, it seemed like you weren't used to having one. Knowing what we do now about Edward's security paranoia, it makes sense he asked you to be armed. And recently.'

'I only got it last week,' Felix confirmed. 'On Edward's request.'

'Whatever Edward was up to, I didn't do anything wrong,' Michelle continued. 'And it's not like I just let the robbery play out. I tried to give up the code.'

'Twice,' I added.

'If everyone knows the goddamn code, can we open the thing?' Winston had a current running through him.

She shot me a wry smile. 'If he's figured it out, why would we rob Ernest of the pleasure? Be my guest, detective.'

It was nice to have a little win in front of Juliette, so I played along, walking over to the keypad. '*Leetspeak*, you called it. *Elite Speak*. A language for gamers and hackers where words are spelled with letters and contractions. And you did try to give it to the thief. "It's *too easy*," you said, if your thirty cents wasn't enough. Your phrasing didn't seem to make sense, but it does now. You thought he might catch on, being in the same game as you. If he was a fellow hacker. Which, unfortunately, he wasn't.'

It was true I'd heard the phrase *too easy* several times that day. But I'd also *read* it.

'Most of all, like you said, you weren't trying to keep Edward out of the vault permanently. After the shock of finding his security compromised, he was supposed to figure it out. I'm guessing you told him what to expect.'

'It's another little game. I told him when he hired me that the code would be right in front of him. He didn't think I'd get in. No one ever does.' There was satisfaction, pride, in her voice.

'You left him the code. You printed your invoice out, using his own printer to prove you'd hacked into the systems – I can tell by the ink defect – and left it on the desk next to the bag of money. Right in front of him indeed. It's written on your invoice – the order number.'

700 345Y

'Not only is it the code,' I went on, 'but it's also a taunt. It's your hacker slang, *leetspeak*, for TOO EASY.'

I typed in the six digits: 7-0-0-3-4-5.

The keypad flashed blue twice, and there was a mechanical clunk within the door. Then it hissed and sighed on its gears, like an old man sitting down in a comfortable chair. I grabbed the handle, twisted it and pulled the gigantic circular door towards me. Despite its size, the hydraulic pistons swung it open easily.

Given the door blocked my view, I had to settle for simply hearing everyone's gasps as the vault was revealed. I hurried around to the entrance.

I learned two things immediately.

First: it wasn't empty. Pallets of money were stacked around the room.

Second: I'll remind you of one of the rules of heists. There is always an *inside* man.

We'd found Edward.

What was left of him, anyway.

CHAPTER 27

'He looks like . . . like a candle?'

Juliette was the first to break the group's astonished silence. I just stared in amazement. We didn't know it was Edward yet, given the state of the body, but I felt it in my gut. Felix ran out to the guard station and vomited in the rubbish bin. Winston had his work cut out for him, pretending not to be relieved at the sight of all those piles of money, in light of the corpse in front of us. Michelle was rapidly shaking her head and backing out of the vault. I could hear her muttering that she wasn't a part of this.

The interior of the vault was gleaming silver on all sides, a rectangular metallic room. It had its own fluorescent tubing lights in the ceiling and several square air vents. Edward was in the centre, sitting in what was left of an incinerated chair: reduced to a metal frame and chalky-white wire springs. Around him were pallets of money and cream cloth sacks stuffed with, I assumed, the same, resting on wheeled trolleys like you'd pop your luggage on at a hotel. The wall beside the body was a grid of numbered rectangles, fourteen rows of twenty: the safety deposit boxes.

'Those are his shoes,' Winston muttered, hand over his mouth. His jaw started to shake, and I could see him trying to hold it all together. 'Who . . .' Given the state of the body, Winston realised it was the wrong question. '. . . *what* did this?'

Edward did indeed take the cake for the strangest corpse I'd ever seen.

He was partially melted.

I mean that literally. His clothes had burned away. His skin had sloughed off his body like clay, puddling around his shoulders and waist like cascading mud. He was still recognisably human, not skeletal, but waxen and glossy. Juliette was right. He looked like a wax figure at Madame Tussauds that had been left in the sun. A rippled lump of a man.

The only part of him that was undamaged were his feet. They weren't burned at all, planted flat on the floor, boots on and laces tied. Problem was, they were on their own – detached mid-shin from his legs. An ash-grey piece of bone poked out from the top of each, but otherwise the severing was very clean: cauterised.

Nothing else in the room was torched. Not a scorch mark on the floor, not a burned hundred-dollar note. If he hadn't been inside a sealed room, I'd suggest he'd been struck by fierce lightning.

I examined the inside of the door. There was a cream-coloured plastic phone that, when I lifted it from the wall, revealed itself to be nothing more than a glorified walkie-talkie because there was nowhere to dial. I held it to my ear; it rasped static. There was no keypad either. I pointed this out.

Felix, wiping his mouth, refused to step into the vault and spoke to me from the doorway, one hand blocking the sight of waxen-Edward. 'There's no way out if you're in here with the door locked. No code, no nothing. The redundancy is that phone, which only has one line. It's basically just a radio to the guard's station. But there's air circulation. If you got stuck inside, even over a weekend, you'd be bored and thirsty, but you wouldn't cark it—' His eyes darted to Edward and he retched again. 'Well, not in any usual way.'

'So Edward figures out that the code to the vault is on Michelle's invoice and opens it, only to lock himself inside. Why?' I wasn't really expecting an answer, just speaking my confusion aloud. 'If he hired a security review in the first place, he was worried about a flaw. What *was* or *is* in here that he wanted to make sure he could protect?'

'And does our thief know his body is in here? Is this what he wanted?' Juliette finished.

This was my same thought process. Bryce might have been trying to lead us to this corpse, under the artifice of opening the vault. He had confessed to murder, though he'd said "I've killed *her*". What else had he said? *I wanted to. But I . . . I couldn't . . . I didn't think I had it in me. And then everything . . . happened. So quickly out of my control.* Had that been about Edward? Did Bryce have a partner on a job in here that had gone wrong? I already thought Bryce had been murdered to stop us finding what was in the vault. Now the motive was clear: to cover up another murder.

The phone call on Bryce's phone played in my memory. *We're in.* A female voice. And yet the vault was still full of cash. The walls, floors and ceilings were intact, the air vents looked too small to fit even a child through, and no safety deposit boxes had been cracked from the wall. No secret tunnel out to the mausoleum.

We're in.

A bank robber who robs a bank for a single dollar, with an accomplice who gets *in* somewhere that wasn't the bank's vault.

Not only that. If there was no way *in* to the locked vault, there was certainly no way *out*. Which meant that Edward had to have locked himself in here and then set *himself* on fire.

The puzzle grew.

'Spontaneous combustion,' Juliette said from beside me, finishing my thought. 'It's annoyingly present, given it's impossible. Same killer, then, as this Bryce fellow that the thief mentioned?'

I flinched, thinking she was talking about the real Bryce, dead and hidden on the rooftop, until I managed to mentally reassemble the lies I'd told. A sudden wave of concern hit me. I figured Bryce's corpse was unlikely to be spotted at night, especially with no helicopters permitted among the butterflies. But it was only a matter of time until the cops outside got antsy and made a go of securing the roof the old-fashioned way.

Juliette noticed my worry. 'What aren't you telling me, Ernest?' Under her examination, I felt a little like Edward, melting. 'Something about these murders.'

'I really need to talk to you,' I whispered. 'Alone.'

Finally she nodded. 'Me too. Let's finish here. Winston'—she spoke to the whole room—'is anything else missing from this vault that we wouldn't know about?'

He had taken to running his hands along the joins between all the deposit boxes on the wall, looking for breaks I assumed, but also an effective excuse to have his back to us so we couldn't see him sniffling. He shook his head. 'Not that I can tell.'

'Do you personally have one of those?' I asked, nodding at the boxes.

'I use my safe.'

'Wise move. Edward clearly didn't trust this vault either.'

'*He* has one though,' Winston said. 'It's number sixty-five.'

'You mean this number sixty-five?' Felix was holding up a small key with an etching of *65* on it. 'It was on one of the pallets of cash.' He handed it to me.

'That wasn't in here when I left. Neither was the . . . body,' Michelle added, talking quickly, loudly, desperate to be heard. 'I broke in just before seven, after Ed headed home. I watched him drive off.' She pointed at a pallet of notes with a corner of cash missing from the neat square stack. 'This is where I took the money from. I walked in and walked out.' She noticed me looking into the corners of the room. 'There's a camera in here. Just like the rest of the bank. But, ah'—she swallowed guiltily—'I turned them off.'

'A security expert who primes a bank to be robbed.' Winston didn't bother to hide the accusation under the words.

'I only show you what any regular thief worth their salt could do. That's what I was hired for.'

'I believe you, but no cameras means no alibi.' I stepped between them, just in case Winston launched at her throat. I tried to distract him with another question. 'Was there any gold in the vault?'

'Like, actual gold?'

'Bars. Bullion.'

'We're a bank, not a reserve,' Winston said. 'I can't speak for everyone's personal boxes, but no, we don't have stores. What does that matter? My brother is *dead*.'

'How did his feet burn *off*?' Michelle was leaning by the corpse, examining the feet, standing like two shoes tucked under a bed. Look, I know Golden Age mysteries aren't supposed to be all that violent, and a melted man really pushes the limits, but it's hard to explain how *unreal* it all felt. There was no smell in the room. The air vents had done their job. The corpse was so curious, I was finding it hard to be disgusted. Yes, even in the presence of severed shins.

Michelle nudged a tiny gleaming shard of gold metal with her toe. It had been sitting under the chair. 'What's this?'

We all peered down at it.

'Give me your name tag,' I said.

Michelle unclipped the magnetic clasp and handed it to me. I hovered it over the metal. Nothing happened.

'Gold's not magnetic. Ed had fillings, I presume?'

'Like *teeth* fillings?' Winston's lip quivered at the grotesque idea of his brother's fillings dropping out of his head. Then he nodded. 'Gold ones.' He'd already known, but the extra confirmation hit him like an arrow. 'Oh, Ed.'

Felix retched again in the background.

'That's the same reason his feet are burned off,' I explained. 'The human body's a bunch of carbon, right? It's got quite a low burning point. Bone is basically coal. So the fire's gone through his legbone before it's managed to travel down through the meat of his shins to catch his shoes. The shins have burned through and snapped off, leaving the feet unburned. It's bizarrely common in spontaneous combustion cases for the feet to be left behind. And as for the teeth fillings, metal doesn't melt at the temperature a body does—'

'Do bodies normally *melt*?' Juliette asked.

'No. I'm still figuring that out. I only know little things about the urban legend, not the whole scientific background. What I do know is cremations. When they burn a body, they sift the ash to find all the metal pieces: hip replacements, teeth fillings. The heat required to turn a human body to ash is lower than what you need to melt metal. A crematorium will pass a magnet over the ashes to pick out any leftovers, so you're not getting Nan's titanium kneecap in the urn. So Edward's teeth have incinerated, but not his fillings.'

Felix dutifully gagged on cue. 'How do you know all this?'

'Because the *wrong body in the incinerator* is a trope of detective fiction.'

'Crematorium's next door.' Winston paced in circles. 'This is supposed to be a bank vault.' He approached me, wild-eyed. 'Get me the thief's gun. I'll kill whoever did this.'

'Why don't we all take a breather,' I offered, before Winston started swinging punches and Felix passed out from the shock: he had paled and started sweating. 'Let's finish this outside, away from the body. Felix, can you get me the bank's master key for the deposit boxes? You need two to open them, client and bank, right?'

Grateful for the relief, Felix nodded and scurried off.

'You're sure there's no gold, no significant amount of money missing?' I said to Winston as I guided him away from his brother.

Winston nodded.

I turned to Michelle. 'Anything different from when you broke in around seven o'clock?'

'Financially, it seems the same as when I was in here,' she said. 'Corpse-wise, there's been an increase.'

Outside, I decided to leave the vault door open. We congregated around the guard's desk, the one without a chair.

'Was there a chair at this desk when you were here?' I asked. Michelle nodded. So Edward had swiped it for somewhere to sit. Which meant he planned to be in the vault for some time.

'It's time,' Winston said.

I didn't understand him, but Juliette gave him a thumbs up. 'We'll catch up,' she said.

Felix had unlocked a mini safe under the desk and now handed me a small key. Juliette and I let the others file past us, heading back into the vault as they made for the stairs.

'What's time?' I asked, but Juliette ignored me. She was busy locating Edward's safety deposit box on the wall: number 65. We slid both keys in and turned them, and the box slid out like a drawer. We opened it.

Empty.

'Why were you asking about gold before?' Juliette asked as we exited the vault.

'Because gold's heavy.' I guided her over to the space in the vault lobby where the wool lift could be lowered down. I was itching to tell her everything, but I was worried people might still be in earshot. I pointed at the scattering of dust on the floor. 'One gold bar is over ten kilograms. I couldn't carry five of them a hundred metres. This'—I scraped my toe through the dust—'has been dislodged from above. It should be caked into the joints and ropes if they haven't been used in decades. Someone's used the wool lift.'

'Which means they've moved something heavy between floors.' Juliette thought for a second. 'And you think gold? Out of this room?'

'They either used this to lift something heavy out or bring something heavy *down*.'

'A dead body?'

'Maybe. Dump it in the vault, light it on fire and close the door . . . a whole lot more likely than—'

'Spontaneous combustion,' Juliette finished. She tapped her lip with a finger. 'Could the same apply to the murder of this Bryce fellow that the thief wants you to solve?'

I shook my head. 'Now that's a problem. There's a witness to that one.'

'A witness?'

I almost told her then, but I could still hear footsteps, echoed voices on the stairwell. I couldn't risk being overheard. 'Yes. They saw Bryce burst into flames. With their own eyes.'

'Are they a reliable witness?'

'Um . . . Not especially.'

The noise from the stairwell had quelled.

I let out a huge sigh of relief. 'Juliette, I need to tell you something.'

She put a hand on my shoulder. 'Me first.'

'It's really import—'

'So's this. Shut up for a second.' She squeezed, and so I did as I was told. 'We've had a chat. The four of us.' I recalled interrupting the conversation in the foyer, thinking it had seemed like a meeting. 'This is getting out of hand. We're going to rush him.'

'Rush? Who?'

'Attack. Kick Winston's office door down. Unless you've got a key?'

I shook my head. I was hoping everyone would think the thief was letting me in each time I returned to swap clothes. 'We have a secret knock,' I said, unconvincingly.

'What are you, pals? He's got Milton in there. I know you have a habit of risking your life, but, Ernest, there's a sick girl upstairs and now a murder downstairs. We *have* to act.' She was charging up the stairs now. I was in tow, protesting, but I knew the decision had already been made. That was why Winston had said *It's time*. I saw that Michelle had hung back for us in the stairwell and my window for confession had closed. We hurried up the last flight and into the foyer.

'Just give him the dollar,' I said, trying to buy any time I could. 'That's what he wanted.'

'You don't believe that. Nor should you. I'm not dragging this out any further,' Juliette said firmly. 'Everyone agrees.'

As we entered the lobby, I saw Winston and Felix on the far side, breaking apart the tables. Felix held one table-top across his front like a shield. In his spare hand, he brandished one of the table's legs, jabbing at an imaginary enemy. Winston had a fire lit in him I hadn't seen before, happily working with Felix now that vengeance for Edward was on the cards.

'I'll talk to him,' I said meekly.

'Time for talking is over.' Juliette caught a table leg that Winston had tossed her. 'This is no longer a murder mystery. It's a rescue mission. Grab a weapon.'

CHAPTER 28

A series of bad decisions, each slightly larger than the last, can lead to murder, or, in my case, to dangling out of a third-storey window.

I could have just fessed up, I know. It was one of those times where the moment was there, dancing in front of me, and all I had to do was grab it. Instead I watched it flit away. I felt like I was so close to *something*. Little pieces were subliminally clicking together. I'd uncovered multiple thefts so far, and I had a suspicion about several others. I couldn't let it end. And if Juliette and her Knights-Of-The-Bed-Bath-N'-Table kicked down the door to an empty room, a thief reduced to a sabre mask and a boilersuit resting in a drawer, then it would be over.

I made a hurried excuse about feeling ill, exposure to a melted man and all, and dashed up the stairs to the top-floor bathroom. I had only one option: I had to get into Winston's office and mask up before they broke down the door. Which meant I had to get in from the outside.

A cool breeze blew in through the bathroom window Remy had shattered, and the walls were peppered with butterflies. I jammed the staff locker against the door with the now-busted lock, took one last second to consider the idiocy of all of this, then pulled myself up into the window.

Remy's stomach had done me the favour of clearing out any residual glass shards in the window frame. He'd got stuck going out forwards, so I went backwards, parking my bum on the sill and pulling my upper body outside the building, my knees dangling inside. I made the mistake of looking down. The drop was dizzying: the ground beneath a murky black. Given the atrium's generous ceiling height, I was at least ten metres high. The wedding-cake look of the bank only applied to the front and sides, and the back was a steep wall, housing things like the elevator shaft, the offices and the stairwells.

The building was ringed with sandstone ledges, only a shoe wide, and while I was able to get a hand on the one above my head, there was no way I could haul myself up onto it. The ledge below was at the internal floor level, which meant I was now a full body length above it, given I was sitting on the sill (which I was realising had *not* been as fully cleared of glass shards by Remy as I'd hoped). There were no handholds aside from the ledges. It was a marvel of architecture, the huge smooth sandstone blocks with so little grouting, but it was a nightmare for bouldering.

In any case, Winston's office was on the mezzanine. I was going to have to find a way down eventually. It was more a matter of how fast I descended. And whether I got off at the right exit on the gravity freeway.

I didn't know butterflies slept, but many seemed to have settled in for the night. They hung from the bottom of the ledges like icing on a cake, a lace embroidery on the building. This was bad news; if too many of the butterflies settled, it meant Tobias could potentially get a helicopter in the air.

I didn't have time to waste; Juliette and the others were ready. Would they wait for me? Winston wouldn't, I was sure. Perhaps a quick strategy meeting would delay them slightly, but then they'd be marching up the stairs and into the office. I pulled myself out the window, gripping the ledge above and putting my feet on the sill, bending at the hips with my arse out over the void. Like the legs and arms of a K. I lifted one leg, then the other and dropped into a hang.

It felt like a bad plan, most likely because it was. I started to swing a little and tried to settle my inertia. A butterfly decided my eyelid would make a good bed for the night. I tried to blink it away and blow it off at the same time. I couldn't see the ledge below properly. I had to be precise to drop down to it.

Then one of my hands slipped off.

My other hand just held on, but I was wrenched to a stop so quickly my shoulder will never forgive me. I was now side on, feet about a metre above the lower ledge. The issue was I was still swinging. If I dropped when I was too far out, I'd miss the ledge entirely. But if I swung in too far, I'd bounce off the wall and plunge to my death. Either way, I'd be reserving my spot in Father Gabriel's mausoleum.

I didn't have the time to make a choice. I let go.

I missed the ledge.

Well, more accurately, I hit the ledge and bounced straight off it, sliding past it and only catching myself by, literally, the skin of my forearms. Butterflies spun up around me like I'd landed in snow.

I paused to catch my breath, elbows on the ledge, body dangling below, like a swimmer taking a rest on the edge of a pool. The bathroom shone a rectangle of light a few metres above. Down here, on the exterior of the mezzanine level, the interior lights were off, and it was harder to see.

There was another ledge within reach below me, and my scrambling feet found it. I gently squeezed myself down. I realised that I hadn't gone all the way to the mezzanine level: I was standing on the ring of semi-circular stained-glass windows. I peered inside: Juliette's homemade commandos were still on the ground floor, in some kind of huddle, Juliette pointing this way and that. Felix had a metallic rubbish bin on his head as a helmet. Winston had duct-taped the chemistry book to his chest, like some kind of rudimentary Kevlar.

I moved along the ledge, keeping my footing steady. I accidentally kicked a stone mount and it crumbled from the wall, landed with a thud in the church graveyard below. It was creepier now, the broken mausoleum door a black mouth in the night. There was a small glow from inside, and I almost expected an arm to come through the gap.

I'd shuffled along far enough to be above Winston's office; I had the advantage of having left the window slightly ajar earlier, which helped me know which one it was. The window opened outwards from the top, like a hotel window designed to stop jumpers, so I could conceivably dangle myself down through it and use it as a slide into the office.

Just my luck though, the window was barred. A rusted iron grille held on by screws. I sat on the ledge and kicked down on it, but nothing moved. I kicked harder, almost spilling myself off my perch. A little sprinkling of dust rewarded me. The screws were corroded enough to loosen.

I looked back through the stained glass. Juliette had her arms folded and was jigging up and down. They were waiting for me, I realised. I didn't have long. Either they'd charge the office without me or bash on the bathroom door. Neither was good for my charade.

Suddenly, a blinding spotlight lit up the side of the building. It was moving left to right and dropping a few feet each time. Someone in the bell tower, scanning for movement. I pressed myself into the ledge, hoping I could dissolve into the stone before the light got to me. If the spotlight operator noticed any movement, the light would surely follow. Then, who knows. A bullet? I turned my head to peek inside again. Through the stained glass, I saw the huddle in the foyer put one hand each in the centre and raise them upwards. *Hoo-rah*. They started to move.

I was out of time. Either I was going to get busted by the spotlight, or Juliette was about to discover an empty room. I wasn't sure which option made me more of a dead man.

'*You!*'

A voice cut through the night. That was it: I was caught. I closed my eyes and waited to be awash with light or riddled with bullets.

But the heat of the spotlight didn't prickle my skin. I opened my eyes. I was in darkness. I looked up. The light was on the far side of the building, the halogen circle instead focused on . . .

'*Are dead!*'

It was Ditto. Looping in circles in the night, his bright green wings illuminated by the searchlight, pecking at errant butterflies as he swooped.

He couldn't have escaped his locked cage. Which meant someone had let him out. I'd have to think about that later. I know better than to look a gift-parrot in the mouth. The clue that wasn't a clue had just saved my life.

Through the stained-glass window, I saw the office-supply battalion start up the stairs.

I had one shot: I was going in or I was going down. I lashed out a final kick, using so much force I lost my balance entirely. I wobbled in place but there was no regaining it. To my delight, the rusted bolt pulled free from the wall. I let myself fall at the same time, bouncing off the angled glass. It cracked but held, and I rolled into the room as the iron cage fell away beneath. The spotlight swung around at the clatter but I moved out of the window quickly and pressed myself to the bookcase, kicking off my polished leather shoes and pulling the army boots on.

On the other side of the room, a flitter of shadow passed under the door. Juliette was coming in.

I bolted to the desk and yanked open the drawer. Pulled the boilersuit on, flying into it like it was skin. I was in such a rush I knocked the voice-changer off the desk, and it clattered to the floor. All I could do was grab Bryce's gun and pull the sabre mask over my head, the silver mesh only just covering my nose as the door splintered off its hinges.

CHAPTER 29

I'll spare you the ins and outs of the improvised yoga positions required inside this cramped space, except to say that I now have a glass jar full of urine.

I suspect it's come just in time. I can feel myself getting sluggish. The pen in my hand moves like someone else is holding it. My spelling is suffering. I'm worse at apostrophes than Ben Huxley at this point. Have I mentioned that's important yet? I hope so. I'm a bit fuzzy on what I've written down. I don't have time to read it back, but I don't want to be accused of not playing fair either.

Did I tell you Bryce's watch was four hours behind in the café? I think I did.

Aside from a screaming headache, the overarching feeling is a sleepiness. Like a hot afternoon. It's almost inviting me to close my eyes, slide into it. Not yet. Once I write this out, I can rest.

I've followed the experiment in *Chemical Insights: Junior Edition* like a recipe. I unpeeled the radio battery's skin, revealing two metal cylinders connected by a wire. If I dip them into the – let's just call it liquid to save the grotesqueness – then the oxygen should be attracted to the positive cylinder and the hydrogen will bubble off at the negative. The negative core is inside the plastic bag, which I've partially submerged in the *liquid* to create an airtight bubble.

It seems to be working. There is bubbling on the exposed metal cylinder, hopefully injecting oxygen back into this airtight cube and diluting the carbon dioxide that will kill me. I assume the same thing is happening on the negative end, because the plastic bag is inflating. That's the hydrogen. I have to keep my non-writing hand in the jar to seal the bag against it leaking. Because I don't want to breathe that in. It's also flammable, remember. I might have made oxygen but, on the other hand, I now have hold of an explosive plastic bag.

I don't know what it's bought me. Twenty minutes? Thirty? Maybe enough to get the rest of this down.

Where was I?

Oh. Yes. Juliette is about to shoot me.

CHAPTER 30

Juliette was first through the door. I aimed the gun above her head. There's no way I'm pointing it at her, remember. I'm an idiot, not a psychopath.

She had a table-top shield held up in one hand and a heavy brass lamp dangling from its electrical cord like a mace in the other. It looked like a very low-budget school play.

'Where's Milton?' Juliette shouted, looking around the room, confused to find it empty. 'Where are you keeping him?'

I couldn't talk without the voice-changer, and it lay agonisingly far away on the floor. I tried to do sign language for *Everyone relax* but Juliette flung the brass lamp out from its cord and clocked me in the wrist.

'Ow!' I protested; screw the voice-changer. The lamp was heavy. But Juliette wasn't listening hard enough to detect my signature whinging, winding up for another swing. I stepped out of the way as the lamp blew woodchips off Winston's desk. Felix and Michelle were ready to rush me, table legs in the air. Felix had two, crossed in an X in front of him. Michelle only had one, given her strapped wrist, but she held it high like a warrior's club.

I could see only one solution.

I ducked under Juliette's next swing and shoved Felix hard, toppling him into Michelle and Winston, sending them into a limb-locked jumble back out through the door. Then I swung the door shut behind me. The lock was splintered now, so I leaned against it. I addressed Juliette.

'Finally. I've been trying to—'

The brass lamp crashed into my forearm. She'd forgone the mace technique and was holding it like a brick. Searing pain shot all the way up to my hand, and my fingers involuntarily dropped the gun. I keeled over sideways, but Juliette was on top of me and raining punches down, the lamp abandoned. All I could do was block the barrage. I certainly wasn't going to hit her back. I tried to yell, but the breath had been knocked out of me. I almost got a word out, but she stood and kicked me in the chest, robbing my confession again.

There was a moment of relief as she either walked away or got a run-up on another kick, I couldn't tell. I tried to get a hand up to rip the sabre mask off, but couldn't. One arm was trying to hold me up, the other in so much pain from the brass beating I could barely lift it. I spat blood while I tried to get my tongue around the words. Tangy, iron syrup had trickled into my lungs, and I was coughing instead of talking.

The old adage is right: communication is the most important thing in a marriage.

I finally hauled myself up off the floor. At least the punching had stopped. Then I realised she'd only stopped hitting me to go and pick up the gun. It was shaking in her hand, but she was far too close to miss. It was pointed at my head.

Strangely, this was a pretty good result. Now she had the power: she'd ask me questions, have me take off the mask and we would come up with a new plan from there. I almost had my breath back. I could explain.

Except she didn't ask me any questions.

I had a brief second to remember Remy's words from earlier that day. *Shoot them dead . . . then take off the mask and find out who it is*. And that Juliette had agreed. Though thankfully not with the killing part, I recalled.

The memory was little comfort as she lowered the gun's aim to my kneecap and pulled the trigger.

CHAPTER 31

Here's a riddle. Who robs a bank with an unloaded gun?

Me, apparently.

The gun in Juliette's hand clicked, refusing to fire. She pulled the trigger three more times, incredulous, which gave me time to finally reach up and pull off the sabre mask. Her face paraded through surprise, relief, confusion, shock and finally anger. I swear I saw her finger dance on the trigger one more time before she hurled the gun to the ground.

She walked across the room, kicking the voice-changer over to me before dropping into one of Winston's meeting chairs, one hand on her brow like a period-set romance where she had the vapours. She was giving me a chance to explain myself.

I dragged Winston's desk in front of the door to barricade it. 'Your rebellion has failed,' I said through the voice-changer. Then, because I figured Bryce might not have known Juliette's name, 'The woman is not hurt.'

Juliette raised her eyebrows. '*The woman* is okay,' she called to the others. 'We're negotiating.'

'How is Milton?' Felix shouted through the door.

'In a much better place than we'd hoped,' Juliette said. 'Give us half an hour. We'll meet you upstairs.'

There was a murmur of whispered reluctance, and then I heard the tramp of footsteps retreating. I slumped down in the chair opposite Juliette, the exact same place I'd started this hellish day.

'You shot me,' I said.

'You deserved it.' She leaned back in her chair. 'This had better be good.'

It wasn't.

I knew it wasn't. The explanation and justification turned sour on my tongue, my stupid decisions somehow made more stupid by the act of verbalising them. I kept pausing and thinking to myself, *Surely, I didn't do that*, when I actually had. The more I tried to explain myself, the more my story seemed to spiral. I told her of Bryce's death on the roof, of his strange threat against an unnamed *she*. I was so desperate, I included show-and-tell, pointing around the room – the abacus (1011) and the photo of Harold and Yang. Juliette, to her credit, could have interrupted hundreds of times with snipes and insults, but she just sat and listened.

'I know it sounds crazy,' I finished. 'But Bryce Fredericks didn't want money. And if he didn't want money, then someone in here has something in that vault worth killing him to protect.'

'Edward's corpse.' She spoke slowly.

'Evidently. It's one of us, I know it.' I was pleading now. 'Someone killed Edward two nights ago, and then they killed Bryce to stop him opening the vault and finding the body. I couldn't let everyone go.'

Her hands were clenched into fists. It was taking all her will to stop from shaking. This wasn't just anger. This was something more. 'You pointed a gun at me.' The words had to stage a jailbreak on her clenched teeth to get out.

'I pointed the gun *above* you.'

'With your aim? Same thing. Did you know it wasn't loaded?'

I hesitated. Which was enough of an answer.

'You pointed what you thought was a *loaded* gun at your fiancée?'

'*Above* my fiancée.'

'That's not the word I'm tempted to correct here.' She ran her hands through her hair. 'What I don't understand is why, after all we've been through, you didn't just *tell* me?'

'I tried. I really did. Things kept getting in the way.' I sighed. 'And by things, I mean me.'

She pushed an imaginary pair of glasses up her nose. 'We're making some real progress here, Mr Cunningham.'

I looked at my shoes. 'I know it doesn't sound like it, but I'm trying to say I'm sorry. I've screwed this one up in every possible way. I mean it when I say that. I *am* sorry. But . . . *if she leaves*. I didn't know who that applied to. Maybe you. I couldn't take that risk. I want to fix it now, though. And the only way to fix it—'

'Is to solve it,' Juliette said quietly. 'That makes you a good detective in a book, but a shitty human in real life. You need some new role models.'

'Help me finish it.' I leaned forward.

Juliette barked a laugh.

'I mean it. Come on. We've been through too many murders for you not to be a little bit interested. Spontaneous combustion, a bank robbery that's not a robbery and a dead man in a locked vault. That's juicy.'

'You're wrong though – it is a real bank robbery. We just don't know what Bryce wanted.'

'Who robs a bank with an unloaded gun?'

'It *was* loaded. It had one bullet in it. He fired it, remember?' She pointed at the ceiling. 'But it's not as interesting as you think it is. You mentioned Bryce had blisters on his hands. So that part's obvious: he lit Edward on fire. Whatever accelerant he used inadvertently set off again, and that's why he died.'

'He had blisters on the *back* of his hands. Not the usual wound for an arsonist. If he'd lit Edward on fire, wouldn't the blisters be on his palms?'

She lingered on that idea, then shook it off. 'No. People aren't puzzle pieces. You can't keep them here. Let everyone go, then solve it.'

'One of them is a killer.'

'One of them might be a killer. *Might* be. But the rest of them aren't.'

'Could be two. I've never faced a duo of murderers before.' I stood up, walked over to the blockaded door and picked up the sabre mask. 'They're sure as hell not all innocent. I just need a little more time.'

Juliette followed, snatched the mask from me and held it out of reach. 'You're not going to solve this with a junior chemistry textbook and a plucky attitude. It's over. You don't need time. You need a shrink.'

'Shrink,' I repeated absent-mindedly, looking at the photo of Harold and Yang. Something clicked in. 'Hey, does that nugget look bigger to you?'

'Don't do that.'

'Don't do what?'

'Don't bring up some obscure clue to try to reel me back in. I don't care.' Her eyes betrayed her by flicking to the photo.

'The one in the foyer,' I insisted. 'It's *shrunk*.'

'People were smaller a hundred years ago. It's perspective.'

'Not by that much.'

'Not interested. It doesn't matter if the nugget in the foyer is fake—'

'I didn't say fake,' I interrupted. 'I said it's shrunk.'

'Gold doesn't shrink. Winston made the pen out of a chunk, remember? Of course it's smaller. They've divvied it up. Edward's tooth, too, I reckon.' She picked up the gun and tucked it into her waistband. 'You're stalling again. It's over. I'm letting everyone out. Christ, it's like talking to a wall. You could have got yourself killed. You'll probably go to jail. This is *criminal*, Ern. You've got a fifteen-year-old kid upstairs. You held a priest at gunpoint! You are keeping a sick woman hostage. Just to solve a murder that you don't even know for sure is a murder!'

I was silent at this. In fact, I was more than silent. I deliberately tucked my lips in. I dragged the desk away from blockading the door in quiet surrender, then opened it and gestured wordlessly out into the corridor.

Juliette couldn't quite grasp that she'd had the last word. She approached the door as if it was booby trapped, but couldn't resist turning back. 'So that's it? No snippy remark? No comeback? No last-minute revelation?'

I shrugged. 'I can't say what I was going to say next. You'll accuse me of trying to reel you back in.'

'Believe me'—she weighed the sabre mask in her hand—'nothing you say could prick my ears.'

'What if I told you that Cordelia's not really sick?'

THE SIXTH HEIST: A HEART

(SEE ALSO: ONE HUNDRED AND FIFTY THOUSAND AND FIFTY DOLLARS)

CHAPTER 32

'Estás atrapada.'

You're caught. I know a little Spanish from my Ecuadorian step-family.

Cordelia, splayed out on her cushion-palace, squinted at me in confusion.

'Are you sure?' Juliette hissed at me from behind, looking at Cordelia, who indeed seemed to have worsened since the last time I'd seen her. She was bleary-eyed, clammy-skinned. In a word: sick.

Everyone else stood around us in a ring, desperate to know what had gone on inside Winston's office. I was back to being Ernest. Juliette had told them the thief had agreed to let someone go, which sent a titter of excitement through the group. As I'd made my way over to Cordelia, everyone had assumed it was to help her up and start moving her downstairs.

'What's the matter?' I said to Cordelia. 'Duolingo not got you past conversation starters and into accusations yet?'

'What do you want?' she rasped.

'I want everyone in here to stop wasting my time. Including you. You're perfectly healthy, aren't you?'

Cordelia gave a dramatic cough.

Laverna pushed her way through the crowd, stopping in front of us and setting me with a glare.

'I should have known the second you asked for your phone back,' I continued. 'You didn't want to drop your daily completion streak on Duolingo: four hundred and eighty days. The whole app's designed around doing a lesson *every day*. Why would somebody who has given up on living keep a commitment to learning a new language?'

'It's called keeping up hope.' Laverna folded her arms.

'That's what it looked like. That's why I didn't think twice of it until I talked to Father Gabriel. He told me that you, Cordelia, had *given up* hope after that car accident robbed you of making it in time for a heart transplant. If dreaming of Spain was the thing that was keeping you going, sure. But once you'd resigned yourself to dying, your daily milestone shouldn't have mattered. Let alone learning a new language you'll never use. Not to mention, your first post on FundAble was on the second of May, last year. In it, you said you were diagnosed on *Monday*. That puts it at the twenty-ninth of April. Which is four hundred and eighty days ago.' I looked at the clock on the wall; it was almost midnight. 'Four hundred and eighty-one in about twenty minutes. Your Duolingo streak is also at four hundred and eighty days. Which means that you had the fortitude *and* resilience, as a then nineteen-year-old, to pass through all the stages of grief and decide to learn a new language *on the very same day you were diagnosed.*'

Look at her. Gabriel held up his pad.

Laverna tried to keep it afloat, growling, 'She is clearly sick.'

'Get that needle out of her arm, and she'll be fixed right up.' I addressed the room. 'Milrinone is heart medication, designed to raise the heartrate for someone with an *irregular* heartbeat. What do you think that will do to a normal heart? Plus, there is a chalky white outline on the tiles in the foyer. It's left over from when the solution in your spilled IV bag evaporated. I tasted it. It's salt. The original bag wasn't milrinone at all. It was saline. Completely harmless IV fluid.

'I overheard Cordelia refusing to take the medication. Laverna explained it away by saying that she'd given up, that she was sick of putting needles and medicines into herself for a hopeless cause. But that's not true at all.' I pointed at Laverna. 'Cordelia was scared of taking the *real* medicine, because she knew it would have side-effects for her healthy system. That it would put her regular heart into hyperdrive, rather than helping a slow heart back to normal. But you, Laverna, forced it on her. You probably knew it would make her sick, but also that it would help the lie get through for one more day. If we went through all the trouble of getting a new IV bag and then you didn't use it, there'd be questions. I'm guessing you thought it might get you out faster, if she did start becoming really ill.' Laverna seemed confused as to how I knew this, not knowing she'd asked me, when I was in the mask, if Cordelia being more sick would help get them get out faster. 'The only medical condition Cordelia had when she walked into Huxley's Bank this morning was being very well hydrated.'

'This is preposter—'

'It's over, Gran,' Cordelia shouted, ripping the cannula out of her arm. 'He knows, okay?' She huffed out through her nose, a breath I have become acquainted with as one that precedes a confession. A dragon with no fire. She turned to me. 'I broke my arm a couple of years ago. Do you know how much sympathy I got? Free meal at the chippy. Cutting lines. The best spots at a gig. People bend over backwards when they pity you. When they think *Thank God it's not me*. And it felt . . . well, it felt good. And I wanted it again. I'd get *concussion*'—she used air quotes—'during sports. I'd feel *oh so faint* on dates. You can be a proper tosser when you're sick and people put it down to a tough day. And then we moved here and this girl in town, Emma—'

'Fredericks,' I finished.

Juliette clicked her tongue at the surname, reeled back in and then some.

'Yeah. She got really sick. Properly. And suddenly I was seen differently. I was troublesome, or difficult, and people didn't have the patience for a dizzy spell or a sprained wrist anymore. But Emma, she was the *great grand tragedy*. She got everything. Every eye and every heart.'

'It's Munchausen's syndrome,' I said. 'You were jealous of her.'

'Not of *her*.' Cordelia hung her head. 'I was jealous that she was dying.'

'Munchausen's is psychological, it's not normally to do with money,' I said. 'Which means—'

'The money was Gran's idea.'

'I shovelled peanuts my whole life with nothing to show for it,' Laverna said, but Cordelia yelled over her.

'Let me speak, damn it! Let me say this for *once*!' She breathed in several deep breaths, then spoke more softly. 'I'm sorry. I want to get this out. Gran helped me with all the fiddly stuff. Paying off the doctor, duplicating Emma's medical records as my own. We're a similar age, similar build. Pop my name on her tests and we were off. It also gave me the advantage of having someone to mimic. If we had identical conditions, I just had to copy her. How she looked, how she moved. And yeah, the money was exciting. I thought I could take a trip to Spain, maybe get myself into university. That's why I started learning the language. But we made a mistake.'

'You chose FundAble as the platform, which doesn't release the money until you hit the target.' I explained it for her. 'And you set the target too high.'

Cordelia nodded. 'Gran said we'd reach it overnight. But we didn't, and then it was a slow crawl. We had to keep it up. I was tired of it. Just like with the broken arm, people's sympathies started to wane. There's always another, more tragic case around the corner. Some family gets poleaxed by a drunk driver or a farmer paralyses himself falling off a horse and again, it's like I'm standing in a corner. I was done. I was begging Gran to let me off. But we were so far in, and we were *so* close to the money. But then the heart.' She bit back tears. 'I don't know. I didn't realise this. But it took so long to reach the target that, in the background, we moved up some queue. Right to the top apparently. We got the call from the hospital a month ago: they were so happy for us. *Get to Brisbane, right now*, they said. *We have a heart*. Six-hour window.'

'It would all be over if we went into the hospital,' Laverna said. 'No money.'

'Getting cut open wasn't part of the deal,' Cordelia added, reminding Laverna of her priorities.

'You ran off the road on purpose,' I surmised. 'Laverna was a professional truck driver; you told me that this morning. Of course, that doesn't excuse you from having a prang, but it does make it less likely. You had to stall, delay having to front up at the hospital. If you got your own tests instead of putting your name on Emma's, you'd be exposed. Or, even worse, you'd get admitted and they'd start slicing.'

Both of them nodded.

'That was when I realised what we were really doing. I didn't know. Okay . . . maybe I did, but I pretended I didn't.' Cordelia burst into tears now. No one ran to comfort her. What she said next was nothing more than a choked whisper. 'They ran out of time.'

I remembered Gabriel writing: HEART'S GOT A TIMER ON IT. SIX HOURS. 'Ran out?' I asked.

'I thought it would just go to the next person. But no one got the heart at all. Because the hospital was waiting for us.'

A sombre mood settled over the room. Cordelia had earned what she wanted, everyone's attention.

'Please,' she begged, wiping away a huge glob of snot. Her cheeks were flushed red, blood pumping just fine from her tip-top heart. 'You have to understand. I didn't think it through. We were supposed to be done quickly, no risk of ever reaching this stage. I'm telling you now because I regret it.' She leaned forward, reached out to us. Even Gabriel turned away.

'You *are* sick,' Felix said quietly.

She collapsed back onto the pile of cushions, utterly defeated. 'I'm tired of dying. I just want to live now.'

Laverna's meltdown was much more internal. Whatever she felt about the revelation, she kept it to herself. She levelled her voice at me in the next stage of confession I was so familiar with: bargaining. 'We haven't taken any of the money yet. I'm too old, she's too young. We'll both do community service.'

I was pretty sure that they'd do more than that, but Laverna had to tell herself what she needed to, and her next question was fair.

'What's this all got to do with a bank robbery?'

'Is Emma Fredericks on that waiting list?' I asked.

A slow nod.

'She was second after me. We stole her heart,' Cordelia wailed from the cushions. 'I know from mimicking her that she's really sick. End of the line. I've probably killed her.'

The clock on the wall clicked past midnight. We'd now spent fourteen hours in this bank. People were fraying, and this discovery had ruptured any sense of community among the hostages. Personally, I felt like I had a major piece of the mystery clicked into place, possibly leading to another, but I still couldn't reconcile it with murder. Edward had donated money to Cordelia's FundAble campaign; I had the thankyou card in my pocket that I'd picked up from his desk. Perhaps he'd confronted Cordelia over it. Bryce Fredericks could have figured it out somehow, too. Were both of them killed to cover up the fraud? It was a possibility, brought down by one thing: I suspected Bryce hadn't known it was a lie.

Why? For one thing, he'd donated $150 that very morning. Not an amount worth murder by anyone's standards – otherwise we'd have a lot more dead parking inspectors. But finding out his daughter's donor heart had been ripped away? That could push someone to any extreme. *Who gets to choose who lives or who dies?* he'd said. *Some stupid list?*

Most telling, he'd used the same phrasing as Cordelia just had. *I've killed her.*

More clues clicked into place, and with them, more questions. What did Edward have to do with all this? Why this bank? I needed a little bit of time to figure it all out properly, but Juliette wouldn't stand for that, I knew.

I assessed the room: every remaining hostage was eyeing the others off. No one trusted each other anymore. Everybody knew there was a dead body in the vault by now. Someone had let Ditto go, I was sure. The words in his beak must be important enough to try to silence. *I am not a clue.* Our firebug was feeling the heat, so to speak. They were cleaning up their mess. The distrust hung thick.

'Given all this'—Winston broke the tension, meekly putting his hand up—'there's a spot going for next one out, right?'

CHAPTER 33

'It needs to be you,' I said to Juliette. We were sequestered in Winston's office picking over cold pizza leftovers, under the pretext of discussing with our fictional thief who would be the next out given Cordelia's revelations. Winston had retrieved and delivered a dollar from the vault, trailed by a curious Eric, whose interest had been diminished to queasiness and regret by the time they returned with the coin. We were figuring out our next lie. In everyone else's heads, the bounty had been delivered and we should all be free. We had to break it to them that it would not be so simple. The hostages had rolled out their sleeping bags and lain down, though I doubted many were sleeping. Cordelia had barricaded herself in the boardroom, bawling, and I expected her howls were keeping most people awake.

I'd checked in with Tobias using the voice-changer, telling him there would be another hostage coming out. He told me Remy was okay, though oddly tight-lipped, both of which were a relief. There seemed to be audible activity on the radio behind his voice, and I figured there was about a fifty per cent chance the police would try to come in quietly in the pre-dawn darkness while they thought

I was asleep, or at least sluggish. I hoped radioing in with the promise of another hostage would hold them off until the exchange, or, at the very least, remind them I was awake.

Juliette shook her head at my statement. 'You have to send the kid. I'll go along with everything but that.'

'I don't know if he's innocent yet.' I was flicking through *Chemical Insights: Junior Edition*. 'Half an hour ago you wanted me to send Cordelia.' Some materials had whole chapters about them, others merely paragraphs. Unfortunately there was no chapter on spontaneous combustion. They must save that for the senior edition.

'She can lie about being sick, but he can't lie about being fifteen,' Juliette said, but stopped short of pushing further. 'And what about: *if she leaves the bank, she dies?*'

There was a chapter on gold, which gave me a rundown of the basic properties. This is where I learned that information about pyrite, or fool's gold, by the way. I'm not one of those detectives who can pluck such facts from their rattling brains like calling a game of bingo. I leafed through to the chapter on iron, hoping to reconcile the spectrometer report I'd found in Felix's locker.

'It's the only way. And I know you can handle yourself, and I'll protect those in here. But we need someone on the outside who can go and find Cordelia's doctor,' I argued back.

'You've reeled me in, okay? I'm interested.'

'You were always interested,' I teased. 'Admit it.'

'People bursting into flames does tend to be interesting. And you're right that something's going on here. But this is still the wrong way to go about it. A *kid*, Ern.'

'I won't use the gun anymore. I don't like it anyway. It feels—'

'Heavy,' Juliette finished for me, her voice weighted. She'd held it – hell, she'd tried to fire it.

I scanned the chapter about iron. There was a breakout box on the page, a picture of a skillet with a little bubble that read

Your parents might use cast iron products at home! Exercise: Check your kitchen cupboards and see what you can find! I sighed. Sherlock Holmes had a wall of encyclopedias to help him solve crimes; I had a textbook for children.

'You know my dad was a thief. Petty stuff, not banks. But I understand him a little better now. Because when I was wearing the mask, I could take what I needed, when I wanted. When we opened that vault, I kept asking myself: if I'd been on my own, would I have taken something? Money's the reason we're all the way out here, chasing a bank loan, and it's just right there in front of us? It felt so wrong.'

'You didn't like it.'

'I *did* like it,' I admitted. 'That's what I hated.'

I handed over the book for Juliette to read the page I was on. It detailed the properties of cast iron. It was made with a majority of iron, a dash of carbon and silicon. All three materials were on the spectrometer report.

'So Felix was testing cast iron? The vault is steel, as are these safes.' She looked at the window. 'The bars on the windows? They rust like cast iron might.'

'That's what I was thinking,' I said. 'But why test the windows? And why is there gold in it? Whatever he tested was one per cent gold. Not much, but it was there.'

'Trace amounts?' She shrugged, handing back the textbook.

I ran my finger down the index for *flammable*. It was all kind of meaningless to me. 'Gold doesn't seem to be incendiary,' I said. 'What I can't figure out is why the murders are the same. Both spontaneous combustion. Given it's so rare – well, not just rare, but impossible – it would be equally impossible for them to have been committed by different hands and yet look the same.'

'So the same person did it.'

'If someone dumped Ed's body, how did they open the vault to get him in there? If he was moved with the wool lift, he'd be unconscious, if not dead. What if Edward locked himself in the vault?'

'That means he set *himself* on fire. It's simple: Michelle's the lead suspect. She's the only one we know for sure was in the vault. And she could get back in.'

'But she's also the only one with a valid reason for being there. Murdering her client would be a really bad business plan. And she didn't take any money. Left a huge trail of evidence. I believe her story.'

'Me too.' Juliette reached over and closed the book. 'Send both Eric and me out.'

'I need to ask him more questions.'

'So ask him, then let him go.'

'Give me your hand.' I took the bank's key to the safety deposit boxes out of my pocket and laid it in her palm. 'I'll go talk to Eric. See if I can convince myself he can go. At the moment, the only ones I can set loose are you and Michelle. She was hiding it, but she was just doing her job.' Then I took out a second golden key and put it on top. It had a little number: 149. 'Meanwhile, I need you to open Father Gabriel's safety deposit box.'

'Gabriel gave this to you?' She frowned.

'I borrowed it.'

'You pickpocketed a *priest*?'

'He wants to protect something. Badly enough to vote for violence at the start. And he's in a stoush with Winston. I think there's more than a jar of water he's keeping in the safe.'

Juliette looked doubtful.

'And I need the sabre mask back, just in case.' I registered her grimace and resorted to begging. 'One more interview, one more lock opened, and then I promise I'll stop doing stupid things.' I reached out and touched her hand. '*Bone-headed* things.'

She laughed as she realised that everything she'd said about me, she'd actually said to my face. 'You know that stuff I said, it was just for show.'

'Uh-huh.'

'To stop you getting more involved. I was doing you a favour. If Bryce thought you were a rubbish detective, I figured he'd let you go.'

'Sure.'

She held out the mask. 'This *is* kinda bone-headed though.'

'Yeah.' I took it. 'You're forgiving me?'

'No.' She closed her palm around the two keys and stood up. 'But at least I'm sure you won't lie to me again. Because now we know who'd win in a fight.'

CHAPTER 34

Eric was easy to find. I just had to follow the sniffling into one of the offices. Everyone else was asleep – even Cordelia had run herself dry of tears and conked out. Eric was curled into a sleeping bag, nose pressed against the cold glass of a window, staring out at the police operation down on the street. The floodlights were now switched on, fierce white suns in the night. The butterflies didn't know what to do; they swirled in the beams. I'd decided against the mask. Eric saw me enter and wiped his eyes, but he didn't look at me.

'Hey, mate,' I said softly. 'Everything okay?'

Eric thudded his forehead against the glass.

'We're working on getting you out,' I lied, sitting down in a spare chair. 'I'm hoping you can help me understand a few things. Mind if I ask you some questions?'

'Sure. I guess.' He kept his gaze outside. 'Provided you don't dangle me out of a window like the French guy.'

'I promise to keep your arms and torso inside the ride at all times.' I held my hands up in surrender. 'Are you watching for your dad down there?'

Eric pointed at the glass. 'There he is.' He turned away. 'Who's next? Now some of us have been miraculously healed.' At my pause, he added, 'It's okay, I know it's not me.'

'Michelle, probably. And Juliette.'

'I've seen *Titanic*. Isn't the phrase "women *and* children first"?'

'I'm not the one calling the shots.'

He turned back to the window, his sigh blasting a haze of fog. 'I really thought he'd choose me. I'm such an idiot.' He thunked his head against the glass again. This time the window shuddered in the frame. 'I should have known he wouldn't.'

'Bryce?'

'Who the hell is Bryce? I meant my dad.'

'Eric, your dad's not the one doing the choosing. He's been trying to get Cordelia out – he doesn't know what we now do, so she was first on his list. You must understand that. And it's the man in the fencing mask making the calls anyway.'

'If Dad really wanted me out, he'd have made demands.' Tears had started to roll. He knocked on the glass. 'He's out there drinking coffee, joking. I can see it. Everyone just standing around. Can you believe that, laughing? No one cares.'

'You know he asked me to look out for you? He cares.' I slid off the chair and sat next to Eric on the floor. He scrunched up his knees to make room, folding like a worm in his sleeping bag. 'You really think if he had a choice he wouldn't kick down that door and get you himself? He knows you can handle it. That you can do what needs to be done.' I squeezed Eric's shoulder. 'The reason you're not out there is only because he knows you're strong enough to be in here.'

This stemmed the tears. Eric turned to me. 'Maybe. What did you want to ask me?'

'I had some questions about *Buccaneers*. I'm not much of a gamer. I knew you were good, but I saw on TV you're ranked first for juniors in the world? That's impressive.'

'Yeah, I guess.' He shrugged, but I could see he was trying to hide his pleasure at being highlighted on the news. 'It's not easy, you know. A lot of people think it's just being a couch potato. Dad's probably pleased I'm in here – toughen me up. He doesn't respect what I do, even when I make more money than both my parents combined.'

'Your father told me he was very proud of everything you've achieved,' I said. He hadn't; rather he'd said that I was doing him a favour making Eric miss his tournament. But Eric didn't need to know that. 'Wait, you make more money than your parents?'

'Easily.' He seemed confused I didn't understand. 'What part of Number One are you not grasping? I was on the university team at *thirteen*. LeBron James wasn't that good.'

'So it's prize money? Sponsorships? Your father said it's just like regular sports.'

'It *is* a sport.' Eric rolled his eyes.

I'd offended him. 'Yeah, that's what I meant. I get it. So it's got everything real sports has? You get paid to play? Tournaments, trophies?'

'Yeah. Obviously.' His voice had the tone teenagers take when they feel they're talking to someone *ancient*. Like, forty. '*Fortnite* World Cup pays three million dollars.' He must have seen my jaw drop. '*Buccaneers* is a little less popular.'

'Gambling?' I asked.

'I'm not old enough to bet,' he said, confused.

'I mean, can people bet on *Fortnite*? On *Buccaneers* matches?'

'Oh, yeah. Totally. You can bet on anything these days. There're probably bets on this robbery. Next out the door. Over-under dead hostages.' He realised I wasn't laughing. 'Lighten up.'

'How does the ranking work? You said you were on the university team?'

'You play, and win, on your own. *Team* is more like a sponsor. The rankings are individual. Earn enough ranking points, move up a competition level.'

'You must be close to moving up, I imagine, being number one.'

'I enter most matches as favourite,' he said, not humbly. 'Missing tonight's tournie doesn't help, though.'

'But Ben Huxley beat you.' I threw it off, almost as an aside, just to see how he'd react. The first-place prize, the gold bar in the red velvet box, was on Edward's shelf.

Eric drew his piggybank towards himself, second prize of silver coins inside.

I doubled down on my cluelessness. 'Wow. First place against the Numero Uno. He must have been really good.'

This tipped Eric over. 'Ben Huxley *cheated*.'

'I thought you said you were friends?'

'We were. We were.' He backpedalled, not wanting to speak badly of his dead friend. 'Friendly rivals, at least. And competition is good – we pushed each other, up and up. When one of us was playing well, it gave the other the drive to beat them. But I was always better. I was number one. He'd never cracked the top hundred.'

'Until he started cheating,' I finished for him.

'He used an aimbot.'

'Aimbot?'

'A computer program that helps aim your gun for you. Basically, you can't miss.'

'Aren't there rules around that kind of thing?' I figured, if Esports was a real sport, an aimbot would be the equivalent of performance enhancement drugs. 'Advantages wouldn't be allowed?'

'Of course they're not allowed.' Eric genuinely seemed upset by this. 'Are you asking stupid questions on purpose? It's why Ben killed himself.'

'Killed *himself*?' This threw me. 'He was shot by the police at home, wasn't he?'

'Yeah, but he swatted himself.' He sighed at my expression. 'Am I going to have to explain every word to you?'

'*Super Mario*, remember?' I thumbed my chest.

'*Swatted*. As in, *hit by SWAT*.' We don't have SWAT in Australia, but I didn't think Eric would care for the correction, and I wanted to keep his tongue's momentum. '*Buccaneers* is a competitive *online* shooter. You play at home. Not on one machine like you'd have had to at the arcade or the milk bar or whatever.' That one felt deliberately cruel.

'I grew up with computers,' I said.

Eric wrinkled his nose like he didn't believe me. 'Think about it. If someone wants to mess up a game, they call in a bogus tip about something suss, the SWAT team rocks up, hears gunshots from the television and kicks down the door. You can't win a game when you've got your hands cuffed behind your back.'

'You mean like calling in a bomb threat so you don't have to take a school exam?'

'If that's what you did back in your day, sure.'

'Just to be clear, *my day* is not the stone age.' I considered the information. 'Someone could have "swatted" Ben if they wanted him to lose, right? Like hypothetically, if someone wanted to be certain of a particular outcome.'

'I'm telling you, he did it to himself. Swatting is usually just harmless fun. A silly prank. But he was playing the game without headphones on, volume up loud. The gunshots and grenade blasts made the cops all antsy. Why would he do that unless he *wanted* them to shoot him? It's his fault, man. Totally his fault.'

'But why would he want that?'

'Because he was a cheater. His reputation was done for. He wasn't even in the university competition anymore.'

'How did you know he was cheating?'

Eric said it with complete sincerity. 'Because he beat me.'

Juliette was in the foyer, holding a little red leather book and a jar of water. The jar was larger than I expected, holding about a litre of holiness, with a wire latch on top. I filled her in as she handed both to me.

'It's a ledger,' she said, slapping the notebook in my hand. 'Money.'

'Wagers, I'll wager.'

I opened it to be proven correct. Inside were neatly ruled columns. On the left, a dollar amount that varied from hundreds into the thousands; in the middle, a smaller amount, one or two dollars with a decimal; and on the right, a date. I knew what I was looking for immediately and turned the pages until I got to entries marked 2024. There it was: 2 September. The date Ben Huxley died.

$220,000 | $2.15 | 02.09.24

'See this bet?' I pointed to it. 'A two-hundred-and-twenty-grand stake, at odds of two dollars and fifteen cents. That pays out, what, four-seventy-five?'

'Four-seventy-three. Struggling with your counting today,' Juliette said. I had, of course, counted the coins on the table wrong, as $4.80, not $4.40, earlier, which Juliette had also corrected me on. She was keeping score. 'Betting on what?'

'On a video game, I'm thinking. This was placed on the day Ben Huxley died,' I explained. I leafed back through the ledger and found the largest sum.

$300,000 | $1.20 | 18.03.24

Three hundred grand, on 18 March 2024, the same date as Ben's first-place trophy, but at much lower odds. $1.20. 'And this one, this was supposed to be a sure thing. Low odds, huge bet.

I'll bet *you* three hundred grand this was a bet placed on a game of *Buccaneers* played between Eric Cuthbert and Ben Huxley. One that Eric wasn't supposed to lose. Certainly not to a player ranked outside the top hundred.'

'How does a priest have so much money?' Juliette asked.

'I'm not sure, but I *am* sure that he was running out of it. Winston said he was cutting him off.'

Another surety: that Gabriel had a bet on tonight's tournament. It wasn't written in the ledger, because it had been trapped in the safety deposit box inside a locked vault the last two days, but it neatly explained the real reason why Gabriel had voted in favour of attacking the thief. I'd always known the holy water story was full of holes. Now I had an alternative explanation: he'd wanted the robbery over quickly so Eric would be home in time for a tournament Gabriel had bet on. It was in his interest for this robbery to end as soon as possible. Did that include getting rid of the bank robber?

Juliette was watching me analyse all this. I noticed something. Her pockets were bulging.

'Don't tell me that's—'

THE SEVENTH HEIST: FIVE THOUSAND AND SIXTY DOLLARS

(WHICH JULIETTE HAS PROMISED TO PUT BACK)

—cash?' I finished. Incriminating colourful triangles poked out the top of her right pants pocket. Red, yellow: twenties and fifties. Her left had a cylindrical bulge.

'I'll put it back,' Juliette said. 'Promise.'

'How much is it?'

'Five grand, couple of loose twenties.'

'You're stealing?'

'Oh, I'm getting a lecture on bank robbing?' Juliette played offended. 'It's not for *me*. If Laverna and Cordelia paid off a doctor to forge medical records over another patient's, I figured the same doc might be open to a little financial lubrication if we need to learn anything.'

'What about the coin rolls in your other pocket?'

She smirked and pulled out a gleaming silver cylinder. Not a coin roll but about the same size. Wordlessly, she had me follow her across the foyer to the gold nugget, where she waved the cylinder over it. She flourished her hands like a magician, as if to say *See, nothing happens*. Then she headed to the rusted teapot on its plinth. The teapot basically leapt off its podium and into her hand, leaving a red trail of rust behind, unmoved in decades. She did a little bow, *ta da*, then pried the teapot off the magnet and placed it back on the plinth. She held the cylinder far enough away for it not to reconnect. 'Magnet. Found it on the floor of the vault.'

'It's strong,' I marvelled, taking it from her. 'How'd we miss that?'

'No idea. Magnets scramble digital systems. Maybe Michelle used it on the security cameras.'

'Or maybe it has something to do with someone getting out of the locked vault?'

'Your guess is as good as mine. At least we know the nugget's not cast iron with a gold leaf overlay, given it's not magnetic. Seems real to me,' she said.

I hovered Winston's pen over the cylinder. It tilted a tiny bit at the nib, a replaceable ink cartridge with metal inside, but the body itself stayed unmoved. Real gold.

I refocused on the ledger, pointed at the three-hundred-thousand-dollar amount on 18 March. 'This was a bet on hot favourite Eric Cuthbert winning a particular video game. A game he lost to an underdog. This one six months later'—I pointed at the two-hundred-and-twenty-thousand-dollar entry—'I think is again a bet on Eric Cuthbert.'

'His odds have gotten worse.'

'Because Ben Huxley beat him, usurping him in the rankings. So Eric's now the underdog. It means if he wins, there's a better payout. Four hundred and seventy-three thousand, to be precise. Enough to almost recoup the loss.'

'You seem confident.' Juliette didn't bother hiding a smile. 'That's a first for today. Are we building up to a parlour scene?'

'I'd bet three hundred grand on it.'

'You don't have three hundred grand,' Juliette mocked and patted her pockets. 'Want to borrow some?'

'Neither does Gabriel, I suspect,' I said. 'He's in a hole and he's digging up. Gambling addicts run a predictable playbook. Just like Remy's scam catching up to him, Gabriel's borrowed or stolen money he can't afford to lose and used it to place another massive bet. Which is why he had to win that bet on the second of September. At all costs.'

CHAPTER 35

Juliette's exchange went seamlessly. A peck on the cheek that was less frosty than I deserved, and a pair of black gloved hands guided her out of the ground-floor window into the night.

The window Juliette had squeezed through was dark. I suddenly felt quite alone.

Two thieves released now: Juliette's stuffed pockets, Remy's insurance fraud.

Seven suspects left. Three known thieves among them: Michelle, a professional; Laverna and Cordelia, con women.

I'm whittling it down like this because I still believe that something worth stealing was worth killing for. It's a handy framework to hang my deduction from. Of course, I still didn't know what Bryce had truly come to steal in the first place. The unluckiest bank robber of all time: burgling a bank that can't open its vault and being killed to protect a secret inside it. That's a tough day at the office.

As for the remaining thieves I've considered: I technically stole a gold pen, but that's hardly a candidate; Winston may have stolen something (or *everything*, as Felix put it); and Felix himself, I suspected, had taken something in revenge. I'll get to that.

Then there was Gabriel. All that money he was losing had to come from somewhere. I headed upstairs to find him.

Gabriel had ransacked Cordelia's cushion-palace and constructed himself a bed in Edward's office; now that it was minus a talking bird, it was a suitable bedroom. Michelle and Felix were in the main room, inadvertently creeping towards each other in sleep, while Cordelia and Laverna were in the boardroom. Eric had stopped sniffling. I was glad he was getting some sleep.

It was tempting to shake Gabriel awake, maybe splash him to life with the holy water. Though, while comic, I figured that would be sacrilegious, even for me. Given I've now drunk and urinated the water, I guess I've crossed that line.

I'd gone in circles on whether to go as the thief or myself, and settled again on maskless. I didn't need a gun to get what I wanted here. But when I gently closed the door to Edward's office and leaned over to shake Gabriel, I noticed that next to the sleeping priest lay his notebook and thick black marker.

I realised something obvious: Gabriel had been writing things down all day and then flipping the page over in the book. But, of course, he hadn't only been talking to me. I'd missed plenty of conversations. I picked up the book and opened it.

Goodnight.

A few more pages back.

That was crazy!

There was a murmur beside me as Gabriel rolled on his back. His lips fluttered. I wondered if talking in your sleep counts as breaking a vow of silence. A ring of gold light from the window framed the safe, the sky blooded by the coming day. I flipped further through the book.

2 Easy!

That one was to me. A few more pages.

KEEP YOUR FUCKING MOUTH SHUT.

I stared at it for a long time. When I looked up from the page, it was straight into Gabriel's open, staring eyes.

He was awake. Watching me.

'Now's the part where I start talking, isn't it?' he said.

THE EIGHTH HEIST: A RED SCRIPT, A LOCK OF HAIR AND A COFFEE CUP

CHAPTER 36

'It's been a while since I've done this.' Gabriel rotated his jaw as he sat up, relearning his tongue.

Of course, I'm sure you expected he was going to break the vow at some point. If we're following the rules of murder mysteries, the very presence of a silent party demands it. His voice was raspy, as if it had been hidden at the back of a cupboard, covered in dust, and needed to be blown off and polished. He had a surprisingly high-pitched tone, soft and youthful. Though whether that was the norm or from disuse I couldn't tell.

'Almost a year, actually,' he continued. '*Hmmph*. So that's what I sound like.' He realised I was waiting and blew air out of his nose. 'Okay. Okay. I knew this was coming as soon as I realised you'd pickpocketed my deposit box key. You have the ledger, I assume?'

'Why didn't you try to stop me?'

'Because I didn't kill Edward. And I thought if I made a scene you'd think I did.'

'Guess what?'

'You accuse, I deny. Is that about right for this bit?' He swatted a hand lazily through the air. 'Let's get on with it.'

Slightly annoyed that he was correct, but not willing to diverge from my planned confrontation, I opened the ledger and read to him. 'In March last year you placed a three-hundred-thousand-dollar bet on Eric to win an almost unlosable game, which he wound up losing to Ben Huxley. Like I suspected when you drew that unfinished dollar sign and almost confessed the debt you owed, it's about money. Losing that bet put you well out of pocket. Like all addicts – and trust me, I know – you thought the way out was to keep going. You just needed one big score to win it all back. And Eric was now looking at some pretty healthy odds given he'd slipped down the rankings. So you placed another extravagant bet on Eric. Except you couldn't leave anything to chance now. You had to be certain Eric would win. Sound familiar?'

'You think *I* swatted Ben?' His mouth hung open. 'To win a bet? Wow – you've got this all backwards. I'm a priest, for heaven's sakes.' He smacked his lips, worked his mouth. 'My mouth is dry. Talking's . . . harder than I remember.'

'I know where I can get you some water.'

'I'm not kidding about that jar.' He waved a finger at me. 'Don't touch it.'

I held up the book. 'You're telling me this isn't a betting ledger? That you didn't vote to attack the thief because you wanted Eric home for his tournament tonight?'

'The opposite. You're right on both counts and still wrong.' He snatched the book from me. 'There was money riding on tonight's tournament. Plus, Eric can qualify for ackle.'

'ACL. Australian Championship League.' I repeated Eric's words from earlier. 'University division for Eric, right?'

'And it'll stay that way given he's just missed the finals. And yes, this is my ledger. But I'm not betting huge sums.'

'You're the bookie?' My mind rattled through the consequences of this information. 'You were taking the bets.'

'Yes, and I made an absolute motza when Ben beat Eric the first time. No reason to kill him. Or my cash cow.'

'Your cash cow?'

'Who do you think was placing the bets?' Gabriel scoffed. 'Man, you should try this silence thing every once in a while. It really helps you listen.'

'Edward.' I put it together. The two million dollars he'd lied about investing in a television show. 'Edward bet on Eric *against* his own son?' I clarified.

'A win is a win.' Gabriel seemed smug at my shock. 'It's just odds. Emotion's how you lose. Like detective work.'

'I don't believe you,' I said, after turning it around in my mind. 'You just brought up the swatting without my mentioning it. How did you know I was going to ask about that?'

'Because you had the ledger. And it's my business to know about swatting. It's quite an issue in the market. You've heard of *Call of Duty*?'

I nodded. And it didn't even have an Italian plumber in it.

'Swatting was rife for a while. Everyone was pranking each other.'

'Eric told me it was harmless fun,' I said. 'I guess it plays havoc with the betting markets, though.'

'It's tantamount to match fixing, not that anyone would treat a bookie as a victim.'

'Especially an illegal one.'

'I'm not saying gambling doesn't ruin lives. But explain to me why it's legal when a multi-million-dollar corporation empties your pockets, and not when I do it?' Gabriel shook his head. 'Swatting is a serious crime. Every time police send out a response team it costs tens of thousands of dollars, taking resources from those in real emergencies, eating up time and money. And that's before people started dying. That *Call of Duty* game – maybe ten years ago someone got killed in America over a bet that totalled one dollar and fifty cents. You think robbing a bank for a buck is stupid, try committing murder over one and a half.'

'Who died in that case? The winner or the loser?'

'Neither. There was a stoush. One player threatened another, who gave them a random address in reply and basically said *Come get me*. The guy who died, he wasn't even playing. Popped out his front door for the newspaper and it was lights out. So yeah, I was familiar, and I thought it was pretty obvious what happened when I heard about Ben. Only I—' He cleared his throat. 'Forget about it.' He chuckled softly. 'What do you know, seems I talk too much.'

'We're past *Forget about it*. You've been silent for almost a year. And now you break it to try and tell me the truth. Is this a vow of commitment, or repentance? One year's silence. One year since Ben's death. They add up. You took Edward's money and backed him into a corner. You suspect Edward called in the swatting so he'd win his money back. And that makes it your fault.'

It occurred to me that a lot of people felt responsible for Ben Huxley's death: Winston, for buying the sound system that made the gunshots sound so loud and real; Eric, for ruining Ben's gaming career by revealing him as a cheater; and now Gabriel, thinking he'd led a desperate gambler to chase a win by deadly sabotage.

'I don't have any proof or anything. Part of me doesn't want to believe he'd kill his own boy, and over a bet. But then again'—he weighed his hands like scales—'a *dollar fifty*.'

I was trying to figure out if Edward had just made a horrible mistake. If he thought the police would simply pull his son away from the game. He might not have realised the danger. I certainly wouldn't have, before this conversation. Swatting seemed an extreme solution. Why not just cut the modem? Flick off the power? Unless he had to be *sure*.

'Ben was winning the game when he died, did you know that?' Gabriel said, as if he could read my thoughts. 'Ed would have been desperate.'

'I figure even an illegal bookie would have to refund that match regardless. Surely it's a forfeit?'

'Of course I gave Edward his stake back. He'd just lost his son! But he was still three hundred thousand down from the first wager. Which he hadn't paid, by the way.' Gabriel wriggled out of his sleeping bag, kicking it away from him. 'I know you don't believe me. And that you think I'm vile. You know that hundred-grand gold-brick trophy on his shelf?'

'Yeah.'

'That's mine. Collateral on the debt. But I let him hang on to it, because of Ben – I'm not a monster.'

I stopped short of explaining that dragging hundreds of thousands of dollars out of this man, which had possibly driven him to hurt his family and then himself, and then letting him hang on to a symbol of that, did, indeed, make him a bit of a monster. 'Why not bet online?'

'First of all, it's traceable. Second, you think someone who's slapping down six figures a bet on a university game is allowed to bet online? That's like taking action on three-legged races down at the school carnival.'

'Why did you take such a large amount of money for each bet?' I asked. 'That's risky for you, surely?'

He answered too quickly, like he was waiting for the question. 'I'd been watching Ben's Twitch streams. Kid was good. Really good. Sometimes the rankings don't match the form.'

'These are children, not racehorses. One of them is dead.'

Gabriel stood, then ran his hand over the letter magnets on Edward's safe. Ben's last words. His voice thickened. 'Why do you think I've been silent for a year?'

I found it hard to summon sympathy. 'Winston thinks Ed invested that money, the money he lost with you, in Remy's television show.'

'That makes sense,' Gabriel said appreciatively. 'A producer comes into town, tosses around cash like it's candy – skipped the collection plate, by the way – so what better cover to say your money's all tied up?'

'And he said Edward had lost a couple of million. That's more than he owes you.'

Gabriel shrugged. 'Do alcoholics drink at the one pub?'

That did make a certain amount of sense. 'If Winston doesn't know about Edward's gambling, why is he messing with your finances?'

'Of course Winston knows about Ed's gambling. I told him. Edward kicking in my mausoleum was the last straw – he must have been drunk and uppity – so I ratted him out to his brother. Well, as much as Winston would listen, anyway. He obviously doesn't know the scale of it if he thinks Ed was investing the money he was losing. Why do you think I was trying to get in to see him? Winston wants me to shut up about it. Puts his fingers in his ears over his brother's gambling and vandalism, says he won't hear another word on either, and flexes by restricting my cash flow. Which means I can't take new bets. Dirty tactics.'

I thought about the plastic-wrapped toy trucks. Winston, having to be a protector so Edward never lacked a plaything. It sounded to me like Winston had been tightening Gabriel's finances specifically to stop Edward's spiral. And he was doing it from afar so as not to shame Edward.

'Have you been inside the mausoleum since it was broken open? Did you happen to see a . . .' I hesitated because the question sounded stupid. 'Tunnel?'

'I mean, I looked in. There's dust and concrete, and now some kids have thrown some beer cans in. I don't know why there'd be a *tunnel*?'

'Me neither. Almost done. Did Bryce Fredericks bet with you?'

Gabriel shook his head. 'I don't know the guy.'

'Who did you tell to'—I read it off the notebook—'*keep your fucking mouth shut*? That's certainly the most aggressive homily I've ever heard.'

'Winston.' He looked like he'd picked the name from a rolodex of hostages. Whether this was because he was lying, or whether he'd told multiple people to zip it and was narrowing it down, I couldn't tell. 'I thought the gambling would give me a motive.'

'And it would also give away that you'd been in Edward's office before the robbery.' I walked over to the photocopier and lifted the hundred sheets of blank paper from the tray. 'Who copies blank pages? No one. But in film and television, if there's a confidential script it will be printed on red paper – it's called a *red script* – so that it can't be copied. There's not enough contrast between the colour of the paper and the colour of the text for an old machine like this to pick up. Didn't stop you trying though, did it? Because you wanted to sell multiple copies of the script. That's how you take the bets. You launder them through eBay.'

Gabriel's jaw tightened. Or cramped. It was hard to tell, given the muscles had been out of use for so long.

'You gave it away when you showed me Laurence Birch's personal items listed for sale on eBay,' I explained, 'though you didn't know you were giving anything away because the robbery hadn't happened yet. You were genuinely curious about Birch's potential murder, figuring my presence was to do with him. Fifteen hundred dollars for a coffee cup? A lock of hair? Birch is famous, but not that famous. A piece of his gum goes for fifty dollars, not five hundred. This is junk sold at an inflated price. *You're* CelebrityEstateSale69. You can't handle money directly, so you find things that *seem* valuable to the untrained eye and inflate them to astronomical prices. The bidders are your gamblers. You sold Edward a collectible Hess tanker truck, worth no more than a few thousand, for two hundred and twenty. That matches the bet he placed with you. I assume you sold him something else for three hundred, six months previously.'

'First edition of *The Adventures of Sherlock Holmes*,' Gabriel muttered. 'Everything's real, if overvalued. It has to be convincing.'

'And you came up here while Juliette and I were meeting with Winston, didn't you?'

'I couldn't get Winston's time of day, so I thought I'd cash in on the collateral and flog back the gold bar. The truck's worthless, I can relist the books. I've been in Edward's office enough that it doesn't look odd me going in. And it's not like he can report the gold bar stolen without admitting his gambling. I picked up the gold bar and . . .' He hesitated, but he was past lying. 'There was red on it. It got on my hand. I wiped it off, but then I worried what it would mean if it was blood, and the gold was in my possession with DNA on it. And I hadn't seen Edward in a couple of days. I think I knew he was dead, instinctually, right then. So I left it.' Gabriel seemed to know it was a weak excuse, but also a believable one. If he had used it to bash Edward's head in, he had more motive to take it than leave it in the office.

'But you didn't want to leave the office empty-handed. You needed a top-up of artefacts to "sell". It's hard to find the genuine article, but Birch gave you that opportunity. So you decided to copy the script while you were here. Or try anyway – all you got was blank pages, so you left them in the printer tray. You stole a few other things when you read Laurence Birch's last rites, didn't you? A lock of hair. The coffee cup.'

'Thou shalt not steal.' Gabriel raised his eyebrows. 'I believe the technical term is *borrowed*.'

CHAPTER 37

The pen is starting to scratch – sorry about any starbursts of ink in the margins while I try to get it going. I am feeling cosy again, warm. The jar has stopped bubbling, my urine bled of oxygen. I've spent what I've earned. It's a race between ink and air now.

We are getting close to The End. Figuratively, in terms of the story I have to tell, and literally, for me. Annoyingly, my suspect list seems to keep growing rather than shrinking. At this stage of a mystery I should be whittling them down. But every lie I uncover only gives new motive: a priest after a quick buck, a gambling syndicate betting on high school students. Another thief to add to the pile. No wonder I can't solve it.

It's even harder when people keep lying to me. Gabriel might have been out of practice talking, but mistruths slid off his tongue like a pro. I didn't know what to trust. Felix and Winston were at war, and I had an inkling what about, but I needed one more piece. And there were the obvious lies. Cordelia's I'd busted wide open, but Laverna had told me some snaky ones too. When I'd exposed her con, she'd complained about shovelling peanuts for a living, not transporting dangerous munitions, which she'd told me earlier. Sometimes it's the small lies that crack things wide open.

'This is your requested wake-up call, thank you for staying at Hotel Huxley.' Tobias came through the radio beside me. I was sitting at reception in the early dawn light, the foyer golden, shimmering. I'd collected everything I had in the plastic bag that Tobias had handed over, way back near the start of all this.

'I'm up,' I said, donning my bank-robber digital voice.

'How is everyone doing?'

'Good. Thanks for not blasting in the windows last night.'

'Pleasure. Look'—Tobias lowered his voice, and it sounded like he stepped away from something, cupping his hand over the speaker—'I'm on borrowed time here. I've been fighting the good fight, and your drip-feeding of hostages has helped, but the SRT are getting ready to come in. My job is to protect *everyone* in there. Including you.'

'I appreciate that,' I said abruptly. Then clicked the button back down and added, 'Whatever happens, thank you. I know you could have shot up the place twenty minutes in. I know you're not doing it for me, but thanks for being good at your job. It's nice to have had someone to talk to.'

'Had?' His voice quivered for the first time. 'Don't talk in the past tense, mate. It makes me jumpy.'

'Sorry. I meant it. But don't worry, I'm not going to do anything stupid. Well, anything *more* stupid.'

'Let me buy you time. How about two more hostages? Cordelia. I know you say she's not sick, but let us examine her. And Eric, I think, would be appropriate at this stage, my self-interest aside. Maybe the priest, as a show of good faith, excuse the pun.'

It was persuasive, but I couldn't agree. Time meant nothing if I didn't have the suspects. I'd already started to regret letting Remy go.

Tobias persisted. 'Or, how about this? Everyone comes out, I go in. No guns. We'll sort something out.'

'Selfless,' I said. 'Do they have a training module on last-ditch ploys?'

'I saw it in a movie once.' He sighed heavily. 'Mate, they're coming in. An hour, maybe two, tops. I'm trying to help you here. Think it over?'

'Yeah.' I looked at the damage around me. Flipped tables, ripped apart and used for armour. A hole in the ceiling, just the one bullet brought for the whole robbery. If I thought, on entering yesterday morning, that this place was the Huxleys' monument to themselves, well, now it was a memorial to me. A museum of my mistakes.

Forgive the melancholy: I'll be dead in a few more minutes.

'While you consider it,' Tobias crackled, 'I've got Juliette here. Says she needs to speak to Ernest.'

'I'll go get him.' I made a show of walking across the room; no idea why. Perhaps I thought my footsteps on the tiles might click audibly. Then, as myself, I said, 'Hey.'

'I assume they can't record this,' Juliette said, in a whisper implying she'd stepped away. 'But let's play it safe.'

'Okay.'

'How are things in there?'

'Everyone's safe. The, uh . . . *thief* has been going around doing interviews. Father Gabriel talked. Literally.'

'Like, actually? With noise?'

'Yeah. The thief cornered him pretty good. It was impressive – this bank robber knows what he's doing.' If I have a superpower, it's the ability to hear an eye roll through a radio. I got to the point.

'Gabriel's not the one doing the betting, he's *taking* the bets. It was Edward placing the biggest bets down. How'd you go with the dodgy doctor?'

She lowered her voice a little. 'A grand to get him out of bed, but legal threats did the rest of the job. His name's Ivan. You sure I can't keep the other four? Could boost the honeymoon funds.'

'Jul—'

'Kidding. Okay. He duplicated Emma Fredericks' medical records, that's for sure. Five grand's the going rate. He'll shill you opioids – medical marijuana too – for a price. Thought I was a junkie when I banged on his window to wake him up. Anyway, because these weren't fake tests per se, but real records with Cordelia's name on them instead of the actual patient, that's why she went into the system and found herself on the transplant registry. I don't think they would have willingly signed up to something so stupid, which is why Cordelia wanted to back out after they screwed Emma out of her transplant a while back. Those two have only been in town less than two years and they must have been bouncing in from some other scam. Lying low. Or planning this. Laverna's not her real name by the way, it's the Roman goddess of thieves – God, we should have seen that! She paid the doctor.'

'One hundred and fifty grand isn't much for over a year on one con.'

'It was supposed to be quick, remember. They screwed up by setting the funding target too high. Sunk cost fallacy: keep pushing through. Like you robbing this bank.'

'Careful. I know a divorce lawyer now.'

'Speaking of names: Cordelia, any guesses?'

'*King Lear*?'

'*Ding ding*. Derives from Latin. Means *heart*.'

'The audacity. Was Ivan the doctor for the whole Fredericks family?'

'Yeah. So there's Emma, who has advanced myocarditis, as you know from Cordelia. Queenie, Bryce's wife, is a local dressmaker. Actually made the dress Cordelia is wearing in the thankyou card on Edward's desk. Imagine that? Smiling as the mother of the girl you're inadvertently killing hands over a dress she made you.'

That explained the Q from *B & Q FREDERICKS* on Remy's bank statements. He said he'd hired local costumers, wasting Laurence's time with fake fittings and the like, but it wasn't Bryce he'd hired, but his wife, as a costume designer. Remy had then paid a two-thousand-dollar kill fee to cancel Queenie's contract. If that seems like a mighty big coincidence, trust me, it's not. It's kind of the reason we're all here.

'Queenie's in perfect health. Oh, before I tell you the really good stuff, I checked the mausoleum. No tunnel. Which is a shame, I was really hoping for one. And I managed to do some research about spontaneous combustion.'

'Don't tell me it's real,' I groaned.

'It's not. There has to be an ignition source. Edward wouldn't have lit up a cigarette in the vault. So someone lit him on fire and escaped the locked vault, or he lit himself on fire. That doesn't matter. The interesting thing is about how the fire burns. You know how he looked like a candle?'

'Yeah.'

'It's called the *wick effect*. As in candle wick. The human body is filled with fats and oils.'

'Especially Edward's – he was chowing down on pistachios to cut his cholesterol.'

'Exactly. So the fire – how do I say this? – *eats itself*. The body melts and the fat becomes liquid, but it can collect again in the remaining body and reburn, turning the torso, where the most fat is, into a kind of core. Because the fire is getting everything it needs from inside this burning centre, it doesn't touch anything else in the room. It looks supernatural – that's why a hundred years ago people believed in spontaneous combustion – but it's entirely rational. Add in that there's not much fat in the lower shins or feet, and bone's lower combustion point, and the shins burn before the fire runs out of gas from the torso-wick. No one cut them off, just as we thought.'

I remembered something. 'Bryce has blisters on his hands. But on the back, not the front. How would he get them from lighting Edward on fire?'

'That is what counts as *the really good stuff*,' Juliette said. 'See, it's easier when you have someone along for the ride.'

I deserved the dig. 'This is a spend-the-rest-of-my-life-making-it-up-to-you thing, isn't it?'

'It might be a spend-the-rest-of-your-life-in-prison thing.' She was whispering now. 'They're getting ready for something. Guns are being loaded, bulletproof vests zipped up.'

'I know. I just feel I'm close.'

'I know you think this is all you're good at. But that's not true. I didn't agree to marry you because you solve murders. I agreed to marry you because you're funny and kind. A little bizarre, a little clever. Because you care about people and you care about me. Life doesn't have to follow any set of rules. Spend as much as you want on a wedding. Accept that a dead body might be unexplainable. Or'—her voice grew thick—'maybe sometimes there *is* an answer, but it's not worth dying to find out what it is.'

'I think it's pretty much over,' I agreed sadly. 'Humour me though, one more time. What's the *really good stuff*?'

'Oh, well, if you don't believe spontaneous combustion, you're not going to believe this.'

'Try me.'

'The Fredericks family have a genetic condition. Bryce has porphyria.'

If she was waiting for applause, she wasn't getting it. 'I'm not a doctor,' I said.

'This condition has many symptoms. It's hereditary, and it can affect the heart, as it has in Emma. But it can also afflict the skin – rashes, blisters. In a very specific environment. One most people go through every day.' She was having fun teasing it out for me. 'You with me?'

'Not in the slightest.'

'Drum roll please: Bryce Fredericks is allergic to sunlight.'

The broken door to the mausoleum flashed through my mind. Concrete, cracked in two.

'He's a . . . *vampire*?'

CHAPTER 38

I've solved crimes with impossible decapitations, teleporting bloodstains, fires that don't melt snow and even a cheeky ghost or two, but vampires were a new one.

Porphyria, Juliette filled me in, is actually one of the conditions that led to the creation of the vampire myth. Other symptoms include receding gums (hence, fangs) and red urine, leading to rumours that the sufferer had been drinking blood. Of course the other half of the famous equation is rabies, which is where the biting and bats come into it. Still, porphyria, no matter how severe, gives blisters, not blazes. I remembered Bryce scratching his neck before he caught fire: the little patches of red, irritated skin. It explained why the backs of his hands were blistered, not the palms.

The mystic, the supernatural, is not permissible in a mystery. I knew Bryce couldn't have been the undead. Then again, a broken mausoleum and a man who burst into flames in daylight is hard to deny.

At least the sunscreen was explained. Bryce had no choice but to escape the bank in civilian clothes, in daylight. He'd asked Tobias for a tube of sunscreen so his skin condition wouldn't flare up.

I had, for once, listened to Juliette. It was over. Maskless, I rounded everyone up, pretending I was under orders, and led them down the stairs promising freedom. I had my meagre collection of clues and artefacts – the magnet, the holy water, Gabriel's marker and notebook, the chemistry textbook, the penlight, the radio and the gold pen – in the bag. The voice-changer, sabre mask, boilersuit and army boots were in Winston's office. I'd wavered on leaving behind Felix's revolver, but decided I'd prefer it to be on me so I could hand it over to the police, rather than leaving it lying around for a potential murderer to commandeer.

My plan was to go out together, all the hostages. Maybe there'd be a few minutes before the police found Bryce on the roof, while they tried to figure out where the disappearing bank robber had gone, in which I could sneak in a goodbye to Juliette. I was almost certainly going to jail; I'd already accepted that.

'Why's he letting us go?' Winston asked as I raised the radio to speak to Tobias, pretending for the final time to be the emissary. And then, because he couldn't imagine a world where he wasn't the centre of it, 'Did he get into my safe?'

'I don't know,' I said. 'The vault's opened. Must be what he wanted. He said I could take you all out the front door.'

'After all this?' Michelle said, then, looking around, 'Where's Milton?'

'Don't question a good thing.' Felix looked like he was packed for school camp, undrunk orange sports drink in one hand, practically bouncing on his toes with excitement.

Cordelia let out a small smile. She had colour back in her skin – life – now she wasn't being pumped full of the right drugs for the wrong condition. Gabriel was silent. Of course he was; I'd stolen his notepad and he was still trying to keep up appearances.

'Milton needs to come out last,' I said unconvincingly. I kept forgetting about my imaginary hostage. I never could keep a Tamagotchi alive as a kid.

Laverna laughed at this. She touched me gently on the shoulder and pulled me away from the group.

'What? I need to make this call.' I held up the radio.

'A liar knows a liar.' She jabbed at my chest. 'Either Milton's already dead, has been for the last twenty-four hours, or he's the man in the mask. Something funky's going on here. What con are you pulling?'

'No con. We're getting out.'

'Hmm.' Her mouth half dropped open in a humouring smile. 'Whatever you say.'

'Speaking of liars.' I held her back from the group, radio forgotten for the moment. 'I understand you said what you had to in order to convince everyone about Cordelia's condition. But why lie about everything else?'

'Everything else?' She seemed offended. 'I lie with intent, thank you very much. Only someone pathological lies about *everything*. I am not that type of liar.' This was like Michelle's burglar/thief paradox all over again: the nobility of crime. Everyone thinks they're a special breed of crook.

I wagged a finger at her. 'No, that's not true. You did lie to me. Your name for one. You also said you were a truck driver. And that you then variously spent your whole life *shovelling peanuts*, but earlier you said you were a *dangerous cargo specialist*. You can't be both. You drove peanuts or explosives.'

'Dangerous cargo doesn't mean guns and bombs. It means dangerous cargo.' She folded her arms. 'You're not familiar with the Transport of Dangerous Goods Code, are you?'

Obviously, I am not. She hissed like a piston in derision.

'Allergies?' I guessed. 'You're allergic to nuts?'

'Some detective. Class 4.2: Flammable Solids includes freshly packed nuts. They have a high oil content. If moisture gets in, it breaks down fats and that decomposition produces energy. Now, energy can be expressed two ways: light and heat. Pack a million of these tiny, self-heating balls in the back of a truck, let a bit of moisture in, wrap them in a bone-dry fibrous shell, and yeah, you've got a serious hazard.'

I was reeling. 'Are you seriously telling me that *nuts* spontaneously combust?'

She counted them off on her fingers. 'Peanuts, brazil nuts—'

'*Pistachios?*' Juliette's incredulousness fizzed through the radio. '*Pistachios* are the murder weapon?'

'They spontaneously combust,' I said, powering up the stairs. I'd told everyone to sit tight while I arranged their release. I'd had an idea, and I just couldn't throw it all in without checking if I was right. But it would be the decision that kills me. I had about two minutes of freedom left, though I didn't know it at the time. Looking back, I wish I'd known someone had peeled off from the group to follow me. 'Self-heating, fat decomposition. It's legit.'

'I just looked it up,' she replied. I remembered she'd now have internet access, which does make murder mysteries a whole lot easier. 'Wow. It's true.'

'It was Laverna who told me.'

'So she's your killer?'

'It's not a good-enough plan for a murder. The conditions you'd need for the ignition, the reaction itself catching. You could never rely on it.'

'So what's the revelation?'

'Edward locked *himself* in the safe. To protect either himself, or whatever was in there. That's why he hired Michelle to review their security and gave Felix a gun, he wanted something protected, wanted to ensure it would be watertight. But something happened and he had to shut himself in there. He took himself into that vault, with a pocket full of pistachios, and that's what killed him.'

'A pocket full of pistachios isn't going to do . . .' She almost retched at the memory of the feet-less human candle. '. . . that. He would have woken up, just patted himself out. Even if he didn't, we're supposing he didn't move at all while he burned alive? And what about Bryce? Could such a thing have happened twice?'

'Edward wouldn't have been able to put himself out if he was concussed when he went in there. I think he got hit, possibly with Ben's gold brick of a trophy. Gabriel told me there was blood on it when he visited the office before the robbery.'

'Could be red dye from the ink pack Winston set off,' Juliette suggested.

'It could be. Say it's blood, though. Edward cops a braining and stumbles to the vault for safety, taking the guard's chair with him to sit on. He might not have realised he had a concussion, so he's sat down, fallen unconscious and when the sweat from his leg adds moisture to the environment in his pocket, the pistachios self-heat. A tiny fire to start. But if he was concussed, he wouldn't wake up, even as it spread.'

'You can't be sure.'

'I can. Edward left a message, on Winston's abacus, that he would be in the vault. 1011. It's not one thousand and eleven, and it's not binary or leetspeak either. It's trucker's code. We all know 10-4.'

'That means *understood*,' Juliette replied.

'Not many people know there's 10-1, 10-2, 10-3 and so on. 10-4 is just the one that's made it into the popular lexicon. 10-11 means: *on radio*. Specifically: *can be contacted by radio but not strictly available*. Edward and Winston both loved toy trucks since childhood. They would have known the trucker codes.'

'So Edward was telling his brother he was in the vault, waiting for his call on the interior phone? *Can be contacted by radio but not strictly available.*' Juliette considered this. 'Why not just highlight the vault code on the invoice?'

'Because Edward was in *Winston's* office. He needed to leave a message fast. And something subtle, so his attacker wouldn't destroy it.'

'So Edward's plan is to sit in the vault all night until someone finds him in the morning? I guess Felix said there's an independent air supply, so it's not that risky. But the person who Edward was running from, they'd be pretty keen to make sure he didn't get out. Why did no one come in here on Thursday? If it was Bryce, for example, and he wanted to open the vault and kill a witness to something, he's robbed the bank a day late. And his accomplice? *We're in.* In where?'

'I haven't figured that out yet. What I have figured out is why Edward was in Winston's office in the first place.' I'd just arrived at Edward's office door. I barged into the room, past the empty birdcage with the open door, and picked up the umbrella from the far corner. I opened it – indoors, yes, I think I've capitalised on that bad luck – and held it against the doorway. It barely fit through when fully opened out. If you leaned slightly wrong, the fabric might snag on the lock. 'You remember the Sherlock Holmes story "The Red-Headed League"? The real-life robbery it inspired?'

'On Baker Street? Yeah, you can't make that up. That's why I thought there was a tunnel.'

'Yes, the tunnel distracted us. But the story *did* influence Edward. The real-life thieves dug into Lloyds Bank from next door, true, but they also cased the joint by renting a safety deposit box ahead of time, purely to access and measure the dimensions of the vault. A tape measure would have drawn suspicion, so they used an umbrella, like you told me earlier.' I turned and now held the umbrella up against Edward's personal safe. It was just slightly wider. Perfect. 'Edward used his umbrella the same way. He wanted to check if the safe would fit through the door.'

It's one of the rules of heists: there's always a *switch*.

Edward Huxley had swapped his safe.

'We know the wool lift has been used from the dust on the floor, but nobody moved any money or gold between the floors as it's all still in the vault. I thought maybe someone had brought Ed's body down, but that doesn't work if he put himself inside the vault. The truth is, Edward was never going to get a person-sized safe up and down the stairs, and it wouldn't fit in the elevator. These safes are heavy – you can wriggle them like a fridge, but only small flat distances. So Edward used the wool lift to transport both his and Winston's safes, one up and one down, between the mezzanine and the third floor, and back into their offices. And the final piece.' I rested a hand on the magnetic tiles: HAPPY FATHER'S DAY, LOVE BEN! 'He had to take down his son's final, magnetic message before he moved it. He put it back up on *Winston*'s safe once the swap was complete, to finish the illusion. Only Edward's better at grammar than his teenage son was, so when he rewrote the message he inadvertently put the apostrophe in the *correct* spot, unlike the photo taken months earlier.'

'That's a lot of effort. Why?'

'Because he knew the vault could be compromised – Michelle leaving ten grand on his desk told him that. He'd planned to use a safety deposit but needed a back-up. His own safe was too obvious a hiding place for whatever he was hiding, and so he figured trading them was another layer of protection. The brothers don't know each other's codes, remember.'

I put my hand on the lock's dial. Talking to Laverna had clued me in on something else, too: most detectives seem to think that figuring out when people are lying to you is the most important thing to cracking a case, but I'd pressed Laverna on what I thought was a lie, only to find out it was two truths. Maybe, I decided, I should start figuring out when people are telling the truth. Starting with Winston.

'One more question,' Juliette said. 'Which safe are you going to open first?'

'The one in Edward's office. So: Winston's.'

'Didn't you just explain that the key to all this is probably in Edward's safe, now in *Winston*'s office?'

'Yes. But I don't know the code.'

Winston had been telling the truth about the combination; I'd just had the wrong safe. For Edward's safe, down a floor, I had a few options – *02-09-24* for Ben's death and *29-39-34* on Bryce's scrap of paper – but it could also be neither. So I figured I'd take the sure thing first. Then try my luck on the second.

I didn't realise I'd only get one shot.

I spun the dial.

79-47-29. Gold-silver-bronze.

The safe door opened.

CHAPTER 39

I'm afraid that's it.

No grand revelation. No parlour scene. Like I said before, two hands in the back and the slam of a door.

I'd had just enough time to see the inside of the safe. The majority of it was empty. A single shelf held several documents in manila folders and a porcelain pot, which I was relieved to see, as it ruled out two suspects. The rest of the safe was one large chamber, with a few scattered bundles of cash on the floor. I'd leaned in to grab the container and suddenly I was careening forward, dropping the radio and my bag and smacking my head on the back wall of the safe. A tumble of limbs, I clambered to turn around. I heard four gunshots, and froze, but felt no impact to my flesh. Then there was a crunch, and the now-stepped-on radio and the still-warm revolver were tossed in after me.

Then, darkness.

It happened in seconds. I'd screamed and banged and yelled, of course. I didn't know how long everyone would wait downstairs, when they'd realise I wasn't coming back. But once they did, they'd be out the door. And then the truth about Milton would come out. That would lead Tobias to the conclusion that I was in on the robbery, which would mean there were no hostages left in the bank. Coupled with the sound of the four gunshots, he would have no choice but to send in the response team. Once they found the body on the roof, they would think I'd simply robbed the bank with an accomplice and turned on them, murdering them and keeping everything for myself. When they couldn't find me *in* the bank, they'd assume I'd gotten away. Everyone would relax: the hostages were safe, and the villain was at large. No need to scour every office and open every safe just yet.

And Juliette. If she told the truth, they wouldn't believe her. Worst case, they'd think she was in on it too. If she was thrown in the clink for the day, I'd already be dead by the time they listened to her statement and checked this damn box.

All I had was my meagre bag of items. And a gift from my killer. The gun, tossed back to me with two bullets in it. A way out.

I'd started writing instead.

It's helped. I think. Laying out all the clues, all the lies and the motives. Reassembling the puzzle from the beginning. Those I haven't slotted yet include: 29-39-34, a coffee cup, a magnet, a slow watch and *We're in*.

And, of course, *I-am-not-a-clue* Ditto. Who must be important, given someone set him loose.

Slotting in what I learned from seeing the inside of this safe, taking in the shrinking gold nugget, a bright-orange energy drink, a spectrometer test and a mausoleum, I reckon I've got to the bottom of seven thefts. Juliette's and my own make nine, and the tenth is whoever stole *a life*. As promised: a gold pen, a single dollar, other varied amounts ranging from a few thousand to twenty-five million dollars, a coffee cup, a life, and a heart have been nicked.

So close to the answer, but I am out of ink and air. The pen is running dry, as you can probably tell.

I figure it's fate we're all in this bank together. Collective consciousness is a funny thing though. I read an essay once about a province in Africa that couldn't stop laughing: known infamously as the Tanganyika laughter epidemic, a communal mass psychological condition in which everyone started laughing and couldn't stop. Then there's the dancing plague of 1518: a town in now-France where everyone got the jitterbug and danced until their toes bled. Was Huxley the same? A mass persuasion in the town that had all the bank's customers deciding to rob it at the same time?

Everyone steals, whether it's product or effort, money or time. There's more you can steal from a man than just his wallet. Air, for example.

Which theft leads me to murder? I don't know. Some private detective agency I was going to end up running. I can't solve my own murder. I can't even count coins: $4.80, not $4.40.

I'm still grasping onto the plastic bag full of flammable hydrogen. And the revolver. There's some kind of ingenious escape plan in there somewhere, but my deprived brain can't handle it. I've thought about using the revolver, just in case suffocating hurt, but it's quite comfortable. Ah, damn. I'm sleepy now. It's warm here. A nice enough place to die.

If you figure it out, come and mention it to my tombstone.

I wish I had more—

CHAPTER 40

Of all the times to solve the damn thing! Right on the death-knell.

Given I've kickstarted this pen, I'll keep it brief. I've got one last burst of energy. I'm getting out of this tomb.

First, I'm going to fire the gun. Right at the join of the door, bottom corner. I expect the bullet to ricochet, but maybe it will do a sliver of damage to the door, enough room for a whisper of air to sneak through. Or at least make a bit of noise.

If that doesn't work, I'll aim at my little hydrogen balloon with the second bullet. Maybe I can blow my way out. There's hardly enough gas in there for an explosion but, again, I'm just looking for a tiny defect.

Last resort: the safe is in front of the third-floor window. If I can rock the safe enough to tip backwards, it will crash straight through it. Gravity does the rest. It's an attention grabbing and almost certainly fatal plan. Like I said, last resort. At least I'll be out of the bank.

As for the killers (yes, plural), I feel it wouldn't be sporting to write their names here without a right of reply. If none of this works, I know Juliette will find enough in these pages. Let me just say one thing:

I am a good detective. And I can count to $4.80.

CHAPTER 41

Ricochet
Bad
Stomach
Blood
No time
Window

You are wonderful.

Celebrating the life of

ERNEST CUNNINGHAM

Born 19-04-1981, Died 23-08-2025

10 a.m., 26 August 2025

Huxley Funeral Parlour, Church Ln, Huxley

Ceremony will conclude with a reading by Ditto the parrot

THE PARLOUR SCENE

CHAPTER 42

'Welcome to my funeral.'

Ernest Cunningham's face flickered to life on one of two wall-mounted televisions in the church. The other television was dark. Bouquets exploding with pinks and whites scattered the top of Ernest's coffin, which lay in the centre of the dais. It was a closed casket funeral. Out of necessity.

'Thank you all for coming,' the recording of Ernest continued on the screen, 'in your mix of grief and celebration. Perhaps more the latter than the former, which is a rarity for an event like this, but I did take you all hostage, so let's call it even.'

There was a murmur among the crowd. They'd, of course, figured out something was amiss when Milton had been safe at home, well slept and uninjured, and Ernest had done his disappearing act, but this was the first time most of them had heard the truth out loud.

It had been a sombre line that entered the church. None of them had seen each other since the robbery. There were some hushed greetings, platitudes and *howzitgarn*s, but no need for condolences: no one had really known Ernest all that well. The handshakes that black-veiled Juliette accepted – double-clasped hands, a requirement at funerals – were offered solely in imitation of real emotion.

After a few minutes of chitchat, people started dipping back into their bonded trauma. *You were there at the vault opening, right?* Or *I never suspected Cordelia, such a sweet girl.* That they'd all been trapped by a psychopath – one now firmly boxed up at the front of the church – for twenty-four hours gave them plenty to talk about. Cordelia and Laverna were allowed to attend under police escort, waiting outside. Remy had his torso strapped with excess bandages, just to remind people he was a victim in all this. Eric was chaperoned by his sombre father, grieving not only Ernest but his perfect record. Winston wore a pale-grey suit, not bothering with black, took the furthest back pew and didn't talk to anyone. Michelle and Felix came in holding hands, so at least something came out of it all. Gabriel stood behind a microphone that, appropriately, wasn't on. He was still holding up his vow. If a priest talks in a forest and only a dead man is around to hear it, has he really talked at all?

'Yes, it was me behind the mask,' the video went on. 'For most of it, anyway. I apologise for putting you all through it. But in my defence, I wouldn't have had to if you weren't all thieves, and if two of you weren't murderers.'

Everyone looked around, most gazes falling on Cordelia and Laverna.

'Once you're done eyeing each other up, I have a few things to say. Last words, if you will,' Ernest's recording continued. 'And then, at the end, Ditto, Edward's parrot, has something to add. If instructions have been followed, he is currently safely housed in the vestry.

'Theft. That's what brings us all together, isn't it? I stole a pen. Juliette stole five thousand and sixty dollars. I hope you've put it back, love. Though funerals aren't cheap. Michelle broke into the bank because she'd been hired to steal ten grand. Father Gabriel contravened the Eighth Commandment, his sticky fingers pinching, among other things, a coffee cup. And Remy was foiled in his attempt to steal twenty-five million dollars by insurance fraud. Sorry I didn't cark it in time for you to cash in the policy without suspicion. Cordelia and Laverna stitched up the community to the tune of a hundred and fifty grand and change, plus a vital organ.'

Ernest took a breath. There were whispers of relief from those he hadn't named.

'But the rest of you aren't innocent. You see, I didn't start off robbing the bank. That was someone else – a man named Bryce Fredericks. He was murdered. Lit on fire in front of my very eyes. In order to solve his murder, I had to don the mask. Take on his role. And to solve that murder, I have to solve Edward's, and by solving those two, I might solve my own.' The recording paused. 'Yes, you do have to listen to all of this.' There was a beat while everyone wondered who Ernest was talking to. 'I'm not sure if that worked given this is a recording, but I figured someone might stand up and heckle. It would have been pretty cool if I pulled it off, huh?'

'I'm not wasting my time with this.' Winston stood up.

'Sit down, Winston,' said the recording.

Winston, shocked, and a little guilty, lowered himself back into his pew.

After another pause, Ernest said, 'Did I get the timing of that one right?'

'Where's his family?' Felix asked, catching on, then leaning into Michelle's ear. 'It's just *us*.'

Ernest smiled a little to himself. 'You know this is my favourite part of a mystery? When we all come together and it all comes out. Normally it's a different kind of parlour, but why let that stop us?'

With everyone's attention focused on the television, it took them a few seconds to register that the lid of the coffin was slowly opening.

Ernest Cunningham, decked out in a black funeral suit, arms crossed over his chest (one in a sling), lay inside on a plush white silk cushion.

Then he sat up.

'Let's have ourselves a parlour scene, shall we?'

CHAPTER 43

My funeral was a small affair. Suspects only.

I, of course, didn't see any of the reactions in the last chapter. It was a closed casket funeral, out of necessity, like I said. And my third-person tangent is a slight betrayal of the usual first-person narration, but I am now typing this out instead of scratching it into a notebook, and Juliette reliably filled me in afterwards. If I'd have been standing up the front welcoming people in, it just wouldn't have had the same impact as sitting up in the coffin halfway through the service.

Forgive me a bit of theatricality, but I think I've earned it.

It's not the parlour scene I expected, but it's the one I got. Luckily I had a contrite priest under my thumb and a convincing enough argument to the police that I needed what amounted to witness protection in hospital. No one knew I was alive. And I intended to keep it that way in case someone decided to finish the job.

I broke six bones in the fall. I don't know their names. What I can tell you is that four were in my leg, one was in my back, and one used to be in my arm but wound up in my stomach. I don't need to know the name of that one to know that makes it a significant injury.

All of that and a self-inflicted bullet wound to the stomach pretty much put me in the ground. The plummeting safe did a good job of imprinting the damp earth with a grave plot for me.

Here's what happened after I fired the gun. The bullet failed to leave anything but a ding on the inside of the door, before it zipped back at me like we were playing tennis and buried itself in my gut. I dropped the bag of hydrogen, breathing in noxious gas. I had no more time for clever ideas, only instinct. Rocking the safe was a last desperate attempt. I managed to throw myself front to back until I could feel it lifting off the ground. I got it to teeter on its heels, then toes, almost landing forwards *inside* Edward's office, which would have been a disaster, but a final shoulder charge from me sent it backwards at the last second. The window stood no chance against the weight of it.

I don't really remember landing. I do recall falling being like the inside of a washing machine, and limbs folded over me that would have won me a world championship of Twister.

I remember lying still in the darkness, my back wet with something warm. The door hadn't opened. Not even a crack, not a sliver of light or air. I'd fallen ten metres out a window and the damn thing hadn't even budged. I started to cry. I'd have traded every case I'd ever solved for one more breath of air.

That was when something tickled my nose in the dark.

Something from the outside.

A butterfly.

CHAPTER 44

I would have felt guilty about almost giving Laverna a heart attack had she not deserved the irony. It was hard to do my best Dracula impression – sitting up slowly, bending from the hips – with a three-day-old bullet wound to the abdomen, a leg reduced to something resembling a smashed candy-cane still in the plastic, and a broken arm, but I gave it my best.

To be fair to my doctors, I should not have been out of the hospital. I was cranked up on all kinds of painkillers. For once my reputation assisted me: I'd solved enough bizarre cases that the police had trusted me when I'd said that if we didn't get everyone to the church today, I'd be dead before I could reveal the truth. I was still their lead suspect, of course, but it's not like I was going to hobble away from them and escape. I also promised, if this church gathering failed, to give them a full confession to both murders and the robbery myself.

The church exploded with noise, everyone shouting over one another that this was ridiculous, against the law, against their rights. Juliette stepped in front of Gabriel and turned on the microphone, flipping up the black widow's veil. She'd insisted on wearing one:

I can't keep a straight face without it, Ern. Felix stood, storming towards me. If it got heated I could just slam the lid down and hide in the coffin, though I had developed some mild claustrophobia given recent events, but he ran out of steam before he got past the pews. Michelle simply sat back and laughed.

'There's police outside,' Juliette said. 'You'll all be better off hearing what we have to say.'

'Thank you, Juliette,' I said, my voice echoing off the polished interior of the church. 'I want to start by talking about why we're all here, and then I'll go back in time a bit.'

'We're all here because you tricked us,' Eric said.

'No. We're all here because Bryce Fredericks robbed a bank. He couldn't have known it was the worst possible bank to rob, on the worst possible day. But sometimes bad luck finds you. Understanding what he wanted helps us understand several other people, so let's start there. *Why* did Bryce Fredericks walk into Huxley's Bank with a gun on the twenty-second of August? What did he want to steal?' I spread my good arm. 'Anyone from the crowd?'

'He wanted a dollar,' Cordelia said.

'Wrong. He *said* he wanted a dollar.'

'What he really wanted was to get in the vault. The dollar was just a ruse,' Michelle offered.

'Warmer, but also wrong.'

'What the hell is the point of robbing a bank if you don't want money or to get into the vault?' Winston asked.

'That is exactly the question that unlocks it. Michelle, remind me again. What did you tell me was the most valuable thing in a bank robbery?'

THE SECOND HEIST:
~~A SINGLE DOLLAR~~ TIME

CHAPTER 45

Bryce had said it himself on the rooftop. *I took the one thing that can't be given back.* It had clicked, when I went to write what was to be my final sentence in the notebook: *I wish I had more . . . time.* Someone had stolen it from me, I'd realised.

'Bryce wanted your *time*,' I explained.

I'd finally understood why the memory of Juliette talking about *backwards* had itched at my brain. How can you rob a bank backwards? By putting something in it.

'Not money, not anything in a safety deposit box. Just time. When he first rounded us up, it was strange that he made such a big deal out of collecting all the hostages; he trashed the place, threatening to kill someone until Cordelia and Laverna came out of hiding.'

Felix and Michelle slowly nodded in memory.

'But he was pointing an unloaded gun. He didn't really want to hurt anybody. He'd fired a single bullet at the ceiling, and from there it was a ruse. Then, after all his effort to acquire the hostages, he had no intention of trading us. He just wanted to make sure we – well, some of us more than others – stayed in the bank. And that's why he flipped out about the hostages. He didn't need ten. He just needed one: Cordelia.'

Cordelia went bright red. 'Did he know I was faking it?'

'He had no clue,' I said. 'Which is the sad part. He wouldn't have done it otherwise. There was a heart up for grabs, you see. The last one you were supposed to get, Cordelia, but you missed out on it due to staging an accident, and Bryce's daughter, Emma, didn't get there fast enough. So this time he had to take your piece off the board. He had to keep you away from the hospital long enough that you'd be scratched off the list and Emma would overtake you. A heart is valid for transplant for six hours. I bumped into Bryce in a café in the morning. I didn't know it at the time, but he was saying goodbye to his family: his sick daughter, his worried wife. I thought Emma was distressed over the death of Laurence Birch because he was her idol; but it was because she knew, on seeing Birch's death, that she was going to live. And she probably knew, deep down, what her dad had done to ensure that happened.

'I saw his watch, and I thought it was four hours slow. At nine thirty a.m., his watch said five thirty. Later, at one thirty, when he died on the roof, I thought he'd fixed it, because it said one thirty.' I shook my head. 'It wasn't the time. It was a countdown timer. He'd set the clock as soon as the victim died: six hours.' The breaking news article had come in while Juliette and I were in the café. 'That gives a time of death as nine a.m. I saw the watch half an hour later. When I saw Bryce on the roof, another four hours had passed and the countdown timer *matched* the actual time. Ninety minutes left.'

I didn't have to explain this to the room, but that was why he'd been getting changed out of his disguise. It's an hour and a half drive to Brisbane hospital, a big enough hospital for transplant surgery, and where the heart would have been taken from Birch's deathbed in Byron. With only ninety minutes left, Cordelia could no longer make it in time and the heart would go to the next on the list. The female voice on the phone – *We're in* – had been Bryce's wife, Queenie. She wasn't an accomplice breaking into a bank vault, she was telling him they'd got into surgery. Top of the list. *We're in.*

And now you know why I called him a *thief*, not a *burglar*.

'You said *victim*,' Tobias spoke up. 'So he's a murderer?'

'If he killed Edward,' Felix added, 'the fire meant he couldn't use that heart. You're saying he killed someone else?'

'Edward's too big anyway; he was never a target. Emma is a young woman with a small build. Transplants are matched by blood type and by *size*. You can put a grown man's heart in a teenager, if it's a small man and a big kid. Bryce had a six-digit number in his pocket: 29, 39, 34. I thought it was a code to something, a vault or one of the safes, but his wife, Queenie, is a seamstress.'

'It's a men's shirt size,' Michelle whispered, understanding.

'A *small* shirt size,' I confirmed. 'Neck, chest, sleeve.'

Remy made a little gasp of recognition ahead of the group.

I ploughed on. 'Those numbers are Laurence Birch's measurements. Queenie was on Remy's payroll for his fake show. Remy, you specifically told me you'd been dragging Laurence around town to costume fittings to keep him from catching on that you were wasting his time. Queenie measured him up. And Laurence was a small man, much smaller than he seems on the big screen. It was the first thing I thought when you hired him to play me: he's too short.' I flipped open my wallet and pulled out a card. 'But Laurence was a method actor: he wanted to *embody* the role. He went through my wallet when we first met to learn about me. He used my name to order coffee, he joined my football club. And he saw that I'd recently signed up to be an organ donor. That's what started all of this.'

'Bryce Fredericks *murdered* Laurence Birch?' Gabriel said from behind me.

'Does he talk now?' Laverna asked.

'Bryce had planned to shoot Laurence last Thursday,' I explained. 'Emma was on death's door. Missing out on the first heart, the one Cordelia was supposed to get, but neither of them did, was the last straw. Bryce decided he was willing to kill to keep her alive. If Queenie was costuming Laurence, she might have glimpsed his new donor card. Once she measured him for a shirt, they knew he was a size match. Blood type can be tested with a home-kit you order online, and you don't even need blood, saliva will do. A piece of used chewing gum, purchased on eBay for fifty dollars, would do the trick. Then a shirt measurement was all it took to decide Laurence's fate. Bryce's plan was simple. One shot, clean to the head, to protect the heart. That's what the single bullet was for. But he told me he hadn't had the stomach for it. He'd been going to walk away, until Laurence came barrelling out of the café after rowing with Remy.'

To be precise, I wasn't actually sure whether Bryce had given Laurence an extra nudge into the path of the van. He'd told me he hadn't been able to do what he planned. And then *everything . . . happened. Opportunity knocks*, he'd said. Never has a statement been so personally relatable. For what it's worth, I think he *did* push him. It doesn't matter though: the result was the same. The donor was dying, the next morning a plug was pulled and there was a heart on the table.

I continued. 'The point of the robbery was to keep you somewhere, Cordelia. Bryce's mask, his outfit, the voice-changer, they were because he planned to kidnap you, hold you for six hours – maybe lock you up with the chain he used on the bank's door – and then just let you go. The bank robbery was improvised. It's why he wasted time with things like yoga, and ferrying you to the bathroom one at a time. It's also why he didn't really know what he wanted. He couldn't ask for anything tangible, because there was a risk we'd just give it to him. The specifics of the dollar from the vault was just a time-killing ploy, and when he discovered it couldn't be opened, it was music to his ears. It was perfect for eating up time. That's why he didn't care about the hostages roaming the bank, or properly keep an eye on everyone. The only person he was watching was you, and because you never went downstairs, he was happy for the rest of us to do what we wanted. But the guilt weighed on him.'

I am killing her. I have killed her. Isn't it all the same? he'd said to me on the rooftop. By keeping Cordelia in the bank, away from a heart, he thought he was condemning her. That's why he'd exploded at me when I suggested he couldn't be *that heartless*. What I'd taken as a threat made sense now, too: *If she leaves the bank, she dies.* He was telling me that if Cordelia left the bank with time on the clock, Emma would die.

'Bryce didn't know that you didn't really need that heart. He thought if you had as little time as Emma did, he was killing you. That's why he donated the last $150 to your FundAble, so you'd be able to cash it out and it might assuage his guilt because at least you'd have the money. But that set off another chain reaction. He was following you, ready to kidnap you, and you walked into Huxley's Bank. Laverna, you would have got the call about Laurence's heart already. You couldn't go to the hospital, but you knew a second missed heart might prompt questions. Your funding goal achieved, you were going to grab the cash and blow town. So you walked into Huxley's. Bryce realised he wasn't going to be able to pluck Cordelia off the street, so using everything he'd prepared for your kidnapping, he decided to keep you in the bank instead and improvise a robbery. And that's why we're all here.'

'So those two are the ones who killed him?' Winston said. 'He finds out about the fundraising con, that it's cost his daughter her chance at life and forced him to put his own livelihood at risk. He'd be pretty pissed off. Laverna and Cordelia had to stop him telling people. And Edward donated too. He had that thankyou card.

I'll bet he confronted them over it as well, so he had to go. It's all to cover up the con.' He dusted his hands. 'Case solved, detective.'

'Not quite,' I said. 'First, Bryce *didn't* know. He checked in about Cordelia's health during the robbery. He donated the final money out of guilt. And, honestly, Bryce was willing to spend the rest of his life in jail to get Emma a heart. I think he'd be delighted to find out Cordelia didn't need one, regardless of the circumstances. As for murder, Cordelia was done with the whole scam when she realised that they might actually be hurting people. They're hardly going to kill over it. And Edward . . . I checked his donation. Forty bucks. Even if he figured it out, what does he have to gain by confronting them?'

Laverna put her hand up. 'So the point of all this was?'

'To eliminate you as murder suspects.'

'Oh.' She seemed surprised and pleased by this. 'Thank you very much.'

'So who *is* the murderer?' This was Felix, the type who flicks to the end of the book.

'Depends which murder,' I said. 'But you know exactly the one I'm talking about, don't you, Felix?'

THE NINTH HEIST: GOLD

&

THE TENTH HEIST: EVERYTHING

CHAPTER 46

'I have nothing to do with a murder!' Felix's shouting bounced off the stained-glass windows. 'This is stupid. Would any of this hold up in court?'

'I haven't even accused you of anything,' I said, turning to Gabriel. 'I think maybe it's time to check on Ditto. We're about ready for him.'

Gabriel nodded and walked down the aisle, over to a side door. He unlocked it with a clunk from the ancient lock, which echoed through the church hall.

I turned back to Felix. 'Besides, I didn't say you committed a murder. I'm talking about the murder you were trying to *prove*.'

'Slander. Defamation!' Winston called from the back.

I heard whispers – 'Who did Winston kill?' – from the front.

Felix did a regal bow, hand out. *The floor is yours.*

'You can't defame the dead, Winston. I found a spectrometer report in Felix's locker.' I unfolded the report. Yes, I'd brought props. 'A spectrometer is used to test the elemental components of a material. At first I thought he was checking if the gold on display was fake, but of course, Felix, you knew it was real. Otherwise, there's no point stealing it.'

'I never—'

'You piece of—' Winston started scrambling over the pews. Remy held him back.

'Don't worry, Winston, your gold nugget is still there. And it's still intact. It's just, well, a little bit smaller.'

Felix glowed bright red.

'You see, Felix, you knew you couldn't just replace the nugget with a fake one, or crack a chip off it. That would be too noticeable. And why are you working for a man you hate? For an economic system that you despise? Why would a banking abolitionist work as a security guard for a bank in the first place? Let alone Huxley's, but we'll get to that. You stole a tiny piece of gold every week, didn't you?'

The drop in his head was enough to encourage me to continue.

'You never drank that bright-orange sports energy drink the whole time we were in the bank. And you snatched it away from Michelle to stop her drinking it. That's because it's not an energy drink. It's aqua regia – a mix of nitric and hydrochloric acid. The name is a literal translation from Latin of *royal water*, given by the alchemists at the time.'

Winston looked like he was boiling, like his suit didn't fit him anymore.

'They call it that because it dissolves gold,' I went on. 'You told me that Winston didn't really care about your job guarding the bank – he wanted you to guard the museum, polish the nugget. That's why you had the microfibre cloth you used to dry Michelle's hair. But instead of polishing the gold with water or gentle soap, like you're supposed to, you polished it with this corrosive formula. Then it's simple: the gold is shaped like a spike. You simply place your open drink bottle underneath it and the solution drips off into your bottle, carrying tiny, incremental specks of gold with it as it erodes the surface. Then you just walk straight out the door. Every day. At home you evaporate the solution and collect the flecks.

Do it once, and there's no value. Do it a thousand times . . . eventually you have a nugget of your own. Congratulations'—I gave him a nod of acknowledgement—'on the world's slowest bank robbery.'

'After all we did for your family,' Winston spat.

'*For* my family?' Felix turned to him. 'It's what you did *to* my family. You owe me!'

At the rear of the church, Gabriel slunk back in and gave me a nod, leaving the door to his vestry open.

Felix whirled back to me. 'I only took what I deserved.'

'Of course you would have felt that way,' I said, watching someone duck out of the room in the commotion. 'After all, Harold Huxley killed your great-great-grandfather.'

I let the room settle before I explained. 'Chinese immigration to Australia had a bump in the eighteen fifties, mostly to find fortune on the Victorian goldfields. As the century neared its end, and each field became more depleted, the prospectors moved north, up to this region. That would include Felix's great-great-grandfather, Yang, who prospected with Harold Huxley. The gold rush was mostly over by the late nineteenth century when gold was struck here, but there were a few late finds. They were tough conditions – which you'd know if you cared for the meaning of *Goldfields* and not just the price tag, Winston – for everyone, but tougher still for the immigrants. Violence, theft. Murder. Winston, you said yourself that if Yang had dug one metre to the left we'd all be standing in *his* bank, *his* town. I don't think that's true, but he'd certainly still be alive. Because he wouldn't have found the nugget Harold wanted.'

'I'm not denying there was violence and all that,' Winston protested. 'But there was also pestilence. Yang died of dysentery – that's on record. It was very common. The water wasn't clean. It's not murder.'

'It was a good cover story, given the symptoms of dysentery are the same as what actually killed him. Vomiting, nausea, stomach cramps. Those are all symptoms of heavy metal poisoning.'

'You won't be able to prove that on a body over a hundred years old,' Michelle said.

'He was cremated,' I said. 'Huxley has one of the earliest crematoriums in the country.'

'Proving it will still be impossible.' Winston leaned back in the pew, stretching his arms. Comfortable. 'You're up shit creek without a paddle. Which is a fine way to get dysentery, by the way.'

'It's not impossible at all,' I corrected him. 'Otherwise you wouldn't have broken into the mausoleum to get Yang's ashes.'

Winston blanched.

'Gabriel thought it was Edward because he saw his car, but you could have easily taken it from your joint property. I saw the urn in your safe. When you thought the thief had opened it, you tried to bargain with him. Your voice was muffled through the door so I misheard it as a threat. I thought you said *Get rid of Ern*. But you were saying *Get rid of the urn*. You were asking the bank robber to get rid of your evidence, because the ashes themselves will indeed prove heavy metal poisoning. You see, metal doesn't break down in a cremation. The usual practice is to pass a magnet over the remains to attract all the loose metal – teeth fillings, et cetera. But certain metals are non-magnetic and they wouldn't have been picked up by this process.' I held up the spectrometer report again. 'Felix wasn't testing gold for traces of fakery, he was testing iron for traces of gold.'

'He was testing the ashes?' Remy asked.

'No. He was testing a cast iron teapot – the one on show in Huxley's Bank's atrium, Harold Huxley's relic. Felix suspected it might have been used in Yang's murder, once he realised the symptoms of dysentery matched heavy metal toxicity. This report shows traces of gold in the old teapot. It's evidence that Harold put flakes in the tea he brewed Yang, poisoning him with the very thing he stole: gold.'

'They put that shit *on display*,' Felix said through gritted teeth. 'Every day, laughing at us. Lying to us. Making us work for them under the same promises they gave Yang, and each of us after that, down to my dad and me.'

'The cremation magnet wouldn't have picked out gold from the ashes, so there'll still be traces in Yang's remains, which can be tested. Winston, that's why you had to break into the mausoleum to steal the urn. You put the ashes in your safe, before, of course, Edward swapped the safes. That was why you were worried about it being opened. Why you asked the bank robber to get rid of the urn.'

'I'm not responsible for the crimes of my ancestors,' Winston said. 'What's a vandalism charge? Community service? I can do that.'

'But you *are* responsible for covering your forefather's crimes up. For propagating them. For not making amends.'

'I didn't realise *amends* was a crime. What's the charge for theft?' Winston pouted at Felix.

'You're really going to press charges against Felix?' I asked.

'*I'm* the victim here.' Winston jabbed at his chest with a thumb. 'So is Ed. It's clear as day. Felix tried to blackmail me! He showed me that stupid report, said he'd go public unless I paid him off. But it's meaningless without the ashes to back it up. So I went into the mausoleum and cleared it out. How am I under scrutiny here? It makes perfect sense: Felix was pissed off about his great-great-granddaddy's murder, so he planned to pick us off one by one. Ed copped it first. I was going to get it second.' Winston seemed to be talking himself into believing this. If he could finger Felix as a killer, his ancestral crimes didn't seem so bad. 'He killed your burglar—'

'Thief.'

'Whatever. He killed them to prevent me from finding out Ed's body was in the vault before I got to it.' Winston brimmed with pride and vindication, but it quickly swerved to anger as he realised what it all meant. 'This bastard killed my little brother.'

There was a murmur of agreement around the room.

Felix stood up to protest. 'I swear I didn't—'

'Hang on.' I cut everyone off and signalled to Juliette, who helped me out of the coffin and into a waiting wheelchair. My leg was strapped into a brace and stuck out at a right angle; I looked like the number four. I wheeled my way towards everyone. 'We haven't heard from our star witness yet.'

'This is a farce,' Winston muttered.

'Ditto, Edward's parrot, overheard some last words. I figured we might like to hear from him. But unfortunately someone let him out of his cage and he escaped. I put him on the invitation because I knew someone couldn't resist a loose end. With me dead, they had one last witness to kill: a parrot.'

'Where's the bird, then?' Felix asked.

'I don't know,' I admitted. 'In the wild, living free. I was in hospital with a Jenga game for leg bones. I'm not out chasing parrots.' I was pleased at everyone's confusion. Well, almost everyone's. 'But someone is worried about what Ditto has to say. I had Gabriel set up his cage in the vestry, cover it with a cloth and deliberately leave the door back there open when he came in before. I'm sorry to air all your dirty laundry, but I wanted our killer to feel comfortable enough to duck out of the room while we were all distracted. Watch this television.' I pointed at the dark screen. 'Whoever goes to kill the bird is your murderer.'

As I said this, there was a slight movement, then brightness. I'd set up a live-streaming phone on the perch. Poised to catch whoever took the cover off.

On screen, Tobias Cuthbert peered into the lens.

THE THIRD HEIST:
A LIFE

CHAPTER 47

Okay, so Tobias wasn't *in* the bank. But Eric was, and this is a team effort. A wholesome family outing, if you will.

Eric got up from his pew and ran into the vestry to join his father. There was nowhere to go; the only other exit from the priest's chambers was a locked door to the bell tower. I wheeled down the church aisle and propped my wheelchair in the door, blocking them in. Everyone crowded around behind me.

Tobias smacked Eric in the back of the head, his hair flicking up. 'I told you to kill the bird,' he snapped. Then, to me, calmly, 'This is all circumstantial. I refuse to play your stupid game.'

'It's a game that started this,' I replied. 'Eric lost to Ben Huxley in a *Buccaneers* tournament, we already know that. Eric picked up six silver coins for second place, while Ben won a gold bar. What Ben didn't know is that his own father lost a whole stack of cash betting on that game. Edward had bet against his son, backing Eric, the firm favourite, instead. He lost three hundred grand. But you lost something worse, Eric. Your pride.'

'Don't acknowledge him.' Tobias squeezed Eric's shoulder. 'It's all guesswork unless you confirm it.' He turned to me. 'None of these detective finales work if no one talks, Mr Cunningham. You're the real criminal here. Armed robbery, aggravated assault.' He pointed to Remy's bandaged middle. 'That's a decade in prison. Maybe more.'

'If I've learned anything by running out of it, it's that time is something we spend so recklessly. Maybe we need to spend it more like we spend our cash – look after it, invest it. And if I have to spend my time, yes, even ten years of it, revealing you as a murderer, I will.'

'Dad.' Eric turned to his father. His face was a puppy-dog appeal, like he was asking for permission to fess up.

Tobias's hand clasped firmly on his shoulder. Too firm.

Eric looked at his shoelaces instead. 'I deny everything.'

'I haven't even accused you properly yet.'

'I, uh, deny everything you're about to say.'

'Well, let's cut to it. *You* swatted Ben Huxley. After he beat you, you spiralled. Lost your ranking, your odds. You scrambled the IP of the call, a rudimentary hack for someone terminally online, and made it seem like it was coming from some passerby who'd heard gunfire. You thought it was just a nasty prank, to mess with him, threaten him a bit. You told me yourself that you thought swatting was *harmless*. You didn't realise the consequences. When you were talking to me, you were trying to justify it. Said it was his own fault. The same thing you'd been telling yourself since last year to try and avoid taking responsibility for what you'd done. You sensed I was close to the truth, so you told me Ben was cheating to try to convince me it was a suicide and deflect my attention.'

'It *was* his fault,' Eric burst out. 'Who plays without headphones? With the volume up that loud? I didn't know he'd *die*.'

'You don't need to respond.' Tobias had a smile carved solid on his face, sweat on his brow. 'He has *nothing*.'

'I told you I'd clean up my *own* mess,' Eric whined. 'You don't trust me. You don't respect me. You think I'm just a little boy who plays stupid games.'

'Am I wrong?' Tobias turned away from us now, addressing his son. 'Ben was better than you. A real man would've shaken his hand, but you couldn't handle it. You got the poor kid killed. And then I had to come in and clean it all up. Bury the emergency call with my connections. You couldn't even kill a *fucking bird*.' He drew a gun from inside his coat, an upgrade from his taser. Evidently he was smart enough to know Ditto's name on the invite might have been a lure, and had prepared accordingly. He pointed it at Gabriel, motioned with a wriggle. 'Unlock the bell tower.'

'There's no exit there,' I said. 'And I don't have "nothing". Picture Edward, in a melancholy mood, going through Ben's old room a year on from his death and finding something. A recording of his son's final game. That's how you make half your money, Eric, right? Other people watching you play online? Ben had recorded the game, only he'd died before he could upload it, so it sat undiscovered on a dusty hard drive. And what father wouldn't want to hear their son's last words? Edward watched it. Then he watched it again, and again, and again. On his office computer. I know this, because he watched it enough times for Ditto to learn the words.'

You are dead. Dead! You can't kill me. Not in here. I am not a clue.

'Ditto was never threatening to kill anyone, he was repeating trash-talk between two gamers, heard over and over as Edward listened to the recording. Ben was bragging that you couldn't kill him, Eric. Because he was better than you. And Eric, you responded with *not in here*. This was you, threatening to swat him in the real world. *A clue*? It's the pronunciation of the Australian Championship League, University as an acronym – ACLU. *Ackle* is how you pronounce the acronym for the general competition, and I realised I just had to add the U. Ben was so good he was going to go pro, away from the university circuit. Where the real money is, no longer playing for silver coins or gold bars. Millions of potential dollars, you told me. He was saying he wasn't in your league anymore. He was calling you a child.'

Eric's lip quivered. His voice took on a haunting monotone, as he recited lines that were clearly a memory. 'You're not good enough. You can't kill me. I am not ACLU anymore. I'll wave to you from the top.' Ben's last words, in full and final form. Eric sniffled. 'I heard the bird repeat it. That's why I chucked him out the window.'

'Murder is often petty, and I thought being a sore loser might just be enough for you to have made the call. But that's not all, is it? Your father told me you were making a lot of money, but how could you be making that much money when you weren't even elevated out of the junior division?' Eric's eyes darted guiltily to the ground. I pushed on. 'The money was coming from somewhere, and you had to explain it to your dad. Luckily he never really understood Esports, so you could fabricate the earnings. The truth is, you *threw* the first game you lost to Ben, the one you shouldn't have lost.'

'How do you—' Eric started.

'You used a betting term that no fifteen-year-old should know: *over-under*. That was a glaring mistake. I think Gabriel paid you to lose. Then, when you were talking too much about *Buccaneers* during the robbery, he told you to *keep your fucking mouth shut*.'

Gabriel glowed red, focusing on shaking his way through his key ring, trying to find the right key, apologising sporadically, not to Tobias, but to his gun. I'd never believed Gabriel had written the threat to Winston; after all, he was in the bank to get Winston to talk to him in the first place. It also explained why he was willing to let Edward bet such a large stake.

'Did Ben know you were fixing the games?' I pressed Eric. 'I think he did. And that you *did* know the true danger of swatting. You wanted him dead.'

'No. No,' Eric stammered. He rubbed one cheek with his palm. 'It wasn't like that.'

'I didn't pay him for Ben's last game,' Gabriel squeaked. I realised he was begging; he didn't want Tobias to think he was responsible for any of this.

'I know you didn't. Because, Eric, your odds had been lowered enough by that game that it was now financially beneficial for you to try to win again. There was only one problem: you couldn't. Ben *was* better than you. And now he had everything you wanted. The career. The ranking. Everything you'd traded for some quick cash. And now when you were really trying to beat him, you couldn't.' Gabriel had given me the key to this: *Ben was winning the game when he died.* 'So you are just a sore loser after all.'

I turned to Tobias now. 'Edward finds the recording, and he calls you, Tobias. Father to father, man to man. He wants to give you the benefit of the doubt. He knows in his gut what's happened, but more than that, he knows what it's like to lose a son. That's why he doesn't want to upload the recording until you've talked. First, he needs to keep it safe. You're in with the police from your part-time gig and he's not confident he can trust anyone. He hires Michelle to check the security of the bank and organises to meet with you on Wednesday evening – he arrived home but then left again, Winston saw his headlights in the driveway. When he gets to his office, Michelle has robbed the bank already. Edward realises his safety deposit box isn't secure enough, so in a rush before your arrival he swaps his and Winston's safes, so the recording is tucked up in Winston's office. You wouldn't have been able to open the safe in Edward's office even if you beat the real combination out of him, just like I found out trying to get Winston's. And good thing Edward *did* have a back-up, because you did not accept his father-to-father talk. Maybe you begged him not to go to the police, maybe you offered money . . .'

Tobias blinked away a memory at this.

'Of course you start with money, you're a negotiator. Edward probably considers it, given he needs cash to cover his gambling. You get out of him that his safety deposit box is number sixty-five, that's important, but things go south from there, escalating until you hit him over the head with the first-place gold bar. Gold is soft – it's why people bite it to test purity – and there's a tiny dent in one end. Gabriel told me he wiped blood off it later.

'It's not enough of a hit to kill him, though it likely knocks him down,' I continued, 'so Edward manages to get away, maybe while you're figuring out what to do, thinking he's dead and scrubbing the blood off your hands. He scrambles down the stairs and into Winston's office, to retrieve the hard drive from his own safe, but you must have caught him, because he realises he doesn't have enough time to retrieve the recording, so instead decides he'll hole up, leaving his brother a message about where he'll be – 10-11 for *available on radio*. Then he runs to the only place he knows he can be safe from you: the vault. He locks himself in. You were foiled. But Edward had a pocket of pistachios and a concussion. When the universe is against you, it's against you. He passed out from the head wound. He would have likely woken up just fine, but a small fire lit in his pocket, caused by the self-heating pistachio nuts, and he was too out of it to wake. It catches onto the rest of him and, well, most of us saw the result.

'You didn't know he was dead, so you had an anxious wait the next day. Waiting for Edward to press charges against you and your son, or to see the video on the news. But . . . nothing. You figure he's coming up with a blackmail plan. Meanwhile, Eric has caught on that you know something.'

'He asked me about the game,' Eric mumbled. Tobias had given up silencing him; pulling a gun on us had kind of ruined his chance at deniability. 'About streaming online. He'd never taken an interest before. I knew something was up.'

'Eric wants to prove something to you. He knows you don't respect him.' I rolled forward as I stacked the evidence in front of Tobias. Eric had told me as much in the middle of the night: *I really thought he'd choose me. I'm such an idiot.* 'And he hopes that if he fixes his own mess you might think a little more of him. So he proposes that you let him try to fix it. You're still assuming the recording is in the deposit box, in number sixty-five, which you tell Eric. He brings in his six silver coins in a piggybank, under the guise of getting his own box. But nestled in the middle of the coins is a magnet. Remy threw the piggybank on the pile of coins when we were conjuring up a dollar to give our thief. I tallied four dollars eighty. When you took the piggybank away, it totalled four dollars forty. I *can* count. Two twenty-cent pieces had been magnetised to the piggybank and taken from the pile. Why bring a magnet? Well, magnets scramble data devices. Eric figured if he could get into the vault with a strong-enough magnet, he could erase the recording without ever having to touch it. I overheard Eric requesting box number eighty-five because it was his lucky number. The boxes are in rows of twenty. Eighty-five would be the box right under Edward's.'

Gabriel finally got the door to the bell tower open. A staircase, turning at right angles, ringed an empty column. Tobias shoved Eric towards it.

'But then Bryce decided to rob the bank.' I kept talking – always good advice to keep distracting a person holding a gun. 'When you and I first spoke, I told you that we couldn't open the vault and that Edward had been missing for two days. And that made you realise Edward was still inside it. From two days ago. Which meant he was probably dead. You knew you'd clocked him pretty hard with the gold brick, so you thought he'd died of the head trauma, which meant as soon as the vault was opened there'd be a murder investigation. You had only one choice: murder the bank robber and pin it on them. But how do you kill someone without touching them?

I made the request for towels and medicine, but Bryce separately requested sunscreen. I thought it was odd that a man in a head-to-toe disguise needed sunscreen, but then I learned that he had an allergic reaction to sunlight. His plan was to try to get away in plain clothes, which meant direct exposure. But you also saw it as an opportunity. You gave him a tube of sunscreen that was laced with white phosphorus.'

'Phosphorus, like in *The Hound of the Baskervilles*?' Felix said, recalling what I'd told him early in the robbery. 'You said the dog would have died.'

'Exactly. White phosphorus is poisonous if absorbed through the skin. Tobias, you expected when Bryce used the laced sunscreen, he'd die from the toxicity. You got the phosphorus from the flashbang grenades the SRT team uses – it's the active ingredient in the razzle-dazzle light show those grenades put out. Hence why it's useful for glowing haunted hounds. You had the knowledge to disarm the grenades because as part of your hostage-negotiation training you'd done a bomb disposal course, you told me that yourself. The last thing you needed was a place to work in private. You snuck into the broken mausoleum to hide from view while you got the active phosphorus out and mixed it into a tube of sunscreen. The remainder of your handiwork is still in there as chemical residue – that's why the crypt was glowing in the dark last night.'

'Does phosphorus explode or glow?' Cordelia asked. 'I'm confused.'

'White phosphorus *is* commonly known to glow in the dark, which we know thanks to Sherlock Holmes, but what's really going on is an emission of *energy*,' I explained. 'Energy gives off in two ways: light *and* heat. It gives off both at the same time: think about the bright glow of a fire, or the warmth of a switched-on lightbulb. Bryce probably *was* glowing, but I couldn't see it in the daytime. And as the phosphorus glows, it gets hot – it self-ignites at room temperature. It also burns the skin. Bryce was scratching his neck on the rooftop before he died. At first I thought this could be explained by his sunlight allergy, but he didn't live shut up indoors. He was casually dressed when I saw him leave the café Friday morning, so it didn't make sense he'd have such an immediate reaction. He was scratching his neck because of a chemical burn. He put on the sunscreen, he started to itch, then he started to feel the heat.' *It's hot up here. Is it hot?* Bryce had complained. 'When he caught fire it was blinding bright. White phosphorus burns hot and white.'

Tobias had heard enough. He pushed Eric towards the tower stairs, but Eric slipped around him towards me. I pivoted my wheelchair to let him join everyone else in the vestry.

His eyes were glistening. 'I have to face what I did. I didn't mean to kill Ben. It was stupid. It was a mistake. I tried to cover it up, first with the bird and then by pushing Ernest into the safe.' He turned to me. 'But every fix created new problems, with even worse solutions. I thought getting you into that safe would, I dunno, prove something to my dad. I fired the gun so the SRT would kick down the doors and everything would get mixed up in the chaos.' He turned back to his father. 'I'm sick at what I've turned into. But that doesn't mean I get to walk away from it. I should accept the consequences. I didn't ask you to hurt anyone for me. You've killed *two people*, Dad. Let it go.'

Tobias gave a grunt of cruel disappointment, turned away from his son and started up the stairs. I rolled through the vestry and into the tower beneath him. Shudders of dust rained down around me as Tobias climbed the disused wooden stairs, which I now saw led all the way up the tower. By my head a rope was tightly wound around an iron claw, which ran upwards to the bell.

'There's nowhere to go!' I yelled up the spire. 'I'm not chasing you in this.' I rocked the wheelchair back and forth.

Bullet sparks zipped around me, one blasting a chunk of wood out of the staircase strut by my elbow, the other off the brick wall. Tobias was shooting from above, leaning over the edge of the stairs. I tried to spin my wheels, retreat back into the safety of the vestry, but got caught on the threshold and tipped myself onto the floor. Juliette made to get me, but the wheelchair was clunky and blocked the doorway. In the seconds it took to dislodge it, I hauled myself up onto the bottom stair, hoping for at least some small cover. My straight-locked leg gave me no help moving; I was like an inconvenient *Tetris* piece.

I looked up. I hadn't found cover at all. Tobias was about three metres up, on the opposite side of the spire, three turns of the stairwell above me. He had a perfect shot.

'At least you won't get to gloat about solving this one,' he said, taking aim.

Then a dash of green, swooping down the tower, fluttered between us.

'*You are dead! I am not a clue!*'

Ditto.

Completely unaware of what he'd sailed into, Ditto was having a grand time soaring back and forth. It lit a rage in Tobias stronger than phosphorus could have, and suddenly I was forgotten. Tobias only had eyes for the bird who had ruined it all.

He fired the gun erratically at the parrot. Once, twice, three times, his aim tracing the flitting bird. One bullet, fired up, sprung a loud *gong* from the bell. He fired again and a bullet thwacked into the stair near my shoulder. Another sparked in the wall by the door. Then nothing more but the clicking of an empty gun.

In the calm, we both saw it. The final bullet had sliced a notch through the bell's supporting rope. The cord started to twirl and fray. It lost tension. The cast iron bell let out a loud creak as it tilted to one side.

Tobias bolted down the stairs. I wrestled with my leg to get moving. Juliette, having sheltered behind the doorframe during the gunfire, poked her head into the bell tower again. People had started yelling, realising what was happening. A major section of the rope twirled loose, dropping the bell a few inches, and ringing out another clang.

Tobias had about two flights of stairs to go. I had about a metre to the door. But he had both legs. It was about an even race.

Then the rope snapped.

It whizzed up and out of sight as the bell crashed into the top of the wooden staircase. The entire tower vibrated. It felt like we were in a tuning fork. The old, rotted planks of wood barely slowed the giant iron bell. It chewed through them as it fell, ricocheting side to side off the tower's walls.

Tobias threw caution to the wind and jumped the last two flights, landing with a crack on the floor. At the same time, I felt a hand on my ankle and a yank firm enough to distend all the broken bones in my leg like a *cut here* line in a children's activity book. The pain was enormous. But suddenly I was moving backwards, sliding on my stomach through a shower of splinters and dust, and out the bell tower door, back into the vestry.

I had a split second to catch a glimpse of Tobias, limping upright on a freshly broken leg, before the bell replaced my view of him. An explosion of debris coughed out of the doorway. The earth shook.

When the dust cleared, Tobias was gone. Only the bell remained.

EPILOGUE

Last words are a funny thing.

Tobias, if he'd got to choose his, might have gone with something kinder to his son. Bryce would have said that what he did was worth it. Edward would have spoken to his brother. Cordelia and Laverna, though they're still alive, had their last words under those names with 'Guilty, your honour'. Remy's last word will be his new movie: *Terror at Huxley's Bank*. A real one this time. I didn't even get to sell him the rights. It's his story, of a heroic film producer trapped against impossible odds.

I've had the rare opportunity to write my own last words and to revisit them. I realised, flicking through the notebook, that although I started this thinking I'd use my final missive to solve my own murder and what I wanted to say was all about the mystery, the actual last thing I wrote, bleeding out from a gunshot and out of options, was to Juliette. Gabriel had chided me early on, when I criticised him for putting himself in danger for a jar of water: *imagine if you had something like that.* Turns out I do.

Would you believe I didn't have to go to jail? Well, not for more than three days. Because my gun was unloaded, it didn't count as armed robbery, and the hostages – even the guilty ones – all went in to bat for me. Even Eric, Zoom-ing in from juvenile detention, made a statement that he was glad I'd confronted him with the reality of his crime. Emma Fredericks fought back tears as she thanked me for what I'd done for her father. That girl has heart.

Like I said about murders, every big bad decision is the last domino in a series of smaller ones. For example, a bank robber who robbed the wrong bank at the wrong time for a heart that he didn't even need to steal.

An envelope I received from Winston felt like placing the first domino in a new chain. He'd been in damage-control mode: I'd seen a big toothy photo of him on the front page of the local paper, handing over Harold Huxley's gold nugget to Felix. To Winston's credit, he'd almost pulled off a smile, though it did look more like he'd stubbed his toe.

I opened the envelope. Inside was a cheque. You don't need to know how much it was for, but there were a fair few zeros.

I tore the cheque in half.

I can always earn more money. I can always solve more murders. I can't earn more time – even with a jar of holy water and a battery. I know that now. So now I'm going to spend more of it with Juliette. The wedding is still on. No one is going to die, I'm going to make sure of that. We'll have it in a locked vault if we have to. No pistachios on the menu.

My concerns about divorce statistics have turned out to be trivial. Father Gabriel is marrying us completely for free. Venue, catering, the whole lot is chucked in. He assumes he'll be off house arrest by then. He even promises to do it verbally and not by writing on a pad.

That gives me some budget to play with. Emma Fredericks recently set up a FundAble to help cover her future medical expenses. So I thought I could put the wedding budget towards that.

I donated $35,999. No harm in following the rules.

ACKNOWLEDGEMENTS

Believe it or not, all of the science in this book is theoretically possible. *Theoretically* being that favourite word of fiction writers everywhere, given how it stretches like mozzarella to cover our arses. To save you googling it: pistachios do spontaneously combust, and Holmes's famous case would indeed be more like *The Hound of the Barbecues*. The rest is . . . well . . . theoretical.

I suppose it's *theoretically* possible to write a book without an incredible group of champions behind you, but I certainly wouldn't like to test that theory.

This book is only possible thanks to many. My team of publishers: Beverley Cousins, Nicole Angeloro and Grace Long, for not only their sharp-eyed storytelling skills, but also their passion for sharing Ernest's stories with as many readers as possible. They have supported every insane idea I've had with all their heart, and I can't tell you how much easier it is to write a book with that kind of enthusiasm behind you. Holly Toohey's and Peter Hubbard's support has been invaluable. I also owe a debt to Katherine Nintzel for launching the series in the US.

My agents – Pippa Masson, supported by Caitlan Cooper-Trent, of Curtis Brown Australia – are my first readers, cheerleaders and therapists all rolled into one. Clair Roberts and Amy Hardman don't get enough thanks for keeping the lights on, too. And to Leslie Conliffe, supported by Kris Karcher, for shepherding Ernest onto the screen. My thanks, as always, to Jerry Kalajian for firing the starting pistol for us.

Amanda Martin, my editor, really pulled out all the stops on this one, doing an incredible job on a very tight timeframe. One day I promise I'll stop asking you whether I can keep that extra comma. But, it won't be today.

I am lucky to have the creative genius marketing and publicity gurus in Tavia Kowalchuk, Tanaya Lowden, Hannah Ludbrook, Maureen Cole, Laura Nimmo, and Jennifer Harlow, and in sales, Adelaide Jensen, Rachel Berquist, Hannah Armstrong, Gavin Schwarcz, Dorothy Tonkin and Janine Brown. Sarah McDuling, Kate Cooper and Anna Ristevski, thank you for turning suspects into sospetti, les suspectes, Verdächtigen, and sospechosos, among many more.

Thank you to Adam Laszczuk for a cover so brilliant that I changed the species of Ditto to fit his marvellous design. James Mills-Hicks, thank you for bringing back-of-napkin sketches of the bank's schematics to such vibrant life. Thanks to Sonja Heijn for proofreading, and to Midland Typesetters for indulging my obsession with white space on the page. Thank you to Veronica Eze for producing another brilliant audiobook, narrated by Barton Welch.

To get to do this magical job called 'writing' once is a dream. To get to do it with four Ernest Cunningham mysteries is only possible thanks to the incredible support of booksellers recommending the books and pushing them into people's hands.

I want to highlight the staff at Dymocks. I wrote part of this book in public, in the front window of the Dymocks George Street store in Sydney, with my words displayed on a giant television screen for the book-browsing public to read along with. There are too many people to name, but a special shout-out to Tim, Kate, Sarah, and Jon, who welcomed me with open arms to take over the store. Legends, all of you.

I also need to give a special shout-out to QBD, who have always made me feel like part of the family. Nick, Gary, Peta, and too many bookstore managers to name, your good cheer and love of books makes every visit to every store a dream.

An author is just fake gold. My name is on the front cover, but it's a shiny plating over a robust and iron core. The iron core that makes a book is every bookseller, library, librarian, and reader who brings the work to life by picking it up. That's the real gold.

Lastly, and always, thank you to my supportive, welcoming family: Peter, Judy, and James Stevenson, Emily and Bud Costello, and Gabriel, Elizabeth, Lucy, Adrian and Salsa Paz.

And Aleesha Paz. You are wonderful.